As If
Women
Mattered

Published by the Piscataqua Press
An imprint of RiverRun Bookstore, Inc
142 Fleet St. | Portsmouth, NH | 03801

www.riverrunbookstore.com
www.piscataquapress.com

Cover Design by Nika Dixon

ISBN: 978-1-939-739-40-7

Printed in the United States of America

For Darwin, Brighid and Forest.

And in remembrance of Judy Popkin,
who changed the trajectory of my life.

Since 1967, consciousness-raising has become one of the prime educational, organizing programs of the women's liberation movement. Feminist groups and individual women who at first didn't think they needed it are all doing it.

Kathie Sarachild
March 12, 1972

So the reason I participate in these meetings is not to solve any personal problem. One of the first things we discover in these groups is that personal problems are political problems. There are no personal solutions at this time. There is only collective action for a collective solution.

Carol Hanisch,
"The Personal is Political," 1970

Consciousness raising groups help women live as if women mattered.

Gloria Steinem, 1972

As If Women Mattered

A Novel

Virginia DeLuca

Winner of the 2014 Piscataqua Press Novel Contest

CHAPTER ONE

The four women met in the fall of 1972, the year *Ms. Magazine* began publication, the year the United States carried out the heaviest bombing of the Vietnam War, and over 100,000 demonstrators protested across the country. It was also the year Alix calculated that she and Sam had had fifty-six serious fights, of which fifty-one involved unwashed dishes, dirty socks, and vacuuming. Five involved three-month-old Davey.

That year, eleven Israeli athletes were murdered by terrorists at the Munich Olympics; Title IX passed, allowing girls and young women access to school team sports; and Vivian's boss at IBM agreed to train her for advanced technical work—if she made it worth his while.

It was the year Gemma graduated from New York University, only to learn her father had saved thousands of dollars for her future wedding while refusing to help with college tuition. Gemma applied to law school.

Millions of American women held a nationwide strike to demand full social, economic, and political equality that year, and *Life Magazine* rejected Emily's photo essay of women and their children protesting the war, saying it was not politically relevant.

The Introduction to the Consciousness-Raising workshop was held September 2 at the Women's Center on Prospect Avenue in Cambridge, Massachusetts. Twenty years later, they would argue about this. Gemma, who thought she remembered everything anybody said or did, pronounced it was at the YWCA on Mass Ave. Vivian, who pretended haziness about such details, waved away the issue. Even Alix, who wrote everything down, said it had to be later, because she remembered it was cold. But Emily knew. Emily had the photos.

September 2, 1972

Vivian tugged on her jeans, looked in the mirror, and then peeled them off. They made her feel fat. She held up a long paisley skirt. No. Too hippie-like. She tossed it on the bed. What the fuck did a person wear to a consciousness-raising meeting?

"Mom-ee. Mom-ee," two-year-old Katie chanted as she bounced on the bed, surrounded by Vivian's rejected outfits.

"Careful there, sweetie." Vivian watched as Katie lost her balance and fell giggling onto the pillows, her blond curls darkened by sweat. "Stay in the middle of the bed. No time for head bumps today."

Vivian held up a peasant blouse, shook her head, and added it to the pile on the bed. "This would be a whole lot easier if it weren't ninety-five effing degrees," she told Katie, twisting her blond hair off her neck.

She dug a tank top out of a drawer. "I want to look serious, but not too uptight. I want to dress like a real feminist." She studied her closet. "Not that I'm not," she assured Katie, grabbing her denim overalls. Living alone, she tended to keep up constant chatter with Katie. Vivian pulled on her tank top and buttoned the overalls.

Katie wasn't paying attention. She lay on her stomach over the skirt, kicking her short legs and hiding her head under the blouse. She slid off the bed and toddled into the next room. "Book. Book. Book."

Vivian looked at her watch. She just had time to get dressed, feed them both lunch, and get Katie upstairs for her landlady to babysit.

As Sonny and Cher came on the radio, Vivian swooped Katie off her feet and danced her around, singing, "'I got you, babe.'" Katie screeched with giggles. Vivian continued to sing along to the radio, dipping and swinging. "'I got you, I won't let go.'" Vivian's voice soared over Katie's squeals as she twirled them. She kissed her sweaty face. "Okay, babe, too hot. No more dancing." She lowered her to the floor.

Katie resumed her chant. "Book. Book."

Vivian had thought about bringing her to the women's meeting, but she would tear the place apart. That past week Vivian had lost her regular sitter and had taken Katie to work with her. She loved it, traveling from office to office where the secretaries ate her up while Vivian did the repairs.

"Are you crazy?" her boss had yelled at her yesterday, when she returned to the main office. Actually, to be precise, he had yelled at her breasts. "Do you know the liability issues of bringing that kid along?"

She shrugged. "It's working out fine."

"You might be the best repairman I have, but customers don't like it. I get calls after you show up. 'Why did you send me that broad? I thought you were sending me a repairman?' I tell them to call me after you've finished the work and see if they still have a problem."

"And do they?"

"I went out on a limb giving you this job. And I could fire you like that." He snapped his fingers.

She had stared with cold calmness into his sweaty face, but even now fear flickered inside her. She could count on two things—she was sexy and she could fix anything with moving parts—but so far neither of those traits was doing much to pay the bills. No matter what it took, she intended to prove to all who'd doubted her that she didn't need a husband to offer Katie the world.

She did need this job.

Vivian dodged the panhandlers, avoided the bald men wearing saffron robes and singing "Hare Krishna," and focused on not catching the heel of her sandals in the brick sidewalks as she raced through the square. She almost collided with a woman who had stopped to lift her camera, parting the foot traffic like a rock in a streambed and just as oblivious.

The woman's black braid swayed, brushing the waistband of her jeans as she bent and twisted to snap pictures from various angles of the house with Women's Center painted in multicolored letters over the doorway. She moved like a dancer, not one wasted movement, smooth and fluid. She lowered her camera, noticed Vivian staring, smiled a hesitant half smile, and then trudged up the wooden steps.

Vivian followed.

The air in the front room was cooler, but Vivian still felt uncomfortably warm and twisted her hair into a pile on her head and clipped it in place. Posters covered the walls. Make Love Not War. A Woman Needs a Man Like a Fish Needs a Bicycle. *Ha.* She would get that one and hang it over Katie's crib.

This past spring, when she'd heard about the opening in the Boston office of IBM, she'd put in for the transfer, packed up Katie, and arrived from California not knowing a soul. She'd been as frantic to leave Berkeley as she'd once been desperate to get there. Some people, like her brother, might describe her as impulsive. She preferred free spirit.

Continuing to wander the periphery, pretending to study the posters, she inhaled deeply, patchouli oil and sandalwood, mixed with floral shampoos. A women's place. It reeked of safety and comfort despite worn, obviously cast-off couches and rugs scattered on the painted wood floor. Woman's Herstory Is a World to Be Fought For.

She adjusted her tank top and wished she didn't feel like a ninth grader in a new school, desperate to be accepted and having no idea what to expect. Her friends in California, working with draft resisters and organizing antiwar protests, had sneered at the idea that women needed liberation and dismissed the movement. But then again, that crowd was mostly men.

The room filled, bright with tie-dyes and paisley, the energy palpable, the noise level rising with excited chatter. In one corner, a woman bounced, trying to soothe her fussy baby in a front pack. Auburn hair frizzed around her face. Vivian moved on to the next poster. What if They Gave a War and Nobody Came? Most of the women looked to be in their early to mid-twenties, around her age, so that was good. The woman with the braid sat on the couch fiddling with her camera and looking at her watch, prompting Vivian to look at hers. The meeting was already starting twenty minutes late and she'd promised the sitter she'd be home by five.

She'd reached the fliers and announcements. Rape Crisis Center Forming. *Our Bodies Ourselves* study group meets Thursdays at six p.m. The baby in the corner began to cry. Vivian gave the mom a sympathetic smile, glad a baby was there; she'd worried that having a toddler at twenty-two disqualified her from being a feminist.

"Hi everyone. Let's get started." A woman with earrings dangling to her shoulders clapped her hands. The thirty or so women settled, sitting in the chairs, on the floor, squeezing onto the couch.

Vivian found a spot on the wall to lean against.

"Consciousness-raising is simply telling the truth about our own lives." The woman's clear, booming voice commanded attention. "For too long women have been defined by men and only in relation to the men in their lives."

"Right on, sister," one woman shouted, and raised a clenched fist.

A small dark-haired woman next to Vivian rolled her eyes at this fervor. The woman was so skinny, she was all angles and edges.

"How often have you played dumb?" the leader continued. "Or purposely lost a game to a man?"

"Or pretended to have an orgasm?" someone blurted, and everyone laughed and nodded.

"Telling the truth about our feelings and experiences is a powerful tool for change," the leader went on. "As the poet Muriel Rukeyser asked: 'What would happen if one woman told the truth about her life?'" She paused for effect. "'The world would split open.'"

The tiny woman next to her sighed audibly and shifted her weight.

"So now, let's divide up into groups of ten, do introductions, tell the truth and"—she paused again—"change the world."

The room erupted in voices and laughter as everyone separated into small groups. With a surge of excitement, Vivian joined a circle of eight women sitting on the floor.

Faces shiny with sweat and offering shy smiles, they glanced at one another, waiting for someone to jump in. Snatches of introductions from other circles of women floated by: I'm Sue, I'm Barbara, I'm Joan. Vivian stared at the scratches in the painted floor and pulled on a loose thread of her overalls, hoping someone else would begin. She hadn't decided which truth to tell about herself.

"I'll start," said the woman with the baby.

Brave woman. Vivian smiled encouragement.

"I'm Alix." She took the baby out of the front pack as she

spoke. "And this is Davey." He was all baby sweat and smiles now that he was free. "I'm new to Cambridge. New to this whole feminism thing." She laughed. "I was a dance major in college. But having a baby has given me a whole new perspective on the need for women's liberation." She laid down a blanket and put the baby on his back. "Does anyone mind if I do a diaper change?" Alix looked at the woman to her right, indicating she should talk next.

"I'm Sarah," the woman whispered. Everyone leaned forward to hear her.

From another circle a woman hooted a laugh. Vivian glanced over, curious about what was so funny. The whispering woman's blond hair curtained her face as she stared at the floor.   Another woman—Vivian missed her name—rambled on about a women's study class she was taking. The facilitators circled the room, leaning in, offering a comment here or there.

Aware of silence around her, Vivian brought her attention back to the circle of women now staring expectantly at her, waiting for her to speak.

"I'm Vivian." She paused, scrambling to think of what to tell. "And I also just moved here. From California. I'm a single mom. I'm the only woman repairman in—"

"Person," interrupted the tiny frowning woman with the black hair. "Sorry, I'm Gemma, by the way. You said repair*man,* it should be repair*person.*"

"Yeah, well, person or not, I'm the only woman," Vivian continued. "And my boss wants me to blow him."

A few nervous giggles surfaced.

"Done?" the woman who'd corrected Vivian asked, not smiling. "Well, like I said, I'm Gemma." She clicked her pen in and out, in and out, as she spoke. "I just moved here from New York and started law school." She clicked her pen again. They waited. She shrugged. "It's not a welcoming place for a woman."

She turned to her right.

"My name is Kathy." The next woman grinned, exposing the whitest teeth Vivian had ever seen. "I'm a teacher here in Boston and am just so excited to be part of all this. I mean is this exciting or what?" She waved her arm to include the whole room and then nodded at the woman with the camera, signaling her to introduce herself. "That's all for now."

"I'm Emily, I want to—"

"What is he doing here?" a willowy woman with a high-pitched voice interrupted. She stood outside the circle and pointed at the baby. "He can't be here."

Alix looked perplexed. "Davey?"

"Yes." The woman nodded vigorously. "No males allowed. He's got to leave now!"

Vivian watched with wonder as Alix finished pinning the diaper, and then in one swift movement scooped up Davey, his blanket, the diaper bag, and stood.

"You are not serious," Vivian said. Her hair fell from its clip.

"I'm one of the organizers." The woman pointed again at Davey. "This is a male-free space."

"Sorry." Alix stepped away, clearly wishing to evaporate but of course, now everyone in the room stared at her.

"No. Don't go." Gemma stood up, all five feet of her, looking fierce. "The baby is what? Three months old?"

Vivian also stood. "This is ridiculous."

"The rule is no males." The woman faced Vivian. "For safety reasons."

"That kid can barely hold up his own head, never mind anything else," Vivian said, trying to lighten the tension. Only the camerawoman, Emily, laughed.

"It's the principle," the woman insisted. "Some women don't feel safe around males and we respect that."

Alix pushed past them, looking close to tears. "It's okay,

really."

"It's idiotic," Gemma pronounced, and strode after her. Emily grabbed her camera and followed right behind.

Vivian watched them leave and then looked back at the woman. She nodded, her expression righteous. *Oh, what the hell.* Vivian turned and hurried after them.

Out on the sidewalk, they all helped Alix gather herself back together. Vivian held the baby while Alix reattached the baby carrier.

"I really am sorry," she said. Beads of sweat dotted her nose. Emily and Gemma folded stuff back into the diaper bag as Alix got Davey secure in the pack again. She wiped at her sweat. "This is so embarrassing."

"That was totally bizarre." Vivian reclipped her hair off her neck, hoping for some air. God, it was hot.

Emily lifted her braid and pulled at her sweaty T-shirt, blowing down the front. The sun glinted off her handful of rings. "If that's what this women's lib stuff is about, I'm done."

"I am sorry you all left—"

"Stop saying you're sorry." Vivian cut her off and fanned herself with an announcement of a rally for abortion rights. "It's making me fucking nuts."

"Coffee?" Gemma asked, shouldering the diaper bag. They walked toward Mass Ave. "What's in this thing?" Gemma switched the bag to her other shoulder. "Must weigh twice as much as the baby does."

"You don't have kids yet, I guess." Vivian really didn't want to get coffee and make awkward conversation, but she didn't want to seem unfriendly.

"Stop," Emily said, and pulled out her camera. "I want to take a picture."

"Now?" Vivian patted her hair, tucked in a loose strand, readjusted her tank top, and watched as Emily snapped picture after picture, circling around them. They stood slightly apart from one another. Alix's hands cupped Davey's rump, her hair frizzing in the heat to a red-brown nimbus. Gemma half turned to follow the camera and looked slightly off balance. They all plastered on smiles, self-conscious and hesitant.

"Okay." Emily took one last photo.

"I need a drink," Vivian said as they continued walking.

"It's three o'clock in the afternoon." Gemma tripped on an uneven piece of sidewalk. Emily grabbed her arm to steady her.

In the dimly lit pub on Mass Ave, Vivian went to the bar and ordered four iced Irish coffees with whipped cream and then settled with the others into a booth. Cigarette burns scarred the table. She shifted to avoid a tear in the plastic seat from digging into her thigh.

"So." She cracked open a peanut from the plastic bowl on the table. "What's a women's consciousness-raising group supposed to do?"

Alix shrugged. Davey emitted little baby snores from low in the front pack. Alix wore that look of a mother content to be anywhere and do anything as long as the baby was asleep. "Just talk, I guess."

"We're supposed to," Gemma began, waving her hand and almost upsetting the tray the waitress carried. She paused while the waitress set down their drinks and then continued. "We're supposed to talk about what it means to be a woman."

"As opposed to what?" Vivian spooned up some whipped cream. "Elephants?"

"Let's do it." Alix's bangles clinked as she reached for the peanuts. "Just the four of us."

CHAPTER TWO

September 12, 1972
Ten days later

"Maybe I shouldn't go," Emily said to her husband as she cradled Jess, who'd fallen asleep at her breast. Next to her, four-year-old Matt slumped against her shoulder, sucking a Popsicle and absently twirling the end of Emily's braid.

Rick stooped over the dining table that served as his home office in their tiny apartment. "Of course you should go." His long brown hair, thinning on top, was caught back in a ponytail. He'd grown a mustache over the summer that still surprised her. He said it distinguished him as a professor and not a student. Although watching as he sorted papers in his jeans and T-shirt, Emily thought he looked like the hundreds of other men in Cambridge.

"Matt feels feverish."

"I've got this, Em." Rick came over and picked up Matt. "He's fine. We'll read a book and—"

"Two books," Matt interrupted.

"Two?" Rick hit his own head in mock outrage. Matt giggled.

"I mean ..." Emily gently swayed as she stood, hoping to transfer Jess to her crib without waking her. "Why am I even doing this?" She wasn't good at meeting new people. In Vermont, in the town where she grew up, she hadn't needed to. She already knew everyone.

"Ten books," Matt said.

"You said you liked the women. Give it a try."

"One of them is in law school. What could we possibly have in common?" In the little alcove that held Jess's crib, she lay her down without waking her. A miracle.

"Four hundred twenty gazillion books," Matt shouted, and he pulled Rick's face toward him.

"Hmm. How many for Jess then?" Rick asked.

"One."

"Okay, that seems fair." Rick laughed and plopped Matt on the couch. "It's a deal."

Emily smiled. She loved the joy Rick took in the kids. Matt slid off the couch and scrambled to get his books. "Maybe I should stay and help you read all those books."

Rick grabbed her around the waist and pulled her close. "Get out of here already. Who knows? Possibly it will even be fun."

Matt staggered back with an armful.

"Say good-bye." Rick took the books from him and piled them on the coffee table. "Your beautiful mom is going off to become a radical feminist and grow a mustache. Better kiss her before her face gets scratchy."

Matt giggled as he kissed her good-bye.

Emily hurried down the stairs, her paisley skirt swinging, both grateful and annoyed at being made fun of and freed at the same time.

She pulled hard on the street-level door; it tended to stick in the humidity.

"Hold that door." She turned to see Marcia Littleton striding up the walkway wearing jeans and a tank top and somehow still looking elegant. "I hear you're going to a meeting to get conscious."

Emily dropped her keys into her skirt pocket and didn't bother to make her smile sincere. Marcia was an associate professor in the sociology department with Rick and had treated Emily with barely contained contempt from the first time Rick introduced her to his friends over four years ago.

"I'll let you know how it goes," Emily said, "in case you ever decide to try"— she paused as she swung the camera bag over her shoulder —"being conscious." She adjusted the strap. "I didn't know you were coming over."

"Oh?" Marcia's eyebrows went up. "Rick didn't mention it? We have some work for classes to go over."

"Have fun then." Emily hoped her tone was breezy, but contact with Marcia always unbalanced her, as if she were an imposter in her own life. At eighteen, she'd rushed headlong out of Vermont, in love with Rick; and five years later, she still danced one beat behind these friends who dismissed her as the mother of his kids, with no need to know anything else about her.

Gemma pulled off her shoes and sprinted the last few yards across the law school campus in her stockings. Her mother had impressed upon her the importance of women wearing high heels when dressing up, especially short women, but she was out of practice and late. Entering the coolness of Parker Hall, she slipped her shoes back on and hurried to the dean's office. She sat where the receptionist pointed and tugged on her suit skirt, carefully crossing her legs at her ankles. The September heat made it excessively warm with stockings and her feet ached. How did women walk in heels all day?

She fiddled with the clasp on her purse. Snapped it open. Snapped it shut. Snapped it open. Snapped it shut. The receptionist coughed and gave her a look.

After twenty minutes the phone buzzed and the receptionist indicated she could go in.

Gemma tried not to wobble in her heels as she entered the office. Dark leather-bound books lined the walls. Red geraniums lined the windowsill.

"Welcome." The dean stood and indicated a leather chair. He adjusted his bow tie and sat behind his desk. It was precisely how she had imagined it and she smiled. She loved being part of all this.

They exchanged pleasantries. Yes, she'd met her class section. Yes, her move from New York to Cambridge had been uneventful. Yes, it was quite warm for this time of year.

"So, Miss Rollando." The dean cleared his throat. He formed a steeple with his hands and touched his chin, right above his bow tie. "You are a very strong addition to our law program."

"Thank you." Gemma nodded and smiled again. She'd worked so hard to get here.

He cleared his throat again. "I've taken this afternoon to meet briefly with all of our first-year women students. I want you all to feel genuinely welcome even if, due to the pressure of the times, you are taking a place that should have gone to a man." He crossed his arms. "I must be candid. I don't fully comprehend this imperative to invade men's arenas. After all, we don't thrust ourselves into your traditional spheres."

Gemma forced her smile to remain.

"Not that I'm old-fashioned, although my daughter might argue that." He chuckled. "We've accepted women into this law school since 1958 and I've always felt there were a few astounding women who had the minds of legal scholars. Of course, there was a bit of debate on that one." He smiled as if to include her in his amusement. "But then again, up until last year women couldn't speak in class unless it was ladies' day." He sighed. "Well. These times are full of change." He stood and offered his hand. "I wish you success in your studies."

Gemma stood, shook his hand. *What a prick.* She whirled and went straight to the ladies' room. She kicked off her heels, stripped off her stockings, and walked the few blocks to her apartment in her bare feet.

"Can you believe it? The utter, astounding, pompous nerve." Gemma paced the length of the small apartment, pivoted, and set off again. Breathless and sweating, she swung her arms as she strode, almost knocking into the furniture. Willie listened patiently, resting against the doorframe, looking cool and elegant with his dark skin and tennis whites. "What was I thinking?" She threw her heels in the trash on her second pass. "Did I really believe they would be happy to include me? Why should I do this?"

Willie grabbed her arm and spun her toward him. He cradled her head against his chest and rocked her. "Listen, if you want to be a lawyer, be a lawyer. If you don't, stay home, and we'll get married and make babies. Either way is fine with me. I just want you to be happy, babe."

She pushed him away. "Why do you always talk marriage and babies every damn time I get angry at the world? You sound just like my father. Believe it or not, making babies is not the answer to every female crisis." She resumed her march.

"Just trying to lighten the mood. Give me some credit." He pulled her close again and smoothed her hair. "You push and push yourself, trying to prove what?"

She relaxed into his hug. So much about herself she hadn't told him yet. "And you don't push yourself?" she asked, looking up at him. "Who was that man who said the other day that no matter what, he's going to be the first black superintendent of schools in Massachusetts?"

"Yeah, well, that's different." He continued to hug her. "I don't make myself crazy."

"Very debatable." She stepped away but felt calmer. "Go play tennis. And remember I have that women's meeting tonight."

"But we talked about this." Alix grabbed the sponge and swiftly wiped the counter. "You knew I planned to work after Davey was born." Her bangle bracelets clinked and jingled. Sweaty curls stuck to her face. No air moved in this apartment.

"But he's so tiny," Sam said. "I thought you meant, you know, later, when he went to school." Sam swayed as he held Davey over his shoulder, patting to bring up a burp. "My mother says it's not natural for a woman to want to leave her infant."

Alix held the dripping sponge and stared at her husband. She had occupied the administration building at Buffalo University and got arrested in antiwar protests in DC with this man. At least he looked like the same man. Blue work shirt, bushy beard, hair in a ponytail, faded jeans slung low on his hips because he was so skinny. She tossed the sponge in the sink. "Well, at least our mothers agree on one thing."

"Maybe you could wait till he's a little bigger?"

"It's the Women's Health Center and the position just opened up." She took the chicken out of the oven. Ridiculous to roast a chicken in this heat. "Anyway, all I did was apply. I probably won't even get it."

"They'd be crazy not to hire you." Sam switched quickly to her defense. He might be concerned about her working but he would challenge anyone else who thwarted her. "I'm not sure how you can manage it, though."

"It's only part-time." She heard the placating in her voice and changed her tone. "I'll figure something out." She held out her arms and Sam passed her the baby.

She settled in the rocking chair in the corner of the kitchen and began to nurse, loving the weight of Davey in the curve of her arm, laughing at his grin when he paused mid-suck, milk dribbling out the side of his mouth.

Last year, when she'd told her mother she was pregnant, her mother had pointed her finger at Alix's nose. "Right out of college? You just ruined all your chances at a life."

"Oh, no, everything is different now. Sam and I will share childcare and housekeeping fifty-fifty," Alix had informed her mother. Perhaps, she thought now, she'd been a bit smug.

Vivian unwrapped a block of cheddar cheese, dumped it on a plate, sprinkled some crackers around it, added a knife.

"Up, up," Katie wailed, clutching her leg and making movement difficult.

"Okay, sweet potato, but company's coming and I'm behind."

After Alix had called around last week and convinced them to begin this consciousness-raising group on their own, Vivian had agreed, but only if they could meet at her apartment so she wouldn't have to get a sitter.

Holding Katie with one arm, she spun around the tiny kitchen, putting grapes on a platter and humus in a bowl.

Still carrying Katie, she hustled to the bedroom, tossing her dirty laundry in the closet and stray toys into the laundry basket. In the living room, she kissed Katie's head and put her down to light the candles. Hopefully the vanilla scent would hide the mustiness of the second-hand furniture. Katie immediately cried and demanded to be picked up again. Vivian sighed and lifted her. The apartment was two blocks from the center of Harvard Square, only four rooms in a three-decker with hardly any furniture, but with piles of bright pillows that she hoped made her home soft and inviting. Covering that old couch with the Indian bedspread she'd bought yesterday was a nice touch. She started Judy Collins playing softly on the record player, straightened the cushions and picked up more toys, wishing she'd gotten home earlier to get everything ready.

Harvey, her boss, had asked her to stay late; and as her coworkers shouted good-byes and the large room cluttered with desks and file cabinets quickly emptied out, she hoped against hope that this meant Harvey was finally giving her the extra accounts, which meant extra money, which meant she could get her transmission fixed. But it turned out all he'd wanted was to go over her invoices.

She surveyed the room, adjusted another pillow, and kicked a ball under the couch. She wanted it all to be just right.

Vivian swung open the door with Katie still riding her hip. "I think I understand why people commit infanticide," she said, gesturing for the three women to come inside and switching Katie to her other hip. She kissed her daughter's blond head. "Love of my life. Only eighteen months and already a terrible two. I'm selling her cheap. Want her?"

Emily laughed. "God, I know that feeling well." Her skirt whirled as she clomped past in her work boots. Alix, her curls bouncing, smiled and followed.

"Let me take her," Gemma said. She scooped Katie from her arms as if to protect her from imminent abuse and with a practiced hand distracted the girl with the tassels on her scarf. "More nieces and nephews than I can count," she said by way of explanation.

Vivian led them into the kitchen. "Sorry, I'm not quite ready," she said, taking down plates and glasses. "I got home from work late and then Katie has been doing her barnacle routine, so I couldn't do a thing. Here." She held out a bottle of red Gallo wine to Alix. "Put this in the living room."

She handed Emily the platter of cheese and crackers and followed them, carrying the plates and glasses. Gemma walked the periphery of the small apartment, crooning to Katie. She wore a black tank top with black jeans and looked hardly big enough to support Katie's weight.

Emily put the platter on the wooden crate Vivian used as a coffee table and sank onto one of the brightly patterned

Marimekko pillows. "This is beautiful."

"Thanks."

"Those plants are so luscious." Alix pointed to the window filled with Swedish ivy, begonias, and spider plants that hung from macramé hangers in pots of various sizes. Alix wore an embroidered peasant blouse and jeans, and her filigree earrings dangled and caught the candlelight. "How do you do it?"

"I just throw them out when they look scraggly and buy new ones." Vivian smiled and hurried back to the kitchen to get a platter of hummus and pita bread.

Gemma walked in with Katie slumped against her shoulder. "I think she's asleep."

"You are a miracle worker. Please, come live with me?"

Gemma laughed as Vivian took Katie from her. "I'll just put her down and then we can get started."

When Vivian returned, Emily held up a cracker with Brie. "You know, I've never tasted this before. This is so, so good."

Vivian nodded. It had been worth blowing her weekly food budget on this spread.

They settled in, poured wine, and filled their plates.

"Thank you all for agreeing to meet here," Vivian said, feeling awkward and formal, but after all she was the hostess. "Anyone need anything else?"

All three shook their heads no.

Alix grabbed a cracker and crunched in the silence.

Emily pulled her braid forward and played with the end, looking like a kid in school trying not to get called on.

Gemma, her body coiled as if ready to bolt, leaned forward in the rocker.

Another record dropped onto the turntable and Roberta Flack sang into the quiet.

"Well, how the fuck do we start this?" Vivian said, and gulped her wine.

"No idea." Alix laughed and spread her hands, jingling her bangles. "But I can't believe how nervous I am."

Gemma reached for her bag and pulled out a mimeographed sheet of paper. "A woman at law school gave me this," she said, waving the paper. "'Guidelines on how to form a consciousness-raising group.'"

"We don't need—" Vivian started, but Gemma kept talking.

"It says: 'One, if you meet at different homes there should be no food or drink served. It's important that there be no competition or pressure regarding providing fancy food or—'"

Emily interrupted, pointing at the appetizers on Vivian's coffee table. "Already we broke the rules."

"Okay," Gemma said, rocking forward, "we'll forget that one. 'Two, each meeting should have a topic and then each woman, in turn, should speak on that topic until everyone in the room has had a chance to speak. Some beginning topics are: mothers, fathers, friends, periods, sex, orgasms, relationships, dreams—'"

"Hey," Alix asked, "aren't sex, orgasms, relationships, and dreams kind of the same topic?"

Gemma lifted her wineglass in acknowledgement and smiled. "'Three, at each meeting a different member should be chosen to be the leader to facilitate the discussion. Four, there is to be no judgment or criticism of each other's experiences. We are here to learn and explore in safe environment.'"

"How many rules are there?" Vivian asked.

"Ten."

"Shit, Gemma. Put away the paper and let's just talk." Vivian held up the bottle. "More wine?"

Emily held out her glass. "Let's choose a topic."

"Mothers," Alix declared, and also offered up her glass.

Emily laughed. "Well, that should keep us busy for months." She speared cheese with her toothpick and went on with, "I love my mother, but my father has put her through ..." just as

Gemma said, "My mother is the most talented, but ..." and Alix said, "I don't want to end up like my mother."

Everyone laughed and Vivian gave silent thanks that Alix hadn't chosen *relationships* as a topic. She wasn't ready to talk about Katie's father. Of course, she could always tell them that her husband had left her like she had told her landlady, but she didn't think lying to a group where you were supposed to tell the truth so you could change the world was the way to begin.

"Why don't you want to end up like your mother?" Vivian asked.

Alix sighed. "Where to begin."

CHAPTER THREE

The day Alix left home the temperature was way below freezing, but no snow. The ground was hard, the dirt frozen into little ruts, the grass brown, the sky that sharp metal gray of early-winter mornings.

"Don't worry. I'm not dying," she said, holding her mother close. She felt wise and protective and laughed to show her mother she was lighthearted and joking.

"We're all dying. Some will take a bit longer than others, that's all." Her mother pulled away and reached for her coffee mug on the end table by the couch.

"Cheery send-off, Mom."

"Tell me why I should be cheery and I'll be cheery." Her mother stood stiff in her quilted bathrobe. "I should be cheery that my only daughter is leaving? Leaving home, moving four hundred miles away to live in tents up north with a bunch of strangers in ten-degree weather in January. This I should be cheery about?"

"Yurts. We'll be living in yurts. And Sam says they're very warm and snug."

"Sam says. Sam says," her mother mimicked.

This was old. This was the refrain from childhood. Alix smiled and fought an urge to ruffle her mother's hair.

Sam would be there any minute and then they were beginning their new life. He had friends who had started a commune in upstate New York, somewhere near Ithaca. They'd been dating for six months and she loved everything about him. He was over six feet tall with black hair that fell to his shoulders, and at eighteen he already had a full beard.

Sam talked passionately about how people had gotten too disconnected from the land, eating processed food, living in little boxes, and only finding meaning when shopping for stuff they didn't need.

He told her she was beautiful and passed her notes in the school hallway, long letters about what he believed in and why the world had to change. He had been suspended from school twice for organizing school walkouts to protest the war.

He suggested she read Aldus Huxley's *The Doors of Perception*, Robert Heinlein's *Stranger in a Strange Land*, and Herman Hesse's *Siddhartha*. It was the dawning of the Age of Aquarius; the body was not shameful, it was beautiful. Sex was not dirty and secretive, it was loving and giving. The musical *Hair* sold out on Broadway. They tripped on acid in Belmont State Park and made love in the dunes. In December he told her that he was leaving to go live on his friends' commune and that he wanted her to go with him.

"I need you," he'd said.

Three little words.

Magic words.

Her mother put down her coffee mug. "Such an independent woman. Talks to me how she will never settle for being a housewife. As if being a housewife was like settling for being a grave digger. As if being a housewife was like choosing to lie down in a grave, so they can see how big to make the hole." She turned. "Ben," she said, and waited for Alix's father to look up from the newspaper. "Ben, do they have such jobs? People who lie down so they can measure the hole?"

"You have to make a scene?" Ben, already dressed in his suit and tie, shook out the paper. "We can't just say good-bye? You have to have a scene?"

He was a salesman on Seventh Avenue in Manhattan and traveled long hours to get to work. Alix understood it was a source of pride to live in the suburbs, but the cost was great. Every morning, all of Long Island would lift, floating lighter on the Atlantic as the railroad carried all the dark-suited men away into the city.

"Do you want a refill?" she asked. "I'll get us a refill." She grabbed her mother's mug and headed toward the kitchen.

Her mother followed right behind.

"Such an independent woman, running off with the first boy who asks her."

"Will you stop?" Alix poured the coffee and took the carton of milk from the refrigerator. "I've described this a thousand times already. This is all different. We're going to live as a group and raise our own food, without chemicals. We're going to share resources."

She had tried to explain it to her mother. "Isn't it weird that in all these houses, each one has a washing machine? Why not one machine for five or ten houses? We don't all need to have our own."

"You try sharing a washing machine with Mrs. Malloy and her ten kids," her mother had said. "You do that and then tell me everyone can share."

In this neighborhood the houses were small, the maple trees were large, and yards were full of kids. Everyone had moved from Brooklyn and Queens; and having survived the Depression and World War II, they were content with watching the game after the big Sunday meal and sipping cocktails before dinner. Most of the parents had finished high school, some had not. College was for their kids.

Her mother had done her best to fit in, sometimes even baking cookies for Valentine's Day, but domestic chores seemed to startle her. Her sewing basket overflowed with skirts, pants, socks—colorful clothes needing buttons or seams repaired. Her mother would take it from the hall closet when she needed a pin and look around as if to say, "Me? I'm supposed to do this?"

Her mother's sister, Aunt Rose, on the other hand, never married, was a teacher in New York City, and went to a lot of meetings about workers' rights. Every Sunday, Aunt Rose, in her sensible suit, with sensible shoes and bright red lipstick, schlepped out to the island with real bagels from Zabar's on the Upper West Side and an armful of books for Alix.

And every Sunday her mother would start some version of the poor Rose song. "Poor Rose, who will love you when I'm gone? Poor Rose, you need fun in your life. Poor Rose, all you do is teach and go to those political meetings."

Aunt Rose patiently listened, winked at Alix, and then said, "Ah, Mimi, who says I'm not having fun?" She laughed, and Alix could see silver glinting off the fillings in her back teeth.

"I'm not talking about that kind of fun, Rose." Her mother blushed. "I'm talking about stability. A real relationship. What are you going to do when you get old? It's just not natural. A woman without love." Her mother broke down and grabbed a pastry, breaking it in half, as if to say, with such stress, a body needed a little sweetener.

Aunt Rose told Alix that her frizzy brown hair was gorgeous, taught her how to play gin rummy and put on makeup, and brought her books.

Alix adored her aunt Rose, but even as a little girl, she knew she did not want to choose between being a housewife or being unnatural, a woman alone and without love.

Her father walked in carrying a tan furry thing over his arm. "I got you this as a going-away present. I got it wholesale. It's rabbit and you'll never be cold wearing this. Try it on." He held it for her.

Alix wrapped herself in the coat, petted its fur, exclaimed about how beautiful, how soft, how warm, how wonderful. She threw her arms around her father and hugged him close as he kissed the top of her head.

It was a shame, because Alix knew she would never wear the coat. She simply could not walk around with a dead animal on her back.

Her father reached for her woolen pea jacket.

"No, I'll take that also, Dad." She held onto it firmly. "I'll wear that when I'm changing tires or something. I wouldn't want to ruin this."

"Do you think being able to change your own tires brings you independence from a man?" her mother asked as Alix sat across the table from her and stroked the fur. "Oh, you think I don't understand that this relationship is different. You let me ramble on about what a mistake you are making while the whole time you feel superior."

"This coat is so warm. I'm beginning to sweat in it." She shrugged it off. Where was Sam? She was tired of arguing with her mother and was eager to be off.

She wanted to ride wild elephants and travel over mountains. She wanted to talk to people you're not supposed to talk to on the city streets. She wanted to say yes, yes, yes, instead of maybe and I don't know and I'm not sure if I should. She wanted to climb way out on the jetty and dance and sing—right there on those slippery rocks with the gray water all around and not be afraid of falling, and let the force of the sea seep through her and be like the ocean and travel the world.

"It's not like we're getting married," she said, trying to reassure her mother.

"That's supposed to make me feel better?" Her mother took another piece of coffee cake. "There are reasons why women get married."

"What?"

"Honey, you love this Sam, he loves you. So off you go together. This is not a new story in history. But who is this Sam to you? Has he said: I'll care for you, I'll work hard for you, I'll stick around? No, nothing. He says, come live in a tent with seven other people in the middle of January with the snow piling up around ..."

"But we don't believe in the man working hard to protect and support a woman. We believe in equality."

"Great. You'll get to cook and clean and change tires, and he'll talk about how progressive he is because he believes in equality." Her mother's fingers drummed on the table.

Her father was silent, staring out the window, probably anxious to get this good-bye scene over with so he could get to work.

Alix opened a cupboard and started rummaging. "Any of those chocolate chip cookies left?"

"At least make sure you always keep your knippel, your secret under-the-sink money."

"That won't be necessary." Alix waved in dismissal. "We have a completely honest relationship. No hiding anything."

"God help you."

CHAPTER FOUR

Gemma, lugging her law books, hurried through Harvard Yard toward Vivian's apartment, brown leaves crackling under her feet. They'd met every Wednesday for the past two months, sharing their stories. Through Nixon's reelection, during the escalation of the Vietnam War, as the words feminism and women's liberation started to hit the media, they came as though their lives depended on it. Not one of them missed a meeting, not one of them was ever late.

She still worried they didn't have a format. Gemma weaved around clumps of students. What was the point of a meeting of women just to talk? It smacked of watching her mother gossip with Mrs. Sipione from across the street. Or her aunts huddled in the kitchen while the men in the living room discussed politics and dealt with real-world issues. Gemma wanted to be in the living-room crowd.

Obviously women had been talking to each other for eons. It was the stuff of stand-up jokes. *Pick a little, talk a little, pick a little, talk a little, Cheep cheep cheep, talk a lot, pick a little more.* The lyrics from *Music Man* ran through her head. But now, women speaking to other women made front-page news and was heralded across the country, from *Ms. Magazine* to Ellen Goodman in *The Boston Globe.*

Even so, Gemma worried. There was so much that needed to

be done. End the war. Fight for abortion rights. Maybe they should be chaining themselves to fences or burning themselves like the Vietnamese monks, or even just getting arrested.

But still she kept coming.

Passing through the wrought iron gates to the street, she stepped off the curb and then jumped back as a honking car sped by.

Willie told her to stop overanalyzing everything and just go if she enjoyed the meetings. Willie had been trying to get her to relax, to take things in stride ever since she'd met him.

When Gemma finally had convinced her father to let her attend NYU, she had put her bags in her dorm room, bounced on both beds to decide which one felt best, grabbed some Scotch tape and put the poster "If You're not Part of the Solution, You're Part of the Problem" on the wall next to the bed she chose. Then she bought a black leotard to wear with her jeans, a warm woolen pea jacket from the Army-Navy store, and a black beret.

She registered for her classes, took a job in the dining hall washing dishes, and joined Students against the War, Students against Racism, and Women for Equality. You didn't have to be anyone special to become an activist—the movements came out and grabbed you off the street.

She became three people.

She was the A student who read everything assigned and did not cut one class, and then sprinted across campus to her dishwashing job.

She was the student protester rushing from meetings to demonstrations.

And then of course, she was the daughter, sister, and family girl. Her mother wanted her to call home every other day.

The beginning of her sophomore year she met Willie at a meeting for tutoring underprivileged kids in Harlem. The black members told the white members to stay home and take care of their own shit.

Gemma argued fiercely for her right to participate. She got put down as a liberal honky bitch. She called them racist assholes.

Willie sat relaxed in a corner, his long legs stretched out into the room, not saying anything. She was distracted by his silence.

She lost her argument and was banned from the tutoring program. She left angry and exhausted. Willie caught up with her.

"You're right, you know," he said.

"Yeah, well, thanks for all your support. A bit late, though, don't you think?" She walked fast. Furious, she just wanted to get home and sleep. She was hungry and had an exam the next day. She was supposed to go home over the weekend to a niece's party, but she also had a big paper due and …

"They're right too, you know," he said.

"Obviously, I don't know." She didn't want to argue anymore. She was all argued out. She'd get the energy back, but not now, and not tonight with this man who didn't even bother to open his mouth before and now tried to consider both sides.

"You must be the kind of person," he said, "who sees every issue in terms of right and wrong, black and white." He kept pace with her easily, just strolled along, while her legs pumped and pumped and she was nearly out of breath.

"I'm not a rigid thinker," she responded, "if that's what you're saying. I know there are gray areas. I know everything isn't black or white. I know …" She stopped mid-sentence when he laughed.

She turned right at the corner. He stayed with her.

"You must be the kind of person who turns everything into a joke," she said. "I believe passionately in certain things."

"You must be the kind of person who needs some help to lighten up."

She stopped short. "Listen. I'm tired. I have a lot left to do tonight. I am not enjoying this conversation. I'm going home."

"Listen," he mimicked her. "I liked your passion. This is going to be a long, long life struggle. I would hate to see you give up."

"Who the fuck is giving up?"

"You will. If you don't crack some jokes, crack a smile. Let's have coffee."

Gemma turned onto Story Street just as Alix and Emily reached Vivian's driveway. It was exactly seven o'clock. Gemma ducked her head behind her books as Emily grinned and raised her camera. Quickly it had become a ritual, Emily trying to get Gemma's photograph before she hid. Gemma hated how she looked in pictures. Alix, her crazy curls bound in a clip, waved.

Inside, Vivian was all bustle and business as she took down plates and glasses. She wore purple and orange paisley bell-bottoms with a long-sleeved V-neck purple top that fell just below her hips. Gemma thought Vivian managed to look sexy and comfy all at once. She could learn a thing or two from her. Vivian was tall and what her mother would call solid, and just a perfect vision of beautiful womanhood. Her blond hair fell from her headband, and she blew it off her face.

"Katie asleep already?" Gemma hoped not. She had been looking forward all day to the usual routine of putting Katie to bed while the rest of them got things set up. Katie toddled out, clutching Dr. Seuss's *The Sneetches and Other Stories*. "Oh, that's my favorite," Gemma said, and scooped her up.

Katie fell asleep halfway through her rendition of "stars upon thars." Gemma tucked her in and went into the living room while Alix and Vivian finished fixing food platters in the kitchen. Gemma pulled a few grapes from their stems and watched while Emily fiddled with her camera. Whenever there was a lull, Emily seemed to handle her camera.

"You know," she said, zippering the camera case closed, "one of Rick's friends told me that if I could capture this women's movement, get photos of real women libbers, I could finally sell something. Editors want to know what happens in these women's meetings." She shrugged, looking chagrined.

"How do you take pictures of ideas?" Gemma asked.

"Oh, no." Vivian laughed, striding in with Alix behind her. "They want pictures in case all the women they ever called a bitch came bursting into their offices to cut off their dicks for revenge. Then they'll have evidence."

Emily smiled but kept on talking. "I don't fit in with Rick's friends, even after all this time. I'm surrounded by these people who think I'm the ultimate earth mother he mysteriously spirited out of Vermont and brought to the city to live. Slightly exotic and from another era—like a wagon wheel. I mean, the women always ask me how to make soup and pumpkin pie and I don't know how to cook for shit."

Everyone laughed, but Gemma thought she could understand the mistake Rick's friends made. Emily exuded tranquility, and with her long braid and flowing clothes, even Gemma wanted to curl up at her feet and ask her to dispense wisdom from a time long ago.

Emily stared at the floor as she spoke, playing with the end of her braid. "I left Vermont in a panic, believing if I didn't leave, the Vermont mud would seize and bury me like it had my mother." She shrugged. "It all made sense at the time, but it's clear I'll never fit in, never belong, coming from Vermont and not being born of this whole Cambridge world."

Vivian sat with her legs folded under her. "You know, I'm shocked at how much I want to belong. Mickey, this guy at work, told me if I wanted to fit in, I needed to stop trying so hard to be one of the guys. I asked him what the fuck he meant and he suggested for one, that I stop swearing so much." She grinned. "He told me that it made the men jumpy, that they'd accept a woman better who acted, well, more like a woman."

Alix laughed and reached for her tea, her bangles clinking. "Whatever that means. I feel like all I do is pretend. Pretending I know how to be a mother, acting like I know how to be a wife. Everyone around me seems to know what they're doing—so I just hope I look the part."

Gemma loved listening to them all, but she wasn't used to so much sharing. Growing up, she'd had to keep so much of herself hidden. It was a hard habit to break. Even now she kept secrets from Willie, not to mention keeping Willie a secret from everyone in her family. Her father would have a heart attack if he found out that she lived, in sin no less, with a black man. Attending law school was as much oddness as he could handle.

Emily flipped her braid over her shoulder. "You know we're always talking about how we're peculiar, how we're not normal women. Gemma's an anomaly at the law school, Alix doesn't match her mother's expectations, Vivian doesn't fit anywhere, being a single mom in a man's profession, and I feel like an alien whose been plopped down from another planet." She grinned. "Maybe *we* are the normal."

"Now, that's a scary thought," Vivian said. "Wine? Water?"

Alix shook her head pointing to her tea. "There's been a lot of talk about this Mickey lately. Anything going on?"

"I wish, but no." Vivian sighed. "He's just nice and he keeps me updated about work opportunities. You know, the stuff they talk about in the men's room or something, because it's never around me.

"But I do think I figured out how to handle my boss." Vivian straightened. "He keeps telling me repeatedly that IBM doesn't promote women to supervisor positions. So, I'm just going to undo one of my top buttons, lean forward like this, and—"

"You wouldn't." Alix sounded horror struck.

"I'm not going to sleep with him," Vivian said. "I'm just going to let him think it may be a possibility."

"I don't know about you," Emily said in an exaggerated country drawl "but where I come from, folks have a name for that."

Gemma laughed, but quieted quickly at Vivian's offended expression. "It's not the same at all. My boss uses his power to try to get what he wants. Why shouldn't I do the same back to him?"

"Hmm. Trading sex for favors?" Alix asked. "I think there's a name for that also?"

"This is different." Vivian reached for the wine.

Gemma held out her glass. "You should be promoted on skill, not on how big your breasts are, and if you play this game you are just perpetuating the whole fucked-up mess."

"Judgmental," Emily said, also holding out her glass.

"Oh, sorry. Right. You should do what you want," Gemma said, and sipped her wine.

Vivian's laugh jiggled her arm, causing wine splatters. She put down the bottle. "It's almost worth getting you upset to watch you swallow your disapproval and try to be supportive."

Gemma shrugged and smiled. "I'm right, though."

Vivian raised her glass in a half salute. "I need this promotion. I'll let you know how it goes."

CHAPTER FIVE

November 16, 1972
Two days later

F our bags! Alix breathed through her diaphragm and unclenched her muscles as they unloaded her mother's car. She planned to stay a week, through Thanksgiving, but four bags?

Sam winked at her and then pivoted toward her mother. "Mimi, you are so good to come." He bent low to kiss her; the top of Mimi's head barely reached his chin. Sam's ponytail curled below the collar of his T-shirt, a few wiry strands of gray threaded among the black. He stepped back, giving her mother a full up-and-down appraisal. "And that haircut makes you look ten years younger." Sam's untrimmed beard filled and rounded his face, and his wide brown eyes completed the fuzzy black-bear look, all cuddly and sweet. Alix covered her snort with a cough and picked up a bag.

"I should take you to work with me and set you up with my boss," he added, and then carried Mimi's suitcases to their second-floor apartment.

Alix thought her mother's hair looked like she had trimmed it with nail scissors; it tufted in uneven clumps. She followed upstairs to help get her mother settled in the small extra bedroom. Sam had moved Davey's crib to their room, along with his clothes and toys to give her mother some space. Alix had even put a vase of yellow chrysanthemums on the dresser to make her feel welcome and to distract her from the painted-over second-hand furniture.

All through dinner, Sam kept up a mix of teasing and flirting, diverting Mimi from what Alix knew was her mission to set her daughter straight. "And that color green is perfect for your eyes," Sam even said as they sat around the small Formica table having the meatloaf her mother had brought in a cooler.

Alix almost kicked him under the table, thinking he was making fun of her mother's lime pantsuit, but her mother beamed. She jiggled Davey, sleeping in her arms, and patted her hair.

"I don't see how you could want to leave him." She bent and kissed the top of his head. "That baby smell, so precious. He's so dear and it lasts such a short time, why would you want to abandon him?"

"I'm not abandoning him. I have friends who are mothers and also work, and their kids are doing great," Alix said, thinking of Emily and Vivian.

Sam jumped in, talking with his mouth full. "She's going to an interview tomorrow for a part-time job, not leaving home. Alix isn't happy just being a mother. And anyway, at this place she can bring Davey to work. Plus, the extra money won't hurt." He helped himself to another piece of meatloaf and smiled at her mother. "This is the best meal I've had in weeks."

Her mother sniffed but didn't say anything more.

Under the table, Alix reached over and squeezed Sam's leg, grateful he'd transformed into her defender, but not convinced she could trust it.

"I got the job." Alix called Sam as soon as she got home and he promised he would leave work early.

"I could have had a career too," her mother said as Alix hung up the phone and turned to take the kettle off the stove. "But I chose to focus on my children."

Alix sighed and put a mug of tea in front of Mimi. "I don't have to choose between work and motherhood."

"Of course you do," Mimi said, waving her hand around Davey wiggling on her lap. Alix and Mimi were built exactly opposite. Her mother was big breasted, round on top, an apple on stilts, Alix thought, thoroughly annoyed with her. But they both had curly hair and talked with their hands.

Mimi shifted Davey to one knee and reached for her tea. He batted at the mug as she awkwardly held it away from his reach while trying to take a sip.

"Can I hold him while you drink that?" Alix didn't like watching her mother hold scalding liquid near the baby.

"No, I'm fine." But she put the mug back on the table. "That's what you young women don't realize, you have to choose. You were the one who went and got pregnant. Don't make Davey suffer for that."

Alix shredded a napkin.

"That's what it means to be a mother. Sacrifice." Her mother again reached for the hot tea, and again Alix tensed. "You just can't go doing whatever you want anymore."

"I think it's time to nurse him." Alix stood to gather Davey.

"I could give him a bottle while you get dinner ready."

Alix paused. She'd left her mother with an emergency bottle and a sleeping Davey that afternoon when she went for her interview, but Davey had slept right through.

"It's Sam's turn to cook tonight," she said, again reaching for Davey. "We don't need to worry about dinner."

Mimi held him tight. "Sam shouldn't be cooking after working all day."

"Mom, you sound like you're from the last century."

"Well, men need attention. They need care. You need to

concentrate on how to keep Sam around."

It had been four years since Alix's father had died, and loneliness and need emanated from her mother like a bad smell.

Alix got the bottle and circled to the stove to heat it up. *Why the hell not?* she thought. She'd let her mother feed the baby. After her father died, her mother's life, which hadn't been that wide before, narrowed to a sliver. During those final weeks, when Alix came home, her father was pasty, doughy; his skin hung and his teeth were yellow against his pale face. His trips to the bathroom left him winded, his legs shaking. He lay on the living room couch with all the windows in the house shut against drafts and the shades drawn. The flickering from the TV was the brightest spot in the room.

Her mother had been pale too. And sharp. As her father's features began to sink and diffuse, her mother's became angular and brittle. In the kitchen, sitting in the one shaft of sunlight at the kitchen table, her mother said, "Well, so it turns out your grandmother was right after all. One way or another, they leave you."

As they waited for the bottle to heat, Mimi riffled through the mail piled on the table and held up an envelope. "You didn't open the card I sent you?"

"I told you I toss mail addressed to Mrs. Samuel Morris." She tested the bottle. "My name is still Alix Goldman. The name you gave me, remember?"

"Keeping your maiden name has nothing to do with being an independent woman."

"Becoming Mrs. Sam Morris has everything to do with eliminating who I was."

"Have you kept up your knippel? Like I told you to?" She took the bottle and adjusted Davey into the crook of her arm. He latched onto the bottle like he'd never eaten before. "Such a hungry boy." Mimi stared at him with adoration and then looked up at her daughter.

"That isn't necessary." Alix waved in dismissal.

"Hmm." Mimi put the bottle on the table, eased Davey to a slumped sitting position, and gently massaged his back for a burp.

Alix laughed. She rarely saw him from this angle, his head tilted, one eye half closed, the picture of debauchery. He gave a loud burp.

"Such a good boy." Mimi smiled and cooed, kissing the top of his head and easing him back to drink more.

"It's ridiculous to hide money from your husband," Alix continued, although she knew she should drop this conversation. She pointedly gathered the mail away from her mother's snooping. "And anyway, now I have a job."

"Just remember, no marriage is an equal marriage," her mother pronounced, and returned her attention to feeding the baby.

Mimi was a master of simply disregarding what she didn't want to hear. Alix turned to wash the dishes, hoping the loudly running water would prevent further conversation.

While drying the dishes, she snuck looks at Davey, milk drunk as Mimi murmured endearments, and wished her mother could be happy that her daughter could be so much more than a housewife.

"Hello," she heard Sam call and run up the stairs, as she dried the last dish. Thank God, good to his word, he'd arrived home early bearing Chinese food and champagne. "We have to celebrate tonight." He kissed her and spun her around the kitchen. "Congratulations, although I had no doubts." She laughed at his enthusiasm and for a grateful moment forgot her mother's disapproval.

"What an amazing daughter you've raised, Mimi!" He presented roses to her mother, kissed Alix again, and popped the champagne cork with a flourish. "Here's to the both of you!" He did his best to keep up the flattery to her mother while feting her.

Her mother tried to look pleased for Sam's sake, but Alix knew that phony smile well.

After dinner, Sam cleaned up while she walked Davey around the apartment, trying to get him to fall asleep. He'd been fussy in the evenings lately, and she found it soothed him if she put him in the baby carrier. Alix thought their apartment looked warm and cozy, but she knew her mother saw only wood planks on bricks that they used for bookshelves, and the bright red blanket covering the holes in the couch. Already she'd suggested improvements.

"You know," Mimi said, watching her pace back and forth across the living room, "you shouldn't coddle him so much. They say that mothers who overwhelm their sons with attention could make them"—she lowered her voice to a whisper—"homosexual."

"Well, going to work should solve that problem." Alix swayed side to side, refusing to engage. Davey was almost asleep.

"What is so important about this job? They say that children who don't have proper nurturing grow up to be emotionally stunted."

"Do you hear yourself?" Alix stopped swaying and shouted. "I pay too much attention and he's a homo and not enough and he's an emotional basket case. You're insane."

Davey wailed.

"Mimi." Sam hurried in from the kitchen. He looked exhausted. "Let me make you some tea."

When Davey was finally asleep and they were alone in the bedroom, Sam cuddled her. "Don't let her get to you."

"Easy for you to say."

He jumped up from the bed. "I have something for you." He brought a shopping bag from the closet and pulled out a briefcase.

Alix grinned. "This is beautiful." It was soft brown leather with her initials engraved in gold. "Thank you. But you do remember it's an entry-level position? I'll be checking people in, filing, that sort of thing."

"Yes, but not for long. You will move right on up."

"It is sexy." She stroked the leather.

"Not as sexy as you," Sam said, and drew her close for a long, lingering kiss.

"My mother," she said when she finally pushed him away.

"We'll be quiet." He tugged her close again.

Davey woke up an hour later. She fed him and he fell back asleep. Forty-five minutes later he woke again. The third time as she dragged herself out of bed, her feet curling on the cold floor, her eyes scratchy from lack of sleep, she wondered if maybe he knew in his little baby soul that soon her energies would be divided. Shivering in her nightgown, she changed his diaper as he wailed. She tried nursing him even though he couldn't possibly be hungry; and when that didn't work she paced the dark living room, the streetlights throwing shadows, whispering how much she loved him and how nothing could be more important than he was.

"Sam," she said as she climbed back into bed after Davey finally fell asleep. "Sam." She shook him awake.

"Are you crying?"

"What if my mother is right? What if my going to work hurts Davey?"

"What?" He struggled to consciousness.

"She could be right. Maybe I'm just being selfish, being a bad mother?"

He groaned. "Don't become as crazy as she is."

CHAPTER SIX

November 29, 1972
Six days later

The Wednesday after Thanksgiving, Emily hurried through Harvard Square, breath clouds puffing into the frigid air. Normally she would slow down and savor the quiet of walking alone, without kids, but today's sun was a total sham. Vermont cold invigorated her, made her want to crunch through the woods, but this Boston cold depleted her and encouraged cowering under quilts. On days like this she longed for Vermont.

At The Camera Shop, she slipped off her gloves and with only her usual difficulty, jiggled the key in just the right way that opened the door. She flipped the closed sign to open and wove her way around boxes and the counter to the back, unwrapping her scarf and shrugging off her coat as she went.

Bernie's store stood on a side street in Cambridge, between Mt. Auburn and Mass Ave. The shop was overheated in winter, perpetually dusty no matter how much she cleaned, and smelled musty, like the used bookstore on Church Street. The front room only had space for a counter, its glass case displaying cameras and lenses. On top were catalogs for ordering all sorts of accessories. The back room held Bernie's desk, invoice files, supplies, and a small darkroom. At least a hundred framed prints covered the walls of the front room. Some were from the late 1800s, brown sepia, and also more recent pictures, compelling black and white studies of Harvard Square buildings that Bernie had taken.

She dumped her stuff on a chair in the back room, grabbed a rag, and went right to work dusting the bottom shelves of the display counter.

When Matt was first born, she would bring him to work most days, but now with Jessica just a baby, she only worked weekends and occasional afternoons, when Rick could be home with them.

The bell over the door jingled, and Emily looked up. Bernie strode in with a gust of glacial air. His gray hair stood up in tufts and the pouches under his eyes were darker and more pronounced than usual.

"Are you all right?" she asked. "You don't look so good."

"I'm old." He shrugged off his overcoat. "Of course I don't look good." He walked around the counter to hang his coat in the back room and put on his tan cardigan. "When you're my age, you won't look so great either."

Emily glanced at her watch. "You're early."

"Did those new lenses come in?"

She nodded. "Out back." She watched with great affection as he walked to the back room. "Why are you limping?"

"None of your business."

When she'd first left Vermont and got this job, she wrote to Dorrie, her best friend:

> *I found this dusty old camera shop owned by this ancient guy with yellow teeth who takes mind-blowing photographs. I hung around until he couldn't stand it anymore and he's paying me to wait on customers and clean a little. You've got to come visit. This place is amazing. Everyone has long hair, and wears love beads and bright colors. I*

bought a beautiful long skirt I wear all the time. There are head shops. Do you know what a head shop is? They actually sell all this stuff for smoking grass, like a 7-11 for freaks. Please come visit. I'll send you the bus ticket money.

Dorrie never did come, but over the years, Bernie had taught her what he knew. He would send her out when the shop was slow. "Go take pictures." They would develop them together in the darkroom, and he would critique her work, asking questions, offering suggestions. He framed the ones he liked best and hung them on the shop walls. She had won a few contests and sold four of her photographs, but she collected more rejections than sales. Her ambition was fierce and gnawed at her insides. It was something the women's group understood. They all were ambitious and determined, and it was the first place she'd ever been able to give full voice to that want, even if she didn't know how to fulfill it.

"Where's the race?" Bernie demanded when she whined. "Art takes meandering."

Maybe. But it also took focus and drive. Emily sneezed and continued her dusting. She was definitely not a be-here-now kind of person. She had rushed to leave home, hurried to have children, and now burned for recognition.

Now, she was working on a photo essay—women in action, women at work, women doing, not just being. Women were the great unseen.

Emily stretched out the kinks in her knees and back, and then grabbed the broom, a futile attempt to remove the grime embedded in the wood floor.

"Okay, Bernie," she called to the back. She straightened and tossed her braid over her shoulder. "I'm leaving now." Two mothers starting a community daycare asked her to do a photo shoot and then she was heading over to Vivian's for the group meeting. Bernie was covering the shop for her. "I'll be back in on Saturday morning."

"Let me tell you something." Bernie came from out back. "You women think you don't get treated right, taken seriously, are ignored as irrelevant. Wait until you're my age. Then you'll see what it means to be looked through as if you weren't even standing on the sidewalk." He scratched his ear. "At least you get noticed for being sexy."

"Elderly women, then, must really have it doubly hard, don't you think?"

Bernie dismissed that with a quick wave of his hand. "Women, women. Let me tell you, being an old man is no picnic."

"How old are you anyway?"

"Here." Bernie held out an Olympus OM-1. It had just arrived. "Take this one with you today to that daycare. Let me know if it's any good." He put it down on the counter and turned to go to the back again.

"I can't— Bernie, if anything happened to this— I couldn't afford ..." It was the best camera in the shop.

"Don't argue. I'm the boss."

Vivian walked in from the kitchen carrying a plate with dark blobs arranged in a circle. "I made these special for group tonight. Chocolate truffles. But I warn you they are addictive."

Emily cupped her hand around her mug of coffee, hoping to get some feeling back into her fingers after the walk from the daycare. They all wore bulky sweaters and Gemma still had her scarf wrapped tight around her neck.

Alix sat on the pillow next to her, reached for a mug and blew ripples across the top to cool the coffee. "God, I couldn't wait to get here. Five days with my mother is four days too long." She laughed. "I know that's mean, but she just wouldn't give up on the whole going to work thing."

Gemma unwrapped her scarf a bit. "I almost canceled but then decided to blow off the meeting with my professor instead." She bit into one of Vivian's truffles. "Oh, these are so good."

Emily reached for one. She wondered if they all weren't falling in love, just a little. They were happy to see each one another and hungry to hear every last detail of the week. She knew sometimes they all got nervous -- maybe they'd revealed too much. Gemma, especially, seemed startled at all this divulging. Yes, it was a lot like falling in love. Longing and fear. Longing and fear. She wasn't sure if they qualified as real feminists, but she was enjoying these women. "Amazing," Emily said around the chocolate and butter melting in her mouth.

"Alix?" Vivian lifted the plate inviting her to take one.

"No, I can't. I'm on a diet."

"Why on earth? asked Gemma.

"What for?" Vivian nodded in agreement. "You're gorgeous."

"Well," Alix scooted back from the food table a bit. "Sam mentioned that my thighs were chunky."

"Brilliant way to make sure he doesn't get laid for awhile." Vivian laughed and put down the plate of truffles.

Alix pointed to herself. "It's hard to see under all these clothes, but I haven't lost all the baby weight yet. And it's time to work on it. He noticed that I seem to be hungry all the time."

Gemma reached for another sweet. "You're a nursing mother for god sakes. Aren't you required to eat when you're hungry?"

Alix sipped her coffee. "I know one of the points of the women's movement is to get past thinking we only have value if we're sexy and stop being all hung up on our looks and all that," she said with a wave of her arm. "But I don't want to be a woman who let her self go, as my mother would say. I want Sam to stay attracted to me."

Emily had to lean forward to hear as Alix almost whispered

this admission and then jumped when Gemma plunked her mug down.

"Oh for god sakes. He should work on being attracted to real women instead of centerfolds. You shouldn't work on trying to look like some model," Gemma said. "You're perfect the way you are."

"I agree," Vivian said. "You shouldn't change how you look; he should change how he sees."

"No." Emily said. Alix looked nonplussed by the number of *shoulds* being flung around the table. "I know what Alix is talking about. Sometimes during sex, I get distracted thinking about my body parts and worrying about their flaws. My belly is too soft, my breasts are too small and I have fat knees."

"Fat knees?" Vivian laughed. "Who gives a flying fuck about fat knees?"

Emily frowned. This was not funny. She was entirely serious.

"I'll show you and then you'll see." She stood up, dropped her jeans around her ankles, and pointed to her knees. "See?"

"You are nuts," Alix said. "Your knees are not fat."

"But look, they do have this fatty stuff that I bet yours don't."

Vivian also stood and dropped her pants to compare. "My knees are bony."

"I really hate my ankles." Alix pointed.

"I have stubby toes," Gemma said.

"You want to see what I hate?" Vivian pulled off her sweater. "You are so lucky your breasts are small," she said to Alix. "Look, one kid and already drooping."

Gemma hesitated and then stood, pulling up her sweater. "Look at these. Stretch marks. And this is with no kids."

"Hey," Emily said, unhooking her bra, "do you guys have hairs on your breasts?" She pulled on one long hair.

And then she started to laugh.

There they were, stripped, in the middle of Vivian's hanging plants and colorful pillows. "Wait, wait. I'm getting my camera." She had never been anywhere else like this. She had never had the experience before of being so closely listened to—to having her stories mean something, to be so intensely curious about everything about these women. It was like being on an expedition, an archeological dig of immense proportions, like the Egyptian pyramids, finding room after room of glittering treasures that had been buried in the desert for centuries.

Emily adjusted her lens.

She'd been raised to believe that women were emotional, weak, dependent, needy, ditzy, not interested in sex, requiring protection, caretakers, fearful, not as smart as men, not critical thinkers, soft, quiet, too sensitive.

And now, all over the country, women were saying, "Oh, wait a minute. I will tell you what I am." All around her women were uncovering, discovering, recovering, and doing it loudly, messily, excitedly, on a deeply personal level. Recreating the definitions, woman by woman, until the very language had to be changed.

Emily snapped a photo. And she was right in the middle of it.

"Well, my mother spent her entire life on a diet and"—Vivian pulled her sweater back on—"both her husbands left her anyway."

Gemma rewrapped her scarf. "My mother and aunts were the women who let themselves go and they happily jiggle when they laugh."

Emily put down her camera. "My mother always changed into a dress when my father was due home. One of them had small blue flowers on a white background. A regular dress, short sleeves, buttons up the front, belted at the waist, the belt covered in the same cloth as the dress with a flared skirt. When she stood up, she blended perfectly with the wallpaper in the living room. The wallpaper was a white background with little blue flowers. I remembering wondering if my mother had dresses to blend herself into all the walls of the house?"

CHAPTER SEVEN

Y ou carry the tribal blood of the Mahican from your grandmother's side, Emily's mother had told her. Our family has lived and died in the hills of central Vermont since the very beginning of time, her mother also said. Emily had always liked the idea of being part of a tribe from way back; and even if it wasn't true, it didn't matter since as it was, she must be related to half the people in Barre and Montpelier.

When she was little, in spring when the mud was so thick it sucked tires off trucks, as her father liked to say, he would take her into town for the first ice cream cone at Jimmy's, and during these walks he always introduced her to some new and distant relative.

"This is our eldest daughter, Emily." Her father's hand would come down heavy on her head. Then he would crouch so his eyes were even with hers and he'd say, "This is Ed. He works over in the quarry. He's the cousin of Martha who is Uncle Jacob's niece. Say hi."

"Hi."

That would be it. Her father would straighten and he and Ed would go on talking about whatever had brought them together. Walking with her father through Montpelier was always like that. He was the editor of the *Barre-Montpelier Times*. He loved to talk, and he talked to everyone.

When she went to town with her mother, it was a different story. Her mother would whip in and out of stores and up and down the block with such sense of purpose and determination, no one did more than nod or smile as they sped by.

Her father called it the Boston walk. When they all went together he'd say, "That's how your mother learned to walk in Boston when she went to nursing school." Emily would be holding her father's hand and up ahead would be her mother's back. "In Boston, you have to walk fast and keep your head down and make sure you don't talk to anyone."

Her mother stopped to let them catch up. "You're telling her stories again. You're going to scare the city right out of her."

"Good. Who wants her to live in Boston anyway? It's fine right here."

"When she grows up, she can live anywhere she wants, do anything she wants. I don't want her scared of Boston before she's even seen it."

It was her mother who got her started with photography.

"Something is not right with Emily," she overheard her mother tell her father one night when she was seventeen. "She's dark, like her soul is murky."

Emily sat on the stairs so she could both see and hear. She sucked on the end of her braid. She wore her hair in a single braid that came to her waist. She liked the solid feel of it, the weight of it as she turned her head, the heavy braid taking its time to travel from one shoulder to the other. This was not a flighty braid. Emily was not a flighty teenager.

Her father worked long hours and her mother, worn out from a day of children and chores, often didn't wait up. But that night she did.

"Her soul murky?" Her father laughed. "You should be the journalist, not me." He slouched in his chair, wearing a flannel shirt, his feet in boots up on the coffee table, holding a glass of Scotch. He waved his arm, as if waving away concerns, and the ice clinked in the glass. "Aren't you taking all this rather seriously?"

"She hardly says two words. And if she does talk, it tends to be accusatory or complaining."

"I wonder where she might have learned that womanly trait."

Her mother ignored him. "Take her down to the paper, find her work, see what she likes, get her out of this house."

Emily climbed upstairs. In her room she pulled up the covers and stared wide eyed into the dark. She had almost run into that room and thrown her arms around her mother, so surprised and grateful that she had suggested Emily work at the paper.

Emily loved it. Mostly, she ran errands for the staff, sharpened pencils, got them paper from the supply cabinet when they ran out, and listened to their gossip when they were avoiding work. Occasionally, she'd be sent out on a story with old Paul, the official photographer, and then she'd help him in the darkroom while he taught her about developing. She fooled around with the camera, trying things out; like the afternoon they were dispatched to the school board meeting and she wandered off to shoot pictures of the kids on the jungle gym.

After she began working at the paper, her relationship with her father changed. He initiated conversations, asking her questions about what she thought, what she noticed. "Emily," he'd say, calling her into his office, "what is the sentiment at the high school regarding the war?" One day, he stopped her on her way to get Wite-Out and asked, "Emily, does anyone in school talk about these women liberationists?" She felt herself grow taller and walk straighter. Anytime she could, she made sure to pass his office, in case he wanted to say something to her.

One exceptionally cold January afternoon, she came into the newsroom after school, stomped the snow off her boots, and unwrapped her scarf, her face tingly and itchy as it thawed in the intense heat of the room. Pat, an assistant editor, came up to her before she had gotten her arms out of her coat sleeves and thrust prints in her face, asking if Emily knew who'd taken the photos. Pat was one of Emily's favorite people on the paper. She was in her late twenties and had left town to go to the Rhode Island School of Design. She was an artist. She actually did the layout for the paper, but at home, when she wasn't working, she painted.

Emily nodded, frightened. She was supposed to be taking pictures for the paper, and when she went off on her own projects, she did the developing when few people were around and took the prints home after they'd dried. Thank God these weren't the breast series of the girls in the senior class. Those were upstairs in her room, under her mattress.

"I did." She turned and hung up her coat and pretended it was no big deal.

"Come with me. I want your father to hear what I have to say."

Pat started off down the aisle between the desks to the back where her father's office was. Pat wore hiking boots and pants and didn't click on the floor like some of the other women. Emily had never seen Pat in anything but pants. Following her down the aisle, her own thighs still numb with cold, she tried to imagine Pat in a skirt or a dress. She couldn't. Pants were perfect for her.

Pat knocked and entered at the same time. "Gene, you need to see this."

"I'm on the phone."

"So, get off."

Emily backed out of the office, expecting her father to yell and wanting him to understand that this trip to his office wasn't her idea; and she certainly wouldn't mind waiting until he was off the phone.

"I'll call you back," he said into the receiver.

Emily was stunned.

"You know, you're beginning—" he started, but Pat cut him

off.

"Emily did these." She tossed the prints onto his desk.

"Emily's here?" He looked up and waved her in. "What's this about?" He picked up the pictures. "Come in. Come in. Don't hang in the doorway." He looked at the pictures as he talked. "I hate people hanging in the doorway. In or out. In or out."

Pat grabbed the photographs from him and walked around to his side of the desk. "Pay attention. Focus." One by one, side by side, over the papers on his desk, she laid the photos out.

Emily stayed by the door, ready to leave the second her father exploded at Pat. She'd never known anyone at work—really, anyone anywhere—who talked to her father like that. Except maybe her mother and that usually meant a big fight was coming. She wasn't sure what this was all about or why Pat was making such a case out of a few photographs done on her own time, but plainly either Pat or she was going to get screamed at and she didn't intend to stick around and listen for long.

"These." Pat pointed to three prints in particular. Emily saw they were the ones of the boys smoking next to the aluminum garbage pails behind the Market Basket. "These are some of the best photos I've seen." She straightened up. "Your daughter is talented."

"Hmm." Her father nodded. "Yes. Very nice." He appeared confused. He smiled at Emily. "I'm glad you're having fun with the camera, Em. Keep up the good work." He gathered the prints and held them out to her. "Listen, I'm going to have to stay late tonight. Pat and I have a layout to work on. Make sure you get a ride home with Bill, okay?"

"Sure." Emily shrugged. "I'm glad you liked these, Pat. I—"

She stopped. Pat wasn't listening to her, but was glaring at her father, her arms crossed, her feet planted.

"Gee, sorry, Gene. I'd forgotten about the late night tonight and made plans. We'll have to come in early instead."

"What?"

Emily backed out. Here it came and she was leaving.

"Is that what you barged in here and interrupted a phone call for? To show me Emily's pictures? Are you nuts? And what the hell, you can't work tonight?"

"How dare you tell her you hope she's having fun? I'm telling her, and you, she's got talent. A lot of talent."

"Can you or can't you work tonight?" Her father's voice was icy.

Emily stayed on the other side of the door, pretending to fix her boot. She wanted to hear more about how much talent she had. But there wasn't going to be any more.

"No. As I said, I have other plans."

"Then we both better get back to our work, hadn't we?"

Pat strode out of the office and saw her there. She smiled and inclined her head. "Let's get some coffee."

For the next hour, at Jakes Diner, Pat reviewed those pictures and talked about form and content and composition. Emily sweated and her hands tingled and the coffee tasted terrible and she barely understood what Pat talked about, but it was clear Pat meant it. And if Pat said she should take pictures and more pictures and stop worrying about sneaking around and developing them in off hours and that Pat would handle her father, then Emily would do it. If Pat had said, go stand out in the snow until your eyeballs freeze, she might have done that too.

A few months later, as the air began to warm, she was out with her cousin Cliff, over in Rutland seeing *Bonnie and Clyde,* glad she was old enough to drive two hours away for a movie. She saw her father and Pat leave the Silver Tooth Pub across the street. They strolled arm in arm, laughing, and then stopped to kiss, quickly, before they got in her dad's car. Emily thought maybe she was wrong, maybe it wasn't Pat because the woman wore a skirt.

She screamed, "Dad!" And waved.

Her father didn't look around and Pat didn't look around, but instead they ducked into the car and drove away.

Her father was up when she got home. He sat in the easy chair with the lamp on low, a Scotch on the end table, a cigarette in the ashtray, still in his street clothes. "It's quite late."

"Yes."

"Don't you have a curfew?"

"Mom trusts me."

"I would appreciate it if you didn't mention seeing Pat and me in Rutland to your mother." He took a sip of his drink. "She might mistake it for something more than it is."

Did her father think she was stupid? "You didn't say hello."

"We just went to unwind after work. But I don't want your mother to imagine things."

"Or wave. Neither one of you waved back or said hello."

"Please, Em."

After that she had a difficult time being at home, watching her mother work her ass off and then listening to her father complain about her mother's hairstyle, the messy house, the noisy girls, and seeing her mother's bewildered and furious face. But she didn't tell her; she didn't know how.

"Doesn't it upset you when he criticizes you like that?" she asked as her mother passed her a dish to dry.

"Not really." Her mother bent her head and with her teeth pulled back the sleeves of her blouse so they wouldn't get wet. "Well, maybe a little." She plunged her hands back into the hot water and the sleeves fell again. She held them up for Emily to roll up more securely.

"Why don't you do something? Say something?"

"I do." She rinsed a glass and passed it along.

"I counted. From the time he came home tonight, he made

eleven nasty comments."

"Emily, this really isn't your concern. We'll work it out. We always have."

"This is different." Emily desperately wanted to say more.

"Listen, hon. Your father's under a lot of pressure at the paper. He'll get over it."

"It's a terrible, terrible way to live. The whole atmosphere around here stinks. You have to do something before it gets worse."

Her mother turned off the water and wiped her hands on the towel Emily was holding. "Leave it alone. You said your piece, now leave it."

Emily avoided contact with her father and worked in the newspaper darkroom. Developing prints in the quiet, with only the light of the red bulb, she couldn't decide who she was more furious at. Her mother was a fool. Maybe that's why her father liked Pat better. Pat wouldn't stand for the crap her mother took.

She watched a wavering image come into being through the liquid in the pan.

"Em, is that you?" her father called from his office. "Come here for a minute."

"Later."

"Now." His voice rose in volume.

"Oh, what is it?" She stomped into his office.

Laid out all over the desk and the table were papers. Pat sat behind the desk with him, smiling. At least they were really working. This was too weird. She didn't want to be in the same room with them. Sweat coated her palms, her breath came short.

Her father handed her an envelope. It was opened already. "Look."

She took out the letter and a check floated to the floor.

Congratulations. You have won the $500 First Prize in the American Photography *amateur photo contest. As first prize winner your photo will be published in the September issue.*

"I didn't enter any contest."

"No, Pat did it for you. She picked out the photo she liked so much and sent it in." Her father was beaming, he was so proud of Pat.

Emily picked the check up off the floor and put it on the desk. "Then this belongs to Pat."

CHAPTER EIGHT

December 2, 1972
Three days later

E mily exited the Park Station T stop, pulled along by the crowd walking to the women's rally on the Boston Common and started snapping pictures. There must be hundreds of women. All kinds of women. All sizes, all ages, all races. Women with sprayed hair and heels and matching pocketbooks. Young women in hiking boots and jeans. Women with gray hair holding signs and shouting slogans. Women holding babies, women holding banners, women holding hands.

And the colors. Bright colors. Primary colors. Women dressed in all tints. Purple hats. Yellow mittens. Emily wore her red woolen jacket.

Women were not invisible anymore. Up ahead on the speaker's podium was Shirley Chisolm, the first black woman presidential candidate. Bella Abzug, congresswoman from New York, was going to speak later. Emily loved her slogan: This woman's place is in the House—the House of Representatives. And Gloria Steinem. And Betty Friedan. And many more. Emily could hear the rumble and screech of feedback from the microphones. Holly Near was going to sing and there were even rumors of Helen Reddy.

The crowd was dense in front of the stage and thinned out along the periphery where tables were set up. Lesbians for Peace.

Mothers against the War. Equal Rights Amendment. Abortion Rights. Women against Violence. Day Care for All.

Emily skirted the crowd, standing on tiptoe, craning her neck as she searched for Vivian or Alix. Gemma would be too tiny to see with all these people. And then she spotted all three of them talking to a woman covered in buttons. Emily waved, and when she got closer she saw the woman couldn't be more than seventeen, maybe eighteen.

Katie was in her stroller, so bundled against the cold she couldn't move, but her eyes were wide, thoroughly entertained by all the action around her.

Emily took several pictures before saying hello.

The young woman had buttons all over her denim jacket, front and back, down the sleeves and up and down the legs of her jeans. She had long blond hair, ironed straight. Large blue eyes. Clear rosy skin. She looked like a model. "Tell me about the buttons," Alix said as Emily circled them and snapped pictures.

"This way no one has any doubt about who I am or what I believe in." The young woman held her arms away from her body and slowly spun. "No hiding anymore."

Emily crouched and took close-ups of the buttons. "What part of NO don't you understand?" "Don't call me sweetie ... it's bad for your teeth."

Vivian started reading out loud. "'I tried to contain myself, but I escaped.' 'Menstruate with pride.'" Vivian smiled. "I love these."

"'Marriage is a fine institution,'" Gemma read, "'but who wants to live in an institution?' 'There are very few jobs that actually require a penis or vagina.'"

Emily laughed and put down her camera. "How much do they cost?"

"They're not for sale and they're not meant to be amusing," The woman dropped her arms. "I'm very pretty and because of that people make assumptions: that I'm a good girl, that I'm compliant, that I like to smile. I don't want any assumptions."

"I see," Emily said, and snapped a picture of her intense expression.

"You're pretty too," the woman said to Emily. "Don't you ever try to pass? You know, smile wide at the gas-station guy. Not get too upset when some asshole thinks he's better than you because he's got a hard-on."

Emily nodded.

Katie screeched and arched her back. "Out, out."

The button woman walked away.

Vivian set the stroller moving again. "Sorry, you have to stay in the stroller, sweetie. I don't want to lose you in this crowd."

Katie twisted and turned against the safety straps. "Walk. Katie walk."

Vivian stopped. "How 'bout a snack?" She pulled out a little bag of Cheerios and handed it to Katie.

"No," Katie wailed, and threw the bag to the ground, cereal scattering.

"Shit," Vivian said under her breath. "It's nap time, sorry. I thought she'd fall asleep in the stroller. I probably shouldn't have come." She jerked the stroller, trying to get it unstuck from an uneven patch of pavement. Gemma lifted the front wheel.

"Can I carry her?" she asked.

"Be my guest." Vivian turned her head and wiped her eyes.

"Jesus, Viv. I wasn't criticizing you; just trying to help." As Gemma freed Katie, Alix hooked Vivian's arm and squeezed. "You are a great mother. And you're tired."

Emily raised her camera and clicked.

With Katie happily settled on Gemma's hip, the four of them pushed closer to the speaker's stand. On the stage a woman Emily didn't recognize spoke with passion about the right to abortion.

"Do you ever try to pass?" Alix asked, banging her mittens together to warm her hands. She had a royal blue hat pulled low on her head and her nose was red from the cold. "You know, pass like that girl—I mean, woman was talking about."

"Pass? Of course, all the time," Vivian said. "God, these conversations drive me nuts. I'm trying to support Katie and myself and live a life. If being pretty helps, and it seems to be helping a great deal with my boss, well then, I think that is great."

"You can't—" Gemma started to say, and then stopped as the woman on stage yelled, "We have the right to control our own bodies."

The crowd roared and clenched fists rose. Emily took more pictures, hoping that one of these, some of these, any of these, would capture the energy and excitement.

"Hey." Alix pointed at the stage. "That's Janet, my boss, the founder of the Women's Health Center."

Emily took another few pictures and lowered her camera. "So how's the job going?" she asked Alix.

"I love it." Alix pulled her hat lower over her ears. "So far we do spend an awful lot of time in meetings. They believe in consensus—abolishing the hierarchy between management and workers. Which is great, but time consuming. There's an idea being tossed around about all of us nonmedical personnel rotating positions, director for three months, receptionist for three months, and so on." Alix grinned and shrugged. "I guess I'll learn as I go. But already, one week in and working only part-time, the house is a disaster and I'm behind on everything. Sam is grumbling. He even joked last night that maybe we should rethink my mother coming to live with us. At least I hope he was joking."

"Let's get to the edge where it's less crowded." Gemma pivoted and switched Katie to her other hip. She pointed to a table covered with boxes of condoms and contraceptive foam. "Did you know that it was illegal to sell birth control to unmarried women in Massachusetts until this year?"

Emily couldn't believe it, but Gemma was a fount of this kind of information.

"Are her eyes closed?" Gemma asked. Katie had slumped on her shoulder.

"Let's see if we can get her back into the stroller." Vivian lifted Katie from Gemma while Emily held the stroller still.

The woman on stage asked a question Emily didn't catch and the crowd quieted. A few hands went up. And then more. Emily took pictures, turning all around to photograph the hands in the air. Vivian and Gemma settled Katie into the stroller without her waking.

"What did she say?" Emily asked Alix in a whisper.

"She asked who here has ever had an abortion."

Hundreds of hands were in the air. Silence descended.

Emily put down her camera.

Gemma raised her hand.

"You never told us," Alix said to her.

"I never told anyone." Gemma hunched her shoulders against the cold and wrapped her scarf tight. "Damn, it's cold."

As the last of the feeble sunlight left, the air turned brittle. People were breaking away from the crowd and trickling toward the Park Street T stop.

"Let's find a place we can warm up," Alix said. "Get some hot chocolate before we go, and give Gemma a chance to talk." She linked her arm through Gemma's.

Gemma jerked her arm free and then tried to cover her abruptness by bending over Katie in the stroller, tucking the blanket more securely around her legs.

"I know a great little bar on Newbury Street." Vivian turned the stroller.

Emily nodded. "And we can catch the T at Copley, miss the crowd."

Gemma straightened. "You go ahead. I need to get home. I'm going to get out of this chaos and grab the Red Line from South Station."

She walked away, hunched against the cold, looking tiny and vulnerable.

Emily arrived home after the rally to an apartment full of Rick's friends. Open pizza boxes sprawled on the kitchen counter and empty beer bottles cluttered the end tables in the living room. Through the kitchen window, in the backyard, she saw two silhouettes outlined in the fading light pass a joint. In the living room, the new guy from the sociology department and the department chair of psychology loudly debated why McGovern had lost in a landslide to Nixon.

"Hi, Em." Rick smiled and headed toward her, a beer in one hand. In the other he held a slice of pizza, carefully folded so it wouldn't drip. He wore a freshly ironed blue work shirt and jeans; not a hair escaped from his blond ponytail. Somehow, even in this chaos Rick managed to look sharp. He leaned in for a kiss. "I didn't see you come in."

She gave him a quick peck and scanned the rooms. "Where's Matt? Did you feed Jessica already?"

"Jess is still asleep and Matt is getting a story read to him." Rick took a swallow of beer and offered her a swig. "How was your meeting?"

Before she could answer, he said loud enough to capture the attention of the room, "Hey, everyone. Emily just got back from a women's lib rally."

"Be careful, Em," yelled Joe, another professor in political science. "That women liberation is full of dykes on the hunt." He exaggerated an expression of mock curiosity. "You're not a closet dyke, are you? Rick will be greatly humbled."

"Naaa," said another man. "Nothing can humble Rick."

Lots of laughter. Emily didn't smile. She went to check on the kids.

In the crib, six-month-old Jessica stirred. Emily figured she had another five minutes before her feeding. In his room, four-year-old Matt was curled up in the lap of one of Rick's many gorgeous graduate students. Emily didn't disturb them. She wandered into the kitchen to grab a piece of pizza before feeding Jess and noticed Marcia with her head in the refrigerator. Emily backed out, hoping Marcia hadn't heard her. She was not in the mood to spar with her.

She wasn't fast enough. Marcia turned and straightened to her full six feet and looked down at her over her glasses. "So you really are into this women lib stuff?"

"I'm checking it out."

"I think it is completely superfluous when there is need for a total working class revolution." Marcia held two beers in each hand. "Don't you think there are more important issues in this world?"

"Hey, Marcia, where's that beer?" a male voice yelled from the living room. Marcia left to bring beer to the men. Emily heard Jess start to cry.

"Oh, don't worry little one, dinner is here." Emily scooped Jess up from her crib and settled them in the comfy chair. Jess latched onto the breast and immediately quieted.

Snatches of sentences floated in from the living room. Even five years after Rick and Emily moved out of the communal house they had shared, many evenings and most weekends the whole group ended up here. Rick frequently held forth. He now taught revolutionary theory in the political science department and could spout off with the best of them. He was charming; people gravitated to him; he loved the discussions, but to her it sounded as if they had the same argument over and over and over.

Her first dinner, years ago, meeting Rick's friends had not gone well at all.

"Where did you study photography?" the bearded man across the table had asked. He turned out to be Joe.

Emily had quickly swallowed her mouthful of brown rice. "Nowhere, really. I just take pictures."

"You should see them," Rick said. "They're far out."

"What do you take pictures of?" the bearded man persisted.

She shrugged. "Anything that catches my eye." She smiled.

"Do you have a political focus or artistic direction?"

"Well, I guess I tend to take pictures of women. Girls, mostly. Though I hadn't thought it through."

No one in the group had asked about her photographs since.

It didn't get much easier over time. "They hate me," she had complained one night after yet another dinner.

"No, they just don't know you yet."

Rick had adored her then and she had focused on that. She thought he was a sophisticated and brilliant graduate student. He thought she was arty, untarnished, and innocent.

They'd married so Rick could get his draft deferment and moved to this little apartment.

"That's bullshit," a voice bellowed.

Jess flinched and stopped nursing. Emily sighed.

"You can't believe that!" the voice continued. "It's idiotic."

"Well, sweetie. I guess it's time to be social." Emily stood and positioned Jess over her shoulder. The arguments had reached their usual level of sophistication and insight for the evening.

She walked into the living room. Marcia jumped away from Rick as if he'd stuck her with a hatpin. Emily nuzzled Jessica and pretended not to notice as they rearranged themselves.

"Wow. Look who's decided to join us." Rick came over and

took a smiling Jess from Emily.

Stan, a professor of economics and one of Rick's friends she actually sort of liked, waved her over and patted the empty place next to him on the couch. He handed her his beer for a sip when she plunked herself down and draped his arm around her shoulders. "The whole evening gets better as soon as you arrive," he whispered into her ear. His breath was a mix of pot and alcohol. "Hmm, you smell like fresh air." He pulled her in for a boozy kiss. She turned her head just in time.

She twisted to put space between them, but patted his knee to indicate no hard feelings. "How's it going, Stan?"

Marcia laughed, high and trilling, and she leaned her head close to Rick's. Emily didn't hear Stan's response. She watched as Rick shook his head, smiled, and said something that must have been oh-so-funny, because Marcia laughed again and she teetered, her breasts brushing Rick's arm.

Emily tensed and told herself she was imagining things. Marcia flicked some lint from his shoulder and Rick glanced over at her. Emily held his gaze and then swiveled her head to kiss Stan full and hard on his lips.

"Hey, sweetie." A man slumped against a door drinking out of a paper bag called to Gemma as she zipped along Tremont Street, far away from the crowds of demonstrators leaving the rally. Neon signs advertising Naked College Girls and 25 Cents a Peep flashed in red and yellow, casting a strange glow onto the sidewalk. Despite the darkness, the night had barely begun in the combat zone, only a few hookers on the corners mixing with tourists ogling the Teddy Bare Lounge and the Naked Eye.

Gemma kept her hands jammed in her pockets and her head down. With one hand raised, in one carried-away moment, she'd let slip a secret she had intended to carry forever.

She stepped around a pool of vomit. She hadn't purposely

kept it a secret from Willie—but abortion wasn't something that generally came up in the flush of new love, and then when was she supposed to mention it? As they were putting away the groceries?

Turning up Essex Street, she walked into the heart of Chinatown. Street vendors were still selling vegetables and fruit on the sidewalk, and old women, carrying cloth bags and holding children's hands, haggled in high pitch. She relaxed her shoulders and walked more slowly. Willie must have secrets also.

The train was not full, and Gemma found a seat and leaned her head against the cool window. In the reflection of the dark glass she watched the two teens holding hands furtively kiss.

CHAPTER NINE

When she was seventeen, Gemma had known she'd passed some unseen threshold of womanhood, when she stepped out of the house wearing old jeans and a T-shirt and her older brother Nick punched his best friend Bobby in the face, knocking him to the frozen ground.

"What the fuck?" Bobby had rubbed his jaw, sitting on the hard dirt.

"Don't you ever let me catch you looking at Gemma like that again." Nick reached out his hand and pulled Bobby to his feet.

"Shit." Bobby brushed off his jeans. "You're fucking crazy."

Gemma hopped off the stoop, shivering without her coat, and told Nick that Mom wanted him to help move the credenza so they could clean behind it.

"Damn." Nick took the steps two at a time. "This will only take a minute,'" he said to Bobby. "Then we can get going."

As soon as the storm door slammed behind Nick, Gemma put her hands on her hips, tossed her hair, and winked at Bobby. She'd been practicing that move, right out of a Chevy commercial, for weeks.

Bobby grinned. His black hair was army short, but he smoothed it with his hand anyway. "You're being a bad girl."

"No." She turned and left him standing on the front lawn. "I'm just curious." She felt his eyes on her butt all the way up the front stoop.

Nick and Bobby were home on leave before they deployed overseas for a second tour of duty. Last time they'd been in Germany, but most likely this time, it would be Vietnam. Her father, so afraid for them, grumbled around the house, furious they'd signed up again. "Idiots. Fools. Still wet behind the ears." Gemma had four older brothers and her father spent a great deal of time in fearful rage. To distract her father, her mother had planned a party for Nick and Bobby. It was clear to Gemma, who was helping with cooking and cleaning, her mother had invited most of Queens.

The next day, her mother told her Bobby's sister was on the phone, but when she picked up the receiver, Bobby was on the other end. "Let's go out," he said simply. He suggested they meet at the Staten Island Ferry on Saturday.

Gemma said okay. No one could know about this, not even her best friend, and if Nick found out, he'd never let her go.

Bobby had a reputation. "He fucks anything that moves," she had overheard Nick tell one of her brothers. She wondered what it would be like with a twenty-one-year-old man who had know-how. Not that she was totally inexperienced. She had done her share of pushing groping hands away from her breasts and avoiding sloppy kisses from the boys in her class. For the most part, though, she had spent high school studying. Of course, her father hadn't actually said yes to college. Yet. But her mother had promised she'd talk to him and to leave the application on her desk.

So on Saturday afternoon, Gemma went into the kitchen. "Mom, I'm going over to Theresa's," she lied easily. "I might sleep over. I'll call you later." She kissed her mother, buttoned her jacket, grabbed her pocketbook, and fled down the back steps. She wondered if there was some magic turning point when you stopped lying to your parents. Clearly being seventeen wasn't it.

"Hey, slut."

She turned to see her oldest brother, Tony, coming up the driveway. Behind him, his wife Fran carried their baby.

"Don't say that," Fran said.

Tony wrapped his arm around Gemma's shoulders and kissed her on top of her head. The shortest of her brothers, Tony was a solid block.

"Hey, I'm just looking out for her," he said. "If I didn't love her, I wouldn't tell her that she shouldn't be seen outside the house with a dress that short. I'm her oldest brother. If I don't tell her these things, who will?"

Gemma slid out from under his arm. "Someone with more brains than to insult his own sister."

"I'm not insulting you." Tony looked her up and down. "I'm watching out for you. Isn't it better for me to tell you that you're dressed like a hooker than some creep in the city?"

"Tell me, how am I supposed to tell the difference between you and some creep in the city?" Gemma ducked as he lunged for her and then laughed as he chased her around the small yard.

She caught the F train into Manhattan and rode standing up, holding onto the pole. She didn't want to sit down, because the seats were sticky and her thighs would adhere to the hard plastic; and anyway, Tony had made her very self-conscious about her short skirt.

At the ferry terminal, the wind whipped off the river and she stood shivering, waiting. She wanted to look casual and nonchalant, but her nose ran from the cold and she no longer could feel her legs.

She saw Bobby ambling toward her, hands in his jeans pockets, shoulders hunched, and the collar on his navy pea coat turned up against the wind.

He grinned when he saw her. Grabbing her hand, he walked her into a little entryway that was less exposed and brushed her hair out of her face. "You could have waited inside. I would have found you." Bobby had a chipped tooth and dimples when he smiled. "My God, you're freezing. We're going to have to find a way to warm you up." He removed his glove and touched her nose. "You're all red like Rudolph."

Gemma needed water. Her tongue stuck to her mouth. She wasn't sure she'd ever seen Bobby like this. He had always been just Bobby, Nick's friend.

Today, he touched her hair, put his hand on her back, and held her elbow, brushing close with his body as he guided her through the crowds to the ticket window.

Gemma, who could usually talk circles around her brothers and reduce them to slamming doors and stomping away in frustration and fury, could think of nothing to say to Bobby. Absolutely nothing.

It didn't seem to matter. While they waited in line, Bobby kept up a quiet, one- sided commentary that only required smiles and nods. He talked about the history of the Staten Island Ferry and how his parents always told the story of their first date. It was during the Depression and the ferry was free. There was this great picture of them standing together at the rail. He said his mom wanted to get married on the ferry, but his grandparents insisted on the church. But a wedding on a ferry sounded romantic, didn't it?

They made their way onto the boat and Bobby guided her to a secluded bench, behind the wheelhouse and out of the wind, but with a good, clear view of the river. He pointed out parts of Manhattan as if he were a tour guide. There's Wall Street. There's the Empire State building; had she ever been? Maybe they should go there someday. There's Battery Park. As he talked, he moved so one arm was around her shoulders, his breath warm on her ear, and his pointing arm occasionally brushed her breasts.

He talked about the Statue of Liberty and Ellis Island. He actually knew his facts about all of this. She was impressed. This was clearly the seduction express for Bobby. She wondered if he had a few different ones. She imagined some women might not be all that excited about freezing their butts off on wooden benches on a ferry heading for Staten Island.

And then somehow, they were in a position so that when she looked up and asked, "What?" to something she hadn't heard clearly, he inclined his head and kissed her. He pulled away and smiled at her. Dimples and chipped tooth. And then he kissed her again, brushing his lips against hers, against her nose and cheeks and chin and her lips once more, and his tongue parted them just a little.

It was so different from the drooling, tongue-down-your-throat boys at school.

She liked this.

She leaned into him and he wrapped his arms around her, wind in their faces, as the ferry chugged over to Staten Island. They didn't get off. They just rode the boat back and watched Manhattan light up as the daylight faded.

Bobby suggested a warm drink and Gemma agreed. She'd love a hot chocolate. He pulled her into a bar on Houston Street, ordered two butter babies and brought them over to the table. Gemma had no idea what a butter baby was, but it had whipped cream on top so she figured it would taste okay. She tried to act as if this was not unusual, as if she'd actually been inside a bar before. She took a sip, tasting butterscotch. Bobby wiped the whipped cream off her upper lip with his finger and then put his finger in her mouth.

He asked if she'd like to go back and see where he was staying with a friend in the Village. They held hands as they walked through Washington Square, passing by young men drumming and draft protesters chanting, "Hey, Hey, LBJ. How many kids did you kill today?" and wandering by a young woman strumming a guitar, her thin soprano drowned out by the drummers.

They climbed the three flights to an apartment overlooking the square, and Bobby let himself in. His friend was in the living room watching TV. Bobby introduced them, but didn't linger and led her to his bedroom.

The entire day Gemma figured she'd said less than ten full sentences. Bobby didn't seem to notice. Or mind. This whole day had felt dreamlike, as if someone else had borrowed her body and she got to watch, curious about what would happen next.

Bobby sat down on the bed and pulled her toward him, kissing her. He slowly unbuttoned her sweater. Then her dress. His hands and kisses everywhere at once, discovering her body, creating sensations she'd never known. She heard herself moan.

His finger pulled on the elastic of her panties.

"I don't … I never …" She started to speak, suddenly nervous that she was supposed to know how to do something.

"Shh," said Bobby.

The Beatle's "Eleanor Rigby" filled the room.

He pushed her lightly so she was lying on her back and he lay over her. She was aware of his arm muscles, the hair on his legs. "You are so soft," he murmured. He was hard against her leg as he kissed her breasts, her neck, her mouth, and she closed her eyes and let herself enjoy the waves of sensation.

He lifted himself off her with one hand, murmuring, kissing, caressing, until her senses blurred, a melding of skin and sheet and song. Bobby continued touching and then began to enter her.

"Wait," she said. The room, Bobby, her naked body, materialized into sharp focus. "Don't you have to use something?" She might not have much actual experience, but she'd done a lot of reading. "A rubber?"

"Shh. Don't worry. I know what I'm doing."

She felt him slide in and out of her, but slowly and not very deep. She had also read enough to know it was going to hurt this first time, and she tensed, waiting. But he kept kissing and gently moving in and out, and nothing hurt and she wanted it to last forever.

Then he pushed up over her with both arms and thrust hard, and she felt a pain. With a soft moan, he pulled away, rolled off her, and she felt him pulse against her leg.

Gemma's period was two weeks late.

She wasted no time. She went down to the free clinic in the Village that all the girls in the high school knew about to find out if she was really pregnant.

Yes. Damn. After only one time?

She huddled in her coat and sat on a bench in Washington Square, chilled by the gray sleeting rain. Nick and Bobby were leaving soon for California and then Vietnam.

That Saturday, afterwards, Bobby had put her in a cab, leaned in and kissed her, and then said, "You are a wonderful girl. But, you know I can't be too serious about anyone—since I'm leaving soon."

He hadn't said much to her in the past three weeks. Not even at the big party her mother threw for him and Nick. She hung around whenever he came by to pick up Nick, but he never did more than say hi, his eyes sliding away from her. He never suggested they go out again.

Now she sat on the bench. Freezing. Fingering the slip of paper in her pocket with an address on Bleecker Street. She watched the NYU students hurrying from building to building. The draft protesters clumped on one side of the park handed out flyers and a man stood at the corner reciting poetry. Next year she could be going to school here.

She walked slowly toward Bleecker Street and stared at the three-story brick building. It just looked like a regular apartment building.

Bobby would be forced to marry her, if anyone knew. Her father might even be relieved. He liked Bobby a lot. An Italian wedding for an only daughter. It would be something to behold. All the uncles and aunts and cousins would be there. Plus the whole neighborhood, and of course, the entire crew at his fire station. And all their kids.

Gemma called Bobby. "I need to talk to you alone," she said, and told him to meet her at the Green Acres Shopping Mall in Valley Stream.

She found him smoking a cigarette, slouched against his blue Pontiac, squinting against the winter sun. The wind gusted around them. "I need $600 for a friend who's in trouble." She didn't bother with hello.

"Theresa?" Bobby looked shocked.

"No," Gemma said loudly and quickly. In this neighborhood rumors spread fast.

"Oh." Bobby got it. He tossed his cigarette. He looked around, to the right and left as if to make sure no one they knew saw them. "How do I know ...? I mean, what if ...?" He rubbed his black shoe against the car tire. "Well, you know, it isn't mine?"

Gemma felt like sinking to the cold asphalt right there in the parking lot and not moving anymore. Miserable. So miserable that this was the boy she chose. And *terrified.* She wasn't afraid of the abortion, but she knew she had to move fast. She was afraid of getting too attached. Someday she imagined having babies, but not now. She had seen what happened to the girls in her neighborhood. Dull, vacant looks and stringy hair. The girls locked away in tiny apartments with a wailing baby while the boys who were forced into marriage did anything to avoid being home.

"Shit." Bobby kicked the tire. "I can't believe this happened to me."

Gemma waited. Silent. The low sun glinted off all the chrome in the parking lot.

"How do I know …?" he repeated, louder this time. Clearly he had decided this was the response to go with.

"You'll never know." She stepped so she was directly in front of him, so he was forced to look at her. "But I will tell everyone it's yours." She waited a moment to let that register and then turned to walk to the bus. "I need it by three tomorrow. Cash."

Gemma went alone. She was not frightened. She had a clear sense of exactly what she was doing and why. She told no one. She was no sissy. She was not like other girls.

The doctor's office was up two flights in the old building. There was no sign on the door, just a number. Everything was clean. The waiting room was empty, the nurse kind, and the doctor young and very matter-of-fact.

There was no exchange of information. She only knew him as "doctor." No names. Only cash was exchanged.

She undressed from the waist down and the nurse helped her lie on the table with a clean paper sheet, put her feet in little metal holders she called stirrups, and draped a sheet over her legs. She didn't have to wait. The doctor came in and did not smile or say hello. He told her from between her legs, behind the draped sheet, that she would feel a cramp.

It was over much faster than she had expected.

When she was dressed, the nurse told her to go home and rest. The cramping and bleeding would continue. If the bleeding became extreme or the pain seemed severe, she should go to her nearest emergency room immediately.

Over the next few days Gemma bled heavily.

In gym class she doubled over and they rushed her to the emergency room. Her mother met her there and held her hand until she was wheeled into surgery.

The doctor came to her in the recovery room. He had shaggy gray hair. His blue eyes were watery, his skin blotchy, his nose had red veins. "You'll live," he said. His voice was soft and gentle. "But there was residual tissue and removal often causes scaring in the uterus. It's likely you'll never get pregnant. I'm sorry."

She didn't ask any more questions. She didn't ask what he had told her mother. She simply watched him, with his white coat flapping, walk away.

Gemma put a pillow against her belly. She turned on her side, curled up around her pillow, and let herself cry. Just this once.

Willie opened the door as she trod up the stairs.

"Am I glad to see you." He pulled her inside and kissed her, running his hands through her hair.

Gemma laughed as they separated. "Sweetie, it was a women's rights rally, not a leave-all-your-men rally."

"Emily called about five minutes ago to make sure you'd gotten home okay. So of course I started to panic. Why didn't you go home with them?"

"I—"

"Tell me in the kitchen," he interrupted, walking out of the hallway.

The kitchen table was set with candles and flowers, and she could smell something with curry simmering on the stove.

"Whoa? You really were running scared." She smiled at him. "It's beautiful."

"I figured with all the excitement today, you might have

forgotten the anniversary of when we first met."

Fuck. "Oh, Willie—"

"And I got a call today from Brian, the principal, and he wants me to head the history department." He turned to the pots on the stove and started to dish out rice. "So I thought I'd do something special. I know it's only because I'm black, but what the hell, I'll take it."

"It's because you are one hell of a gifted teacher and Brian is smart enough to know it," Gemma said, and hugged him from behind. They were so lucky to have found each other. They'd pretended last year when Gemma was applying to law schools and Willie for teaching jobs that it would be okay if they didn't end up in the same city, but it turned out they both only applied in Boston—secretly, without telling each other.

See? Gemma thought. All couples kept secrets. And she'd tell him, but not now. This wouldn't be a good time.

After getting them settled with the food on the table, Willie poured wine and lifted his glass in a toast. "Here's to us. To you being the first female justice on the US Supreme Court. And to me being the first black cabinet member, Secretary of Education."

"Yes." She clinked glasses with him and smiled. "So does this mean you're finally coming to New York for the holidays with me?"

"You marrying me?"

She shook her head, smiling. It was an old routine. "Told you I'm not a marrying woman."

"Then no way am I heading into northern racist country with everyone knowing I'm a black man screwing their white sister-daughter-cousin and living in sin."

CHAPTER TEN

December 6 1972
Four days later

V ivian sat on her desk, swinging her legs and stealing the occasional french fry from Mickey as he told her a story about the office manager from one of the Watertown offices who had legs that went from here to there, and who he was trying to get the nerve to ask out. It was almost time to leave to pick up Katie from daycare and she was all packed up and ready.

"I offered to buy you some," Mick said, moving his fries out of her reach. "I told you they were the best in Boston. You should listen to me."

"What happened to Liz?" Vivian asked, stretching to reach the fries.

Mickey groaned and ran his hand through his hair. "She told me that her kundalini yoga instructor insisted she give up sex for six months in order to center her chakras."

"Poor man." Vivian laughed. "You dumped her just because of that?"

"No way. She left me. She said I was too tempting to be around."

Vivian laughed again. "I believe *that.*"

She knew she shouldn't flirt or do anything mildly suggestive with Mickey. He was hard to resist, though. Coffee-colored hair, big shoulders, a chest wide enough to imagine curling up against, and a great butt. And those liquid chocolate eyes.

Gemma had groaned and did an exaggerated eye roll when Vivian had described Mickey to them.

She enjoyed him— he was one of the few repairmen in the office that made a point to talk with her. The others were nice enough, nodded and said hello when she arrived, but still silence rolled in like a dense fog when she came too close.

"Are they telling dirty jokes that they think might offend my delicate feminine sensibility?" she had asked him once, in what she hoped was an I-don't-care-just-curious tone.

"No, you're just the first dyke they ever met and they're not sure how to act around a woman who doesn't find them irresistible."

"I'm no dyke," she had shouted, and then felt her face flush as heads turned.

Mickey had winked. "I know that."

She had refused to talk to him for a week.

Mickey relented and moved the fries closer to her. "The next time she calls, I'll make her office the last stop of the day, and then take an extra long time, and when she's fuming because she's had to stay late, I'll ask her out for a drink to make it up to her. What do you think?"

"I think making a woman angry is a great way to go." She dipped the last fry in the little glob of ketchup.

Their boss Harvey had made the rules very clear when he hired her. "No screwing around with the other repairmen. And I mean that literally. I'll fire your ass at the first whiff of anything like that." Harvey was boxy. He was like a snowman built out of squares instead of balls. His cheeks crowded out his eyes. "And nothing with the clients either. It's bad business. You're a sexy broad, but keep it under wraps. Unless, of course, you can't resist me." He laughed to show he was joking, but any chance he got, he brushed against her breasts. Accidentally, of course.

"Seriously," Mickey said as he cleared the food debris off his desk and tossed it into the trash, "you don't think she'll go for that?"

"Why not just say you think she's beautiful and ask her out."

"I think she's married." He shrugged those huge shoulders and looked crestfallen.

Vivian laughed. "You're fucking pathetic."

Harvey stuck his head out of his office. "Viv, I need to see you."

"Now?" She looked at her watch. "I was just about to leave."

He didn't answer, just went into his office, leaving the door open. She slid off the desk, shrugged at Mickey, and followed.

"Close the door behind you."

Harvey's office was barely large enough to hold his rickety desk and two chairs. He waved at a sheaf of yellow job orders on his desk. "You know, for a dame, you're doing damn well better than I thought you would. I think it's time to expand your territory and give you the North Shore accounts."

"Really?" That would mean a substantial increase in pay. "I thought those were Al's."

"Don't worry about Al."

"Wow, Harvey." She bent over his desk to take the papers and lingered a beat, letting him get a good view of her cleavage. "I don't know what to say."

His smile almost closed his eyes. "Thank you is good."

She put a lot of breath into her thank you.

"What was that about?" Mickey asked as he pulled on his coat.

"North Shore!" She grinned and did a little dance. "Harvey gave me the North Shore accounts."

He frowned. "Those are Al's."

She grabbed her purse and coat and walked with him to the street. "Harvey said not to worry about Al."

"Be careful," he said as they waited for the light. Mickey's entire face folded into a frown of disapproval. "Harvey does not do good deeds for free. And the rest of the guys know that. It won't look good."

"Damn it. How 'bout congratulations." She strode across the street and whirled to face him when she got to the sidewalk. "What the hell are you insinuating? I'm a damn good repairman."

"So are the rest of us," he shouted back at her. "And you are a woman. A repairwoman. We see how Harvey looks at you. Don't think that gets lost on the rest of us."

"And that's my fucking problem?"

Vivian weaved and honked her way from her office in Central Square down Mass Ave, furious at Mickey. He was just jealous. Getting those accounts would mean a new winter coat for Katie, maybe even some good boots for herself. She leaned on her horn again and swerved in front of a station wagon. Damn holiday traffic was going to make her even later than usual picking up Katie.

She pulled the Plymouth into the bus stop in front of the daycare center and put on her flashers. She ran up the walk and up the stairs, almost losing her footing on the slippery wooden steps.

Sylvia, her least favorite teacher, waited in the doorway by Katie's room. "We're going to have to charge you for the extra twenty-seven minutes, Vivian." Sylvia crossed her arms over her maroon corduroy jumper.

"I know. I'm so sorry." Vivian tried to slide past Sylvia and spot Katie. She mumbled, "Work emergency, traffic bad." Katie saw her first and came running.

"Hi, my baby girl." Vivian crouched for a big hug and inhaled deeply Katie's smell of shampoo, little girl sweat, and crayons.

"Mommy, come see."

"It's very important," Sylvia said over Katie's words, "to be timely. Structure is essential for two and a half year olds. Meeting your child's expectations builds trust."

Vivian straightened, scratching the back of her neck. Talking to Sylvia always made her itch. Katie tugged on her hand. "Come, Mommy."

"Katie," Sylvia said, "go get your pictures ready to take home and then when I'm finished talking to your mother, she'll come see what you built."

Katie let go of Vivian's hand and ran to the art table where two other children with late parents were drawing.

"Inside we walk," Sylvia called. "Running is for outside."

Vivian thought Katie slowed down, but not much.

"Katie said another swear word today," Sylvia said.

Fuck.

"You're going to have to talk to her about her words."

"Absolutely." Vivian stepped toward Katie. "Thank you for alerting me." She escaped Sylvia, admired Katie's building, helped her pack up her artwork, bundled her into her winter jacket and boots, and off they went, almost colliding with another parent bounding the slippery outside stairs. "Traffic sucks," he said, embarrassed, as if she needed an explanation. She nodded in sympathy.

"Daddy?" Katie smiled, almost dropping her picture.

"Hi there," he said as he kept moving.

Recently, Katie had taken to calling every man Daddy with a question mark. Vivian thought she should talk to the women's group about it, see what they thought, but then she'd have to go into the whole Jerry story and she wasn't ready yet.

She opened the car door and lifted Katie in, and then bribed her with Goldfish crackers to stop fighting and let Mommy buckle her in. Once she eased the car into the traffic on Mass Ave, Vivian began to relax. "Look at all the pretty Christmas lights." She pointed and then swerved to avoid the car that cut in front of her. She hit the horn. "Goddamn fucking asshole."

In the apartment, as soon as Katie was free of her bulky winter clothes, she zoomed through the three rooms chanting, "Mommy play. Mommy play." She paused to pick up her beach ball and a doll. She dropped the ball, bent to pick it up, dropped the doll, and started the process over again, the tip of her tongue curling over her lip in concentration.

Smiling, Vivian pulled out the bottle of Johnny Walker she hid in the back of a kitchen cabinet for emergencies. She poured a generous amount over ice and added a splash of water, and then with her glass clinking sank into the couch to watch Katie's progress.

Katie had gotten distracted by her fire truck and now made *woo, woo* sounds as she ran the truck around the doll and into the ball. She looked up and grinned. "Woo, woo." She held up the truck. "Mommy come."

"In a minute sweetie." Vivian took a large swallow and felt the scotch sooth as it went down.

Katie scowled." Now."

Vivian sighed. This was the hardest part of the day. They were both exhausted and they both needed someone to come in and take over for just a minute. Vivian didn't think she could get a husband for only five minutes at the end of the day—but it was worth fantasizing about.

She took another sip, stretched out on the couch, and with her other hand reached toward the truck. "Bring the truck here, sweetie."

"No," Katie shouted. "No."

Vivian winced and shut her eyes. "Mommy's tired, honey. Let's play with the truck here."

"No." But she turned around and attempted to gather the doll and the beach ball again.

Vivian took another sip. Damn Mickey. She should be feeling

elated and dancing with Katie over the new account, not slimy and drained.

The truck landed on her belly. "Want Mommy play." Katie tugged on her sweater.

"Just need to rest a second, then Mommy will play." She closed her eyes again and felt something else land on her chest.

"Catch ball."

"One more second, sweet potato." She took another sip of her drink, and then her arm jerked as the ball hit her. Scotch spilled down her chest.

"Damn it, Katie." She sat up, swiping at her sweater. "Leave Mommy alone for a fucking minute."

Katie's eyes got big and her face crumpled a second before she howled.

"Oh, honey." Vivian scooped her up, hugging her close. "I'm sorry, baby. So sorry."

"Poor Viv," Emily crooned after hearing the story. "We all have monster mother moments. It's the dark secret."

Gemma and Alix were sprawled on her couch, while she and Emily stretched out on the floor. Alix had started the meeting by asking Gemma about her abortion, but Gemma stiffened and cut her off stating she was not ready. Vivian had poured Gemma wine and changed the subject. She understood that not all pain was eased by talking.

Vivian picked up her glass. "I read Katie five extra books as penance before putting her bed. My heart just aches."

"Katie will be fine," Alix said.

"Not me."

Emily said, "You'll be fine too."

"Not me. I was never going to be like that. Never!"

"That's what we all say." Emily nodded.

CHAPTER ELEVEN

V ivian's memories of childhood were sharply divided into before and after her father—no, her stepfather—left. She was careful now to refer to him always as her stepfather. When she was fourteen years old, he left to visit his relatives in Illinois and never returned. Before he left, he'd been her father and read her the *Little House on the Prairie* books by Laura Ingalls Wilder. He told her she was beautiful, even when she was in fifth grade and her older brother Charley called her lard-o and her mother said, "Don't worry, Viv. You're just chubby." Sometimes he called her his golden girl when he smoothed back her hair that always was escaping its pigtails. He wore Old Spice aftershave, and for years she got him a new bottle with the ship on it for Father's Day.

Her mother also had blond hair, but she sprayed it, and not one hair ever was where it wasn't supposed to be. Everything about her was the way it was supposed to be. She was soft spoken, slender, and small boned. She wore shirtwaist dresses and always had the house clean, the laundry done, and extra home-baked goods in the freezer in case she had unexpected guests for coffee. She fixed lemon chicken for dinner with baked potatoes and salads of crisp iceberg lettuce and firm tomatoes.

Her stepfather was tall and told great stories about the west. He made Illinois sound like it was still wild pioneer country, with the powerful Mississippi River and river boats taking grain all over the world and miles of farm land as far as the eye could see.

For years, she played pioneer women under the oak trees with her best friend Judy, driving the covered wagons over the great prairie, toting rifles and a brood of children. In these games the husbands were killed off by Indians and she and Judy were alone under the big sky.

Her stepfather had four brothers and two parents and lots of nieces and nephews back in Illinois, and she never met any of them. He visited the relatives once a year for four days in September on his mother's birthday.

"Why can't I go with you?" she asked when she was little.

"Oh, it's just a boring old place with lots of corn. Nothing much is happening. You'll have much more fun here with Charley and Beth."

Her mother's lips thinned and her face got blotchy whenever he mentioned his relatives. Vivian learned later that his family thought of her mother as *that woman* who had tricked their boy into marrying and taking care of her and someone else's kids.

That last time her stepfather left to visit his relatives, he stayed longer than usual because someone was sick, only it turned out no one was sick, he simply never returned.

At first her mother didn't act any differently. Vivian would come home from school and read the note left on the kitchen table. It usually said something like: "Ran to get groceries for dinner. Will be back in five." Or, "Out shopping, will be back for dinner. Please turn oven on 350 degrees."

In fact, everything was so much like normal, Vivian didn't find out her stepfather had left for over a week. She didn't find out until Charley called from California.

"Hi sis. How're they hanging?"

She giggled and then pretended great offense. "Pardon me. There is nothing I possess that hangs."

"Oh, yeah. I forgot. You're a girl. Tough break. So …" He paused. "How're they bouncing?"

She giggled again. She stretched the phone cord so she could reach the living room couch and flung her legs over the arm. A position her stepfather hated. "Nothing much is happening here. Dad's still away. Mom is out shopping, I think. What are you doing? Tell me about California."

She planned to head out to California and go to Berkeley when she graduated from high school. If her mother wouldn't let her, she'd just hitchhike. She read everything she could find about Berkeley. The Beatles had been there. Or maybe she'd go out to Ann Arbor where her sister, Beth, was at the University of Michigan. Beth wrote long, wonderful letters about the coffee houses and the teach-ins and the brutal cold.

"Did Mom tell you about Dad?" Charley asked.

"Yeah, the usual, he went for the annual pilgrimage and someone was sick or in trouble or something and he couldn't return right away."

"He's not coming back, Viv. He's gone for good."

"No. All his stuff is here."

She quickly got off the phone and took the stairs two at a time the way Charley did when he lived there. Beth's telephone number was upstairs in her room.

"Charley said Dad isn't coming back. Is he telling the truth?" she said when Beth answered.

"Viv?"

Beth was stalling. "So, it's true. Was anyone planning to tell me?"

She went outside and sat on the stoop. It was September fifteenth and almost sixty degrees. Yellow and orange mums surrounded the Japanese maple. The large oak trees were golden, and she remembered her pioneer women days with Judy.

Her mother's Mustang turned the corner and slid into the driveway. Mustard colored. "Help me with the groceries, Viv." Her mother opened the trunk.

"When were you going to tell me that he wasn't coming home?"

The brown paper sack her mother was holding ripped and lemons rolled down the driveway.

Her mother lay down on the couch to rest her eyes and ease a headache and didn't get up. It seemed that as long as she could pretend with Vivian that her husband was just gone for a visit, was simply staying longer than usual, she was okay. Once Vivian knew, she couldn't seem to stand up.

Vivian was the only one left in the big Tudor, with its wide lawns and wide trees, to watch her mother disintegrate. The woman simply became dust. It reminded her of what her freshman biology teacher had told them about the giant water bug. It injected venom into frogs that turned their insides into soup, and then it sucked out everything and all that was left was flattened frog skin.

That first morning Vivian woke to bright daylight and sat right up. She thought she'd overslept, but when she looked at the clock, it was only seven fifteen; she had plenty of time to get to school. Her mother was snoring with the couch blanket wrapped around her. The TV flickered with no sound.

Vivian got herself breakfast_and then put away the dishes in the sink.

Wiped the table. Wrote her mother a note. Ripped it up and went in and gently shook her mother awake. "Mom, I'm going to school now."

Her mother opened her eyes and shifted her head on the pillow, wiping her mouth with her hand. "Good idea."

Good idea? Vivian had expected, Oh, I'm sorry, I overslept. Do you have everything you need? But good idea? Like it was a choice.

She went to school and came home to her mother sleeping.

The first week, Vivian cooked grilled cheese sandwiches, soup and crackers, and brought her mother tea.

She hadn't really known what her mother did all day anyway, so she assumed that life was limping along as usual when she was in school—and her mother was just incredibly tired.

So she let her mother sleep and cooked for her. She did the dishes and answered the phone.

Her mother didn't want to talk with anyone.

When they ran out of milk and orange juice, she took some money and walked to the corner store.

When Beth called, she told her that Mom was sleeping. "Don't bother to wake her," Beth said. "I'll call back."

Vivian tried to get her mother to change her clothes. Her mother smelled.

It was at this point that Vivian realized she knew little about her mother's life. They had no relatives. Two couples sometimes came over to play bridge, but Vivian actually didn't know them. The neighbors were remote. She didn't even know if her mother had any friends.

Her mother had always been distant, slightly removed from the world, not an affectionate, mushy, cuddly woman. Much later, Vivian would think that a woman who could sever all the major relationships she had in the world was not a woman comfortable with intimacy.

The living room began to stink from oversweet body odor. Her mother lay on the couch, moving occasionally to get a drink and pull the throw blanket up under her chin. She had positioned the TV so that the little light that came through the drawn curtains and blinds wouldn't reflect off the screen and make it difficult to see.

"What do you want, Viv?" her mother said when Vivian tried to talk to her. "I'm just tired, sweetie, really tired."

Vivian wanted some real food. She wanted her mother to get

dressed.

She did not know where the rule for silence came from, but she knew it was important to keep operating as if everything were normal. That was the trick. She was fourteen, she couldn't drive, her stepfather was gone, her mother lay on the couch, and the trick was to keep operating as if everything was exactly the same. That became her goal.

The first two weeks, when she and Judy walked home from school, Vivian told Judy that she probably shouldn't come in because her mother wasn't feeling so good. She'd call her later and maybe they could get together over at Judy's house. She walked in through the back door to the kitchen and could hear her mother snoring on the living room couch. Thank the Lord, she'd told Judy not to come in. She searched the kitchen for signs that her mother had been up, dishes in the sink or crumbs on the counter. No dishes in the sink. But when she got to the living room, she could see her mother had been up. On the coffee table was a glass with amber liquid and a bottle of Scotch. Johnny Walker.

She went to the couch and shook her mother's shoulder. She hated her mother's snoring. It was disgusting. Her mouth was slack and she blew stale air out with a soft rumble. Vivian's stomach churned.

"Mom." She shook her shoulder again. "I'm home."

Her mother's eyes fluttered open for just a second and then closed.

Maybe she would go over to Judy's house. She'd do some homework; she'd be back in time for dinner. Vivian started to leave quietly out the back door, and then remembered she should leave her mother a note. She put it on the coffee table, next to the glass.

Later, years later, when she would tell this story to friends, they would ask—Didn't you miss your father? Weren't you angry at him?

No. She remembered feeling none of that. Her father got away without having to bear the brunt of disappointment and hurt from the youngest daughter left behind. Not that he would have known about those feelings if she'd had them, because he never came back to check on her. Maybe it never occurred to him, since she wasn't his real daughter, that she might have feelings that would need attending. If she had had them, maybe she could have sent them out like radio signals, and they would have altered the sound and light waves around his being and he would have felt, momentarily, that the world, his world, was out of sorts.

But she never remembered having such feelings. Her mother was lying on the couch, drinking, not eating, not washing, and she smelled. That was much more of a concern.

Two goals consumed Vivian: making sure no one knew her mother was in the living room not taking showers; and getting her mother into the shower and walking around before anyone found out. She went to bed with the terror that someone would see her mother like that, and woke up worried someone would sneak in in the middle of the night and see her. Vivian started sleeping downstairs on the chair in the living room, in case there was a fire. Then she could grab all the blankets off both couch and chair as she hurried them out the door, and people would think they came from their beds.

She even, after a few days, pulled down the bedspread on her mother's bed upstairs. She rolled around on the bed and messed up the sheets and punched the pillows, so in case there was a fire and she pulled her mother and all the blankets off the couch downstairs and the firemen came upstairs, they would assume her mother had been sleeping upstairs all along.

She also worked out an elaborate story for Judy's mother.

That first month she walked home from school with Judy, checked on her mother, and then went over to Judy's house to do some homework but mostly to eat. They still had food in the house, but a lot of it was stuff she didn't know how to cook, and Judy's mom usually offered a snack of leftover lasagna, or chicken wings, or whatever from past dinners. Judy's mother asked how her mother was, she hadn't seen her around, and Vivian told her about the cold that had turned into the flu.

"My father is out visiting his folks in Illinois. His mom is real sick and so is his brother and uncle. Isn't it weird that they all got sick at once? Anyway, he has to stay and help for a little while, and he calls every night to see how my mom is. And she just has a cold, so she'll be better soon. So he stays out there."

"He's been gone quite a while. Over two weeks now, isn't it? I hope it's nothing too serious with his family. Maybe I'll call your mom tomorrow and see if she needs any shopping done."

"No, we don't need anything. We have a refrigerator full and a freezer full and even the cabinets in the basement are full. No, we don't need more food in the house."

Judy's mother laughed. "Well, I'll just call and see if she needs anything besides food then."

When Vivian got home, she took the phone off the hook. She brought in the mail and added it to the pile on the table by the door. She opened the window to air the room.

"Mom."

"Hi, hon. How was your day?" Her mother smiled.

Vivian felt better. Maybe it was over. But her mother's smile just stayed. It was strange. Her mother closed her eyes and brought her arm over her forehead and leaned back against the pillow, and the smile stayed as if she needed to be reminded to stop smiling.

"I don't have any clean clothes," Vivian said.

"Oh, dear."

Vivian waited. "Aren't you getting up soon?"

"I'm very tired."

"Do you want me to make coffee?"

"That would be nice. Very nice." Her mother rolled onto her side. "I'll be up in just a minute, hon. I promise."

Twelve weeks to the day after her mother lay down on the couch, she got up. Vivian came home from school, pushed open the back door, and there her mother sat surrounded by papers and yellow legal pads and dirty cups of coffee. Vivian grinned. No one had found out.

She didn't ask her mother one question about her father. She figured if she never brought him up, then her mother would be okay. They drank shakes whenever they wanted. They had sandwiches for dinner and sometimes even ate in front of the TV. Vivian loved it. It was casual and relaxed and the two of them just hung out together.

Two weeks later, Charley called. He couldn't register for the spring semester because the tuition check hadn't come. Then the bank called to say the mortgage payment was overdue.

"Don't fathers have to support their kids when they leave?" she asked when her mother talked about selling the house.

"He's not your father."

"Don't husbands have to pay wives?"

"I got the house in the agreement."

"What agreement?"

"The divorce agreement."

"You talked to him?"

"Of course."

"Did he ask about me?"

CHAPTER TWELVE

January 8 1973
One month later

R ick closed his book as Emily came into the bedroom. "I thought you'd never finish putting them to sleep. Come, sit." He patted the bed.

"I think Jess is cutting a tooth." Emily sat and rolled her shoulders, trying to relieve the ache.

"Here let me help." Rick shifted position and she felt his hands, warm and strong, begin to knead her muscles.

"Mmm," she murmured. "That's good. So good."

"Your shoulders are knotted."

As he worked his magic, she relaxed. He gently pulled her toward him, so her back was against his chest, and his hands slid down the top of her blouse, unbuttoning as he went.

"I should do the dishes," she said but didn't move, enjoying this moment, loving the feel of his hands as they slipped under the waistband of her sweatpants, groaning as her body awakened and her mind slid away from chores and children.

He pulled away.

"Don't stop," she said.

"Don't worry," he whispered, turning her to unbraid her hair. She closed her eyes as his tugs loosened her hair and everything about her.

She twisted around to kiss him.

"No, not yet."

He took off her blouse and laid her back on the bed. Pulling a long lock of her hair over her shoulder, he brushed her nipples and then, finally, he stripped off his clothes and joined her on the bed.

Emily turned off the lights and sat by the window. Snow was just starting. Rick loved playing with her hair. Sometimes he'd ask her to pile it on top of her head with bobby pins and then he would pull out the pins one by one and watch her hair fall, curling down her naked back. Or like tonight, carefully arrange tendrils over her breasts.

It had begun to irritate her.

She stared out the window at the falling snow. What would happen to their sex life if she cut her hair?

"So Congress finally ratified the equal rights amendment," Joe said as he took a chicken leg. "But I guarantee it isn't going to pass through all the state legislatures."

"Why not?" Emily asked. They were having dinner with Rick's friends and she was doing her best to participate. "All it says it that women should have the same rights under the law as men. Seems pretty obvious to me." She passed the mashed potatoes. "I mean it's—"

"Sweetheart, you are beautiful and maybe even talented," Stan interrupted. "But very naïve." He turned to Joe. "Didn't it pass New York and California already?"

Stung, Emily concentrated on chewing, wishing Vivian or Gemma were there.

Before Joe could answer, Stan kept right on talking. "But to be honest, I just don't understand the narrow focus of feminists." He was serious. "I mean, don't you think there are a lot of really important issues to consider? Men are dying in this war. And poverty. Do you know how many people are living below the poverty line in the US? Still?"

"Yes, but who cleans up your shit?" Emily's breath came fast. She waved her fork. "Have you ever cleaned a toilet?" She speared a Brussels sprout.

"Honey, isn't that off topic?" Rick chuckled, but his eyes narrowed. She'd embarrassed him. "Not to mention that your tone is a bit strident?"

"Strident?"

"After all, it's men who go off and get killed in wars. You have to admit that's not exactly in the same league as cleaning toilets."

Two days later, during yet another snowstorm, Emily lugged Jessica, asleep in her car seat, up the dark staircase to their second floor apartment. Along with two bags of groceries, along with coaxing four-year-old Matt up the stairs.

"I'm so tired, Mommy." He slumped against the wall.

"A few more steps, Matty. You're such a big boy. And when we get upstairs I'll let you watch *Mr. Rogers* and *Sesame Street.* And you can have a fruit pop."

Might as go all the way. Rick was intent on limiting television watching, even if it was *Sesame Street.* He wasn't too crazy about the sugar in fruit pops either, but then he shouldn't have forgotten to come home. That's what he'd said when she called him to ask where he was. "Oh, babe, I'm so sorry, I completely forgot. The department meeting went longer than I thought, and well, I forgot." She could picture his little shrug and the sweet, chagrined smile on his face. She had hung up.

Emily stuffed a bag of peas into the freezer and quickly shut the door before it fell out. Jessica, still in her snowsuit, slept on in her car seat on the kitchen floor.

She needed to get the food away and dinner started before

Jessica woke up. Her movements felt stiff and choppy. When she got this angry, it was as if there was a time lapse between her brain and muscles.

The phone rang as she was stacking cans of tuna in the cabinet. Probably Rick saying he was going to be even later. "What?" she said into the phone.

It was her mother. "Hi, sweetie. You sound tense."

Emily cradled the phone between her head and shoulder and kept unloading the groceries. "Rick forgot to come home. I had to drag the kids out food shopping in this weather and now I have to get everything ready before I go to work. Who forgets to come home?"

"Well …"

"His parents are coming to visit tomorrow," Emily kept going. "I have to get to the darkroom, the house is a wreck." She heard herself whining and stopped. "How are you? What's up?"

"Isn't Rick going for tenure? He probably can't drop everything just so you can go food shopping."

Emily didn't want to get into this with her mother. She tried to change the subject. "Did you guys get all this snow up there yet?"

"You know, honey, maybe you are trying to do too much. Maybe you should concentrate on the house and kids and let Rick get his tenure. Then you can take your pictures."

"Mom, have to go. Jessica is waking up."

When Rick got home, she was sitting on the living room couch cuddling with Jessica and Matt, trying to talk herself out of her anger while they watched Big Bird and Cookie Monster. After all, Rick adored her. He was a great father.

"Hey, babe." He shrugged off his coat. "Wow, did I have an amazing class. I might be good at this professor stuff, if I do say so myself."

Emily's anger surged again.

Matt launched himself off the couch. "Daddy, Daddy." And then Jessica crawled over. Rick scooped them both up and held them upside down, kissing and saying hello to their feet, and they screeched and wriggled with pure pleasure.

He looked at her, grinning. Carefully, he turned Jessica and then Matt, settled them on the floor, and kissed them on their heads. "Okay, wonder kids, now its Mommy's turn."

"Again, Daddy, again."

"One minute. Okay?" He came over to the couch and leaned down for a kiss. Emily turned her head away.

"What's up?"

"You 'forgot' to come home?"

"Oh, shit." He hit himself on the forehead in mock exaggeration to send the kids into giggles again, the he smiled at her. "I am really sorry, babe."

She didn't say a word, just headed toward the bathroom.

"Come on," he shouted after her. "What's the big deal? Why are you making a federal case out of this? I always take the kids food shopping."

She leaned against the doorway. "When you take the kids grocery shopping, and Jess is in the backpack and Matt is bouncing out of the food cart, no one looks at you thinking you are a bad father and your kid is out of control. They're thinking, isn't it wonderful, a father spending time with his kids, isn't he sweet."

"Okay." Rick nodded, his face serious. "But why does this make you angry at me?" He looked so puzzled.

"Look at this place." She waved her arm over the toy-strewn room, the cracker crumbs on the rug, the dirty socks under the chair. "Your parents are coming tomorrow." She turned to leave again.

Rick grabbed her from behind. Cupping her breasts, he whispered loudly in her ear, "I love you." He spun her around and kissed her on the lips, his tongue forcing its way in. "Fuck the house."

On Monday, when Jess went down for her nap, she plopped Matt in front of *Sesame Street* and started on the dishes left from breakfast, hoping for half an hour to get the house back in order. Yet again. She grabbed a plate from the table, swearing when she stepped on the grapes Jess had thrown from her high chair, squashing them into the floor.

Leaving the mess, she went to bedroom to grab her camera. She returned, focused the lens, and took a close-up of the sink piled with dishes and globs of jelly on the counter.

For the next three days, Emily took pictures of the messy closets, the unpaid bills, the dust under the bed. She photographed the heap of dirty laundry and the newspapers piled on the floor. She kept going and photographed the junk drawer, the dirty refrigerator, the calendar with all the pediatric and other kid appointments, the toys strewn around, and the garbage needing to go out.

In the darkroom, she blew them up into black and white 8 x 10s. Then she bought frames and hung them all through the house. Women's magic powers were often disguised as simple domesticity, she thought.

She loved them. Bernie loved them. Vivian, Alix, and Gemma all wanted copies.

"Interesting," Rick said, nodding. "Interesting. But do they need to hang in our living room?"

CHAPTER THIRTEEN

January 29 1973
Two weeks later

G emma hurried to her torts class, her bag bouncing painfully against her hip as she clutched the casebooks that must weigh fifteen pounds. Up the stairs, around the corner, out of breath, she reached the bathroom. There was a line of six women ahead of her.

She let her bag slip to the floor and leaned against the wall to catch her breath. The law school had accepted twenty-five women that year, which was progress, but they had designated only one bathroom for women and allowed just five minutes between classes. Of course, they also had only one woman professor, which might explain that oversight. Her next class started in four minutes. Gemma moved another step forward and resigned herself to being late. Again.

"Nice of you to join us, Miss...?" The professor looked up as Gemma finally made it to class. It was a large lecture hall with stadium seating and the professor was down in the well at the bottom.

"Rollando."

"Speak up, speak up."

"Rollando." Gemma projected her voice. "I apologize for interrupting. There was a long wait for the ladies room."

"No need to discuss your personal business." The room

tittered. "Just make sure it does not happen again."

Gemma glanced at the other women in the lecture hall. One shrugged and rolled her eyes as if in sympathy; a few looked away, embarrassed to be associated with her.

The seats for the first-year law class were assigned and hers was in the middle of the third row, most of the way down those steep stairs at the front of the room. Gemma sighed and made her way down the steps, her bag bumping behind her, peering over her books so she wouldn't fall. Everyone in her row had to stand and let her squeeze through. She tried not to wallop anyone with her pocketbook, stomp on any toes, or drop any of her books.

The professor waited in silence until this process was completed.

"Miss Rollando, since you've already commandeered the attention of the entire room, why don't you begin the discussion of the case assigned for today. Give us the background on Nelson vs. Washington."

He was being a total prick. She hadn't even gotten her notebook out yet. Her upper lip was sweaty. Her scalp itched. She had read the case just last night. She hadn't been unprepared for any class yet and was proud of that, but now her mind was a blank.

"Sorry. Could you repeat the question?" She forced herself to appear relaxed and assured. Occasionally, this happened. Under pressure, her mind just erased itself like a faulty tape.

"Nelson vs. Washington?"

Nothing. She could not remember anything about the case. "I don't know."

"Did you read the assignment?"

"Yes."

"So what was the precedent in this case?"

It was not helping that he'd asked a slightly different

question. The people around her started to squirm. She heard coughs. The tension was getting to everyone.

Her mind was gone. "I don't know."

"Mr. Norris?" The professor peered around the seats until he located him. "Can you illuminate us?"

Gemma studied her unopened notebook and willed herself not to cry. Four older brothers had trained her well. She forced her head up and her eyes front. Never let them see your fear or your hurt, her brothers had pounded into her.

The class finally ended and the lecture hall erupted with sound as people stood, gathered their books, and started the slow file out. No one met her eye, as if she could taint them by association.

The next day, Gemma rounded the hall again with her bouncing bag, and again there was a long line for the ladies room. She looked at her watch and decided she wouldn't be humiliated by being late again and hurried to class, hoping she could ignore the pain in her bladder, hoping she could last the two hours.

Damn.

She turned and ran back down the hall to the bathrooms.

"You may go in now," said the Dean's secretary.

Gemma rose and entered the room with the mahogany bookshelves and leather chairs.

"Good afternoon, Miss Rollando." The Dean's hair was cut very short, and he wore an ugly plaid jacket with his ridiculous bow tie. "Please sit."

Gemma sat.

He cleared his throat. "Miss Rollando, it has ..."

"Ms. Rollando," Gemma interrupted.

"Excuse me?"

"I prefer to be addressed as Ms. Rollando."

"Ah. Of course." He put his hands together to form a steeple. "Mizz Rollando, it has been brought to my attention that you are frequently late to class. This is not acceptable. I trust in the future this will be remedied. Otherwise there may be consequences."

Gemma nodded.

"You may go now, Miss … Oh, excuse me. I mean, Mizz Rollando."

The following week, when yet again, Gemma faced a long line waiting outside the ladies room and a short few minutes before class, she almost groaned out loud. She looked at the line. She looked at the men's room door. No line. She asked the woman beside her, "Shall we?"

The woman shook her head.

Gemma shrugged and pushed open the men's room door. A male student by the sink gave a questioning look, but didn't say anything. Gemma went into a stall.

The walls did not crack. The building did not fall.

As she washed her hands, another woman came in. Then another.

"And this is how a revolution starts," Vivian said. "Feminist battles are fought on all sorts of fronts." She lifted her coffee mug in a toast to Gemma. They were all in the Pewter Pot having a quick bite before going to see a new movie, *Lady Sings the Blues.*

"And this is how it ends." Gemma waved the note she'd found in her mailbox in the law school office and then read it out loud. "Miss Rollando. Dean Graham requests a meeting with you at 8:30 Wednesday, January 24."

Vivian laughed. "Wow, at twenty-two you're being called to

the principal's office? I bet it's the first time ever. I bet you were a goody-goody."

Gemma hadn't thought it funny, but Vivian made it hard to take things seriously. She slouched in her chair and lit another cigarette. "But that wasn't the worst part. The worst was I couldn't say anything to the dean, because I thought I might cry. Typical girl." She sat up and tapped the cigarette against the ashtray. "I can't tolerate women who get angry and cry instead."

Emily raised her eyebrows. "Whoa. I'm beginning to see that compassion for other people's weaknesses may not be your strong point.

"Maybe." Gemma shrugged. "But I'm beginning to wonder what I'm doing in that place. Every day is such a struggle. I'll never fit in that world."

"Shit, Gemma, you've got to learn to laugh at this stuff." Vivian ground out her cigarette. "What are they going to do? Expel you for peeing in the men's room? Now you are a true trail blazer."

Gemma finally laughed and gave her the finger.

Alix nudged Emily and said, "so tell them."

"It isn't anything, really. Bernie handed me an announcement about the Center Street Women's Book Store in Jamaica Plain calling for artwork. They're planning to start hanging local artists and Bernie thought I should apply." Emily played with her spoon as she spoke. "But, I don't really have…"

"The housework photos would be perfect," Vivian interrupted.

"Yes," Gemma said. "Of course you should use that series." It astounded her whenever she realized that Emily didn't know how good she was.

Emily put money down to cover their bill and pushed away from the table.

"Something to think about. Let's go. I hate being late for movies."

CHAPTER FOURTEEN

February 21, 1973
Two weeks later

V ivian ripped the sheet from the typewriter, even though she always told the secretaries not to do that because it ruined the feed roller alignment, then crumpled it and tossed it over her head. She was finishing up invoices before she headed over to group. She scrolled in a clean sheet and tried again. She was a great repairman, or as Gemma would insist, repair*person.* She could fix almost any machine, from mimeograph to the new IBM electric typewriters to cars. But she sucked at typing. And cooking. And sewing. In junior high she got suspended from school for conducting a sit-in during Mr. Silver's shop class. She was forced to take home economics.

She stretched in her chair and looked at her watch. She had time before group. June, her landlady who lived upstairs, had offered to pick up Katie from daycare and watch her, so group was meeting at Alix's apartment for a change. Placing her two index fingers on the keys, she searched and pecked.

"Come have a beer with me after we're done?" Mickey asked from behind her, rustling paper as he gathered her rejected invoices.

"I can't." Vivian didn't bother to look up.

"You do have a wastepaper basket, you know." He stood in front of her desk, rolling onto the balls of his feet and arcing the crumpled paper over his head, aiming for the trash basket.

"I know." Still she didn't look up until she heard him step away. Then she looked, watching his butt as he walked off.

"Damn." She made another mistake. She ripped out the invoice, tossed it, and looked at her watch again. Four p.m. She had to get these invoices in by 4:30.

On her desk were two photographs Emily had taken, one of the dirty laundry and one of her and Katie from the rally back in December. She picked up the picture and studied it. Anyone who could make her look that good had to be talented. Vivian was in awe of Emily. She put the picture back. Too bad she wasn't a lesbian. It would eliminate so much grief, although her lesbian friend told her the same shit went on in relationships between women.

Vivian finished the last invoice and put it on top of the pile. She picked up the rest of her rejects, threw them away, and straightened her desk.

"All done?" Mickey had his coat on. "Come on. Just one beer?"

"I told you, single mom, baby waiting, and no beers after work." She grabbed her coat and swung her bag over her shoulder, and then dropped her typed invoices in the box on Jan's desk and picked up her work orders for the next day.

Mickey followed behind as she headed out. "What? One baby and you're out of commission for life?"

She weaved around a desk and out the door. "Damn, it's cold." She wrapped her scarf tight against the chill. "Who said I'm out of commission, as you so delicately put it?" She held the door for Mickey. "I only said no beers after work." They started walking down Pearl Street in the direction of the Central Square T stop. "And anyway, wasn't it just a week and a half ago you were telling me about working things out with Liz?"

"What does that have to do with anything?"

"Well, in my limited experience, asking one woman out for a

drink while 'working things out' with another doesn't bode well for the 'working things out' part."

"Oh, did you get the impression I was asking you out for a drink?" Mickey's eyes widened. "Like as a date? I apologize." He shook his head. "I was just asking as a fellow worker."

He let her step in front of him up the curb. Vivian felt her face flush. Was she acting like some desperate woman, making up a whole flirtation?

"Wasn't it a few weeks ago," he continued, "that you were complaining how everyone treated you like a visitor from Mars and you just wanted to be treated like one of the guys?"

"In that case," she said, "as one of the guys, let's get that beer." At least she'd be out of the wind for a minute.

"Great." Mickey grinned. "We can go to Monahan's. It's a great little Irish pub, probably a cover for gun running for the IRA. A tough broad like you should fit right in."

Vivian made sure she got to the door first, opened it, and waved Mickey in ahead of her. The elongated room was taken up with a huge, dark wooden bar polished to a high sheen. A haze of cigarette smoke made the room waver. Behind the bar, an ornate mirror reflected shelves of colored liquor bottles, but this was a beer-drinking crowd. Most of the stools were filled. All men. They explicitly checked her out as she followed Mickey. They plainly felt no need to pretend to be polite. She was on their territory. Men having a wee wet one after their shift ended, before they headed home to families.

"Hey, Mickey." A man in a grubby T-shirt and jeans nodded.

"George." Mickey smiled, clapped George's shoulder, and kept walking.

"Good to see you, Mickey," said a clear-faced boy who looked too young to be legal.

"Johnny, my boy." Mickey shook his hand.

Mickey was hailed and greeted all along the bar as he led her to two stools near the end. A few winks and head shakes in her direction showed Mickey their approval. The bartender brought over two drafts without asking.

"Come here often?" Vivian asked, grinning.

"Enough."

"Maybe you'll tutor me then on how one of the guys acts." She purposely let her thigh touch his as they settled at the bar. "I really would like to fit in better." She leaned across him to grab the ashtray, giving him—and a few gawking patrons—a clear view of breasts. She smiled. He blushed.

Except for the blatant stares from men walking from their stools to the bathroom and back, the bar returned to normal and conversations resumed as if she weren't there.

Vivian sipped her draft and ate peanuts while Mickey told funny stories of growing up in Cambridgeport with five sisters, his father working in the Polaroid factory down the street and his mother a schoolteacher. A few other repairmen wandered in from work and came down to their end of the bar to tell tales. Vivian stopped touching and torturing Mickey and just enjoyed herself, actually grateful to be out with the guys.

The smoky haze got denser and the decibel level increased as everyone moved on to their second or third beer and talked over Ike and Tina Turner belting "Proud Mary" on the jukebox.

"I've got to get going," Vivian said into Mickey's ear. She slid off her stool. "I have a meeting."

He nodded at her while listening to one of the guys explain the spread on Friday's Celtic's game. "See you tomorrow," he said.

She started to squeeze her way out of the crowd, when her boss blocked her. "I didn't know they even let women in here."

"Hi, Harvey. I didn't see you." Harvey had the kind of voice that stood out, like a tall man in a crowd. A few of the men stopped talking to listen.

"Don't you have a kid to go home to?" he asked, using the

crush of bodies to move in close.

"I'm going now."

"Is Mickey going with you?" A few more conversations around them ended.

She used the press of bodies to step on his toes. Too bad she didn't have heels on. "Oh, sorry," she said when he winced. "No. I'm leaving alone."

"Leaving alone?" Now his voice demanded the attention of the entire room. "We can't have that." He held his drink out, clearing some space as he pivoted. "This gorgeous babe came into a bar and you fellas are letting her leave alone?"

"Got to go, Harvey." Vivian stepped sideways and men gave way.

"No. Dance with me." He dropped his drink into a waiting hand and pulled her arm. "Honky Tonk Woman" was playing.

"Hey, Harv." Mickey appeared at her side. "Game's starting. Should we deal you in?"

"Yeah. I'm playing." He smiled, holding tight to Vivian's wrist. "Just having a dance first."

Mickey shrugged and walked toward the man dealing cards.

Vivian swore under her breath. She could struggle and create a big scene with her boss in front of all his drinking buddies. Or she could dance with the asshole, be totally humiliated in front of Mickey and a few coworkers, and keep her job.

"You don't want to dance?" Harvey asked her. "Isn't that why women come into bars to be with a man? I'm here." He grinned, swaying a bit. "Ready and willing."

Other than the Rolling Stones wailing on the jukebox, the room was silent.

"Come on. Just one dance."

"Not now." She jerked back, but he wouldn't release her.

"You like to dance, right, sweetie?" He smiled and forced her closer to him, her face so near to his chest, she smelled Scotch through his skin. His leg worked between hers.

The music blared, pounding her skull, and a man shouted, "Hey. Harv's finally got lucky."

She wriggled and pushed against him, but he had her like a vice, both arms pinned.

"Who-ee," someone yelled.

One of his arms circled around her back and squeezed the side of her breast as his other arm stretched low, his hand cupping her ass, forcing her into him, forcing her to feel his hard-on. This could not be happening to her.

"How come he gets the only action in this fuckin' place?"

She went slack and stopped struggling, and as Harvey focused more on groping her, he loosened his hold. She twisted and used her shoulders to gain some air space.

"Can't get enough, can you?" he said. "I knew it." He thrust his hips forward, and as she strained backward, he tightened his grip again.

"Go, Harv. Go, Harv." A chant started, and she tasted terror.

"My turn."

Vivian felt a hand on her shoulder, felt herself being dragged from behind, being pulled from Harvey, and she stomped hard on someone's foot. With her arms freed from Harvey, she started swinging wildly, blindly, fighting with all she had, reduced to pure panic, no awareness of sound or smell. *Must get away. Must get away.* She bucked and hit something fleshy with her forehead.

"Fuck."

Arms encased her again, unyielding muscle.

"Viv. It's me. Mickey. Mickey."

The cold air hit her face as he got her through the door. He let go of her immediately.

"You okay?"

"Yes." She couldn't look at him. "Cigarette?"

He shook one out of his pack and angled it for her to take. She reached for it, but her hands shook too much to grasp it.

He put it to his lips, lit it, and handed it to her.

"I have to quit my job," Vivian said after she told the story to group.

"No," Alix said, her bangles jingling with emphasis.

"How can I ...? I mean every time I see him ..." Vivian shuddered.

Emily poured her a glass of wine. "He won't remember with that much Scotch in him. Or he'll pretend not to."

"She needs to call the police," Alix said.

"And say what?" Gemma asked.

"The man assaulted her in front of witnesses." Alix dropped the bowl of popcorn with a thud.

"A woman walks into a bar, sees she's the only woman, sits down anyway, and has a drink. What do you think she wants? And this is no innocent virgin either. She has a child out of wedlock. The police will simply snicker." Gemma salted the popcorn. "But stay away from him. Never be alone with him. And for God's sake stop flashing your boobs at him." Gemma stood. "Napkins?" she asked Alix.

"Next to the sink."

"Damn Gemma," Emily said. "That was harsh. Very harsh. Are you blaming Vivian for this?"

Emily sounded appalled. Vivian felt tears well; she dragged on her cigarette and slid her pendant across her chain.

"I'm not blaming her. The guy is an asshole. But it's important to not set yourself up. Men like that are dangerous and until things change, women need to take care of themselves." Gemma plunked a handful of napkins in the center of the table. "He's your boss. He wanted to let you know he could do what he wanted. And that is scary." She grabbed a handful of popcorn. "In another few years, I can sue his ass."

Fuck Gemma. Vivian's whole body shook as she drove home. Damn arctic front. Even the full moon looked frozen, and the heater on the Plymouth took forever to get going. How could Gemma say she'd set herself up for that scene? All she'd done was go out to a bar with coworkers.

She lit a cigarette with shivering fingers and wondered if maybe she should call in sick tomorrow. Facing Mickey might be more humiliation than she could handle. The one other time she'd felt this mortified, she'd been hitchhiking on a blazing hot interstate ramp, trying to get far away from Ann Arbor, Michigan.

CHAPTER FIFTEEN

Vivian finished her last exam, English Literature, on Tuesday at eleven a.m. on June 14, 1968. She was sure she aced it, but she didn't stick around to find out; it was irrelevant. Martin Luther King had been killed in April. Bobby Kennedy had been killed last week. The world was fucking crazy. She had decided against college. She was finished with school, finished with grades, finished with Westchester, NY. By three o'clock Tuesday afternoon, she and her best friend Ellie were on the Greyhound Bus. They had enough money for two tickets to Ann Arbor, Michigan.

The bus slowed to a full stop at the bus terminal at one in the morning. Vivian's eyes felt gritty, the sand in your eyes sensation. Her mouth stank, her skin felt slimy, and she knew her hair was stringy. She shook Ellie awake. "We're here. Let's go."

She grabbed her pack and slid into the aisle, waiting her turn as the bus emptied out. She wiggled to adjust the straps on her pack and smoothed the front of her dress. A favorite long, Indian cotton paisley dress, with hiking boots. She'd been right, it was comfortable to travel in. No jean waistband sticking into her waist for two days, like Ellie who'd had to unzip her jeans after awhile just to keep sitting.

"We should have called from Detroit," Ellie said. She stood hunched over between the seats, waiting to get out. "What happens if they're not there? It's one in the morning, they might all be asleep."

"No, they'll be awake. Beth said we could come anytime, remember? I'm her sister, they'll go for it."

Beth had written from Africa, where she was in the Peace Corps, and told her to look up her friends in her old house in Ann Arbor as she went cross-country. She hadn't really told Beth about her plans to leave home, and she didn't think she should tell Ellie that Beth's letter telling her to stop in was over six months old. Ellie had gotten awfully nervous as it was on this trip.

They walked so close together that Vivian could feel Ellie's jeans through her dress. No one else was out and the trees cast moving shadows as they walked. And walked.

"We should have called," Ellie said again, stopping to readjust her pack. "Maybe they would have met us at the bus."

"I didn't know it would be this far."

"Let's call now. They're probably all asleep. Look, the whole neighborhood is asleep. Let's call."

"Where the hell are we going to call from? Do you see a phone or a store?"

"Shh," Ellie whispered. "You don't have to yell."

They made the next right turn, and there in the middle of the block was a two-story house with a light shining in every window. They could hear the Grateful Dead playing from where they stood.

Vivian poked Ellie. "They're not asleep."

The woman who opened the door had straight brown hair hanging down to her hips, pale skin, and huge eyes. She just smiled and held the door, looking at them.

"I'm Beth Parker's sister," Vivian said.

She nodded and waved them in. Without saying a word, she floated away into another room. Vivian closed the door behind her.

"This is too weird," Ellie said.

"Shh." Vivian walked down the hall into a room. She stood and smiled. Two women swayed to music over by the unlit fireplace. They wore long blue work shirts and not much else as far as Vivian could tell. A woman and man were entangled on the couch in what looked to be a dreadfully uncomfortable position, sort of crooning at each other. Another man sat cross-legged on the floor in front of the speakers, singing as loud as he could to the music. The bass boomed. His ears must hurt. Vivian stood there, her smile in place, waiting for one of them to notice her and Ellie.

Two men deep in conversation walked in from another room and stopped when they saw them.

"I'm Bill. Who are you?" Bill wasn't wearing a shirt and he had curly chest hair, jeans slung low on his hips, a beard, and long hair pulled back in a ponytail.

"I'm Vivian, Beth's sister. This is my friend Ellie. We were wondering ..."

"Hey everyone. Beth's sister. Come in. Come in." He waved his hand at the group. "Don't mind them, they're tripping tonight."

Ellie raised her eyebrows.

"Hey, Arnie, can you believe it? Beth's sister." Bill reached his long arms around both of them and ushered them past the stairs and into the kitchen. Arnie followed.

"Ruth, Beth's sister is here."

"Oh, my God. How'd you get here?" Vivian was enveloped in a hug, backpack and all, by Ruth, who was short and big breasted.

"We walked," said Ellie. "A lot."

"You walked from the bus terminal? At this hour? Well, never mind. Put your stuff down. You can crash in my room tonight."

The table was full of food. A loaf of white bread and peanut butter, and bagels and cream cheese, and all those sitting around the table smiled and said hi and made room as Bill pulled up chairs. The man sitting next Vivian nudged her and passed a joint. "Do you want a toke?"

Vivian inhaled deeply and passed it on. Her eyes watered and her throat constricted, but she counted to a full seven before exhaling. She grinned at Ellie. "We made it."

Bill with his curly chest hair squeezed in next to her.

"Tell me who everyone is," she said.

He gave a brief run down on the house: who was staying for the summer, who was just crashing for a few weeks, who lived there during the school semesters, who was working at the food co-op, who was counseling draft resisters, and who was setting up the daycare in the projects.

As she watched him talk, a feeling of well-being passed through her in waves. Slowly, people said good night and left the table. Ruth suggested they put their packs in her room, and Ellie unrolled her sleeping bag and just about fell on it, she was so tired. Vivian went back into the kitchen to talk to Bill.

He talked on, telling her about the work he planned, the liaisons he'd set up with draft evaders in Canada, how he wasn't planning on going back to school in the fall, so he would lose his student deferment and might have to flee to Canada. His hand rested on her thigh. "You have eyes to get lost in," he said. "So, what brought you to Ann Arbor?"

She told him about her high school years, her mother, her plan to see and learn before she went to college. His hand felt warm and his breath was sweet with dope as their heads moved closer together.

"You have the softest hair." He twirled strands at the back of her neck. Outside it began to get light. Finally, he kissed her.

"Would you like to crash in my room, so you don't wake up Ruth and your friend?"

She nodded yes and smiled. Her life had begun.

Vivian woke late that morning filled with the sense of having finally come home. Lying next to her on the dirty sheet was the body of this man, Bill. Even in his sleep his hand came around her shoulders and gently hugged her. This was what she'd been waiting for her whole life. She played with some of the hairs on his chest. Feeling his other hand trace her cheekbone, her jaw line, she looked up. He smiled, awake now, and kissed the top of her head.

As the sun streamed through the curtain-less window, she watched the dust dance in the rays as his hand smoothed her hair and felt such peace and contentment and pleasure, pure pleasure, safe and pure pleasure. Mattress on the floor, piles of books everywhere, piles of clothes in between, a light bulb hanging from the ceiling, the wall covered in psychedelic posters, some corners curled where the thumbtacks had fallen out. She wanted to stay forever. She shifted position so she could more easily kiss him.

That day Bill had to post leaflets announcing a rally and teach-in against the war and the draft. He offered to take her and Ellie around the city and show them the campus. It was one of those glorious summer days, with clear air, the sky so blue she wanted to breathe it in, with the tiniest breeze that wafted away the sweat on her upper lip.

She was giggly. She felt like skipping and twirling, and her mood was catching. She had pulled Ellie out of the kitchen to the dirt of the backyard and whispered in her ear.

"No way," said Ellie.

"So do I look different? I feel different. I feel wonderful. I feel..."

"'... pretty. Oh, so pretty,'" Ellie sang from *West Side Story*. She grabbed Vivian's hands and they spun around, laughing and dizzy.

And Bill was wonderful, just like the day, just as she'd known he would be. He took both their hands and swung with them, making Ellie feel comfortable and wanted and not like a third wheel at all.

They tacked up posters and walked for miles and stopped at a playground. Bill pushed them on swings, and then they ran around and around the go-round, and he grabbed her by the waist and pulled her close to him. He kissed her and swung her down and then did the same to Ellie, and Vivian loved him with total abandon. Anyone who could be so open, so generous that he could include Ellie so that Vivian didn't have to worry, was perfect. She'd write Beth immediately and tell her that coming to her old house in Ann Arbor had changed her life and she owed her big.

On the way home, they stopped to buy spaghetti and the makings for sauce and loaves of French bread and fresh garlic.

That night they drank wine and smoked dope and all around Vivian was laughter and fun and togetherness. She grinned at the whole table. This was the way people were supposed to be. This was alive and great and not dead like her house in New York and *oh my God*, she was so glad. Here was purpose and work to do and people to love you as you did it.

After dinner, she had coffee with the group in the living room, who were planning a demonstration. She had a difficult time concentrating. Her mind kept slipping away into the night with Bill, and she waited until she thought it might be appropriate to say she was tired, but also hoping he would come find her and take her away. She squirmed and wiggled, although she knew the discussion of the war was very serious and important. But after all—she was new to all of this and full, full of joy.

Finally, she couldn't stand it anymore and went to find Bill, planning to whisper in his ear that she was thinking of going to bed soon. The group in the kitchen had cleaned up and were devouring brownies and playing poker for toothpicks. Bill wasn't around.

She checked out the back room, but saw only a guy watching TV whom she hadn't met yet. He didn't look up as she came into the room, didn't move, and she had the fleeting thought that maybe he was dead and no one had noticed he was even missing. She went back to the kitchen to ask Ruth if she knew where Bill was.

"Oh, he went to bed a while ago."

She wouldn't feel bad, because after all they'd had a great afternoon and there were no guarantees in this world, and she certainly didn't want to be a clinging, demanding type of person. No, she wouldn't feel bad. She'd just go find Ellie and maybe they could go for a walk or something, or maybe Ellie could explain to her what this meant. Ellie had had a boyfriend. Maybe it didn't mean anything. Maybe he was just tired.

After another round of the house, she couldn't find Ellie either. She checked out Ruth's room—maybe Ellie had gone to bed too—but she wasn't there.

She got worried. She wanted to go to bed, but she needed to know that Ellie was okay and not out wandering around stoned. After all, she had dragged her into this, so off she went to make the rounds of the house again, and finally she asked Ruth if she'd seen Ellie.

"I think she crashed."

"But she's not in the bedroom."

"I think she's sleeping in Bill's room tonight."

Vivian asked Ruth if it was okay to crash in her room.

"Of course. Of course." Ruth pushed away from the table, sliding her chair back with what looked like slow motion, and then sort of floated toward Vivian. "My God," she said to the others at the table, laughing. "Those brownies were some sort of weird shit. I mean, this floor feels like sponge. It's not sponge, is it?" Everyone at the table laughed. Ruth put her arm around Vivian. "Do you want one? A brownie? Only half. You can have only half since you aren't used to it."

"No, thank you." Vivian felt stiff and uncomfortable with this woman's arm around her. "I'm just real tired. Must be the trip. I just need to lie down."

"Listen, hon," Ruth smoothed Vivian's hair and then took it up between her hands, slowly stroking it, as if her hands were the softest brush. And as she brushed with her hands, she said, "I know how it feels. But don't be upset. Ownership is a bad thing. Sometimes we have to just go with the moment. Sometimes we get overtaken by the moment and it would be wrong to push those feelings away, right?"

Vivian felt her bones tighten and shrink away from this touching person. "I'm not upset. What gave you that thought? I'm just tired. Real, real tired."

Ruth gave her hair one last stroke. "The single mattress on the floor is for guests. There are clean sheets in the trunk if you're tired of your sleeping bag. I'll try not to wake you when I come in."

Vivian lay in Ruth's room and stared at the patterns on the walls and ceiling in the soft glow from a red light bulb. Ruth had covered every inch of wall space as well as the ceiling with Indian bedspreads in reds, blues, and browns. It was like lying in a tent, those tents she pictured Arabian princes erected in the desert, all soft, protective, and warm. The material hung loosely from thumbtacks, and the breeze from the window made the fabric waver, as if the walls and ceiling moved.

She stared. Again the mattresses on the floor, heaps of clothes and books, but the effect was distinctly different from Bill's room. This room smelled of sandalwood and laundry soap.

So, she was just like her mother. Big fucking deal. Actually, she was worse than her mother—or better, depending on how she looked at it. Her mother could keep men around for years before she drove them away. Vivian could drive them away in twenty-four hours.

"Are you upset?" Ellie asked the next morning as they walked to the draft-counseling center.

"No. Why would I be?" Vivian hoped she sounded vastly cool and sophisticated. She stopped and checked the numbers on the buildings, clutching the sheet of paper in her hand. They were going the right way.

"Oh, good. I worried about that, but Bill said you were the kind of woman, he could tell, that was a free spirit and uniquely generous and not bound, gagged, and tied by traditional societal conventions. Look." Ellie pointed across the street as two long-haired men went into a church. "I bet that's it. I'm so glad you're not jealous. I couldn't stand it if you were jealous and weren't talking to me or something."

"No, that can't be the center," Vivian said. "It has to be on this side of the block. I think it's up there." She checked the paper again. "Did he really say those things about me? You're not making it up are you?" She slowed her pace, not liking that possibility at all—but then looking at Ellie, she remembered Ellie was a terrible liar. It wouldn't even occur to her to make it up. She walked faster again. "A free spirit. Uniquely generous. Ha!"

Six weeks later she sat on her pack in the hot sun, on the ramp to the interstate, staring at sticky road tar. Fucking free spirit, she thought. More like fucking idiot. She was hoping for a trucker. A shipment that was going all the way to Seattle maybe. Then she'd only have to make her way down the coast to Berkeley and her brother Charley. She couldn't wait to see the Pacific Ocean where she could watch the sun set over the water.

She couldn't wait to get out of fucking Michigan, away from

that house and all those schmucks she'd slept with, hoping to impress Bill with what a free spirit she was so that he would want her and only her.

That morning as she walked down the hall from the kitchen to the front door, setting off for the meeting at the Unitarian Church to plan the demonstration at the Democratic Convention in Chicago, she had heard a few of the men talking.

"Vivian's something else." That was Tom's voice. She'd smiled and stopped out of sight, pretending to retie the laces on her boots.

"Last night," Bill said, "I thought I'd died and gone to heaven. That mouth is golden. We could set her up and raise more money for the movement in two nights than we do in two months."

The men laughed. Crouched over her boots, Vivian was having a hard time breathing. All along the edge of the floorboards were dust balls and dog hair.

"Yeah," Tom said, "but we'd have to give her a new body. She's getting to be a little too much woman. How 'bout Janet's?"

"No, Janet's too skinny," someone else said. "I like my women big."

"That's because you're fat too." The men laughed again. "Who's on for tonight? I think … Shit. What the fuck?"

Tom ducked as the candlestick Vivian threw missed him and flew out the open window behind the couch.

"Hey," Bill said as she grabbed an empty glass off the end table and threw that. "Stop it. Goddamn it, Viv, what the hell are you doing?"

That was it. Vivian shoved her clothes and belongings into her backpack and left. Now she sat on her backpack, wishing she'd thought to bring water and watching the ant columns travel in long, busy lines across the road dirt. Fuck the convention. She wanted to start the life she knew she would lead forever. She would be a serious political activist. She would find the people that were as committed to change, to honesty, to a sane lifestyle, as she was. And she knew they were in Berkeley, California.

A little Volkswagen bug rumbled past and then stopped. It might at one time have been green; now it was mostly rust. Vivian walked toward it. She peered in as the driver rolled down the window. Someone had told her never to get into a car with two guys. Women were fine. And truckers were okay. If it was one guy, you had to engage in conversation for a few minutes, get the feel of him.

This was a one-guy scenario. "Where are you headed?" he asked, smiling, his beard waggling.

"California. By way of Seattle, probably."

His car was jammed with stuff. Lots of stuff. Sleeping bag, duffle bags, stereo, boxes of records.

"Hey. Wow. Far out. Me too." He grinned. "I'm taking a little side trip first, up to the Olympic Mountains, but I could drop you in Seattle."

She nodded. How do you get a feel? "Where are you from?"

"All over. Traveled all over this summer. What a trip. What a trip. Country is going fucking crazy. It's great. Amazing."

"Why are you going to California?"

He had long hair caught back in a rubber band, a dark beard, and blue, blue eyes. But she'd learned already that ponytails and beards didn't mean trustworthy. Didn't even mean nice.

He didn't seem to mind the interview. "Live there. School, you know. Got to keep the old deferment."

"Do you go to Berkeley?"

"UC at Santa Cruz. The most beautiful place in the country, and I've seen some beautiful places. So? You getting in or what? We could talk as we drive."

She nodded yes, but didn't open the door. *Are you going to try anything weird or funny?* How the hell do you judge this shit? "It's beautiful here," she finally said.

He stuck his head out the driver's window. "Yup. It sure is." He opened the door and uncoiled from the seat. Tall, skinny, jeans, and T-shirt. Looked like a million other guys. "I think I'll take a leak, since I've stopped anyway. Just throw your pack on top of the other junk."

She watched him walk back into the tall grass, wandering until he found a thick clump of bushes. She opened the door. A good enough feel.

Vivian pulled into her driveway, the car finally warm, and sat with her head on the steering wheel before going up to relieve the sitter.

God, she missed Jerry.

CHAPTER SIXTEEN

February 26, 1973
One week later

E mily screeched, startling the kids, when she opened the letter offering a place in the art show.

"Happy. Mommy's so happy," she squealed, jumping up and down and twirling Jess. Matt had no idea what was going on, but he giggled with pleasure at his silly mommy.

She waited to tell Rick until the kids were asleep and the two of them were cozy in bed.

"That's great, babe." He lightly circled her nipples with his index finger. "I always knew you were great."

"I got a babysitter for the opening."

"Why?" He brushed her chin, her shoulder, with his lips. "I promise I won't forget to come home to watch the kids." He lifted his head to see how she took his little joke.

She smiled, turned toward him, and kissed the spot right below his ear. "I want you to come."

"Oh, that's okay." He pulled at her nightgown. "Art shows aren't my thing."

"I'd really like you to come." She felt his tongue on her lips.

"It's okay," he murmured, caressing her hip. "Anyway, I don't really like those pictures."

Emily stiffened.

"That's not what I meant, sweetie." His eyes went wide. "I just meant I don't understand them." He laughed. "You have to admit, they're a bit hard to relate to." He stroked her rigid frame and pulled her toward him. "I love your work. You take amazing photos. You deserve this." He kissed her eyes, her nose, her lips. "You're so talented."

He kept desperately throwing out words. "Of course I'll come. I'm so proud of you."

Emily saw his mouth move. His eyebrows furrowed with concern, maybe even love. She stared at his long hair, his beard, and wide chest and wondered who this man was.

Gemma trudged through the slush, her backpack digging into her shoulders, her fists thrust deep into her coat pockets, her chin burrowed into her scarf, not even attempting to avoid puddles, just hoping to stay upright. Cold and tired, she might have skipped group that night if she hadn't agreed to pick up Alix from the health center and walk over to Vivian's with her.

Still irritated from the meeting the previous week, she kicked a frozen chunk and sent it skittering down the sidewalk lit by yellowish street lamps. If women like Vivian persisted in using sex to get what they wanted, then there was no way men would stop seeing women as sex objects. Vivian saw *herself* as a goddamn sex object. Plus, it was dangerous. It had consequences, often unseen consequences. Tonight she'd definitely confront her again on that one.

The Women's Health Center was a block from Mass Ave, centered on a residential street between Harvard and Leslie College. A discreet sign to the left of the door on the three-family house with peeling clapboards was the only indication it wasn't student housing.

She climbed the thoroughly sanded steps, pushed open the heavy front door, and followed the arrow pointing toward the waiting room. It glowed with a soft light from lamps on the end tables next to overstuffed chairs and two couches. Magazines obscured the top of the coffee table. A couple huddled on one couch, and three way-too-young women sat on the other couch. The one in the middle looked wide eyed and pale, while her two friends wrapped arms around her and whispered.

Gemma walked over to a woman with the biggest afro she'd ever seen, sitting behind a desk in probably what had originally been the dining room. She said hello and told her she was there for Alix Goldman.

The woman gave a welcoming smile and asked if she had an appointment.

"No, I'm just a friend meeting her."

"Have a seat and I'll let her know you're here."

Gemma sank into a chair across from the three teenagers. Alix, holding a clipboard and dressed in a corduroy jumper over a turtleneck sweater, rushed in and gave her a kiss hello. "I'm running a bit late," she whispered. "Will maybe be another ten minutes. Help yourself to the cookies and coffee in the kitchen."

Then she turned to the young women on the couch. "Amy Wells?" The one in the middle nodded.

"I'm Alix." She offered her hand. "And I can take you back now. Do you want your friends to come with you or stay here?"

The young woman looked petrified and about to burst into tears. She turned to her friends as if she didn't know the answer.

"I'll tell you what," Alix said. "Why don't your two friends"—she paused so they could supply their names—"come with us. I'll tell you all what to expect where we can talk in private and then you can decide?"

Amy nodded.

"Just follow me."

Alix looked so warm and competent, Gemma thought, people would follow her anywhere.

Two more women, laughing, one of them obviously

pregnant, came from the back through the waiting room and stopped at the desk. "I need an appointment for next month," the pregnant woman said.

Watching the easy interactions of the women staff and women clients, Gemma wondered how it might have been different for her if abortion had been legal, if she'd had a place like this. She remembered shivering in the gray sleeting rain, all alone, stunned, trying to get up the courage to walk up that flight of stairs to the address she'd been given.

"I'm so sorry." Alix startled her, standing over her, her coat on. "I didn't think I'd be that long."

Gemma stood, feeling disoriented, but she made herself smile. "Don't worry. It's a great place to wait and it's fun to see you at work."

As she spoke, she realized she was jealous of the all-women atmosphere, the informal room, and the easy laughter. She knew from Alix's stories that there were also endless meetings, circular discussions, tears and arguments as the staff tried to forge a way to take charge of women's health care delivery, but she was bone tired of the man's world of law that she struggled in. Jokingly, last week, Vivian had suggested she form a women's law caucus at the school and really freak the dean out. The idea was growing.

"I can't wait for you to read this." Alix reached into her huge bag and pulled out a book. "It's by Erica Jong and called *Fear of Flying*." They'd gotten into the habit of trading books. Alix lowered her voice to a whisper. "She does a great job describing women and sex and the fantasy of the zipless fuck."

Gemma laughed. "Now that's a phrase I won't forget." She'd never had a friend before who loved to read as much as she did.

"Just have to wait one more second while I call Sam and remind him I'm not coming home because there's women's group tonight. And Viv called and told us to stop and get some flowers. Em has news."

Gemma nodded and looked at the book, pulling out a newspaper article wedged between the pages.

Alix grabbed it. "My mother sends me clippings on a weekly basis about the rupture in the mother-infant bond when mothers go to work, and I send her clippings about fifty-year-old women who return to school and get degrees." She strode over to the reception desk and picked up the phone.

After buying the flowers, they crunched their way to Vivian's house. Gemma kept her head down, watching for icy patches and trying not to slip. Tonight, definitely, she'd tell them the whole story of her abortion and what followed. She'd practice on them, before she told Willie.

Inside Vivian's, Gemma pulled off her hat and unwrapped her scarf. Katie toddled in waving a book. "Gemma come."

Gemma swung her up to her hip. "*Goodnight Moon*? Is this what we're reading tonight? Good choice."

"Freesia!" Vivian grinned. "Alix, you are wonderful. I am so fucking tired of this gray weather."

Emily reached for another one of the bags Alix had put on the counter.

"Don't touch." Alix snatched it away before she could open it. "It's a surprise for later."

"Did you cut your hair?" Emily frowned at Gemma.

"Yeah. Is it too short?" Gemma patted the back.

"It's beautiful," Vivian said. "You have the cheekbones for short hair."

Emily nodded and smiled, but Gemma didn't think she agreed.

"I just did it this morning before I left for class." Holding Katie, Gemma bent so she could see her reflection in the toaster. "I don't have time for hair."

"Great." Emily said. "You're shrinking under the pressure of law school, you've lost weight, and now your hair is gone."

"Let's go read this book," Gemma said to Katie, deciding to ignore that comment. Emily put way too much stock in hair. She carried Katie to her bedroom. A bedtime story from Gemma and Katie always went right to sleep. Vivian joked that she drugged her.

After Gemma finished, everyone settled in the living room. Alix, still carrying her mysterious brown bag, sat on the floor and asked, "Okay, Emily, what is this news we've been hearing about?"

"That bookstore accepted my photographs," Emily said with a grin. "I still can't believe it. I'm having my first showing. It's not a real gallery, like downtown, but critics will come and another artist canceled at the last minute, and they called me and … well, it's less than two weeks. March ninth. I am so goddamn nervous. I got you all tickets for the opening."

"To Emily!" Vivian lifted her wineglass.

"Mazel tov!" Alix said.

"We'll be there. Would never miss it," Gemma said, though she thought Emily sounded more disjointed than excited and even her hair seemed limp.

"That's good. I'll need the support."

"You sound like you're expecting to be executed," Gemma said.

At least Emily laughed at that and nodded. "This is it, you know." She wrapped Vivian's afghan closer, making a cocoon. "I can take the pictures, send them off and get rejected, even occasionally accepted, and moan about wishing I was successful and respected—but this? This is public, this is exposure, this is putting it all on the line. Do I have it or don't I?"

"It's a bookstore in Jamaica Plain," Vivian said. "I think it's great and all, and I'm totally excited for you, and I know it's scary, but this is not going to make or break your career."

"Rick can't go."

"Why not?" Alix said. "You can get a sitter."

"Well, I should have said Rick doesn't want to go. He doesn't like my photographs."

"He actually said that?" Gemma asked.

"Well, he said art wasn't really his thing and he probably just didn't understand them." She twirled her wineglass. "I know I shouldn't let Rick's reaction influence ... I mean, we're supposed to be beyond the opinions of ..." Her voice trailed off.

"Oh, sweetie," Vivian said. "You mean he doesn't love the photo of overflowing garbage you hung above the TV?" She leaned back, exhaling smoke. "Bastard."

Gemma knew Vivian was trying to be funny—and maybe prick Emily's dramatic balloon—but Emily was serious. Gemma poured more wine.

"Maybe you should just stop fucking him for a few days until he agrees to go?" Vivian said, trying again when Emily didn't smile.

"Or explain how important it is to you." Gemma scowled at Vivian. The woman brought everything back to sex. "Communication."

"No. She couldn't," Alix said, who usually advised compromise and patience. "You shouldn't have to explain things to someone so they'll notice your soul."

Emily nodded. "You got it." She took a sip of wine and a handful of popcorn. "I'm livid and at the same time so heartbroken that he ruined this moment, this one evidence of success. I watched my father deflate my mother over and over. I don't want that to happen to me."

"Maybe he's jealous," Vivian said. "Worried that you'll get rich and famous and leave him."

"Doubtful." Emily crunched popcorn. "Anyway, I'm happy you all will be there."

Vivian shrugged. "Maybe, he's feeling—"

"Have you ever noticed," Alix interrupted, "how much time we spend guessing what men might be feeling?"

Emily nodded. "Let's not talk about this anymore."

"But—"

"Really, Vivian. Change topics." Emily pointed at Alix's bag. "What do you have in that thing anyway?"

"I'm not sure this is the time."

"Come on."

"All right then." Alix reached into the paper bag. "I brought this as a special surprise for us." Grinning, she pulled out a small round mirror and a speculum.

Vivian blew out smoke. "You are not serious. This is not happening."

"Have you seen yours?" Alix asked.

"Who gives a shit?" She lit another cigarette. "I haven't seen my liver either."

Emily leaned over and took her camera out of her bag. "This could be better than my high school breast pictures."

"Come on," said Gemma grinning, feeling wicked for enjoying Vivian's discomfort and grateful for the reprieve. This obviously would not be the time to talk about her abortion. She poured more wine into Vivian's glass. "It's part of being in a women's group. It's like a rite of passage."

"I am not putting anything that has been in another woman's vagina inside mine." Vivian said this as though it should end the discussion.

But Emily looked at Gemma and Alix and then at Vivian, and all three of them just burst out laughing.

Vivian looked startled, and then stubbed out her cigarette. "Right. Well, anything that's metal."

CHAPTER SEVENTEEN

March 9, 1973
Less than two weeks later

"**D**avey is down for the night," Alix said as she sat at the kitchen table and pulled on her boots. She was already late for Emily's showing.

Sam stood doing dishes. He sniffed the air. "You smell wonderful."

Surprised, Alix looked up from lacing her boots. Sam usually wasn't too free with compliments. "I just tried this sample perfume that Viv gave me," she said to his curved back. Too tall for the sink, Sam stooped. His ponytail curled around the neck of his shirt.

"Hmmm," he said. "I like." He turned, dried off his hands and massaged her shoulders.

"Oh, that feels very good." Alix was impatient to get going, but it was important to reward good behavior.

"Maybe you don't have to go?" He winked.

"I can't miss this." She twisted in the chair to better see his face.

"Yeah, but…" he squeezed her shoulders and winked.

"Emily is having her first photo show." She bent to finish lacing her boots. She couldn't believe he'd winked.

"Between work meetings and women's group you've been out

four nights this week."

"You know how important this is."

"More important than me?" Alix felt her whole body sink. His hands slid from her shoulders to her breasts. Sam attempted to lighten his tone. "Davey is asleep." She could feel his breath on her hair. "We could have some fun."

She shook her head. "I'll be home by eleven – let's have fun then." She kissed his arm.

He took his hands away. "Never mind." He turned back to the sink.

"Don't be mad."

He was silent. A loud sulking silence.

Alix looked at the clock over the sink and sighed. She stood, wrapped her arms around him, and leaned into his back. The top of her head barely reached his shoulder blades. "How about a quickie before I go?"

"Really?" He turned.

"Sure." Alix forced a smile.

He kissed her. "I'll meet you in the bedroom."

Alix bent and undid the laces she had just finished tying. She didn't know who she was more appalled at—herself for suggesting it or Sam for agreeing so goddamn fast.

Alix counted eight people in the storefront bookstore and Emily, Viv and Gemma were three of them. The room was narrow but long, with a children's section up front. Spotlights lit Emily's photographs on the brick walls above the bookshelves and near the back a table had been cleared of books and held wine and cheese.

"Thank god you're here," Gemma greeted her holding a glass of wine. She wore one of her lawyer suits and even pumps with heels for the occasion. "Why are you so late?"

Alix ignored her question. "Did I miss the crowd? Do I look

okay?" She should've worn a dress, but at least she'd put on her silver necklace.

Gemma appraised her. "You look beautiful. No crowd, yet. But Emily's classy and has been gracious to the few people straggling in." Gemma gestured with her chin to where Emily was talking. "And she's so thrilled to see her pictures on the wall and have people here talking about her work she's actually glowing." Gemma smiled.

Emily wore one of her long flowing skirts and it swayed as she gestured and laughed. She did look radiant.

Turning back to Gemma, Alix asked, "Any sign of Rick?"

"No. Not yet. The schmuck."

Alix noticed Vivian on the other side of the room in a cream silk blouse and long dark skirt, tossing her hair and touching the arm of an elderly gentleman.

Gemma again pointed with her chin, scowling. "That's Bernie. He's already besotted. And if Vivian doesn't turn it down a notch, by the end of the night he'll be leaving her his entire fortune."

"Lower your voice," Alix said laughing. "I'm going to say hi to Em.

"I'm going to circulate and look like extra people," said Gemma. "And if Rick shows up, keep him far from me or I might make a scene."

Emily greeted another woman who entered and Alix wandered the room looking at the pictures while she waited for her to be free. Most of them were ones she recognized: the messy house series, the daycare, and the rally. But there were a number she hadn't seen of Vermont, of women and children in the playground, of Boston. As soon as Emily was alone again, Alix went and hugged her hello. "Your photographs look great. I can't believe how proud I feel."

Emily squeezed her arm and grinned. "Thanks. I think it did

turn out okay." She scanned the room. "The show will be hanging for the next two months." The air around Emily was electric she was so excited. "The art critic from the Globe came and said she loved my work."

The older man stepped close and tapped Emily's shoulder. She turned. "Oh Bernie – this is Alix."

He shook Alix's hand. "So nice to meet you. Excuse me and sorry to interrupt, but I should take Emily over to meet someone. He's from the Boston Phoenix." He held Emily's elbow and guided her away.

Alix spotted Vivian and Gemma in intense conversation over by the wine and cheese table. Gemma faced Vivian and Alix couldn't see her face but her hands waved obviously making an emphatic point and Vivian's answer came in a loud hiss that was audible across the room.

Vivian rolled her eyes as she noticed Alix walking toward them.

"What's up?" Alix asked as she took a slice of cheddar from the plate.

"I think Gemma's calling me a slut," Vivian smiled but her face flushed. Alix couldn't tell if it was from wine or anger.

"I did not say that," said Gemma.

"Too loud," cautioned Alix, seeing a few heads turn in their direction.

Gemma lowered her voice, but not by much. "I said you play a dangerous game when you flaunt your sexuality all the time." She finished her wine.

Vivian turned to Alix as if she were going to referee. "And I said that there is still this fucking double standard crap. All this women's lib and free love didn't change it at all." She put down her glass. "I still can't fuck around like a man."

"You can, obviously," Gemma said. "And that's all fine and good as long as you don't end up raped and dead in some hotel room after picking up some guy to prove how independent you are."

"Jesus Christ!" Vivian exploded.

"Where the hell did that come from?" Alix said, appalled.

"It's risky, is all. And anyway, the feminist movement has more important issues to deal with than making sure you can have sex without consequences. Sex always has consequences."

Vivian pointed her finger and leaned forward but before she could say anything, Alix jumped in and whispered. "Maybe we should discuss this at group. This is Emily's night." A few more people appeared curious.

Gemma poured herself more wine. "If women use sex as their only means to power, we will never be taken seriously in this world."

Alix thought about her quickie with Sam and wondered what Gemma would say about that when she saw Emily walking toward them looking worried. "Stop. This is not the time or the place," Alix said.

Gemma ignored her and pointed at Vivian. "For example, why are you wearing cleavage tonight?"

"This is a blouse, Gemma. A blouse." Vivian leaned in and spoke softly. "And why the hell are you criticizing me?"

"I'm not criticizing, I'm worried. Women get injured all the time. I should know," she murmured, but then her voice rose again. "Look what happened with your boss."

"That was not my fault," Vivian said. Too loudly.

"Shhh," said Alix.

"No, no. Of course not," said Gemma. "But if you're not careful…"

"I'm not listening to this shit." Vivian shrugged on her coat just as Emily reached them.

"What's going on?" Emily looked stricken. "Why are you leaving?"

CHAPTER EIGHTEEN

Vivian balanced Katie on her hip as she kicked snow off her boots and opened the front door. "Let's have dinner before we fall asleep." Katie's face felt hot and damp against her neck.

Once inside, she bent to let Katie down, but Katie clung to her. Her legs dangled and then went spaghetti-like when her feet brushed the floor. "Up, up," she cried. She rarely asked to be lugged around anymore.

"Hey, sweet pea, just stand for a second, till Mommy gets off her coat."

She tried to lower Katie again, but Katie wailed.

Vivian sighed and carried Katie over to the couch, her wet boots making splotches on the rug, and sat them both down. Katie leaned into her.

"So, sweetie, tough day at daycare?"

Vivian shrugged out of one sleeve of her coat, then transferred Katie to the other side and slipped out of the other one. "Mommy's day sucked too."

She smoothed back Katie's hair. Usually when she picked Katie up from the toddler room at daycare, Katie screeched "Mom-eeeee," high pitched enough to break glass, and Vivian quickly dropped whatever she was carrying and crouched low, ready with open arms as Katie hurtled into her. What possible love with a man could compare to that? And then Katie would start to talk, naming every random thing she saw or thought of on the way home. "Lights, Mommy, lights. Truck. Big truck." And if Vivian didn't respond right away, Katie would just up the volume. "Dog, dog, *dog*, *dog*!"

"Yes, sweetie, there's a dog," and she'd wish for just a second of silence.

But today, Katie was much too quiet. "There were no real emergencies," Vivian went on as she maneuvered Katie out of her coat. "Just the usual crisis calls about typewriter breakdowns. What about Jell-O?" She really wanted Katie to perk up. Katie shook her head and sat wide- eyed, sucking her thumb.

Katie's jumpsuit was damp and sour smelling. "And then Alix called to tell me how upset Emily was that Rick never appeared at her showing and how my leaving early didn't help any. Why am I getting the blame?" Katie's whole body was limp. "Damn Gemma and her sanctimonious shit." Katie radiated heat.

"Uh-oh, baby cakes. I think you have a fever."

She carried Katie to find the thermometer. With one hand she rummaged through the medicine cabinet, moisturizing creams, Band-Aids, toothpaste piling up on the side of the sink. But of course no thermometer. She had to get better organized. She went to Katie's dresser and searched through the bin of diaper lotions and pins.

She switched Katie to her other arm and went back to the medicine cabinet to find the baby aspirin. She hesitated to call the pediatrician because all he would tell her, with that slightly amused tone that indicated she was overreacting, was not to worry, babies often spiked fevers. Just give Katie a Popsicle, baby aspirin, and call in the morning. She probably should also find a different pediatrician.

Vivian gave Katie a sponge bath and cuddled her on the couch until she fell asleep.

Through the night, Katie woke every few hours, feeling hotter each time. Vivian finally found the goddamn thermometer in the junk draw and at three a.m. called the pediatrician. Katie was listless and her fever was 105 degrees. He told her to bring her to the emergency room at Cambridge City Hospital. Vivian grabbed her coat, but realizing she should put real clothes on, stripped off her nightgown and pulled on jeans and a sweater without worrying about finding underwear. She wrapped Katie in a blanket, then decided that wasn't enough and eased her into her coat and hat. Carrying Katie, she snatched her bag and then couldn't find her keys. Her panic rose.

It was late morning when the emergency room doctors finally decided to admit Katie. They couldn't get her fever under control and worried about dehydration. The hospital room was small and crowded with a crib, a chair, and a metal cabinet with diapers and equipment. Katie was hooked up to an IV, her arms strapped to stiff boards so she couldn't pull out the tubing.

At five in the afternoon the pediatric resident took Katie down the hall for a spinal tap to test for meningitis. Vivian was not allowed to stay with her and she heard Katie screaming for the full fifteen minutes.

Now two hours later, Katie was back in the room, sleeping, and they just had to wait for the results of the culture. Vivian leaned over the crib and watched her breathe.

"Bastards," she whispered, stroking Katie's forehead. She knew she was being unfair. The doctors were only trying to help. But she'd abandoned Katie, left her alone with needles and strangers. "Assholes."

"Are you okay?"

Vivian glanced at the nurse and nodded. She tried to smile.

"It's probably a good time for you to go while she's sleeping. Get something to eat. Get some sleep."

"I'm not leaving." Vivian put her chin down on the crib bar again and rubbed Katie's belly.

"Well ..." The nurse checked the IV. "Visiting hours ended over an hour ago."

Vivian sat up. She hadn't notice daylight leave or darkness arrive. Hospital time operated outside normal time. She remembered calling work to tell them she'd be out, and Alix to say she'd miss group, but she couldn't remember eating. "I'm not leaving." She lowered her head and stroked Katie's hair.

"I'm sorry," the nurse said, "you can't—"

"You can't make her leave." Gemma's voice startled Vivian. There she was, all five feet of her, looking powerful and stern. "Family members of young children are allowed to stay."

"Who are you?" asked the nurse.

"I'm Vivian's sister."

Vivian almost laughed out loud. The nurse looked completely unconvinced.

Gemma went on. "We could stay out of the way, in the waiting room down the hall, and then Vivian could check on Katie when she wanted?" she stated and asked at the same time.

"I'll ask," the nurse said, shaking her head at Vivian and Gemma but smiling as she left the room.

In the waiting room were Alix and Emily and two bags filled with snacks and drinks.

"Do not hug me," Vivian ordered when they started to stand up. She could feel the tears; her nose tingled. She was not going to cry. She sat near one of the bags. "Why are ...? I mean, how did you ...?"

Emily reached into the bag and handed her a tuna sandwich. "When Alix called and told us why you couldn't make group"— she popped open a soda—"we decided it was going to be a long night for you alone."

Vivian bit into the sandwich to keep her face from

crumpling. "I really am okay. You guys didn't need to come."

"I know you're fine." Alix tore open a bag of potato chips. "But Sam offered to babysit." She handed the bag to Vivian. "Never should waste those opportunities."

In between bites of her sandwich she filled them in on Katie. "So now we're just waiting. She has an infection and they're trying to identify it. If it's bacterial meningitis, the antibiotics should take care of it. If it's viral meningitis, well, then ..." Her voice wavered.

Alix leaned toward her, her arms open wide.

"No hugs," Vivian repeated.

"When will we know?" Gemma asked.

"It depends." She put down her sandwich. It tasted like cardboard anyway. "She might respond fast to the antibiotics, in which case we'll know soon, or it could take a few days, or she might not respond at all."

Gemma came and sat next to her. "I'm sorry. She put her hand on Vivian's knee. "And I'm so goddamn sorry about how I acted and what I said to you at the show. I don't want to hurt"-- she turned to Emily--"I ruined your big night. Maybe I'm... I know this is not the time to go into it"-- she looked at each of them, her eyes glistening –"but please know how sorry I am." Gemma stood without waiting for a response. "I'm getting us some blankets. I never understood why they keep waiting rooms so goddamn cold." A few minutes later she returned with four thin cotton blankets and some extra pillows.

Emily grabbed a blanket and tucked it around Vivian's legs. They were making it awfully difficult for her not to cry. She unwrapped from the blanket. "I'm going to check on Katie."

The corridor was dim and quiet as the unit settled in for the night. She could hear little hisses and beeps from various machines in the rooms she passed. Her stomach felt leaden from the sandwich, her muscles ached from clenching, and her brain had shut down, numb with terror. A nurse was leaving when Vivian reached Katie's room.

"Her breathing is labored," the nurse said.

Katie was fast asleep, her hair matted. Vivian sat, arms resting on the crib bar, and watched her daughter breathe and made bargains with a god she desperately wished she believed in. She smothered a sob of solid fear.

"She's sleeping," said Vivian as she walked back into the waiting room, trying for an upbeat tone of voice. "And she doesn't feel as hot." If they noticed she'd been crying, none of them said a word.

"That's good. That's a good sign." Emily handed her a pillow. "Maybe you should close your eyes. We'll check on her."

"I won't sleep. Talk about something else. Anything else."

"A real live stranger bought one of my housework photos from the show," Emily said.

"Which picture?" Vivian asked.

"The one with the sink overflowing with dishes," Emily said as she stretched out on the couch.

Gemma dragged another chair close to the couch, creating a circle. Alix handed out more pillows and put the food within grabbing distance on the end tables.

Vivian gulped her soda. "That's one of my favorites. Reminds me when Katie and I lived in Berkeley with my brother and his friends."

"You always make it sound like you loved living in California with your brother." Alix settled into one of the chairs. "You never told us why you left."

"God, that story would take all night." Vivian curled under her blanket on the other end of the couch.

"You going anywhere?" Gemma inched her chair forward so she could put her feet up on the couch.

Alix did the same. The four of them huddled under blankets within whispering distance, with partially eaten sandwiches, bags of chips, cans of soda, and packets of cookies strewn on tables around them.

Vivian saw they were determined to distract her and decided to give in. Maybe if she talked about Jerry, she could conjure him up.

"Well, I should start with Jerry who I met hitching to Berkeley. He looked like a million other guys looked that summer: skinny, tanned, blue work shirt, blond hair in a ponytail. He pulled over in his crazy Volkswagen Beetle, bursting with everything he owned. I was feeling so wounded and discouraged and Jerry, bless his soul, seemed to sense that. He talked and shared and made me laugh.

"I had never met a person I was so relaxed with. He asked little about me or where I came from. I mean he did ask, but when he saw me get teary or hesitate, he would just babble on."

"There's a country," Gemma said, "where the people believe that to ask a direct question, to request information from a person, is such an affront, such an invasion of privacy." Gemma always shared odd tidbits of knowledge that cluttered her brain.

Vivian nodded. "Yes, yes. Jerry never intruded. It was so restful being with him. Not that he was restful at all. He was jumpy and drove erratically and was always taking side trips and finding little waterfalls.

"But he required nothing from me. It was the first time I could just be, and I knew he somehow would get me where I needed to go. And he made me feel beautiful and sexy without making one sexual overture."

Emily laughed, stretching her legs. "Now that's a trick I'd like to see."

"Seriously. I'd change in the morning and he'd say, 'God, you look beautiful in that shade of yellow. Wait, I've got something,' and he'd rummage in the back of that car and pull out a scarf or hat or something that would go with my outfit.

"The first time we made love, it was on a cliff overlooking the Pacific Ocean." She smiled. "Jerry took me all the way to San Francisco. We watched the Democratic Convention at some bar in Oregon with men cheering as the cops beat people bloody. Jerry sat with me, holding hands, tears streaming down his face."

Vivian picked up her pack of cigarettes. "He and I said goodbye in San Francisco. He went back to school and"—she tapped out a cigarette, lit it, and shook out the match with a quick flick of her wrist—"and I began life at my brother Charley's house."

"That's it? That's the end of Jerry?" Emily asked like a little kid at the end of a chapter. "I really hope not. I like Jerry."

Vivian blew out smoke and continued. "I loved living with Charley and his friends. We worked the soup kitchens and with draft resisters while the campuses fucking exploded. People were pouring into Berkeley and San Francisco, pot smoke hung in a cloud over the streets. It was a whole new world being born right before our eyes. Anything was possible."

Emily passed Vivian the ashtray to catch the ash that was about to drop. "Jerry came and visited every few months or so, and well ..." She slid her turquoise pendant on its gold chain. "That spring, I got pregnant."

Emily grinned. "Oh. I guess that wasn't the end of Jerry."

"What I never told anyone, until now, was that it wasn't an accident. Jerry was the nicest of all the men I'd been with and so I chose him. I just wanted someone to love who was guaranteed to love me back, no matter what."

"God, you're like the stereotype of teen pregnancy," Gemma said.

Vivian laughed. "I was not a stereotype. I was what the fucking stereotype was based on.

"I loved being pregnant, the feel of my body expanding. I felt powerful. I felt invincible. Actually, with Katie I still feel like that, even now. When she's around, I am untouchable. I am a mother. She's my shield."

"I'm not sure how that'll work out for Katie down the—" Gemma stopped when Alix nudged her with her foot.

"After Katie was born, I took her with me everywhere. My sister had sent me this front pack thingamajig and Katie lived in it. She would burrow down and sleep curled up on my chest, and I could go ladle soup at the People's Park or scream slogans at the antiwar demonstrations.

"I vowed she would never feel alone or overwhelmed, that she would know in every cell of her being that she was loved.

"And when my shoulders started to ache, then Gary or Charley or Steve or Paul would take her. It was so much fun to see these gangly, tall men, with their long hair and bushy beards, with a baby strapped to their chests.

"Charley got me a job at the agency where he worked, helping out the kids who were coming in by the busloads with no money, no food, and living on the streets. Because I have this odd talent to be able to fix things with moving parts—engines, mimeograph machines, typewriters, anything—everyone appreciated me, because everything was old and always breaking down.

"I decided I'd stay forever. I'd finally found my home. We protested, smoked dope, cried at the killings at Kent State, and threw things at the TV when Nixon gave speeches. Katie was thriving. In the evenings people took turns playing with her. And Charley told me all the time what a great mother I was, and I cannot tell you how good that felt." She blinked back tears.

"A little over a year ago, about a week after Thanksgiving"— she wriggled upright so she could drink her soda—"I was doing the house dishes and I could hear Charley reading Katie a book in the living room. Charley's new friend, Jack, came in and started drying for me. He had that surfer blond hair and a strong clean-shaven jaw.

"He started quizzing me about how long I planned to live with Charley, who my friends were besides Charley's, what I wanted to do for work besides be at Charley's agency. And I was thinking, who the fuck are you, but luckily before I got nasty, Charley came in with Katie who needed to be changed. Uncle Charley didn't do shitty diapers.

"So, it turned out that Charley was thoroughly in love with creepy Jack, and over the next few weeks he kept asking me, 'What do you think? Don't you just love him? Isn't he great?' Blah blah blah.

"So, finally Charley and I talked and he said yes, it was time for me and Katie to go. I mean it was a long, drawn-out conversation over days and days. He cried and I cried, but clearly he wanted his life alone with creepy Jack. So." Vivian shrugged and gave them a sad grin. "Now it's just me and Katie against the world. And that's fine with me."

"But what about Jerry?" Emily asked. "Where was Jerry in all of this?"

"I don't know. I kind of lost track of him."

Gemma stared. "You lost track of the father of your baby?"

Emily sighed. "I can't believe Jerry turned out to be a schmuck and just disappeared on you like that. He sounded like such a great guy."

"He was a great guy." Vivian played with her necklace. "I refused to see him again after I got pregnant. He doesn't know he has a daughter."

There was a moment of stunned silence, and then Gemma asked, "But why?"

"Fathers and husbands tend to leave, and I didn't want Katie to go through that heartbreak."

"That's—"

Vivian cut Gemma off. "I'm going to check on Katie again."

The hospital lights were low; it was past two a.m. Only one nurse sat at the nurse's station, doing paperwork, and Vivian hurried past, not wanting to draw attention and get thrown out.

In Katie's room, two nurses hovered over her crib, and she could hear Katie whimpering.

"What's happening?"

The nurses turned. One was the nurse from earlier; she didn't recognize the other one.

"What are you doing here?" the unfamiliar nurse asked.

"It's all right. She has special permission," the other nurse said. "Katie's IV infiltrated," she told Vivian. "We need to start another."

It was hard for Vivian to see, since the nurses were on either side of the crib. "What does that mean?"

The first nurse stepped aside so Vivian could get close. "It's good that you're here. You can comfort her while we try to find another vein." Katie's arm where the old IV had been was twice the normal size.

"It's fluid," the nurse explained. "It happens with kids. Their veins are delicate so they break and the fluid goes into the tissue instead."

Katie was barely awake, mewling.

"It's okay, baby. Mommy's here." Vivian stroked her head and murmured while the nurses got the IV started in the other arm.

"How's she doing?" Vivian asked the nice nurse.

"We just have to wait and see."

Vivian stroked her hair. *Please let her be okay and I'll never get impatient again. I'll give to charity. I'll stop swearing. Please let her be okay.*

The light outside was melting from black to gray when Vivian finally returned to the waiting room. Hospital sounds were increasing. She found the other women curled in their various places sleeping.

They woke up, stretching and groaning, stiff from bad sleeping positions.

"Mrs. Jenkins?" Vivian stood as a gray-haired man in a white coat walked in. "I'm Dr. Lang." He held out his hand. "The nurse said you wanted to see me?"

"Yes." Vivian shook his hand. "Thank you. I have some questions."

The doctor looked around the room. "Where is your husband?"

"He's not here."

"Maybe we should wait then, so we don't have to go over this twice. I'll be on the unit doing rounds. The nurse can find me."

"I'm not married." She mumbled the words, feeling herself shrink. Her gaze fixed on his expensive black shoes, and then she made herself straighten and look him in the eye.

"Let's step into the hall, shall we?" He gave the women a questioning glance. "For privacy."

Gemma immediately followed and Vivian nodded, feeling grateful. All she could do was watch his lips move as he told her what she already knew: that Katie was quite ill and they would know more in a few hours.

Vivian walked back into the room rubbing the back of her neck. "You know, maybe it was just selfish of me—" She stopped, distracted by the squeaks of nurses' shoes on the linoleum. "Selfish to believe I could take care of—" The tears were coming. She tried to smile and ended up choking on a sob.

"Stop," Gemma said. "Kids get sick. That's all." She looked at her watch and then sat next to Vivian. She put her hand on her shoulder. "Alix and Emily have to go, but I'm staying."

"Really, I don't need you to—"

"Of course you do," Alix said. "We'll be back later."

§　§　§

Alix arrived at noon bearing clean clothes and the new *People* magazine. She sent Gemma off to school, arranged with the nurses for a place for Vivian to take a nap, and promised to check on Katie every fifteen minutes.

During most of that day Katie was listless and slept nearly all of the time. When Alix left, Vivian met other parents up and down the hall. It was terrifying. She never knew so much could go wrong with these little bodies. Everyone told their stories. Harrowing emergency trips by airplane; mystery illnesses that turned out to be cancer; kids with pneumonia under special breathing tents. She learned this was a parallel universe where children suddenly stopped eating, or developed high fevers, or got smashed by unseen cars. And things didn't often turn out well in this universe. Children couldn't be fixed and children died, while parents sat in the waiting room with stunned, this-can't-be-happening looks on their faces.

Alix, Emily, and Gemma arrived back at seven p.m. with snacks, again ready to spend the night. Vivian didn't bother to argue. She did not want to be alone during the hissing, dark hospital night.

Over the next few days the three women took turns visiting, bringing her food and clean clothes. Vivian refused to leave the hospital. She knew that just her presence in the building was keeping Katie alive.

During Katie's naps, she let herself go to the waiting room and hang out with the other greasy-haired, pacing relatives. She helped the nurses with Katie's bathing and feeding. She watched the IV, calling immediately if the drip rate slowed or quickened. She made them come get her no matter what the time when they had to find another vein.

Some of the parents she met went home smiling, carrying balloons and stuffed animals. Some, she hugged as they fought for control.

On the fifth morning, Katie let out a screech, startling Vivian out of her chair. Katie wailed, outraged, banging her IV boards, furious she couldn't use her arms.

"Whoa." Vivian pulled her upright and hugged her close. "Easy, girl." She pushed the call button. The nurse came in, saw Katie struggling, and smiled.

Vivian started to cry.

FIVE YEARS LATER

CHAPTER NINETEEN

November 9, 1978

"I hate women's group." Katie's face flushed as she stomped off in eight-year-old indignation, her blond ponytail bouncing with emphasis behind her.

Vivian sighed. All their kids at some point said it, objecting to this rival in their lives. Over the past five years, Emily, Alix, and Gemma had showered Katie with attention and love; and she had preened and grew in front of them, knowing, but not understanding why, that whenever these women appeared, she felt like the smartest, best, most special girl in the world.

But the words *women's group* also meant that Mommy was leaving, that Mommy's attention had turned, that Mommy was nodding and murmuring as she listened to stories, but her mind had left the room.

Vivian looked at her watch and then followed after Katie. She found her sitting on her bed, scowling and hugging the brown bear that was almost as big as she was. Vivian smothered a laugh as she sat. "The hot dogs are almost ready. And June told me she was bringing chocolate pudding mix when she comes to stay with you."

Katie's frown deepened, letting it be known she was not so easily bribed, but her eyes brightened. Chocolate pudding was the new favorite. June, their landlady, lived upstairs and had declared herself an honorary grandma years ago. Whenever she stayed with Katie they baked sugary treats that Vivian didn't usually allow and created a complete mess in the kitchen.

Vivian pulled a limp, resistant Katie and her bear onto her lap, showering them both with noisy raspberry kisses until Katie screeched and giggled.

Vivian blew one more kiss and squeezed a hug. "Go pick out one of my hair ribbons and I'll braid it into your hair."

That worked. Katie slipped from her lap and ran off, excited at having permission to touch her mother's stuff. Vivian straightened the animals on the bed, knowing she didn't have many years left in which she could so easily mollify her daughter.

She checked the time again. She still needed to get ready for the dinner celebrating Alix's promotion and she didn't want to be late. She picked up dirty socks from under the bed and tossed them in the laundry basket. Alix deserved this promotion; she'd worked her ass off. In the past few years, the women's health movement had exploded. Working at the center Alix had been in the forefront, and now she'd been invited to participate in the new edition of *Our Bodies Ourselves.*

Vivian was jealous as hell.

She kept putting her name in as jobs were posted and … nothing. But still she hoped, as foolish as it might be, that she'd get the Northeast Regional Supervisor position that posted yesterday. She sank onto the bed. She was so tired of waking at two in the morning sick with dread over money and bills. She wanted to give Katie her ballet lessons and maybe take her to a play.

Mickey was convinced she'd get the position. "Women are taking all sorts of jobs that belong to men," he'd said the night before to explain his certainty, causing a big fight. They were seeing each other on a regular basis now, however comments like that made it clear they could never be serious.

But it was an amazing time to be a woman. Doors she hadn't even known were closed were being pried open. Alix had discovered that her mother had been forced by the school district to leave teaching when she married. Were they trying to protect children from women who had sex? Well, that couldn't happen now, and Vivian thought it explained a great deal about Alix's mother.

When Gemma had informed them earlier that year that Nebraska was the first state to outlaw marital rape, Vivian had sat dumbfounded. Who'd even think that marital rape was legal?

Much had changed, but still, even though she outperformed every man in her office, even though she kept picking up more and more accounts, she couldn't make it onto the managerial track no matter how hard she worked or how many hours she put in.

Katie ran back in waving a scarlet ribbon. She kissed her and spun her around to rest between her knees while she braided the ribbon into her blond curls. Last week Gemma had handed her paperwork to file a job discrimination suit with the EOCC and said, "Let's do this."

Vivian tugged Katie's braid when she was done. "Now, sweet pea, come help me get ready."

In the bathroom, bending toward the mirror, Vivian carefully applied eyeliner with one hand and snatched the eye shadow Katie had opened with the other. "Here." She handed Katie a jar of cold cream. "You can put a little of this on."

Katie dipped her finger in the jar and smeared the lotion on her cheek. Then she stretched for another of Vivian's cosmetics. "Chelsea's daddy bought her a Barbie doll when he came to visit."

"That's nice." Vivian plucked the tube of foundation from Katie's hand before she squeezed and splattered the bathroom. Katie opened a lipstick and watched as the red column rose and fell as she twisted the canister.

"I wish my daddy could visit and bring me a Barbie doll."

Fuck. Vivian smeared the eyeliner when her hand slipped. She grabbed a tissue, hoping this was more of a Barbie-doll wish than a daddy-wish. So far, she had sidestepped the third-grade fervor for Barbie dolls, but recently the daddy questions came in cascades.

Only two years ago, when Katie asked questions about her father, Vivian had gotten away with describing different kinds of families. Some kids lived with just a mommy, some with just a daddy, some with both, or grandparents. At some point last year, she'd invented Jerry the hero and told Katie how he helped men escape to Canada so they didn't get killed in the war and how he couldn't talk, or write, or visit or he'd go to prison.

Gemma had groaned when she heard this. "Well, Carter pardoned the draft resisters. At some point you're going to have to also."

Putting on blush, Vivian looked at Katie in the mirror. "I could buy you a Barbie doll. We could go this weekend."

"Okay." Katie kept the lipstick cylinder going up and down.

"Did you want me to put a little of that lipstick on you to surprise June?"

"I told you to plead this case out. Get it settled." The district attorney handed the file back to Gemma as she stood in his overstuffed, overheated office. His shirtsleeves were rolled up, his suit jacket hung wrinkled over the back of his chair, and the pouches under his eyes told of long nights of overwork. He opened another file from the heap on his desk, dismissing her.

Gemma refused to budge. "Her boyfriend broke her arm and her jaw. I have pics and hospital records. She wants to press charges."

"It's her word against his, and there are no witnesses. Nothing places him at the scene." He lifted the phone receiver. "Get him to take a plea."

Over and over again, they had perpetrators and victims, but not enough evidence to go to trial. Domestic-disturbance calls were not treated as crime scenes and so evidence was not gathered. If the case was built around victim testimony, there was always the chance the victim would recant.

Gemma vibrated with rage. "Do you think she fucking beat herself up?"

The DA didn't look at her. "Go take a walk or something. Get yourself under control and then settle the damn case."

She charged out of the office, furious at herself for having to blink back tears, and collided with Tim, almost spilling his coffee.

"You have to understand something," Tim, an older prosecutor, said as he followed her to her office. "Everyone hates victims." He sat on the molded plastic orange chair at the side of her desk, coffee in one hand and a powdered doughnut in the other. He held out the doughnut, offering her a bite as if hoping the sugar might calm her down.

"I'm meeting friends for dinner," she said, shaking her head and sank into her chair behind her desk. Through the small window, cloudy with decades of grime, she saw the grim November afternoon spit rain. She tugged at her suit skirt and kicked off her pumps into the desk well.

Two years ago, after passing the bar, she took a job with the prosecutor's office. As the only woman there, she'd been handed all of the domestic and rape cases. She'd been incensed. These were abysmal cases. Everyone knew they were dreadful. But in addition, she'd been (and still was) outraged at how the cases simply got thrown at her to be settled with no expectations they'd go to trial.

Tim, who'd been there forever, had taught her a great deal, but right this minute, she didn't want him in that awful orange chair he was too big for, staring at her as she struggled not to cry.

"Everyone hates victims," he repeated as if it was a mantra and sipped his coffee.

"Ridiculous. How can you hate some innocent woman beaten up by her boyfriend?" She tossed the pictures of the bruised woman face up on the desk.

He bit into his doughnut. "No innocent victims." White powder drifted onto his dark suit.

"What?"

"There are no innocent victims."

"Don't give me that crap. Look at this one from yesterday." She opened another file and read the details. "This woman was raped. Twenty-eight years old. Walking home from work."

"What time?" He broke off a piece of doughnut, and more powdered sugar floated over the desk. He offered it to her.

She shook her head. "Eleven p.m. When her shift ended at Mass General Hospital. She's a nurse."

"Alone? She was walking alone?"

Gemma nodded.

"In her nurse's uniform?"

Gemma nodded.

"Walking alone, eleven p.m. in the dark, in her nurse's uniform, down a deserted street. Is she an idiot?"

"No. You are." She flipped the file closed as if the woman would be violated again if Tim saw more.

"I'm not saying the guy was right, but no jury will convict." He brushed sugar off his suit. "And they will find a way to make it her fault. The defense attorney will paint it that way of course, trot out every sexual encounter and stupid thing she's ever done, and the judge and the jury will be grateful. They'll go along willingly. And that's if she doesn't recant and refuse the stand."

He leaned back in his chair and swallowed some coffee. "Everyone hates victims, and soon you will too. You see, if she really is a victim, then these things could happen to anyone. We can't tolerate knowing that. And so." He put his coffee down on a pile of manila files on her desk, making a little brown ring, and patted his chest pocket for cigarettes. "We make it her fault. She did something wrong or was just plain stupid."

Gemma stood up. "I might not be able to bring the case to trial, I might lose if I do, but I will *never* hate her."

Gemma weaved around chairs and tables to where Vivian, Alix, and Emily sat holding menus they weren't even pretending to look at. Emily obviously had just said something funny, because Alix and Vivian cracked up. Gemma felt herself smile along with them, even though she had no idea what was said.

They looked so beautiful and vibrant in the soft candlelight. In fact, all the women in the place looked relaxed and glowing. No men were visible. This was Bread and Roses, a restaurant opened by a feminist collective in Inman Square.

"It isn't as if men aren't allowed, they just wouldn't be too comfortable," Vivian had told them when she chose the restaurant. "It's my kind of activism. Eating out."

Gemma laughed to herself. She was careful not to bump anyone with her huge shoulder bag filled with papers and books.

Emily noticed her and waved.

"Hi. I didn't think I was late." She looked at her watch, shrugged off her coat. Her shoulder bag slipped to the floor and opened. Coins, papers, makeup, cigarettes, the entire contents scattered under the table. They all bent to help her retrieve it. "Damn, I'm sorry," Gemma said as she grabbed her wallet.

Coming up from under the table with a lipstick, Vivian said, "We just got here." She looked around as if afraid of being seen and stage whispered, "I'm not sure it's cool to carry lipstick in this place."

Gemma laughed, grabbed the lipstick, and concentrated on

sitting down and not jostling the table or sending anything else flying.

Emily leaned forward, handing over Gemma's comb and brush, and also whispered. "You should see what they have hanging on these walls."

"What?" Gemma looked around.

"Shh." Alix laughed, handing her a handful of coins. "They're menstrual prints. You can see them on the wall near the bathroom."

"What? How do they ..."

"Do you remember as kids we used to dribble paint on a piece of paper and then fold it in half?" Emily asked.

"Oh, gross."

Emily giggled.

"Hey. Congratulations." Gemma toasted Alix with her water glass.

"Thank you." Alix grinned. "I'm so excited. It's like I've been asked to play with the big kids. Plus I get to develop programs and, this may be the best part, we're putting in on-site daycare so I can bring both the boys. Although when I told my mother that soon I'd be working full-time, she acted as if I was selling the kids to gypsies."

Alix's silver filigree earrings almost reached her shoulders and caught the light as she talked. Vivian's hair was twisted up on her head, and she looked elegant and sophisticated. Emily wore a scoop-neck peasant blouse with red embroidery around the neck. It was fun to see them all dressed up, thought Gemma, and out of their T-shirts.

"To Alix!" she said, waving her water glass again. "And her continued success. We really should do a real toast with real liquor." She looked around the room. "Where's our waitress?"

"Everything okay?" Alix asked, her dark eyes focused on her with concern. Alix had the most uncanny ability to read moods from a mile away.

"I'm fine." Gemma rummaged through her bag for her cigarettes.

"You look exhausted," Vivian said.

"I always wondered how one is supposed to respond to a statement like that. 'Thank you, I know I look like shit'?"

Emily laughed. "You look gorgeous. Just tired."

It's this job," Gemma said as her match flared. She really wanted a drink. She leaned back, inhaled, and blew out a long stream of smoke. "Listen, when the waitress comes, order me a gin and tonic." She stubbed out her cigarette and pushed away from the table. "Rest room?"

Emily pointed and called after her, "Check out those prints on your way."

Gemma only glanced at the walls as she walked down the corridor. She knew it was art, and she knew maybe it had a point, but it made her angry. She'd seen enough pictures of women's blood.

In the bathroom she splashed water on her face. She felt feverish and hot despite the November chill. Seeing her face in the mirror, she agreed—she did look like shit. Her skin was blotchy, her eyes dark and huge, only slightly larger than the dark circles under them. She grabbed a paper towel and blotted at her face, hoping not to smear her mascara and really complete the ghoul look.

Lately, sleep didn't come easily, food tasted like sawdust, and she fought images of slapping the DA's face when her cases were dismissed. She didn't know how to explain what was happening to her, she didn't know how to manage the frenzy that threatened to reduce her to tears.

Tim tried to help, talking to her after particular bad sessions.

"I know it's hard to see them walk when you know they're guilty," he'd said last week, balancing the coffee he'd bought her on top of her tower of files.

She hadn't bothered to lift her head from where it lay on her arms on her desk. All she could see was her client, Louise, turning to her as she walked out of the courthouse. "He's going to kill me," she had said, just stating a fact, no emotion left.

"What if he kills her?" she'd asked Tim, finally raising her head and taking the coffee.

"It's not your fault. You did everything you could." He said it kindly, but she almost threw her coffee at him.

At home last night, Willie sat up with her, cradling her head against his chest and calming her. "We are failing these women and they are dying because of that," she told him. He didn't argue with her, he didn't tell her that she worried for nothing, he just nodded and she loved him more.

"I think it's time we got married," he said later into her hair. "I picked out a name for our first son."

She was half asleep, head on his shoulder, not sure she'd heard him right. She lifted her face and kissed him.

He grinned. "Is that a yes?"

"Someday. Right now there's still racism, sexism, and classism to eradicate." She spoke lightly, but her body had gone rigid and she sat up, all sleepiness gone, worried about all she hadn't told him yet.

He guided her head back to his chest. "We can do it together. But we'll talk later, over this weekend."

Their drinks were on the table when Gemma returned and Alix was asking Emily if maybe her photos should be hanging on these walls.

"I don't really have anything. Nothing new, anyway. I haven't been out shooting for awhile." Emily grabbed a breadstick and flipped her braid back. She turned to Vivian. "So what happened to your idea of finding Jerry?"

Gemma sipped her gin and tonic. Emily hated talking about her photography now and that was a clever way to get the focus off her. Over the past few months, Vivian had been bringing more and more Katie-asking-about-her-father stories to group, upset the topic wasn't going away like it had when Katie was younger. Vivian smeared butter on her bread with care. "I've called around, but nothing so far. And there is a big part of me that wonders why I'm doing this. I mean, Katie and I are fine. Doing really well. We have something special, just the two of us, and it all could be ruined."

"Knowing who her father is won't change what you and Katie have," Alix said.

"Well—"

Gemma jumped in. "I can help. We have investigators in the DA's office. It would be nice to actually help one person, accomplish one positive thing for once. I'm so tired of being useless facing women's broken bodies."

CHAPTER TWENTY

Gemma's earliest memories were of bodies. In her house it was men. Big, hairy bodies: hairy legs, large knees, huge hands, wide mouths, and big laughs. When her four older brothers sat on the couch, they looked ridiculous. Their shoulders scrunched together, their large palms resting on their knees that, if their feet were on the floor, rose at funny angles so it looked like they might bump their chins. They sat still only for a few moments and then were moving again: bouncing, dancing, punching, a blur of limitless energy barely contained.

At her nonna's house it was a world of women. Jostling upper arms, big breasts, large hips, soft bellies, smiles and hugs that gathered her into folds of softness. In nonna's kitchen she sat and listened and watched all the flesh around the table jiggle when they laughed at Aunt Marie's off-color jokes and then go silent when an uncle walked in.

To cover their silence, the women directed all their attention at him. "Joe, what are you looking for? Can I get you anything? You want coffee or just that beer? Are you hungry? Dinner isn't for a while, but I could fix you a snack?"

When she was much older, Gemma thought it was no surprise the men in her family grew up thinking that women sat around waiting to jump up and serve them food and get them drinks. All those women sitting silently around a table until a man walked in, and then they came alive, offering food and concern.

But of course as soon as the uncle left, the women turned to one another again, cups were picked up, hands grabbed a nibble of cheese, and the story continued right where it had left off.

Her nonna on her father's side bore ten children. All boys. The first five did not survive until adulthood. The remaining five, including her father, married and had sons. She was the only granddaughter among nineteen grandchildren. Her aunts brought her dolls with dresses they had sewn by hand. Her uncle Joe built her a dollhouse with real wallpaper on the walls. It was a blessing. Finally a girl. But being female was dangerous, and she felt that too.

In late spring, when everyone opened their windows, the scent of roses mingled with the garlic, sweet sausage, and oregano, and neighbors spilled out of their tiny houses. Her neighborhood, Rosedale, in Queens, New York, was mixed, but the groups did not overlap. Gemma's street was all Italian. The teenage boys fiddled with their cars, heads underneath the hoods, or rags in their hands as they washed and waxed. The teenage girls sat on low concrete walls between driveways, swinging their pale legs, rolling up their sleeves to catch as much sun as they could while they flirted and giggled. Old Mr. Moretti, bent over near his chain-link fence, pruned and fertilized his roses while Gemma avoided playing with the other kids on the street.

Being small and skinny always made her a target in the street games. The bigger boys body slammed her and sent her sprawling to the asphalt, and she'd get up scraped and bleeding. When she was little her brothers would swagger out and have a talk with those boys and it would be okay for a while.

When she turned twelve, her brothers wanted her to fight back. If she cried, her brothers accused her of being a baby. Don't be like other girls, they pounded into her head. Don't be a sissy. She was not allowed to walk away bruised and hurting. She had to bruise and hurt back. It was a rule, but she was no good at it.

Instead, Gemma sneaked through the back door and went straight downstairs; no one knew she was home. She curled up in the faded blue chair in the corner that they couldn't get reupholstered because it cost an arm and a leg, but that her mother wouldn't throw out because it was the one thing she had left from her own mother and someday she'd get it fixed.

There, in her chair in the basement, Gemma read books about fearless girls like Pippi Longstocking and Scout from *To Kill a Mockingbird.*

Her brothers were proud, thinking she had stopped being pounded on the street because she was tough, because the bullies had learned their lessons. They thought she walked without fear. They were wrong. She was always on guard, always ready to get out of everyone's way.

Don't be like other girls, her brothers insisted.

She remembered one day, near the end of the school year, she and Theresa had taken the shortcut through the alley toward Ray's Candy Store. They were hot and sweaty and wanted a vanilla egg cream from Ray's.

That weekend they had to finish their final public speaking project on heroes and heroines. Gemma was nervous and wanted to do well, because then she would end up with straight As, and Mr. Wilson from guidance suggested she might want to take advanced classes the next year.

Theresa asked her who she'd picked, and Gemma answered, "Rosa Parks." Her teacher had talked about the Montgomery, Alabama, bus boycott. Gemma dreamed of doing something that would take courage and change the world.

"But she's colored," Theresa said.

"Negro. You're supposed to say Negro."

"So she's Negro. You're white. That's my point. You have to pick a white heroine."

"Why?"

"I just explained." Theresa looked at her as if she were retarded.

Gemma sighed. "Who's your heroine?"

"Okay, okay. Let me think. I want to be just like Audrey Hepburn."

"I didn't know you wanted to be an actress."

"I don't." Theresa kicked a stone. "Audrey Hepburn is so beautiful, so glamorous, and so elegant." Theresa twirled. "I want to be just like her."

"But how can you be like her and not be an actress, if she's an actress?" Gemma asked.

"Don't be stupid. I've seen her movies. I know what she's like."

"But she's acting in those movies. Maybe in real life she's a drunk."

"Don't say that." Theresa looked horrified.

"But how do you know?"

"I don't want to talk about this anymore. I'm thirsty."

They stopped to count their leftover lunch money.

Gemma felt a hard push on her back just before tumbling into Theresa. They both went down among the gum wrappers and cigarette butts littered along the alley. Their books thudded to the packed dirt, flopping open.

Gemma landed on her elbow, and shocks of pain shot to her shoulder. A dime wobbled and rolled to the brick wall.

"Watch where you're going." Jimmy Murphy stood over them. "You might bump into something." He laughed and poked his friend, Dan Malloy.

Dan laughed a high screechy laugh. He was younger than Jimmy and almost as skinny as Gemma.

Maybe if they just lay there like possums, Gemma thought, he'd go away. Jimmy wasn't all that big, but everyone at school was pretty sure it was Jimmy who'd pushed that fourth grade girl off the slide, breaking her arm. Jimmy bent and picked up their scattered coins. "Give me more." He held out his grubby hand near her nose. Gemma ignored him and looked at Theresa, who was swiping tears and smearing dirt over her face.

"I see underpants." Dan laughed and chanted and pointed at their tangled limbs, their bare legs showing where their skirts had ridden high. "I see China, I see France, I see Theresa's underpants. I'm telling the whole school I saw your underpants."

Theresa's eyes widened.

Gemma pushed herself to standing and pulled Theresa up.

"I'm telling the whole school I saw you punched by a girl," she yelled at Dan as she picked up their books. "Let's go," she said to Theresa.

"That's not true." Dan's face was red, and he stood so close that his spit sprayed her face. "Take it back."

"And I'm telling that you cried after a girl punched you," Gemma said, and tugged Theresa's arm.

"They took our money," Theresa said.

"Never mind. Let's go."

They started walking away. Not running, walking, so Jimmy and Dan wouldn't feel they had to chase them, but Jimmy ran in front and blocked their path and Dan came up close again.

He pointed at Theresa's blouse. "I'm telling I saw your titties." He poked Theresa's chest. "Show us your titties and we'll let you go."

Theresa didn't move.

Gemma yanked at Theresa's sleeve to keep them walking. Jimmy grabbed Gemma's arms, forcing her to drop her books, and then twisted them around her back. "Not you." He laughed. "You don't have titties. Go head Dan, lift her shirt." He laughed again, indicating Theresa while he held Gemma fast. "Lift her shirt."

Theresa froze as Dan giggled and reached for her blouse.

"Don't you dare." Gemma twisted and kicked, but she was

small and Jimmy was big and he just laughed.

"Ooh, a bra. Pull it off. Pull it off," Jimmy said as Dan grabbed at Theresa.

Gemma kicked and yelled and stomped, and he must have lost his grip for a second, because her arm got free. She tangled his feet somehow and they both went down in a heap, but she got up fast and grabbed Theresa's hand. "Run!"

They ran in the direction of Jericho Boulevard, toward Ray's Candy Store, which would be crowded with people.

Theresa stopped at the corner, heaving to catch her breath, and pointed. "Frankie."

Down the block were her brothers, Frankie and Nick.

Frankie slouched against his car, smoking a cigarette. He was eighteen and about to go into the army. Nick was smoking too, but he was only sixteen and not allowed to.

Theresa ran up to them, crying hard now, big, gulping, hard-to-breathe sobs. "Jimmy ..." Before Gemma could stop her, Theresa spilled the whole story between gushy sobs, even about Jimmy asking to see her titties.

Frankie listened closely, and then bent and kissed the top of Theresa's head. "Go home."

Gemma started to walk off with Theresa, but Frankie pulled her back. "You're coming with us."

They found Jimmy and Dan sitting on the curb in front of Ray's store, licking chocolate off their fingers. Frankie yanked Jimmy up by his shirt collar and roared in his face. "What the fuck are you?" He shook him. "You coming near my sister again?"

Nick held Dan by the elbows.

"No," Jimmy answered, his voice muffled.

"I can't hear you," Frankie bellowed.

"No," Jimmy said again.

"Or her friend?" Frankie turned to Dan, who looked crazy

eyed with fear. He shook his head violently back and forth.

"Get out of here." Frankie shoved Jimmy and turned to Dan. "You too."

Dan took off and Jimmy stumbled after him.

Gemma watched them go, standing behind Frankie. She wasn't so sure this would work. This could make it a lot worse for her and Theresa.

"Thanks," she said to Frankie's back. He did try, after all.

He turned. "We taught you to fight." He pushed at her shoulder, forcing her to step back. "Not run away like a girl." Gemma blinked fast. "Or maybe you wanted them to see your tits?" Frankie pushed her again, stepping forward as she stepped backward. They were not strong pushes, not meant to knock her down, just put her off balance. "You're not always going to have us around, you know. Girls who don't know how to stand up to bullies get in trouble. Bad trouble."

CHAPTER TWENTY-ONE

December 11, 1978
One month later

A lix lay on her back on the living room rug, reading Adrienne Rich's *Of Women Born* while two-year-old Mikey used her body for a jungle gym. He climbed on her bent knees and laughed his belly laugh when she straightened her legs and he dropped. She bent her legs again, and again he climbed to the top of knee-mountain, and again he laughed when she straightened them. Six-year-old Davey was over in the corner, concentrating on building his block tower. His tongue licked his top lip, just the same way she did when she focused. Outside, she glimpsed the first of big, fat snowflakes falling in the fading daylight.

She turned another page and switched positions, sending Mikey into giggle fits as he tumbled from her thighs. She loved her days off with the kids. She had raised her babies lying on the floor, letting them climb over her, around her, borrowing her body, knowing someday they would give it back. She loaned them her mind and energy too, believing those would also be returned when no longer needed. Of course, on occasions she yearned to reclaim herself after a day of lend-lease with the kids. Then she craved time alone, private time, no one wanting anything. Sam tried to understand, but she could see the hurt as he wondered why she could give so much to the kids and not to him.

She glanced at the clock; still another half hour to go before *Sesame Street.* She rolled onto her belly and started a new chapter of Rich's book on motherhood. Mikey began to inch toward Davey's tower, and she captured him with her legs. Time with young children was different from other time. The constant, ever-present background worry about safety and illness overlaid everything. The day moved to a rhythm of breakfast, naps, outings, play dough, with time snatched for reading; or the suspended time of walks around the block that took forever as every path was explored and every puddle jumped in—and then the day was over. Exhaustion. The measurement of work done in adult terms was nil. No papers written, no deals made, even the vacuuming didn't get done. And children days passed slowly, far removed from adult time, while the weeks and years sped along.

Mikey grabbed for her book. She distracted him with a ball and hid it underneath her, reading one more page as he poked and prodded, trying to find it. Gemma had loaned her this book that talked about the politics of motherhood, insisting she read it immediately so they could talk about it. Gemma inhaled books and was always passing them on to be stacked in wobbly piles throughout Alix's house.

Women were writing and publishing like never before in the history of the world. Book after book, writer after writer, article after article, turning long-held assumptions about women upside down and exploring beliefs that resonated in her soul. Maybe mother-love wasn't instinctual or unconditional like she'd learned in her developmental psychology courses. Maybe women could claim their sexuality and not try to have only vaginal orgasms, like Freud had argued. Maybe childbirth didn't need drugs and forceps and scalpels. Maybe this divide of mothers staying home to bond with infants while fathers left to earn the money damaged both parents. Maybe women weren't lacking in moral development or stamina or brainpower.

She and Gemma had begun sneaking off on Saturdays, leaving the boys with Sam so they could go off for an afternoon of browsing at New Words, the feminist bookstore, buying books and feminist journals and taking them to the coffee shop across the street. They read and talked over cigarettes and endless cups of coffee. This past Saturday Gemma had discovered *Witches, Midwives, and Nurses: A History of Women Healers,* by Barbara Ehrenreich and Deirdre English, and read passages aloud. "Did you know that during the witch burning in Europe, some small towns were left with no women at all? It was organized genocide against women," she said, and waved the book at her. Gemma believed that if you reimagined the past, you could reinvent the future. Occasionally, the intensity of Gemma's passion and anger troubled her. Gemma had such focus and drive, she often overlooked nuance, like in this new fixation on helping Vivian find Jerry. Alix didn't think Gemma was paying attention to how ambivalent Vivian was about actually finding him, and she worried this was not going to come to any good.

Mikey grabbed at her book again. She held it out of reach. He toddled away and knocked into Davey's tower, sending blocks everywhere.

"Mo-om!"

Reading time was over. She folded a corner of the page and closed the book. "Time for snack. And then it's *Sesame Street!*"

She let Davey help spread peanut butter on the crackers for being such a big boy and not bashing Mikey over the head when he toppled the blocks. Work, her work at the health center, honed an edge, made her razor sharp. Domesticity flattened and dulled her edges. Housework, childcare, being attuned to others' rhythms, doing repetitive tasks, smoothed her like rocks in a streambed.

This wasn't necessarily bad, she thought. It was important to understand, though, so that when she let go of domesticity, she would know what she needed to keep smooth and what she planned to sharpen to deadly points.

With the boys settled with snacks and *Sesame Street*, Alix started dinner, dumping onions, carrots, and chicken into a pot with cups of broth. She spread her papers on the kitchen table. She had fifteen minutes, or maybe a little more if she let them also watch *Mr. Rogers*.

She wrote: *playground–1:00-2:30 pm* on that day's chart.

She'd decided she needed to calculate the amount of time she spent taking care of the kids and doing housework, to understand how undone chores threatened to tumble on their heads and to convince Sam he needed to take on more household tasks, when she started full-time. She'd created a month's worth of charts to catalogue every task she did during the day. Sam had no complaints about her working, and he threw in a load of laundry or picked up groceries whenever she asked. Still, the running of the household fell under her domain and he appeared disappointed when there was no toothpaste or when finding boots in the hall closet required a major excavation

Last week she had shown the group her colored pie charts and graphs.

Vivian had examined them for a minute and then handed them back. "You need to put it more bluntly. Just tell him that washing the dishes is foreplay."

The soup bubbled and Alix got up to adjust the heat.

The phone rang. "There was another abortion clinic bombing. In Buffalo." It was her mother. "Did you hear?"

"I haven't listened to the news all day." She hooked the phone under her chin and stretched the cord so she could cook and talk at the same time. "And anyway, I don't work at an abortion clinic. It's a women's health center."

"These crazies don't know the difference. Your clinic does

abortions. You've gotten bomb threats."

"You worry too much, but I can't talk now, I'll call later. I have to get dinner ready. Emily's coming over later to help me design some brochures."

"Are you taking care of yourself? I'm not sure you can keep up your pace. Do you want me to come up and help when you start full-time?"

"I'm fine, Mom, really. I'll call you back after dinner."

In her junior year of college, Alix had taken her first women's studies class in the sociology department. That evening, as Sam cooked dinner in their one-room attic apartment, she tried to explain to him why her head, her world, had burst open.

"And then the instructor put this study on the overhead projector, and all these words that people consider bad human traits, they also just happen to be what people consider feminine traits." She took down two plates from the cupboard. "You know, words like irrational, emotional ..."

"What's wrong with emotional?" Sam asked. He opened the oven to check the chicken he was roasting.

"Nothing. But this study showed that most people think of emotional as a negative human characteristic."

"I don't." He fluffed the rice with a fork.

"Yes, you do. You always say I'm 'too emotional.'" She set out forks and knives.

"No, I don't. I say you're too sensitive."

"Okay, that's another one." She pointed with a fork as if the list were in the air in front of them. "'Sensitive' is another negative word that's associated with female."

"But you are too sensitive." He put the pan of steamed carrots on the table. "Do you want butter?"

"That's not the point." Alix tried to keep her hurt feelings (too sensitive) tamped down. "The point is that there are all these negative characteristics and they're all associated with being female."

"Who says?" He cut up the chicken, all crispy and golden, and put a thigh on her plate. Her favorite part.

"Peggy had a study that—"

"What kind of study?"

"I don't know. Some research study."

"People can make research studies say anything they want about anything they want." He dished her out some rice. "You have to be careful about believing something just because it's a research study."

"But it feels so right, so true to me."

"Doesn't feel right or true to me."

Arguing with Sam made her head cloudy. It was the strangest feeling. How could he be arguing about this? It seemed so obvious to her. It was like looking at those optical illusions, seeing a vase and then suddenly it's a face. She wanted him to see the face.

"Women weren't even considered human," she said. "The council of cardinals voted women were human by one vote!"

"That was in the fucking Middle Ages. Are you crazy?"

Sam arrived home just as she tasted the stew.

"It's snowing." He kicked off his wet shoes and shook out his jacket. "You left the bikes out front."

"Oh, damn, I forgot about them." Alix stirred and added salt to the stew. "Did you bring them in?"

"Yes." He sighed. "But we need to be careful. They could get stolen."

"How was your day, honey?" Alix asked herself out loud as she added pepper. "Fine, Sam. We went exploring, a little walking, a little biking—and then Mikey needed to go to the bathroom. So I hurried inside with two little boys and got the boots off and the coats off, and the pants down before there was a catastrophe. And then it was time for lunch. And then nap time for Mike and now you're home and somehow the bikes got left out."

Sam smiled his apology and bent to kiss her. His hair curled just above his shirt collar. He'd cut off his ponytail last year when he became assistant director of the affordable housing unit. She still wasn't used to it. She thought he would look better if he shaved his beard also, but that hadn't happened yet. He emptied his pockets into the basket on the counter and then poked his head into the living room, but didn't call out to the boys.

"They are totally mesmerized," he said. "Do you think they should watch so much TV?"

"They don't watch so much TV. It's *Sesame Street* and *Mr. Rogers*." She dumped egg noodles into the boiling water.

"Maybe we should throw out the TV?" He opened the bag of potato chips he'd brought home and offered some to her. "What do you think?"

She shook her head. "Do you want me to heat some rolls, or are you okay with just the egg noodles?" She opened the refrigerator and took out butter.

"I don't think we're supposed to eat so much butter." He munched on a chip.

She put the butter back into the refrigerator and stirred the noodles.

"I've been thinking," he said. "I don't think you working full-time is such a good idea." He perched on the stool with his chips. "It's not like you'll earn that much money and already it's hard for you to keep up with everything around here."

"You'll just have to help more."

Mikey came into the kitchen and grabbed her leg, just as she started draining the noodles.

Sam swooped up Mikey, who giggled, delighted. "Hey, where's my hug?" He turned back to Alix. "My job is very demanding; it's not like I can just call in when one of the kids gets sick."

"I'm taking the new position." Alix plopped the bowl full of noodles on the table. "And this is not the time to talk about it."

After they finished eating, Alix looked at the leftovers to be put away, the dishes to be washed, the toys scattered everywhere. And the kids needed their pajamas and stories.

"Sam, would you start getting Mikey ready for bed while I clean up?"

"Sure. Can he wait a few minutes?" He looked at the clock. "I just want to catch that special on the Jim Jones suicide pact in Guyana." And he walked out of the kitchen.

Alix picked up a dirty plate. She knew she could fight about it and lose some love for him, or not fight about it and lose some love for him.

Did he realize how damaging these little lapses of consciousness were?

CHAPTER TWENTY-TWO

December 19, 1978
One week later

E mily was washing the glass on the display cases as Bernie came in. Already she was exhausted. She'd been up since six that morning, averting Matt's homework crisis (his fifth grade teacher had no tolerance for lost reports), discovering a stray mitten under the couch, making lunches, and getting the house picked up a little. And then Jessica, the only first grader who rode the bus, threw a fit, so she had to drive them to school, with Matt complaining the whole way that he wanted to take the bus.

"Why aren't you taking pictures?" Bernie always started right in with whatever he'd been thinking on his walk over. He declared he didn't have time to waste on hellos and nice days. He was getting too old for all that.

"Good morning," she said. "You're in early."

He removed his coat and carefully put it on a hanger in the office closet. He lifted her jacket that she'd thrown on the back of the chair, shook it out, and hung it up also.

"You haven't been shooting any film." He patted himself down, looking for which pocket his glasses were in. "Why not?"

He opened his ledger tally of the previous day's receipts and looked at her over the top of his glasses. "Well?"

"I'm a working mother with two kids." She started unpacking boxes of film and putting them on the shelf. "Was it busy yesterday?"

"Don't change the subject."

"I think they forgot to include lenses in this order," she said, reading the packing slip.

"Check that box." He pointed to the corner. "Take pictures of the kids then, if you're so busy being a mother."

"Who wants pictures of more children?"

"You will, for one." He sharpened his pencil on the pencil sharpener attached to the wall. "And you know, you shoot a hundred pictures, maybe you'll get one that's good." He checked the point and sharpened it some more. "You take no pictures and none are any good."

"Where do you want me to put these?" She held out the new photo albums.

"Out front in the display case, where people will see them when they pick up their photos." He erased something and blew on the paper. "Don't waste your talent."

"Who's wasting anything?" Emily snorted. "I'm just really busy."

"You're sulking, throwing a temper tantrum because *Rolling Stone* didn't want your photos. So you'll show them. You'll stop taking pictures."

"What do you know of taking care of kids?" Emily flattened the box she'd unpacked. "You had a wife."

"I didn't have the gift. But I was given talent to recognize the gift when I saw it."

"I'm going to dust the inside of the cases." She walked out to the front room.

"You know if you don't keep shooting," he shouted after her, "if you don't keep using the gift, it will dry up like an old woman."

"Do you work at being a sexist pig," she called, "or is it natural because you're a dirty old man?"

He pointed when the bell over the door rang and a customer entered. "Do your job."

The next evening, Emily heard the women clumping up the stairs to her apartment. She kissed Jess on the top of her head. "You can say hi, but then it's really, really, really bedtime."

"I'm really, really, really thirsty." At six, Jess had mastered all the delaying tactics.

Her hair flopped over her large eyes. Emily smoothed it back and pointed to the glass of water on the night table.

"Can I have orange juice? Please?"

Emily knew she was being had. She scrunched her face into an exaggerated frown so Jess would know that she knew she was pushing it, but that she wasn't super mad. "Okay, go get some juice."

Jess slid off the bed, bounding out her bedroom door. "But then you have to brush your teeth again," she called after her, and hurried down the hall to open the door.

Vivian came in breathing hard. "You had to move to the effing third floor?" Vivian had resolved not to swear after Katie got sent to the principal's office last month for saying *shit.*

Emily peered over the banister. "I told you to quit smoking. Where's Alix and Gemma?"

"We're coming." Alix's voice echoed in the stairwell.

Vivian unwrapped her scarf. "I'll get this stuff on plates." She headed to the kitchen with her bag of goodies. "Hey, Jess," Emily heard her say. "Help me find the glasses."

She and Rick had recently moved into this railroad flat, which meant all the rooms were off one narrow hallway that ran from front to back. Supposedly it gave them extra space, so Rick could have a home office, not that he used it. Emily hated it. It was gloomy and claustrophobic. When she and the kids ate dinner, they could watch the older couple next door eating sausage and potatoes. But it was cheap for the space.

Earlier, Emily had walked into the kitchen and seen her neighbor with three other women pointing at the poster Gemma had given her. It was a great poster of an angelic woman in a lacy medieval gown, with long, flowing curls that cascaded to the floor, holding a broom she'd just broken. The words Fuck Housework were across the bottom. Emily had smiled and waved, but the neighbor shook her head in disgust and pulled the shade.

She wanted to run over and explain that she wasn't dirty. She wanted to explain how it wasn't a statement about them, but a statement about how a woman's worth shouldn't be judged by how clean her stove was.

"I wanted to invite them in," Emily explained when the group was all settled in the living room, "and show them my housework photos and let them know I wasn't putting them down, that I understand how hard they've worked. I don't want their feelings to be hurt." She pulled her braid forward. "I want to show the value of women who have been doing this domestic work forever."

"That's why your pictures are so great," Gemma said.

"Yeah." Emily nibbled on her hair. "Then why doesn't anyone want to buy them?"

"You're just ahead of your time." Alix leaned back against the pillows. "Maybe I should hang one of your old housework photos in our bedroom. Now that I'm working full-time at the center, I can't keep up with laundry and there are dust balls big enough to hide shoes. I can't figure out how to do it."

Gemma frowned. "We need to read about great women who combine worldly success with domestic bliss and do it with balance and satisfaction. Or else write those books."

Vivian started humming a song Emily recognized from some commercial, but couldn't place. Vivian stood. "'I can bring home the bacon.'" She sang the lyrics to the Enjoli perfume commercial, thrusting her hips forward and twirling an imaginary belt tassel.

Emily shook her hair loose from its braid and joined her. "'Fry it up in a pan, and never let you forget you're a man. 'Cause I'm a woman ...'" Their voices soared over the last notes, and they collapsed giggling against each other, with Alix and Gemma laughing along.

"That commercial should be banned from the airways," Alix said when they'd all settled again. "It's worse than pornography."

Vivian and Alix sprawled on the daybed covered with a bright red blanket that served as the couch and Gemma sat cross-legged on the floor. Emily put Roberta Flack on the record player.

Vivian leaned forward to take a slice of cheese and a cracker. "So, you know, Mickey insists I'm finally going to get that promotion. Of course, I won't believe it until it happens. But it would be great." She grinned. "And he also set me up for a date with that new guy, Neil. By the way," she interrupted herself, "do you know that Mickey thinks that in another ten years, people will have computers in their homes?"

"Viv, stick to the interesting parts," Emily said.

"Neil has these deep dark eyes ... and such shoulders? I'm a sucker for shoulders." She paused. "Well, really, you guys can't blame me. It's been a while, since, well ..."

"Is this the one," Gemma interrupted, "that Mickey warned you is juggling two women who don't know about each other? And might be married?"

Vivian frowned.

"What about Mickey?" Emily asked. "You aren't seeing him anymore?"

"We're better as friends and anyway Mickey has gone back to Liz." Vivian sighed. "Neil has this curly hair that is almost impossible for me not to run my hands through. So what do you guys think? Am I being stupid?"

Gemma asked, "Do you want to really know what we think or just have us support you no matter what?"

Alix kicked her.

"Of course," Gemma went on, "we support you no matter what." She paused. "I just don't think he should be sleeping around and cheating on his other two women."

"Yeah, but he is, so why not with me?"

"It won't be possible to have a society in which woman are valued, aren't diminished, if you don't value yourself."

Vivian sat up. "Since you've been working in the DA's office, you've been coming to group even more outraged."

Gemma ran her hand through her hair. "It's important to be passionate about change. Don't you want that for Katie?"

"Hey." Vivian held up her hands. "Don't lecture me on this feminist shit. I stopped shaving my legs and I read *Ms.* cover to cover every month."

Emily grinned, loving these women. Gemma could slice and dice and skewer with her words, Vivian swore every other sentence, Alix could peer into your soul's innards, and Emily knew she was often impatient, but they flourished together as if placed under a benign grow light. They stopped trying to hide or change and became more of who they were.

She passed around the cheese plate. "Bernie gave me such a hard time yesterday about not shooting more film. I don't know why I stay in that dusty old shop."

"Because he pays you more than minimum wage?" Vivian asked.

"Because he believes you're one of the most talented photographers he's seen in a while?" Alix asked.

"Because you can create your own hours around childcare issues?" Gemma asked.

"Because he gives you free use of the darkroom whenever

you want?" Vivian asked.

"Because he displays your photos on the wall of the shop?" Alix asked.

"He's so fucking annoying sometimes." Emily drank her wine. "He has no idea what raising kids is like. He's never even changed a diaper."

"Well, why aren't you taking pictures?" Gemma asked.

She shrugged. "How do I justify to Rick spending money on sitters when I can't sell a thing and all it has become is just an expensive hobby?"

CHAPTER TWENTY-THREE

January 9, 1979
Three weeks later

"**B**ut why not get married?" Willie ladled tomato sauce and meatballs on top of steaming plates of spaghetti and carried the plates to the table.

"I don't believe in it." Gemma took a bite of a meatball. It was good. Very good. "How did a black guy from out west learn to cook sauce like my nonna from Sicily?"

"Cleveland is not the west. Someday I'm going to have to take you west of New York City." He served them each a plate of salad with his homemade Italian vinaigrette. "And don't think for a minute that I'm such a fool you can distract me with blatant flattery."

Often, Gemma thought, distracting him with blatant flattery worked brilliantly. She ate a forkful of spaghetti, made a big show of closing her eyes and murmuring with pleasure and appreciation.

"So?" He snapped a cloth napkin open onto his lap.

"I told you when we met, I wasn't a marrying woman." She grinned. "And, come to think of it, that's probably why you stuck around. I was safe."

Willie frowned but didn't say anything. He just dug into his food. He was definitely stuck on this whole marriage thing. Gemma ate another forkful. She was hungry.

Willie's chair scraped the worn linoleum as he pushed back from the table. "Can I get you anything, babe? Another meatball?"

She held out her plate. "Thanks." Soft light suffused the kitchen, in contrast to the dark of the windows. They hadn't pulled the shades yet, and there were no curtains. The cabinets were old white metal with doors that no longer quite closed. The table was chipped Formica. Willie had lit the candle they'd stuck in a fat wine bottle, with red and yellow wax carefully dripped down its sides.

He kissed the top of her head when he put her plate down. "For the record, I did not stick around because you weren't the marrying kind."

"Something happens when people get married." She looked down at her plate and mixed the spaghetti around in the sauce. "I don't know how it happens, but no matter how innovative or groundbreaking you want to be, the ancient codes of what is expected from a wife and what is expected from a husband emerge. I've seen it ruin great relationships." She raised her head. "Look. We've been living together for more than five years and it's wonderful."

"So that's a perfect reason to get married. Make it official."

"Does this have anything to do with visiting your mother over the holidays?" That wasn't really fair since one version or another of this conversation had been happening a lot recently.

"It's because I love you and we're great together. Name one other couple that is better than us."

"Your sister said I'm just some white bitch who trapped you."

Willie gave a dramatic sigh. "That was years and years ago. Time to give it a rest. Now they think I should make an honest woman of you."

"I don't want to be anyone's property. You should understand that."

Willie's eyes widened. She could see his jaw muscle tighten in his effort not to roar. But she'd grown up with four brothers and a father and many uncles; she was not intimidated by the male roar.

"Are you equating marriage with slavery?" he finally asked in a soft, tense voice.

This conversation was not going well. She put her fork down on her plate and her hands in her lap. "Throughout recorded history, women have been either the property of their fathers, brothers, or husbands."

"You do remember we are in the twentieth century?" She could tell he was working at keeping his voice even. He spun spaghetti onto his fork but did not lift it. "You're afraid I'll start making you darn my socks?" He slid into sarcastic. "Refuse to let you go out alone?"

"It's bigger than us. The roles. The pressure to conform." She thought of Alix's struggles. Sam was such a progressive guy, and yet last week Alix told them that when six-year-old Davey was crying and Sam told him that big boys don't cry, Davey told his father: It's okay to cry. They had been listening to the record *Free to Be You and Me*. Sam said that was not the way the world was. That it was just the way Mommy thought the world should be. There was a big difference. Alix told this as a cute story. Gemma was horrified that Sam could put her down like that in front of their son.

And then there was Emily fading away like overexposed film as Rick took on more and more responsibilities in his department. The only one who seemed free of all this was Vivian, but then she had other issues.

"I don't want to fight about this," she said. "I just don't want to get married." That was true, but it wasn't the whole truth. That, she couldn't tell Willie.

"Why do you get to set the rules?"

She twirled her fork in the spaghetti. "Why is this so important to you now?"

He smiled an exaggerated, suggestive smile, and a sexy glint shone in his eyes. He lowered his voice into an overstated huskiness. "I think it's time to make some babies."

She laughed in spite of herself. He could always do that to her. "Babies? As in plural?"

"Okay, I'll let you grow them one at a time, if that's truly your preference."

She really loved this man; more than she'd thought possible. And she knew she was going to break his heart. And then he would shatter hers.

"I need to tell you something ..." She paused, having no idea how to begin what she had to say. Instead, she reached across the table to squeeze Willie's hand.

"It's yes?" he asked, mistaking her gesture for assent and folding her hand between two of his. He rushed on, not giving her a chance to respond. "I promise nothing will change. We can even write a special contract about how we think marriage should be, a partnership between two equals, how to stay friends and lovers. We'll make it impervious to ancient institutional codes, whatever that means, and I'll even teach you how to make my sauce."

He picked up her hand and kissed her fingertips one by one and then held it again. She knew, when he left her, she'd never love anyone this way again.

"People can try to make babies," she said in a whispery voice, batting her eyes, hoping to tease him off this topic, "and still not be married."

He jerked his hand away and sat back. "Oh, so it wasn't a yes."

She could see he felt rejected, his vulnerability exposed, as if she had played him for a fool. She wanted to cradle his head and tell him all would be okay and beg forgiveness.

He turned back to his food. "When we have babies, we need to be married. I'm not perpetuating the stereotype of fatherless black kids." He spun more spaghetti onto his fork. "You do remember any baby we have would be black? And you know nothing about being black." He waved his fork, and sauce sprinkled the table and floor.

"It would be half white. I know a lot about that." And she also knew she should not be letting the conversation veer in this direction.

"Would be a black baby. Black. Black. Black." Sauce was everywhere. "Shit." He dropped his fork and went to get the sponge.

He came back to the table and stood over her chair, forcing her to look up to see his face. "You're willing to consider having a black baby but not a black husband. That's where you draw the line?"

Gemma sat behind her office desk and moved piles of folders from one side of it to the other. Over the past few days she and Willie had been painfully polite to each other, but she knew she had dealt him a brutal wound and wasn't certain how to make it better. She opened a file and then closed it again.

She hadn't made much sense during that entire conversation. When trying to hide something by telling half-truths, people created gaps in their stories. In her work, she could spot it a mile away and obviously Willie had sensed that and filled in the gap of what she was trying to hide. Only he filled it in so wrong, believing it was race.

She opened her drawer and took out a pen. So this was how love ended. If she told the whole truth it would be over, and if she didn't, it would be over.

She opened the file again and quickly closed it. She couldn't deal with this now. She had to get out of the office for a while.

Driving to one of her favorite spots, she angled the car across the empty parking lot so she could see the rise of land and the edge of trees against the sky, and not see the radio towers and tall office buildings off to the right.

It was called a park, but in truth it was a paved road with parking spaces that wound into undeveloped land. On sunny weekend days, she supposed there would be kite flyers and joggers, dog walkers and gardeners. But during the week it was usually empty, especially on a day like today, rainy and cold, her windshield blurry from the water.

A car door slammed, making her jump. She watched a panel truck pull away. Lunchtime was when she saw other people in cars, mostly reading newspapers as they munched on a sandwich. Car people. Cops. Delivery vehicles. Plumbers. Everyone ignoring one another.

She opened her book. It was a new mystery by Sara Paretsky. V.I., the female protagonist, fought bad guys too. Lately Gemma spent more and more time reading in her car. She had a thermos, her coffee cup, her snacks, and her bag with books. She was prepared to travel to remote areas of the city and sit protected and warm, away from humans and their noise and needs. She often felt she could handle anything life threw at her as long as she could read. Maybe even losing Willie.

"Hey Viv," Mickey called from across the office. "Come have dinner with me."

"Don't you ever work?" She knew it was only four o'clock, because she'd planned to leave early and meet Gemma. She put her worksheets from the morning on Deb's desk and grabbed her bag from the back of her chair.

"A man's got to eat. And anyway, I have some news."

"If it's not about that asshole friend of yours getting his legs broken, I'm not interested." She took her coat down from the hook on the wall. The date with Neil had not gone well.

Mickey sighed. "I'll treat."

"Great, but not tonight. I'm meeting Gemma for coffee before group."

Winding his way around desks, Mickey caught up with her, took her elbow, and steered her into the empty conference room. He pulled out a chair, indicating she should sit.

She leaned her thighs against the table instead. "I'm late."

He dropped the blinds on the glass wall and turned to face her.

"So, what's with the cloak and dagger routine?" she asked.

He just looked at her.

"Out with it."

"I got it," he said.

Fuck that.

She pushed away from the table and hooked her bag over her shoulder. She didn't even need to ask. He got the position of assistant regional director—all of New England and most of New York—that she'd been counting on.

"Great. Congratulations," she said, and looked at her watch. "Shit, I'm late."

"I wanted to tell you myself. I knew you'd be upset."

"I'm not upset, just late. Really, it's great, you deserve it." She left him staring at her, but instead of turning toward the elevators, she went right to Harvey's office.

"Hey, knock first, why don't you?" He swung his legs off his desk and straightened in his chair as she strode in.

"You said that promotion was mine. You said it was in the bag."

He shrugged. "Really, I tried. Really. But the higher-ups don't think a broad can be a manager. Too much trouble with the other regional supervisors who might feel their dicks shrinking because a woman has the same level position as they have."

§   §   §

"He actually said that?" Gemma put down her coffee mug without sipping. "He used those exact words?"

Vivian nodded.

"Well, you definitely have a sex-discrimination suit now. Did you file those papers I gave you?"

She shook her head and laughed. "Might be a whole lot faster if I just went ahead and finally fucked him."

Gemma didn't laugh. "Goddamn it, Viv. If we don't take action, men like that just keep control and companies keep doing this crap. A big sex-discrimination suit was just won this year against the feds. And more are being filed against major companies every day. There might even be one against IBM that you could join."

"Not happening. I'm a single mom, remember? I'm *it.* I can't afford to rock this boat." She waved for a refill, praying Gemma would let it go.

"But …"

"Drop it." She watched as Gemma fought with her urge to persist. "Although this all makes it difficult to be a financially independent single mom."

Gemma picked up her coffee mug and, her voice low, said, "If you found Jerry, he'd be required to help with child support, you know."

"Wouldn't that be sweet?" Vivian stirred cream into her coffee. "I can picture that call now. 'Hi, Jerry. Remember me? By the way you have an eight-year-old daughter. Oh, and just so you know, you owe a hell of a lot of child support.'

"Jesus, what kind of role model would that be for Katie? I want to show her how it's possible to be a woman of distinction and means, powerful, independent, sexual, financially secure. A full life, with friends and lovers and all possibilities. I don't want Katie for a second to think she needs a man to be complete." Vivian pointed her spoon at Gemma. "You of all people should get that."

"Yeah, I get it, but if you find him, you don't have to ask for money. I spoke to the investigator at the office and he said he could look for Jerry for you." She pulled out a notepad and pen from her bag. "I just need his last known address, or where he worked or went to school and his telephone number if you remember it."

"As I've said already, I'm not so sure I want to find Jerry."

"Why not?"

"Probably for similar reasons you don't want to marry Willie. Who needs another boss?" She threw some bills on the table. "Let's get to group."

CHAPTER TWENTY-FOUR

Emily sat at the worktable in the back of the camera shop sorting developed pictures into envelopes for customers to pick up. Pictures of babies with dirty faces, couples on beach vacations, blurry group photos of posed families, nothing unique but fun all the same to see what people wanted to memorialize.

At the tinkle of the bell over the front door, she looked up and saw Bernie out front arranging a new display of cameras. No need for her to wait on the customer.

She went back to work. The man had a British accent and she listened with pleasure as he chatted about cameras and asked questions about the shop, while Bernie gave his usual brusque responses.

"You have intriguing pictures displayed. Are they for sale?"

"Some."

Emily sighed. Sometimes she wondered how Bernie remained in business all these years with his horrible customer manners.

"That one is rather remarkable."

Curious, she stood and tried to see where the customer was pointing without being spotted.

"Boys on the verge of manhood, that sort of thing. Captures it brilliantly, I'd say."

Bernie grunted.

Emily positioned herself so she could hear better. That was her photograph he was talking about.

Bernie saw her, but the man couldn't. Bernie winked at her. "Would you like to meet the photographer?"

She jumped back and waved no. No.

"Em," he called. "Someone wants to meet you."

Damn. Filthy and sweaty from moving inventory, she brushed at her jeans.

"Em," Bernie called again.

"Yes?" She walked to the front room as if she had no idea what Bernie wanted and hoped her face wasn't smeared with grime.

"This is ... I'm sorry, I didn't catch your name."

"Evan. Evan Marsh." He held out his hand. His eyes widened, probably with disgust at how grubby she was. "Pleased to meet you."

"Emily Baxter," she said, and shook his hand.

"I've been admiring your photograph and was inquiring if it was for sale."

She nodded yes. "Thank you. I'm glad you like it."

"Grand." His sandy-colored hair barely brushed the collar of his corduroy jacket and his smile revealed slightly crossed front teeth. "May I ask the price?"

Emily wondered what number to give. "Fort—"

Bernie swayed as if having a sudden attack of vertigo, stepped on her toes, and said, "Four hundred."

"Ah." He stared at the photograph. "That's a bit dear." He turned back to her. "I'll have to think about it. But it was a pleasure to meet you."

She turned on Bernie as soon as the door closed. "Four hundred dollars!"

"Don't sell yourself cheap."

"Four hundred?"

"Value yourself and value your work."

"I do. I do," she said. "But there are other ways of valuing myself besides charging too much for a photograph. Like making a sale for one."

"There's a reason my mother told my sisters, why buy the cow when you can get the milk for free."

"How does that fit here?" She stomped into the back room, too angry to find out what the hell he meant.

Jess got sick and Emily didn't go into the shop for a week. Bernie called and told her Mr. Marsh had returned and purchased the photo. She couldn't believe it.

"Rick," she yelled and ran into his study. "I sold one." She swiveled his chair so he faced her and kissed him hard.

"Great." He smiled and then spun back to his desk. "I have a ton of work. Can we celebrate later?"

When she finally returned to work, Bernie told her that Evan had been into the shop again twice, staring at one of her other photographs and asking about her.

"I told him you were out shooting film. I thought that sounded better than being at home cleaning up vomit."

"Probably." Emily laughed and went out back to finish the inventory.

A little later, Bernie called to her. "Here he comes. Right on time. Quick come to the front, so I don't get that crestfallen look when he sees me and not you. It hurts my feelings. It's not good for my self-esteem."

After almost daily visits from Evan, Bernie asked, "Are you going to put this poor man out of his misery and ask him to go have coffee with you at least? I mean, I don't mind that he comes in and buys stuff just to be near you, but even I have some scruples."

During coffee and then lunch at Grendel's Den, Emily learned Evan was a visiting painter and art history professor from Cornwall and lonely this far from home. "I grew up in Padstow, a small fishing village on the coast. Families have lived there for generations and everyone knows everything about you. I miss that"-- he paused, staring into the distance--"those connections." He shrugged and smiled, ducking his head a bit as if to cover shyness or vulnerability. "Must sound odd to you. There don't seem to be communities like that in the States."

"In Vermont, where I grew up," Emily said as she buttered a roll, "women would come to my mother's kitchen, roll up a pant leg and ask if a cut was infected, or pull off their kid's shirt so my mother could look at a rash. She'd been a nurse before she married," Emily explained. "She'd pour them coffee and they'd sit at the table, and my mother would tell them she didn't think there was anything to worry about, but they could always have Dr. Peterson take a look. And if they weren't going to Dr. Peterson's, they would sit and talk and talk and talk.

" Long after I left home, long after those afternoons at the kitchen table with my mother, seeing the same faces over and over, I realized that in small towns you might not get to meet many different people, but the people you knew—you knew. You knew whose grandmother had run off with whose uncle and had settled over on Cobbs Hill and was raising sheep and doing quite well, and it turns out that the grandmother had never even really married the grandfather and all those years everyone had thought different. Imagine."

Evan laughed and nodded.

"In my mother's kitchen, the stories of love and disaster and betrayal and the constant keeping track of lineage flowed around and over my head. This was the stuff I grew up on. No one was shocked. Not like my city friends are shocked when people don't behave the way they expect they should. Up where I come from, everyone assumed anyone could do anything. People just made the best of it and reported it along the kitchens so everyone could keep straight what was happening."

"Exactly." He smiled. His crossed front teeth an endearing imperfection. "Maybe that's why I'm so drawn to…" He halted, as if steering clear of too much exposure. "Drawn to your work," he continued. "We have similar sensibilities."

"How did you"—Emily forced her thoughts away from the way his hair curled, brushing his jacket collar and how his hands, boney and calloused, might feel on her skin—"end up an artist?"

"The Cornwall coast is rugged, the sea crashes on rocks and the area is filled with caves that go far inland, underneath fields covered in bluebells and grazing sheep. Long ago pirates stashed their bounty and as boys we explored and imagined." He laughed and did that shy head duck again. "All bloody romantic. When I started to draw I wanted to capture the mystery." He gave a diffident shrug.

When their meal arrived, Evan went on to describe the London art world, how he couldn't resist his chance as a visiting professor at Harvard and best of all how good he thought her photographs were. It was intoxicating.

Over the next two weeks, when Evan dropped by the shop, they went out for coffee or took walks along the Charles during her lunch break. She took him to the Harvard Fogg museum and he invited her for a concert at the Isabella Stewart Gardner Museum. They compared favorite artists, and he gave mini-lectures on their lives and the era in which they painted.

"I'm finally getting the education I missed," Emily told Bernie when she got back one afternoon after a snowy walk with

Evan. "I've never known anyone who could talk about art like that, who knows so much. And he values my opinions, my thoughts on it all, as amateurish as they may be."

She stamped her feet to get some feeling back in her frozen toes. "I haven't had such fun in ages. Of course it helps that he thinks my pictures are fabulous and wants to see my full portfolio."

Bernie didn't look up from his ledger. "Probably not all that he wants to see."

Emily laughed. "He knows I'm married with two kids."

"Since when has that prevented anything?"

Evan kissed her as they pored over art books in the back of the Harvard Book Store. "You are a beautiful woman. Beautiful." His voice was husky and he folded her hand between his.

Emily knew she should pull away, that she should tell him she was flattered, but couldn't possibly … Sorry but he'd gotten the wrong impression … She was faithful.

She looked at him. "I've never seen where you live."

That night, after putting Jess to bed and listening while Rick, so gentle and patient, helped Matt with his book report, Emily scrubbed the inside of the oven and wept.

She remembered in the beginning of their relationship, Rick told her he loved her sense of humor, and suddenly she was cracking jokes and people around her laughed. He told her he loved the unique and creative twists her mind took, and her conversation became scintillating. He told her she was beautiful and sexy, and she walked the street with confidence and pleasure. When she first met Rick, she had expected to be dazzled by this sophisticated graduate student, but she had not expected, was totally unprepared for, being loved. At first she didn't know how to react. Rick told her she was stunning, her hair was gorgeous, her breasts were magnificent. He brought her wildflower bouquets, and he cradled her head and smoothed back her hair. She discovered she liked it. She didn't know if she loved him, but she did know that she loved being loved by him.

Over the years, things changed. He forgot to come home, he didn't like her photos, they scarcely touched and rarely talked. In Rick's eyes she'd become insubstantial, ephemeral, and she was terrified she might vanish altogether.

But that was no excuse. She vowed never to be with Evan again. No one would ever have to know, not even group.

CHAPTER TWENTY-FIVE

February 13, 1979
One week later

G emma sat on the floor alongside Vivian and Alix in Emily's living room, surrounded by the fundraising letters and the photo montage Emily had created to go with them. Since the Hyde amendment passed, banning federal funds for abortions, the health center was always on the brink of financial collapse, like a tattered dress held together with safety pins.

"These are just great," Alix said, picking up the sheet of photos. "Who could resist giving money to such a place?" The photographs showed the outside of the building, the staff, the patients waiting in the reception area filled with flowers and magazines, and the warm, cozy consulting rooms. Emily had donated her services and that night they were helping Alix get the mailing out. "Thanks again."

"Sure," Emily said, folding paper into thirds. "At least this way people will get to see my pictures." She handed the papers off to Vivian, who was stuffing the envelopes. "It looks like it's going to be a long night, I'll get the coffee."

"Willie's stuck on this whole marriage thing," Gemma said, straightening a pile of envelopes.

"And?" Alix asked.

"Why is he making such an issue about this?" she said as Emily returned with coffee and mugs. "We were so happy and now it's like I'm watching this relationship crash and burn."

"His feelings are hurt," Vivian said without looking up; she just kept stuffing. "Why *are* you making such an issue of it? Just get married already."

"You know." Gemma lit a cigarette. "I read this article by Robin Morgan, and she thinks that marriage for women is like slavery."

"I wonder," Emily said, pouring coffee all around, "if she's talked to any slaves."

"You didn't actually say that to Willie?" Alix took a mug.

"I still don't get it." Vivian pushed away her pile and stretched. "Why not get married?"

"Why didn't you?" Gemma snapped.

"I'm not good at sharing. I didn't want to share Katie, or my bathroom, or decisions about what to make for dinner. But you're past all that. You've been living together for years."

"He wants to have babies."

"Why do you sound as if you're doomed?" Alix asked.

"That's wonderful." Vivian stirred her coffee. "You're great with kids. No one can deal with Katie like you can."

"There's too much to do. Too much still needs to be changed. When we were in grade school, we learned that women were given the vote in 1920, which when you think about it is bad enough. Only fifty-four years ago. Only thirty years before we were born, for God's sake, and I remember thinking that was a long time ago, probably right after Columbus discovered America. But last week I met a retired professor who actually was in law school before women got the vote."

"Yeah?" Vivian leaned back. "Your point?"

"What we weren't taught is that women fought and struggled and were jailed and harassed and demonstrated to get the vote. They weren't *given* anything. We were taught that men *fought* for freedom and women were *given* the vote.

"And now we're trying to get the ERA passed, which you think should be a very simple thing, but no, it's a pitched battle and it might not even pass."

"Oh, stop distracting us with all that noble talk." Vivian stubbed out her cigarette. "You love Willie. You're a basket case when you guys are fighting. He wants kids. You want kids. So get married and get over it."

Gemma didn't say anything. She knew she was making little sense, trying to talk about something without actually divulging it. But she wasn't sure she wanted to. If she talked about it, she'd cry and she didn't want the fuss. She'd accepted this a long time ago.

"You do remember you're talking to three women who work and also have children?" Emily sipped her coffee.

"You do want kids right?" Vivian asked.

"Yes. But …" Gemma felt the tears come and stood. "But I can't."

"What do you mean you can't?" Vivian went back to stuffing envelopes. "Why the hell not?"

"I'm sterile," she blurted. She had to get out of there before her tears started. She turned and ran from the room, clattering down the stairs

Gemma sank onto the porch stairs and leaned against the icy railing, finally letting the tears fall.

Just this once.

She hunched in her sweater and wiped her nose with the sleeve. Fucking cold.

She wanted to disappear, to go home, to go somewhere all alone, but she'd left her coat and keys upstairs. She didn't want to go back up there and talk and answer all the questions that would come and have them try to comfort her.

She heard someone walking down the stairs and felt for her

cigarettes. Left those upstairs too. So cold it felt like her tears would freeze on her face.

Alix opened the door, handed over her coat and cigarettes, and sat beside her. She didn't say anything and didn't touch her, and Gemma was grateful for that.

She lit a cigarette. "I never told Willie. Too scared."

She saw Alix nod in the glow of the streetlight.

"What am I going to do about Willie?" she finally said.

"Come inside. It's too cold out here to think."

She let Alix pull her to standing.

Upstairs, Emily handed her a glass of wine as she came in and ushered her to the living room, away from the unfinished mailing.

Vivian gave her a hesitant half smile and patted the seat next to her on the couch. "Tell us," she said. And then quickly added, "Only if you want to, of course."

Gemma sipped her wine. "I had an abortion."

They all nodded. This was not news.

"But what I never told you is that there were complications, scarring of the uterus, and they told me I couldn't get pregnant.

"As a little girl, I always wanted children." She laughed. It mingled with a sob and came out like a croak. "I come from a huge family, my cousins and brothers pop out babies like ... And I remember sitting with my aunts as they talked in hushed tones about barren women they knew, the disgrace, the shame, the women's shame, always the woman's shame. Because if a woman couldn't have children, what was she?"

They all sat quietly, listening, sipping their wine, letting her talk.

"The women's movement saved me. It came along at just the right moment, when I could believe as a woman I had worth beyond making babies. And I do good work. I'm proud of the work I do. I have value." She jutted her chin out, looking at them, daring them to contradict her.

Vivian's eyes glittered with tears.

"It never seemed a good time to tell Willie. When we first got together, I didn't think we were going to be a couple for very long, you know. We were young and I was trying for law school. And then when we moved up here, moved into our apartment, I was busy with school and he was busy being the first black teacher, then first black department head, then the first black assistant principal. We weren't talking about babies or marriage. And it almost seemed premature to bring it up, as if I were assuming our relationship might be more than it was.

"I have come to terms with this. And so that is why I cannot marry Willie. He wants to be a father and he deserves a woman who can give him babies."

"But why didn't you tell *us*?" Emily asked.

She shrugged. "Embarrassed, I guess, for being such an idiot."

"But you were seventeen," Alix said, "and a victim of circumstances beyond—"

"I am not a victim. I chose to have sex with that boy and I have accepted the consequences."

Vivian shook her head. "You are making my brain hurt. On the one hand you declare your value and on the other you feel such shame, you didn't even tell anyone."

Gemma didn't know what to say to that. She faced this issue all the time at work—woman who felt such overwhelming humiliation at being beaten or raped. She understood it and yet it frustrated her no end.

"I don't know what to do about Willie," she said after a minute.

Vivian lit a cigarette. "Tell him."

"I can't imagine how."

Emily filled her glass. "Secrets are terrible things. Believe me, I know. "

Vivian nodded in agreement. "I'm telling Katie everything. No hiding anything."

Gemma didn't believe that one for a second.

Neither obviously did Alix, who laughed, breaking the tension. "Come on. You're going to tell her about sleeping with all those guys in the Ann Arbor house?"

"Not to mention the whole daddy thing," Gemma said, knowing that was mean and not caring.

"But you want to be with Willie," Vivian said. "I didn't want to be with Jerry."

"We all fool ourselves one way or another."

Vivian didn't rise to the bait. "I know it's scary," she said.

"This will be the end of me and Willie."

"Why?"

"There is no reason…"

"Ridiculous…"

All their voices jumped at her, trying to change what she knew.

She had to give Willie his chance to find someone else. And she would have to be the one to end it, because he would never do something so hurtful. He would stay and they would limp along together forever, while she worried constantly that he resented having settled for damaged goods and she struggled to find ways to make it up to him. No. That was no way to have a relationship.

It took her three days, but on Thursday, Gemma put down a deposit on a studio apartment on Mass Ave in North Cambridge. A converted attic with skylights and wood floors, available March fifteenth.

That evening after they'd washed and dried the dishes and Willie headed to his desk to do schoolwork, Gemma said, "We need to talk."

He nodded. He filled the kettle for tea and returned to the kitchen table, waiting for her to start.

"I know you think I don't want to get married because of the whole race thing." She took two mugs out of the cupboard. "And how you could think that after all our time together, and knowing me so well, is painful." The mugs landed angrily on the table.

"I think—"

"Wait. Please." Realizing she was going on the attack and still avoiding the issue, she took a breath to regroup. "I need to tell you …" She paused. She still had no idea how to begin. She took out tea bags. "When I was in high school," she said, sitting across from him and dropping a bag into each mug, "I had an abortion. There were complications and I am not able to have children." There, it was out.

He didn't say anything. The kettle screeched, and she got up and removed it from the burner. With her back to him, she said, "I'm moving out the first of April. I've found an apartment."

She turned around, poured the hot water into the mugs, and looked at him. The rage on his face, never seen before, stilled her. She stood, holding the kettle, waiting, but he remained silent.

"How dare you?" he whispered, but it was almost a hiss. He seemed unable to continue.

She straightened to her full height, bracing herself for what she knew was coming, how she'd tricked him, how she'd hid this from him. She placed the kettle on the stove.

"Not trust me," he finally said. His voice, although soft, was sharp, blades through her heart. "I thought we had a relationship. A partnership. And you are suggesting we end? Without talking? Who the hell are you?"

"But you want children."

"I love you. Or thought I loved whoever the hell I thought

you were. I would love to have children with *that* woman. Not with some nameless, faceless woman I haven't even met. You have no fucking idea who I am."

He stood, grabbed his coat, and slammed the door on his way out.

CHAPTER TWENTY-SIX

February 27, 1979
One week later

"**W**hy can't I wear a dress to school?" Davey swung his legs, kicking the table leg as he moved the apple slices around his plate.

"Not allowed." Alix swung Mikey to her other hip and rummaged through the freezer, knowing that was a poor excuse for an answer but really too tired to do better at the moment. "How about fish sticks?" She also pulled out a bag of corn and one of peas. Not the best dinner she'd ever made, but she needed something fast. She'd been late getting home because Pam had called an emergency meeting at the health center, and later she had to go back to work for the evening group she led for pregnant and postpartum women. She turned on the oven.

"Anna wore a dress today." Davey punctuated his sentence with a thump.

"Sweetie, don't kick the table and Anna's a girl." She tried to lower Mike into his high chair so she could use both hands to get dinner, but he clung tight and yelled, "No. Mommy. Up." One-handed she bent and pulled saucepans from the cupboard, and got the water heating with the vegetables and the fish sticks into the oven.

"Why can't I wear a dress if Anna wears pants?"

A few minutes later, she heard Sam bounding up the stairs.

The goddess had offered a reprieve.

"Fish sticks," Sam yelled as he barged through the door. "I smell fish sticks. I love fish sticks. Yay for fish sticks. " And he did a little dance with his briefcase before taking off his coat.

Davey giggled and ran for a hug, and even Mikey gave a tired grin as he leaned against her shoulder. Sam dropped a kiss on Mikey's head and then her head and then checked the oven.

Grateful Sam was taking over, she sat down, Mikey snuggling into her lap.

"You'd have let Matt wear dresses to school in first grade?" Alix felt skeptical as she and Emily crunched through the snow on their way to meet Vivian and Gemma for lunch.

Emily shook her head. "No, I couldn't do it. He'd have been pummeled. But Davey does have a point that it's not fair. I did let Matt take his doll to nursery school. And that started a whole run on boys wanting dolls. It was gratifying."

They'd met up to take a walk before meeting the others, although slipping and sliding along the half-cleared sidewalks didn't make for easy conversation.

"So what are you going to do? Are you going to let him wear a dress?"

Alix sighed. "Probably not." They tramped on in silence while Alix tried to think how she would explain to Davey the different rules for girls and boys she wanted him to follow, while at the same time having him listen to the album *Free to Be You and Me.*

Emily banged her mittened hands together. "Damn, it's cold. Have you spoken to Gemma?"

"I've called a few times and left messages, but …" Alix grabbed Emily's arm as her feet slid out from under her.

"Yeah, I was relieved when Vivian said Gemma would come today."

Alix pointed to the Pewter Pot. "I'm having hot chocolate first thing." The cold was brutal.

Emily nodded, pushed open the door, and headed toward the booth where Vivian and Gemma were waiting. Gemma looked like she hadn't slept in a while and she'd chopped at her hair again.

They all hugged hello and then huddled in their coats and scarves as they gave the waitress their order. Alix wasn't sure she'd ever feel her feet again.

"By the way," Emily said as the waitress left. "Did I mention I had lunch with that guy who bought the photograph a few weeks ago." She released this information like steam from a pressure cooker valve, not bursting, but just for safety. "He's a visiting professor from England, so we've been talking art-talk and yesterday spent two hours at the MFA."

"Uh-oh." Alix cupped her hands around the hot chocolate when the waitress put their mugs down.

"I feel like an old house plant," Emily continued. "that's been rescued from the dark den and set out on the bright windowsill, watered, fed, and misted. My leaves are perky. Do you know what I mean?"

"Really, Em? Perky leaves?" Vivian laughed.

Gemma stirred her coffee. "Does he know you're married?" Gemma looked more defeated than Alix had ever seen her.

"Oh, it's just fun." Emily dismissed the question. "But he's good for me. I think I took some amazing photos yesterday."

Alix studied Emily's face, wondering what she wasn't saying, but this wasn't the time to get into it. She turned to Gemma. "So what's the story with you and Willie?"

Gemma shrugged. "We've settled into a sort of armistice while I wait for my new apartment to be ready. He brought me coffee this morning before I got up. No matter how angry he gets, no matter how upset he is at me, Willie is unfailingly kind.

It breaks my heart."

Vivian leaned toward her. "Don't do this. Don't move out," she said. She sipped her coffee as if she were done and then added, "Don't *you* be the one to end it. Let Willie have some time to digest things and come to his own decision. Don't run away,"

"How would I survive it if he decides he wants to leave me? That he wants children more than he wants me?"

"Fuck him then!

Gemma briefly smiled at that. "You do see how bizarre you sound, the irony of this, the weirdness. You being the one giving me advice to have faith and not flee."

"That was totally different. I was terrified and I hardly knew Jerry. And you are much stronger than I am. You can handle anything—even if Willie leaves you."

That Saturday, Sam had to go into work and Davey and two friends careened around the apartment, jumping from couch to chair, wielding cardboard swords, with Mikey toddling after, desperate to be included. An icy March rain fell in sheets, creating puddles the size of small lakes as it melted snow, keeping them all inside.

"I killed you. You have to be dead." One of the boys pointed at Mikey.

"I not dead. I not dead." Mikey's wail was pitched high enough to make her wince.

She didn't know what she felt about Emily and her British painter. *That way lies danger* kept coming to mind, followed rapidly by wishing she had a British painter, followed by how lucky she was that Sam was so supportive of her work while Rick behaved as if Emily's photography was playtime, followed by wondering what it would feel like to have perky leaves again, and then she laughed at herself for adopting that expression. Sam was just getting on her nerves. It happened to the best of marriages.

She just didn't seem to be able to explain to him how totally exhausted she was from trying to care for house, kids, and job.

"Maybe you're trying to do too much," he'd said when she tried the other day.

"Maybe you could do more?"

"Why do you always look to me? I'm doing as much as I can, and then I come home and help out here."

"Help? Help? Is this my apartment you're visiting? Are these my kids that you're playing with?"

An ear-piercing wail caused her to rush into the living room. One of Davey's friends writhed on the floor in full imitation of death by stabbing. Where the hell did he get that from, she wondered. Mikey stood staring, wide eyed and terrified.

Alix pulled out the dress-up box, desperate for less screaming.

She'd made a trip to the secondhand store and loaded up on half-slips, colorful scarves, shiny old jewelry, and fancy hats. Then she collected all the old Halloween stuff—wigs, gorilla masks, and capes—and stuffed those in the box too.

She dragged the box to the middle of the living room, not saying anything, just leaving it there, knowing they'd get curious eventually, and went back into the kitchen to call her mother.

She stretched the phone cord so she could watch as the boys, distracted from their swordplay, started pulling out the contents of the box.

"Why not move home to New York?" This was a recent refrain of her mother's that had crept into their weekly phone calls.

"Sam has a job in Boston. I have a job in Boston."

"There are jobs in New York. Sam wants to work with poor people—there is poverty in New York. You want to work with women. There are women in New York."

Her mother's loneliness and need pulsed through the wires. Alix dreaded every phone call.

"You're exhausted," her mother continued. "I can hear it in your voice. If you moved to New York, I could babysit the boys, help out with the house. You wouldn't have to rush around so much."

"We're not moving, Mom." Alix wanted this latest idea of her mother's to stop. What she didn't suggest, and it made her shoulders ache with guilt, was that her mother move to Boston.

Davey had pulled on a black half-slip that flowed down to his ankles and the eye patch from the pirate costume. He hung red beads over Mikey's head. One of his friends slipped his feet into high heels.

"Aunt Rose thinks I should get a job," her mother complained. "But who wants an old woman with no skills?"

"You're not old, Ma. You're fifty-five." But she thought maybe her mother was right. "How about you volunteer to read to kids or something?"

"I'm done with kids." And yet her mother insisted she wanted to babysit the boys? Alix didn't think it would be kind to point out this contradiction, but she really wanted to. Davey's other friend had pulled on a wig like a hat. She heard her mother light a cigarette. "I don't understand why you have to stay in Boston."

By the time Sam came home, all the boys were darting around the living room, hollering and wielding swords again, but with feather boas draped over their shoulders, beads hanging from their necks, and skirts swinging in colorful array.

Alix had even scrounged up some old lipsticks and created dramatic facial effects.

"Whoa. What happened here?" Sam called as he stepped into room that had been rearranged with blankets and pillows into caves and tents.

"Mom got us dresses," Davey yelled as he chased an escaped friend into the pillow hideaway.

"I see."

Alix got up from the floor, laughing. "Pretty good work for a rainy afternoon, eh?"

"Maybe you should clean up these guys before their parents pick them up."

"Oh, it all comes off easily with cold cream." She gave him a kiss.

"They might not appreciate this." Sam waved his arm at the scene. "Some parents don't think boys should wear dresses and jewelry and makeup."

Davey looked at his father, his floppy hat sliding from his head.

"They look ridiculous," Sam continued. "Do you really think Davey wants to look like a girl?"

"Lower your voice," she said, and tugged at his arm to steer him to the kitchen. "They're just having fun. Don't make them feel bad."

But it was too late. The older boys unwrapped their scarves and pulled off their skirts.

"How could you?" asked Alix as Sam grabbed a beer from the refrigerator. "Now, instead of simple silliness, they feel embarrassed and ashamed."

""Boys shouldn't dress up like girls. They should feel embarrassed." Sam took a swallow of his beer and leaned against the counter.

"No," Alix said turning away from him. "It's you. You're the one who should feel mortified for what you did to those boys."

CHAPTER TWENTY-SEVEN

March 6, 1979
One week later

V ivian arrived at the nurse's office of Katie's elementary school and saw her daughter perched on a chair holding a bloody cloth to her nose. Blood spattered her shirt, even her pants. Blood congealed on a cut over her eye and God knew where else. Her face was a mess of tears, dirt, and snot. The nurse, her white hair perched like a soft cloud on her head, sat at the desk filling out paperwork.

"Whoa," Vivian said. She put her arm around Katie, kissing her head. "How does the other guy look?"

"I wouldn't make light of this." The nurse stood and offered her hand. "I'm Mrs. Gaines and you must be Katie's mother."

"Vivian." She shook the nurse's hand and pulled up a chair to sit next to Katie. "What happened here?"

"It wasn't my fault." Katie moved the cloth from her nose to say this, and blood started pouring again.

Mrs. Gaines got another ice cube wrapped in cloth. "Hold this against your nose. Your daughter decided the way to solve a problem was to beat someone up."

"Craig," Katie started. "You know that kid I told you about who steals lunch boxes?"

"The fifth grader?" she asked, not liking the look of the cut over her eye.

"Yeah, he …" Her nose started bleeding again.

"Hold the cloth tight." Mrs. Gaines turned to Vivian again. "In this school we use words, not violence."

"I still haven't heard what happened." She didn't think the cut over her eye needed stitches.

"Katie hit another child," Mrs. Gaines said. "According to people who saw it, she started the fight. A teacher broke it up and tried to steer her to the principal's office." She gently took a fresh cloth and wiped Katie's face. "It seems she was also yelling and kicking at the teacher and then you got called."

"Well," said Vivian. "There must have been a reason."

She looked at Katie, but before she could speak, Mrs. Gaines repeated, "There is never a good reason to use violence."

"So can I take Katie home now?"

"Yes, but you must call the principal."

"So?" Vivian asked Katie after she was buckled in the car.

"Craig started it," she mumbled from behind the cloth at her nose. "He stole John's lunch box and dumped it and stomped on it." Katie forgot about holding the ice cube against her face as she got into the storytelling, but it looked as if her nose had stopped bleeding. "John gets picked on because he's weird and only in third grade. John just stood there and cried. I told you he's weird. And Craig started pointing at him and calling him names. And I told Craig to cut it out and he laughed and said 'make me.' And he pushed me. Right here." Katie pointed to her chest. "So I punched him in the face. And then he punched me. Then Mr. Tiechart came and maybe I hit him, but I didn't mean to."

Vivian patted her knee. "Let's get home and get you out of those yucky clothes."

With Katie resting on the couch in clean pajamas, Vivian

called Mr. Andrews, the school principal. He informed her that Katie had been suspended for the rest of the week.

"On Monday," he went on, "before Katie can return to school, you must meet with the social worker, the school psychologist, and myself. The meeting is at seven."

"Suspended? And a social worker? Is all this really necessary?" Vivian paced as she talked. "Obviously I'll talk to Katie about it, but—"

"She attacked another student. For a fourth-grade girl, that is highly unusual behavior."

"But suspending her? She was defending a little kid."

"Her choosing to use force is very disturbing."

"But what was she supposed to do?" She was proud of Katie, although she wouldn't admit it to Mr. Andrews. "I thought we wanted to teach children to stand up for what is right."

Monday morning, Vivian sloshed through the rain to bring Katie to meet with Mr. Andrews, the social worker, and the school psychologist.

They sat on tiny chairs in the empty waiting room. It was too early for students to be allowed in.

Mr. Andrews opened his door. He gave them a big, welcoming smile. "Katie, you wait here while your mother and I have a little chat." Mr. Andrew's hair was graying and he was tall with a round belly. He was the perfect combination for an elementary-school principal, warm yet large enough to immediately command attention.

She patted Katie's knee and followed Mr. Andrews into his small office and sat where he pointed. He introduced her to Ms. Dana, the social worker, who had such a friendly smile, Vivian immediately relaxed. He then explained that the school psychologist was running a bit late and they'd start without him.

"So," Mr. Andrews started. "I assume you comprehend the

seriousness of the situation." He waited for her to nod in agreement and then continued. "Craig's parents are understandably concerned about violence on the playground. We need to understand why Katie, a little girl, would start punching someone who hadn't done anything to her. It may indicate antisocial behavior. " He cleared his throat and looked toward Ms. Dana. She nodded encouragement. "Other parents have expressed concern. Rightfully so, I may add." He smiled his big smile. He looked at her; he looked at Ms. Dana. "We have decided Katie needs a psychological evaluation before being allowed back to school." He nodded. "We can start today."

Vivian leaned forward. "You're serious? Is this boy Craig being evaluated also?"

"That is confidential."

She stood up. "No evaluation. Katie starts back to class today. Her behavior has been addressed at home and it won't happen again."

"But—"

"Mr. Andrews, I will not sit here while you determine if my daughter is safe to be around other children." She turned toward the door. "If you don't allow her to go back to her fourth grade class today, I will have my lawyer sue you, the school board, the Town of Cambridge, and the Commonwealth of Massachusetts, if necessary." She carefully closed the door behind her.

"Can we actually sue?" Vivian asked Gemma, who sat across from her in Friendly's Ice Cream Parlor. "Is it legal? Can they do that?" She scooped up some hot fudge. If possible, Gemma looked like she'd even lost more weight.

"Don't worry. I'll help if you need it, but you won't." Gemma swirled her spoon in the dish of ice cream but she didn't eat any.

Vivian sat back feeling greatly relieved. "Do you think they're really worried she's an incipient Lizzie Borden or something?

That she might start a rampage at recess?"

She at least got Gemma to give a tired smile.

"My brothers would be impressed," Gemma said. "I have to admit it's not every fourth grade girl who can pack such a wallop."

"So did you tell Willie you've changed your mind, that you don't want to leave?"

"No."

Vivian sighed. "Don't wait too long."

Later that night, Gemma heard the key in the door and looked up from her book. It was after nine. Willie had been staying away most evenings since she'd announced she was leaving.

He nodded hello as he hung up his overcoat and emptied his suit pockets. He headed to office where he'd been sleeping on the couch.

"I'm sorry. So very sorry," she said.

He paused and looked at her. "I know." He continued to his office.

"Come sit?" she asked. "Just for a minute."

He returned and sat opposite her, glancing at his watch as if to time her.

"I should have told you about all this a long time ago."

"You think?"

"I was scared and…" She didn't know what else to say. "I was wrong."

"Yup." He looked at his watch and started to rise.

"Willie, I'm trying here."

"What do you want from me?" He stood. "You dump this secret,"—he paced—"something you didn't trust me enough to tell, and then"—he stopped walking and stood in front of her— "you tell me we're finished. No talking. No discussion." He resumed his pacing. "A total disregard of me."

"I'm sorry."

"And now you're sorry? What am I supposed to do with that?"

"I don't want us to end. Not like this."

"It's too late." He stood rigid. "How can I ever trust you?"

Gemma rose. "That is something you will have to decide. I can't convince you." She walked to him, but did not attempt to touch him. "I am telling you that I love you and I'm sorry I hurt you. I let fear win over love. That is not an excuse; it is an explanation. I have fought being afraid my whole life and I'm sure the struggle isn't over."

She looked up at him. "But I am saying to you that in this instance I was wrong." His expression was severe and his body unbending. "Only you can know if your fear is stronger than your love," she said and turned away, walking to the bedroom and closing the door.

CHAPTER TWENTY-EIGHT

March 13, 1979
The next day

E mily gave Evan a quick good-bye kiss and got out of the car. They'd stayed way too long at the DeCordova exhibit.

Last week, she'd tried again to end it.

"I respect your decision," he'd said in his clipped tones when she'd stammered, blushing, and told him she just couldn't do it. "But I do hope that we can continue seeing each other. I value your company."

So they made arrangements for the DeCordova. Emily walked toward her apartment. Sleeping with him today was cruel. To both of them. To all of them

But when Evan took her arm to steady her on the icy street and brushed against her as he pointed at a painting, her body's intense arousal betrayed her, jamming her thoughts and jumbling her conversation.

It would have to stop. Definitely. That was the last time.

As she climbed the stairs to her third-floor apartment, she heard Jim Morrison blaring even through the solid wood door. She let herself in. The usual crowd was over.

"I'm home," she called, hanging her coat, but who could hear over this music. She'd jump in the shower, saying she needed to warm up. She poked her head into the living room to wave hello.

Marcia, pressed against Rick on the couch, adjusted his collar and then reached up to ruffle his hair. Rick looked at Joe and laughed at whatever he'd said, and squeezed Marcia's thigh.

She stood mesmerized, repulsed by them and disgusted with herself. It was all so pathetic.

Rick eventually noticed her staring and jumped away from Marcia, his expression horrified. She met his eyes. "How was the exhibit?" he asked.

Without saying anything, she turned and walked down the hall to the kitchen to fix some tea. What was there to say?

Marcia followed and leaned against the doorjamb. "'I wouldn't take this seriously, you know," she said.

"No?" Emily filled the kettle and turned on the burner.

Why was this woman standing in her kitchen talking to her?

"He flirts." Marcia shrugged. "It's what Rick does. It doesn't mean anything."

Emily looked at her. Marcia gave her an odd smile, as if they could bond over Rick's little indulgences.

"He's done this since I've known him. And I've known him a lot longer than you."

"I know." Emily nodded. Damn if she was going to show this woman how shaken she was. "But get out."

Rick came in and looked questioningly at them.

"I've made tea," Emily said.

"Jess is eating with Susie and her mom," he said. "Matt's not home from practice yet," he said.

"Great." She turned the burner off. "Marcia's just leaving and I want everyone else gone."

Rick followed as Emily brought her tea to the living room and placed the mug on an end table.

She whirled to face him. "When were you planning to tell me

you were screwing Marcia?"

"What the hell are you talking about? I'm not sleeping with Marcia." At least he had the good grace to appear sincerely shocked. He watched her as she paced the room. "Sit. Tell me what's going on."

"I've suspected it for a long time, maybe forever, but I guess I didn't want to believe it." Emily's tears shocked her. She swiped them away. Ludicrous to feel this hurt, given…everything.

"You're being crazy. Marcia and I are old friends."

"I think I've known for awhile this marriage was over, but I was hoping…for the kids, you know…"

"What are you saying? I told you I'm not sleeping with Marcia."

"You can't keep your hands off her. You can't keep your hands off any woman come to think of it. Except me, maybe." Emily laughed, but it sounded harsh, even to her.

"No. Oh God, Em." Rick stood and pulled her to him. "I love you. I just tease, play around, flirt." He hugged her close. "If I knew that's what you were thinking… I'm sorry, so sorry. Oh god, I would never do anything to jeopardize what we have, this family, our kids." He kissed her hair and the held her face in his hands, kissing her cheeks, her fore head, then pulled back and looked at her. "Please believe me. Please." His eyes glistened, begging.

Every part of her collapsed. Maybe he was telling the truth? What did that mean about her? Her knees buckled and he caught her and they sank to the rug together.

"I love you. I love you," he murmured holding her tight and then kissed her hard and fierce.

"No, not here." She pushed at him. She needed to take a shower. What if he could smell Evan? A moan of anguish escaped and he mistook it for something else and pulled at her jeans. "We shouldn't. What if Matt comes home?"

"Shhh," He was intent, beyond caring.

§   §   §

The next day, Emily kissed Vivian hello and carried the wine bottle into the living room. She smelled the flowers before she saw them. "Oh, my. What is this?"

White and yellow freesia filled the top of the bookcase. Bunches of yellow daffodils lined the windowsills. Purple hyacinths with their heavy aroma clumped together in vases on the end tables. Blue and yellow irises stood tall and stately among the houseplants.

"Vivian is impatient." Gemma, wearing a big cable-knit sweater, was curled into the corner of the couch, a pile of books next to her, her cigarette burning in the ashtray. "She decided to hurry the season along."

Vivian reappeared from the kitchen with a tray of nibbles. "Isn't it great?" She wore a strappy bright yellow sundress over a turtleneck. "I have vases for you all to take home with you when you go. And ..." She pulled Emily over to a table in the corner. It was covered with little square containers of dirt. "Katie and I started seedlings for your garden."

"I'm shocked." Alix's loud voice startled them both. They turned to see her appearing from the direction of Katie's room. "What is this?" Alix stood with her hand on her hip, waving a naked Barbie doll.

Vivian blushed and stammered. "Well ..."

"Emily and I don't allow guns in the house with our boys." The bangles on Alix's wrist jingled with accusation as she continued to wave the naked Barbie. "Do you think it's appropriate for Katie to have this—this ... doll to represent the ideal feminine form?"

"I—"

"Do you know how scarred I was"—Alix pointed the Barbie at Vivian—"by not developing breasts that point?" And then she collapsed into the nearest chair in giggles.

Vivian's face was blotchy pink.

Emily choked on her wine as her laugh burst out. "She's teasing, silly."

"But I do feel guilty," Vivian said. "I mean, it is a terrible image to give her." She fiddled with her necklace. "I've tried with the Legos, but she really wanted that doll."

"Davey really wants a gun," Alix said. She sat up and sliced a piece of cheese. "Any stick he picks up turns into a spear. What am I supposed to do about that? He struts and squints, intent on his latest pretend foe, with his cheeks still round with baby fat."

"You're going to have to relax," Emily said. "Just a little."

"Hey, I'm not the one who won't let her eleven-year-old son see *Star Wars* with his friends for fear he'll want to battle the evil empire when he grows up," Alix said.

That was true. Emily lived with a constant dread that some asshole in power somewhere would start a war and try to kill her son. She'd started a war watch and had started to plan escape routes. She showed antiwar movies to Matt. She was going to train him away from violence.

"Jessica loves to play with dolls, she loves to wear dresses. The frillier, the better." Emily looked down at her jeans and work boots. "I don't know where she gets this shit." She shrugged. "One of her greatest pleasures right now is playing with my hair."

Gemma leaned forward. "I have no doubt that there are differences between the sexes." She dipped her cracker into the humus. "But what exactly they are, and what is culturally proscribed and what isn't, will take a long time to figure out." She cupped one hand under the cracker to catch any drips. "In the meantime, what is at issue is that the characteristics attributed to women, whether biologically based or culturally determined or both, are—in this culture as well as many others—valued as less. Less important, less necessary, less human. And that is the issue."

"Oh, fuck," Vivian said. "Do we have to think about this shit all the time? Let's just do our nails." She left the room.

Gemma looked at Alix and Emily and shrugged.

Vivian came back with a small quilted bag. Emily and Alix cleared the coffee table and they all watched, speechless, as Vivian laid out cotton balls, emery boards, nail polish remover, and about fifteen shades of nail polish.

Gemma picked up a bottle of red. "Brazilian Night," she read. She put it down and picked up another. "Are you planning a second career we didn't know about?"

Vivian explained about only filing your nails in one direction and the importance of using cuticle softener. They all got busy.

"I got called to Katie's school." She applied bright orange polish to her hand, splayed on a magazine that protected the coffee table. "She got into a fight."

"Uh-oh." Emily laughed and smudged her thumbnail.

Vivian passed her the cotton balls. "Yeah, well, they didn't think it was funny. They think she's trouble." She waved both hands in the air to dry the polish. "I want her to stand up for herself. I want her to be spunky. But she needs to… pick her battles? I don't know." She carefully struck a match without smearing her nails and lit a cigarette.

"She's a great kid," Alix said, also waving her hands to dry her polish.

Emily concentrated on brushing on the pink polish. She was glad Alix was doing the talking. Truth be told, Emily thought Katie was too demanding and maybe a little out of control. Alix always worried about not having a talent like photography or skills like Vivian and Gemma, but Alix had a gift of attunement. People would expose to her parts of themselves they'd hidden for years. She listened with her entire being, hardly even registering the words but understanding what was being said through the glance, the unsaid, the catch in the voice, the level of anger.

"I'm fucking up." Vivian blew out smoke. "She embarrassed me before all those holier than thou people thinking, *disturbed kid, single mother.* And she doesn't have a father to run to when her mother goes crazy."

"Having a father doesn't make this easier." Gemma's knee hit the table and all the little bottles jiggled, but none of them tipped. "Every failure of the child always gets blamed on the mother, whether or not there's a father in the picture." She held out her hand to see her bright red nails better. "I don't think this color is me." She picked up a cotton ball and the nail polish remover. "That's why I came up with the grandfather theory of dysfunction." She started taking off her polish. "It goes like this. Right now everyone says if a child is fucked up, it's because of the mistakes of the mother. But if you trace that back, the mother is a mess because of *her* mother. But that still doesn't seem fair. Because, probably, given what we know of history, that mother was a mess because her husband treated her badly. So the blame goes to the grandfather." She smiled. "So what do you think? Brilliant or what?"

Vivian frowned. "You think too much."

Alix laughed and turned to Emily. "We haven't heard much about your hunky professor recently."

"Nothing to tell." Emily shrugged. That wasn't exactly a lie since she'd ended it. "Rick and I had a fight. I accused him of having an affair with that Marcia. He denied it of course and…"

Vivian interrupted. "Of course he would deny it. He…"

"Shh," Gemma broke in. "Let her talk."

"I believed him. He…"

"How"--Vivian cut her off again—"can you believe…"

"Viv, please shut up and let her speak," Gemma said.

"It's all a mess. And so sad, considering… well…everything." Emily paused. "I remember overhearing my mother talk to a neighbor, Evelyn Baker, when she was at our house having her baby checked for some rash on her arm, and moaning and groaning about maybe having to divorce Scooter because he'd been screwing around since she's been pregnant with number two. My mother said, 'Evy, there are worse things than getting divorced.' So Evy stopped blowing her nose and said, 'Name one.'

"And my mother, my own mother said, 'Staying married too long.'"

After she went home, Gemma sat in bed going over some legal briefs, hoping they'd make her tired. Sleep didn't come easily these days. She wondered if eventually they'd all end up single.

"Okay," Willie said as he walked in carrying a wicker basket with clean laundry. "I've decided we don't have to get married right away."

She had no idea what this meant.

"If you're so sure getting married will ruin everything between us, I certainly don't want to be responsible for that." He put down the basket and walked around to the other side of the bed. He slid in next to her, slipping his arm around her back and leaning in close for a kiss.

She put down her pen. His hands cupped her head and he gently drew her face to his. "I agree marriage would never work." He pulled away, staring at her, smoothing her hair off her face.

"Right," she said. "You're too snotty, too upper-class."

He kissed her. "You're too deprived. You'll resent my privilege."

"You'll always think you're too good for me." She rubbed her face along his cheek, breathing in his smell, rooting for his mouth.

They kissed long and hard, hands touching, stroking, exploring. He leaned his chin on her head as she sank into his chest. "What about your brothers Vinnie and Vito?"

"Don't stereotype. Your sister is no model of tolerance herself." She could feel his heart beating against her cheek. She closed her eyes.

"She's just upset that our great-grandma was enslaved, is all."

"Not by my great-grandmother. She was a peasant in Sicily tilling the soil with her teeth."

His hands slipped under her pajama top. "We'll just do the best we can and if it doesn't work out"—he ran his hand down her back and thigh—"I can go my way and join the Black Panthers and you can join lesbian feminists and denounce all men, black and white."

"Right," was all she could manage.

"And my father wants me to try to be the first black president. A white wife would never do."

Her pajama top was somehow unbuttoned, his shirt already off. He stopped touching her.

"What?"

"I'm just wondering why those I-talians have such great lover-boy reputations if they let someone like you pass on by."

"So we should probably talk seriously about all this, don't you think?" She hesitated to ruin his loving mood, but this turnaround unsettled her.

"We have plenty of time." He loosened the string on her pajama bottoms. "We have our whole lifetime to talk. And talking may be very overrated."

FIVE YEARS LATER

CHAPTER TWENTY-NINE

January 14, 1984

S now mixed with sleet made the streets glassy and treacherous. The street lights didn't begin to penetrate the sticky gloom. Rick insisted Emily ride with him into Harvard Square that morning. Not being married, not living together, was the best thing that had happened to their relationship. It had taken Emily a long, horrible period of indecision and uncertainty, but she'd finally asked Rick to leave.

He dropped her off at the corner near the camera shop, promising to pick her up again by five. She thanked him for the ride and slid through the slush to the shop. Pulling her gloves off with her teeth, she fumbled in her coat pocket for the key and got the door open. She flipped on the lights and, without taking off her coat, went to the back to start the coffee.

"I promise I'll change," Rick had pleaded, dumbfounded that Emily actually planned to end their marriage.

She had understood the marriage was over long before he did, and she began, without him, the long road to growing up. By the end, Rick clearly was relieved to be away.

Now, a few years later, things between them couldn't be more amicable. Emily believed there was no need to rehash everything, to relive every crime and miscommunication.

"Of course it's all extremely amicable," Vivian had said. "You're not asking for any support money and you're still screwing him."

Gemma gasped every time that was mentioned. Emily was not sure if Gemma was more upset at the lack of alimony or the sex.

She poured herself a cup of coffee and sat at the desk in the back room, idly sorting through photos. She loved coming in early, before the shop opened, before Bernie showed up, sitting with her coffee and flipping through pictures.

She and Rick still had dinner together with the kids a few nights a month. Usually he'd pick up takeout from his favorite ethnic restaurant of the month. Recently it had been Indian. It was hard to remember what she had ever found so compelling about this man. He was a tenured professor, pushing forty, hair a little too shaggy and now bald on top, dating a series of graduate students, although he swore they weren't from his department.

Of course, her disinterest had a lot to do with Evan. Emily decided that it took two men to make a perfect man. Rick was not the greatest husband material, but he was attentive with the kids; and Evan was too self-absorbed to be aware of details, like children, but he made her feel exquisite—sexy and wild.

Maybe it took three men if you counted Bernie. Emily rose to refill her mug. Bernie was now teaching her everything about the business: he kept threatening to retire and travel the world. In the meantime she took pictures of birthday parties for extra money. She would arrive early before preparations and stay through the cleanup. Jessica, at eleven, thought she was the luckiest of luckiest to always have a birthday party to go to on Saturdays.

Emily divided her pictures into sets. The ones with the radiant child, the friends, the presents, and the cake—those she got paid for. The ones of the mother cleaning, the mother decorating, the mother comforting the over stimulated child, the cleaning again of the house sticky with popcorn and chocolate—

those she got thanks for.

"So you always remember what you go through," Emily said when she gave them the pictures.

But what she really wanted to do was to make a difference. She still wanted her pictures to change the world, but she had reconciled herself to maybe having to wait until the kids were older. She tried to remember to be proud of herself, like Alix told her. "Remember, you're a single mom, supporting two kids, working, running a house. Maybe this has to be enough for now," Alix had said.

It wasn't, though. Emily gathered the pink invoices strewn on the desk and began to put them in files. She wasn't sure where this ambition, this far-reaching, star-reaching ambition, came from, but it made her life uncomfortable. It meant she never could be where she was. If she was at the camera shop, she should be home. If she was home, she should be shooting film. If she was shooting film, she should be food shopping.

She retrieved two invoices that fluttered to the floor. She had recently got a picture into the *Boston Globe* of women demonstrating against the nuclear power plant in Seabrook, New Hampshire. Alix kept telling her to revel in all the successes, even the small ones, not only the big stuff.

"Why don't you ever do anything? Why do you let things just happen?" she remembered yelling at her mother. "I will never let a man do that to me."

She rose and went to refill her coffee cup once again, and then stood staring out at the street as the traffic increased along with the snow. The judgments of daughters. Her poor mother had withstood five of them. She no longer faulted her father for his affair. She now understood how these things happen, but she'd never forgiven him for the fissure in her relationship with her mother—and she vowed she would never create such a breech between Jess and her father.

On the slippery sidewalk, treacherous with hidden ice and accumulating snow, some people teetered as if any moment their feet would go out from under them. Others walked as if it were summer, while others wore shoes with treads, totally prepared. She saw Bernie striding, hatless, his scarf around his neck, his cane offering a sense of invulnerability.

Of course it was unfair of her to blame her father for her betrayal of her mother. He had not forced her to keep his secret. She could have told her mother at any moment that he was having an affair. But she hadn't. And that meant she still felt the secret wedged between her and her mother. No, she would never do such a thing to her children.

The low heels of Gemma's boots clicked on the linoleum, echoing down the deserted hall. Most everyone cleared out of the courthouse by five in the afternoon. A few straggling lawyers in the prosecutor's office stayed late, like she did, finishing up paperwork with the overhead fluorescent lights flickering in the winter gloom.

During the day the courthouse was a bustle of shouting voices and scurrying people on their way to meetings, files flung into briefcases, suit jackets thrown on as they skipped down the marble stairs.

But in winter, at night in January, the windows were dark behind the blinds and the shadows felt deep. She poked her head into John's office, one of the few that had a light on.

"Leaving soon?" she asked. Of course it was a stupid question. His shirtsleeves were rolled above the elbow, his tie was curled like a dead snake on top of a teetering pile of folders. A few remaining fries smeared with ketchup sat on a paper plate on a slightly lower pile of files.

"I have to finish this by tomorrow." He sighed and rolled back in his chair. "Probably another three hours. Want to stay and help?"

Gemma laughed and shook her head no as she was expected to, but part of her wanted to say yes so she could avoid walking to her car alone in the cavernous parking garage.

She checked in on Joan in the public defender's office, but her office was dark. In the past seven years, more and more women lawyers had been hired in the prosecutor's office, and President Reagan had even appointed Sandra Day O'Connor, the first woman to the Supreme Court, in his first year of office. She sighed and headed back toward the exit. Nothing to do but go for it. She pushed open the door to the stairwell and headed downstairs to the lobby.

She generally was more careful about making sure she wasn't the only one staying late. Casually at lunch, or in the copy room, she'd mention having to work late, and listen for the groans of "Me too" and then tag along when they straggled out. Tonight she had women's group, so she'd planned to leave right at five, but she'd let time slip away and now had to walk alone.

She called Willie from the lobby pay phone, postponing her trip to the garage a moment longer. She'd tried to reach him before leaving her office, but he hadn't picked up. Probably still in meetings. As principal of the high school, he spent hours in meetings after the school day ended.

"Yes." Willie's voice snapped into the phone.

"Hello is the accepted convention for answering phones."

"Hey, babe." With those two syllables he somehow conveyed comfort, wide shoulders, easy smiles, and an undertone of sexy.

"I'm done for the day and heading off to group. Just wanted to say hi and see how late you'll be working."

"Board meeting, but shouldn't be too bad. And yes, I did eat. And yes, I did remember to drink lots of water. And yes, I did take a walk at lunch." He laughed, making fun of her worries and clearly pleased at her continual concern. "I should be home about ten."

The elevator took Gemma from the lobby to the parking garage. Why, she wondered, as the sound of her steps rebounded off the concrete pillars and slabs, if the garage was still so full of cars, were there never crowds of people walking in it? There were only distant sounds, a car door slamming, some footsteps echoing down a ramp, a motor starting. She detested parking garages.

Of course, she knew that parking on the street was no guarantee of safety. Her newest client was a case in point. Mother of three, out shopping, got into her car to pick up her kids from school. A man hid in the backseat. He forced her to drive to Forest Hills Cemetery and then he raped her.

Gemma heard footsteps behind her but didn't turn around. She was spooking herself. The other thing she hated about this garage in particular was that it was a winding, loopy thing and the walk to the car from the elevator was long.

Mary, the woman in the new rape case, was insisting on going public with her name. When the story came out in *The Globe,* it reported that *Gary Stevens, age 33, was arrested and charged with assault on a woman in Forest Hills.* Mary called the paper and gave her name and said the charge was rape. The editor said it was against the *Globe*'s policy to publish the name of rape victims. Gemma had promised she'd call the editor for her.

The footsteps were definitely closing in on her. Definitely male, loud clear, not heels and not threatening. Threatening would be if they were hesitant, or trying for soft. Her car was just around the last bend.

"Why should I hide?" Mary had asked her. "This happened to me, not some nameless, faceless victim. They're acting like being raped is some terrible shame. Women need to come out about this, give their names, tell their stories. I will not be made invisible." Then she had burst into sobs, but kept talking. "Make no mistake." Mary wiped her tears. "I can weep and be fierce at the same time."

The footsteps were right behind her. Maybe she should carry a gun. Great, the way her adrenaline was flowing, she'd end up killing someone. The person behind her could be a judge, or another lawyer from any of the downtown firms. This whole garage was full of the legal profession. Time to get a fucking grip. Why the fuck was no one else around?

When she had finally reached the *Globe* editor, he said, "You can't let her do that." His voice was kind, almost fatherly. "Listen, honey, she'll become fair game to every crazy who feels she's no longer off limits. People will look at her differently. She'll be seen as broken, damaged goods. Her kids will be teased at school."

So much was wrong with those statements, it made her weak with exhaustion. Here was this nice man, with all his power, trying to be protective, and instead was insulting and didn't even know it.

The man was still walking behind her. Her car was right up ahead, but she didn't want to get trapped in her car like Mary.

She spun around. "Halt." She yelled it at full volume; her voice reverberated down the ramps.

He stopped so fast, he wavered on his feet, and he looked up, startled. He was a good ten feet away. He was thin, his suit rumpled from the day, and carrying a briefcase. He was younger than she was, maybe in his late twenties, probably a first year in some downtown law firm.

"Don't you know fucking better than to follow a woman in a deserted parking garage?" She gave her voice power, hoping some other person somewhere would appear.

"So then I got in my car," Gemma said, taking the tea Vivian held out to her, "and left this poor schlub of a kid, who was probably doing nothing more than daydreaming how he could impress his boss or screw his secretary, standing frozen with his mouth open as I drove off."

"You're losing it." Vivian lifted the teacup out of Gemma's hand and replaced it with a glass of wine.

"Yeah, not my proudest moment." She sipped the wine. "But how are we supposed to know? Am I feeling fear because I really am in a dangerous situation and it's an instinctive signal that I should get the hell out of there? Or am I feeling fear because I have an overactive imagination? I mean, women get into bad situations all the time because they think their fears are crazy or paranoid or they're overreacting."

Vivian shrugged. "Just park on the street."

Gemma nodded as if considering it, but thought of Mary who hadn't seen the guy in the backseat. She didn't need to tell that story.

"Or take the train," Emily said.

Logical and reasonable, but why couldn't she park in the same garage as all her colleagues and half the legal profession of Boston without her heart jumping out of her chest?

"I'm scared of so much these days."

"Gemma," Alix said, "you work every day with women who are beaten and raped, and you try to get the bad guys put away in a world that doesn't consider violence against women to be such a big issue. Doesn't it make sense that you might feel vulnerable?"

It made sense, but she didn't like it. She was raised to be fearless. And if she hadn't actually achieved that, she had at least been able to pretend. But now even that was becoming difficult.

She thought of Tim, the prosecutor who'd trained her. If anything had happened in that garage, people would tsk and shake their heads, and then they'd ask: Why was she walking alone in a deserted garage? Was she nuts? The question would not be, Why isn't it fucking safe for a woman to retrieve her goddamn car after work? How was it that the questions were about why would women take such risks, as opposed to, How do we make it safer?

She grabbed a slice of cheese and a cracker and tuned back into the conversation as Alix said, "... there Dave was, shivering on the curb, jacket hunched around his ears, in the dark and the sleeting rain. He wasn't wearing hat or gloves, of course, because that's not cool for middle-school boys. He looked so wet and dejected."

She flopped back against the couch. "How do I say: 'Sorry, sweetie, I forgot you'? Or 'my work is so much more important than you are'?

"He told me he could have hitched a ride with one of the other drama-club kids, or walked home, but he didn't want me to worry when I showed up and he wasn't there. He said he knew I probably had an emergency.

"But I hadn't, of course. I just simply forgot."

Gemma arranged her face to appear sympathetic, but she was thinking, Where was Sam in all this? Why wasn't Sam feeling this guilt? Gemma wanted to scream at them all, *It's not fair.*

"I'm also losing it," Alix said. "I'm dropping balls everywhere."

Gemma wasn't surprised. Alix was now co-directing the Women's Health Center, and the pressure was intense as the antiabortion movement gained momentum.

Alix blew out a stream of air. "It actually was easier when they were younger and I wasn't trying to coordinate between school projects, drama club, soccer, my meetings, Sam's meetings, not to mention making sure we have food."

Emily nodded and passed Alix the plate of fruit.

"When I called my mother this week, I told her she'd been

right all along." Alix popped a grape in her mouth. "It may be possible to work full-time and raise a family, but it's not feasible that both can be done well."

Both Emily and Vivian started to object, but Alix continued, "I expected her to be a little smug with the 'I told you so's'. Instead, she says, 'I can't talk long, ketzalah, because I have to get to my board meeting.' But don't just kvetch, figure it out.'" Alix laughed, pulling more grapes from the bunch. "Ahh, the tables turn. But I did tell Sam last night that we need a wife. A nice asexual, 1950s wife."

Vivian dumped flyers on the coffee table, along with staplers and a list of addresses. "Speaking of not whining, let's get to work."

Gemma groaned as she picked up a flyer. Vivian was on the organizing committee for the upcoming rally on the Boston Common of the Women's Truth Squad on Reagan, which hoped to get the word out about his anti-choice policies and to increase voter registration. Now that she'd finally gotten a promotion and was lead trainer on the new IBM computers, she had volunteered to print out the flyers for the group. So whenever the women met at Vivian's, they were pressed into service to get out the mailings.

"Katie got detention for cutting study hall," Vivian said as she folded a flyer into thirds. "When I confronted her, she asked me, didn't you get in trouble for demonstrating against the Vietnam War? Didn't you used to refuse to wear makeup and shave your legs to prove you wouldn't be bought by the capitalistic regime?" Vivian put her folded flyers in a pile next to Emily. "I'm thinking, she's kind of got the history and protests of the times a little mixed up, though the general gist is there, but I'm still unclear about what this has to do with cutting study hall. Then she asks me why I haven't held tight to my values?" Vivian waved a flyer at them. "And then she stands very straight, thrusts her chin out, and pronounces: 'I will not go to study hall. I will not waste my time following stupid rules that even the teachers who enforce them cannot tell me what they are for. I have a life to lead and I will not waste my time.'

"So, I say," Vivian said, taking a new pile of flyers, "we all have to do shit work sometimes. And then Katie says: 'If I start compromising now, I will compromise my life away and not even remember what I was so upset about, just like you did.'"

Emily was stapling, Alix was addressing, and Gemma was stamping. Vivian stood and stretched, arching her back. "It's going to be a long, long adolescence." She turned to Gemma. "And no, I haven't called that number you found for Jerry."

Gemma raised her eyebrows. "Did I even ask?" It had been over six months since she had located Jerry and given Vivian the number, and Vivian still hadn't found the courage to call. Gemma understood that, understood that she might never call, but at least she had the option now. When it had taken so long to find him, Gemma had wondered if maybe Vivian had made him up—the story of a really nice guy who was Katie's father. Now she worried that maybe Vivian had simply made up the nice guy part, and the reason she wasn't calling was because Jerry was really a jerk, maybe even dangerous, and Vivian knew she had to protect Katie from her father.

Emily pushed herself off the floor. "Well, Matt had his first heartbreak. Sixteen and just miserable." She picked up a pile of finished flyers. "So miserable. He finally got the courage to ask this girl out and she said no. There is nothing that causes me to obsess like unhappy children."

"Tomorrow," Gemma announced as she also stood and stretched, "I'm signing us all up for Model Mugging." She headed toward the kitchen. "Katie and Jessica should come too." She paused to ask if anyone wanted tea.

Following her, Vivian said, "I've heard of Model Mugging. Isn't it where women beat up on some guy in padding?"

"And why would we want to do this?" Emily asked, taking out the mugs.

"It's a self-defense class," Gemma said. "I want to learn to fight with my body. I need to know I can do it. And next week we're all marching in the Take Back the Night Rally. I'm done being afraid."

"Afraid?" Vivian said. "You're the toughest broad I know."

Gemma smiled. "Didn't your mother ever teach you that only scaredy-cats act tough all the time?"

CHAPTER THIRTY

February 15, 1984
One month later

"Ouch." Emily sat cross-legged on her living room floor in her T-shirt and jeans while twelve-year-old Jessica stood behind her brushing her hair.

"Oops. Sorry, Mom." Jessica slowed the brush. "But don't wiggle and it won't hurt." Jessica loved playing with her hair and was practicing how to braid.

The kids had reached the perfect age. She had cozy moments like this with Jessica, and just last week she and Matt, at sixteen, had discussed apartheid in South Africa. The workings of his mind intrigued her, just as she'd been enthralled by his learning to walk.

Jessica's fingers combed through her hair as she took out a braid and started over. "Hmm," Emily murmured. "That feels nice."

"Going to Steven's," Matt called from the hall, opening the front door.

"Homework?" Emily called back.

"Done."

"Kiss?"

He clumped into the living room and bent low to peck her cheek. She felt the stubble on his face and marveled at the coming man. He grinned and poked Jessica. "Great job, Jess. Now

Mom looks like the wicked witch of the west."

Jessica swung the hairbrush at him.

"Take your warm jacket," Emily ordered as he left the room. "It's freezing out there." He pretended not to hear her and closed the door.

Emily reached for her coffee cup, trying to keep as still as possible while Jessica concentrated on her braiding. She'd moved the kids into this first-floor apartment last fall, a rent-controlled apartment in a cul-de-sac outside of Harvard Square, full of sun and only four houses down from Rick.

"This is a good thing?" Vivian had said when she told group about it. Emily had nodded, ignoring Vivian's sarcasm. It meant Matt and Jessica could go back and forth between the houses on their own.

The house faced south, and the living room had a bay window that Vivian had filled with plants she grew from her own cuttings. The sun streamed in and lit up the bright pillows and colorful quilt placed strategically to cover the holes in the secondhand couch. The people upstairs were grad students and studied at the library, so Emily and the kids pretty much had the backyard to themselves. She planned to put in a big garden. Two large maples stood out front, big old respectable fellows, older already than she'd probably ever get to be, who had greeted them with a show of red the day they moved in. On one side were a lilac bush, a scraggly forsythia she could tend and bring back to bushy life, and a pussy willow beginning to bud.

She even could walk to the camera shop from here. In the mornings she dropped Jessica at her school bus, bought the *Boston Globe* from Pete on the corner of Mt. Auburn, and gave Laura, who carried everything she owned in a shopping cart, whatever change she had in her pocket and chatted with her about the weather. It had taken a while, but she finally felt part of this little neighborhood in Cambridge.

She straightened her legs with a groan. "Hey, sweetie, I really need to move my head soon or it will freeze like this forever. Almost done?"

"No. Don't move yet." Jessica's fingers were still fiddling. "I had to start over."

"Just a few more minutes, sweet pea." Emily shifted her weight.

"Mom, will my hair ever be as long as yours?"

She smiled. "Patience. It will grow. Remember, I am a lot older than you."

"You are so beautiful." Jessica let out a big sigh. "I hope I'm as beautiful as you when I grow up."

Emily spun around and grabbed Jessica, pulling her onto her lap. "Mom," Jessica screeched, clearly torn between twelve-year-old dignity and childish delight.

"You're already gorgeous," Emily said, and kissed her head. But, she noted, this was a question Matt had never asked. At twelve he'd been much more concerned with his batting average than his looks. She sighed. Tonight was movie night and they were watching *Grease.* Maybe that wasn't the best choice.

Monday morning, Emily felt the pea-sized hardness in her breast while taking a shower, before getting Jessica and Matt breakfast. She wiped the steam off the mirror.

"I have no clean socks," Matt yelled through the bathroom door.

"I can't find my backpack," Jessica added.

"Come down to the clinic now," Alix ordered when Emily called her. "I'll ask the nurse practitioner, to check it out for you."

"Oh, it feels like a cyst," said the nurse. "Don't worry about it. Go to your doctor and have him check it out just in case. He might want to aspirate it, just so you'll absolutely know not to worry."

"We really should have this biopsied," Dr. Rosen said. "I don't think there's any problem, but I like to be safe."

One week later, Dr. Rosen called before dinner. "It's positive. Call the office tomorrow and tell Harriet I want to fit you in and we'll talk about what we have to do next."

Emily went into the bathroom feeling sick. She sat down across from the toilet, leaning back against the towels. The tile grout should be cleaned. She remembered a few years ago, when she first found out about cleaning the tile grout. Up until then she hadn't noticed; she just thought it was discolored. But no, there was a special tile-grout cleaner. It would clean off your skin too. The kind of cleaning agent that said on the label to open all windows, be in a well-ventilated area, use only for short period of times. The grout came up white. She thought maybe her mother never cleaned tile grout; maybe that's why she hadn't known. But when she went up for Thanksgiving that year and checked out the bathroom, the grout was sparkling. She was always finding out about new things to clean that everyone else somehow always knew about.

She heard the front door close. That must be Jessica. She got off the floor, washed her face, flushed the toilet, and called out hello.

She hadn't told Matt or Jessica about going for the biopsy, because she'd been so sure it would turn out to be nothing. Now she wished she had. They at least would be prepared. Now she would have to come out of the blue and tell her adolescent children that their mother had cancer.

"Mom, can we drive Marta to gymnastics and her mom will drive us home?"

"Sure." Emily headed for the kitchen. "Are you hungry?" She would be leaving with Jessica before Matt got back from basketball practice. She would make spaghetti and let everyone eat whenever they were hungry.

She wanted a cigarette. She deserved a cigarette. After all, when you find out you have cancer, don't you deserve a cigarette?

She called Alix.

It turned out there was a lot of work involved in a diagnosis of breast cancer. Many decisions to be made; a great deal of research to do. No one talked about this part of it. Everyone spoke of the horror of losing a breast, or the fear of dying, but no one talked about the work of interviewing doctors, making choices, the exhaustion of so many options. This was part of the benefits of the women's health movement. It used to be you went in for a biopsy, and if you were lucky you woke up with all your body parts still there. If not, you woke up without a breast and half your chest wall. She knew this was better, but she felt overwhelmed with the decisions.

Over the next few weeks Gemma did the research, spending hours in the medical school library reading outcome studies of chemotherapy vs. radiation, lumpectomy vs. radical mastectomy. Vivian brought her bags of fresh fruit and vegetables that she also cooked into delicious meals for her. Alix took her to the doctors' appointments and made her write out lists of questions because her brain had gone fuzzy with fear.

Emily wanted her mom. She wanted someone she believed to tell her it would all be okay.

"So call your mom," Alix said, and handed her the phone.

Two days later Emily sat by the window at Vincent's, in Concord, New Hampshire waiting. She saw her mother walking toward the restaurant, hatless, her gray hair twisted on top of her head, somehow looking elegant even wearing a down maroon vest over her flannel shirt and jeans, with her wool scarf wrapped around her neck against the cold. Her mother was fifty-six. Emily wondered if she'd get to be that old.

She waved as her mother entered the restaurant.

Her mother smiled and walked over, pecking her cheek as she slid into the booth. "What's all the fuss?"

Emily suddenly felt silly and melodramatic and selfish. Just as she'd felt as a teenager.

"Can we walk first or are you starving?" She stood before her mother could fully unwrap.

Emily told the waitress they'd be back, and then linked arms with her mother as they left the restaurant and headed toward the river path.

"So," she began, "remember the summer before I left home?"

Her mother stopped. "You're the mother of a sixteen and a twelve-year-old? Do you think you'll forget when Matt leaves?"

"Right." Emily felt chastised. Were you ever not a child with your parents? "Well, anyway." She started walking again. "There's something I never told you, and I've felt guilty for years and …" She paused and right then decided not to tell her mother. She realized finally, after all these years, what would be the point?

"Please, Emily, just get to it. You're making me crazy with anxiety with all this lead up."

"Well, when Rick and I split, I blamed it all on him. What I never told anyone was that I also had an affair." She had to tell her mother something.

Her mother let out a big sigh. "I know." She squeezed Emily's arm. "God, you had me so scared this was going to be some extremely bad news."

"You knew? How could you possibly know?"

Her mother smiled. "A mother knows these things. And anyway, for a while there all you talked about when I called was some painter you'd met. Just count yourself lucky you don't live in a small town. When your father and I went through similar troubles, everyone knew."

"You knew about dad?" Emily slipped on an ice patch, and her mother steadied her.

"Honey, as I just said, we live in a small town."

Emily felt furious and foolish at the same time, not a great combination for rational behavior and thought. She forced herself to remain silent.

"Your father and I had an unspoken understanding," her mother went on. "I pretended I didn't know and he pretended I didn't know, as husbands and wives have done in our town since they stole it from the Indians."

Emily stayed silent. Their boots crunched in the packed snow.

"But everything was all upside down back then in the sixties. Everything was changing, and I thought, why is it okay for him and not me?" Her mother gave a little laugh. "What really almost ended our marriage was when I had an affair with Al Sweeney."

Emily sat quickly on the nearest bench. Ice flows drifted with the current of the river. Her mother said this as if it didn't change the cellular makeup of memories.

"Can we go eat now?" Her mother stood by the bench.

"Sit for a minute. There is something else."

"It's cold. Can't we talk inside?"

Emily looked up at her mother, silhouetted against the sun and said. "I have breast cancer."

Her mother sat, grabbed Emily's mittened hand and pulled it onto her lap. "You will be fine. I have a ton of questions; but I know as only a mother can, that you will be fine."

CHAPTER THIRTY-ONE

March 24, 1984
Six weeks later

"**I** don't know what the hell you want from me," Sam bellowed, rising from his chair, his eyes both angry and panicked.

But then again, she'd interrupted *Miami Vice*, where muscled men, much younger than Sam, successfully fought the bad guys and bedded the beauties with fake breasts.

"I work hard," he said. Alix watched from her perch on the ottoman as he paced from the television to couch, barely suppressing his urge to bolt from the apartment and be done with this. "I don't screw around; I food shop; I cook dinners when you have to be at meetings; I make lunches." He pivoted. "I even supported you going back and taking classes toward your master's degree. I could keep going, but it doesn't matter. It's never enough."

He held up his hands. In surrender? In supplication? "What the hell do you want?" His voice was a low growl.

"I want you to feel despair and self-loathing when Mike has to wear a wet basketball uniform because I, never *we*, forgot to move the laundry to the dryer last night. I want your insides to clutch with panic when you see Dave's permission slip and money for today's field trip still on the car seat, and if you turn around and speed through red lights you might get back to the school before the bus leaves; but you'll miss the board meeting where you're supposed to do a presentation on the recent clinic bombings."

He stopped pacing and looked at her. "You want me to be miserable?"

"Stop being an asshole and listen." She stood to face him. "I'm failing here. I can't do this all by myself. It's too much."

"Don't blame me," he shouted. "I told you you couldn't manage." He waved his hand through the air. "Give something up."

"Like what?" she yelled back. "A kid? The house? My job?" She stepped toward him. "You?"

This was not anything serious. Alix sipped an amaretto brandy, sitting in the rocker wrapped in a blanket. It was three a.m.

It was a slow unraveling. It had started with leaving Dave on the curb in the rain and escalated with Emily's cancer diagnosis. Running late for work almost every morning this week didn't help.

It was a slow unraveling. Maybe she was naive, believing the world had changed completely for her generation of women, that she was now mistress of her own life. When she was little, her aunt Rose gave her biographies of women to read. Marie Curie, Florence Nightingale, and she tried to imagine herself into those lives, determined to be as courageous.

"I don't know how to knit it all back together," she told her reflection in the dark glass of the window. There was no one else to tell at this hour.

After Davey was born, she realized her life course had changed. Her very bones and muscles had been twisted into new shapes. But for Sam, his life simply became busier, harder to schedule. She kept trying to get him to understand this, so it wouldn't be so unfair.

Or maybe she was the one who was being unfair?

After all, she grew up with images of women on TV reaching orgasm as they removed ring around the collar. He grew up with images of men going off—to war, to work, to the moon, to other women—and kissing the sleeping kids on the forehead when they returned.

Part of her understood Sam's frustration. The women's movement had exploded into the world and women had said YES. It felt right; it was intuitive. It gave a language to things they had felt since little girls. *Of course I am equal. Of course I have value.*

The men in their lives were baffled. Why are you upset? What is wrong?

This made sense to Alix. They were being toppled from the top of the pyramid and it would take a while for them to grasp that living on a point like that gave them precious little room to maneuver. It would take a while for them to grasp that they might have more if they gave up a little.

But the men were bewildered. They didn't feel powerful. How could they give up what they didn't have?

Vivian and Gemma had both jumped down her throat when she said that the other night.

What do you mean they don't feel powerful? What do you mean they don't have power? They control all the purse strings, all the positions.

Alix held her ground. *Some* men hold all the purse strings. *Some* men have these positions of power. But most men are just bumbling along, hoping to get laid.

Alix understood.

The rules were changing and women were saying, "Oh, finally!" As if they'd been confined to a room with not enough air or space and really hadn't noticed until the door swung open. But the men were saying, "What room? What door? What the fuck are you talking about?"

She went to the kitchen, turning on the overhead light, and watched the cockroaches scurry. She hated this part of living in the city. She grabbed a wooden spoon they kept for this purpose and started killing. She heard Sam stir.

All the women she knew were involved in map making, re-envisioning the contours of a woman's life. For them the change risked being a narrative of failure—failure of floors to sparkle, of children to thrive, of careers to be recognized.

For the men, the change provoked a narrative of heroism — look, I take the kids food shopping; look, I make lunches and *still* I provide.

She returned with more brandy to the rocker and her blanket by the window.

Monday, Alix dressed in her navy suit and stockings, put on full makeup, and went to her appointment with the director of the Jamaica Plain Multi-Service Center, to talk about her idea for groups for adolescent girls.

Alix liked Jim well enough. As an experienced fundraiser and political organizer, he was well known in the progressive, liberal human-services community. And of course, like all service agencies, the center needed private funding to stay afloat as more and more government programs were cut as a result of Reagan's belief in trickle-down economics.

Jim smiled broadly as she entered, coming from behind his desk to clasp her hand in both of his. He was charming, the kind of man that made you feel you had made his day just by crossing his path. Today he was dressed in a suit and tie for a fundraiser later that day. His hair was almost completely gray and he trimmed his beard close to his face.

"Coffee?" He pointed to the coffee maker.

"No, thanks." Alix smoothed her skirt as she sat on a chair in the conversational grouping he'd arranged at one end of the room.

She handed him a file folder as soon as he got his coffee and settled behind his desk. "I want to do a class on growing up female." When she had said that in group, Vivian told her she made growing up female sound like an affliction.

Jim was silent.

Alix continued. "I want to start offering sex-education classes for girls thirteen and over." She pointed to the file. "I wrote up a syllabus and plan for you to look at, but basically we would cover sex, birth control, menstruation, pregnancy, changing bodies, preventing sexually transmitted diseases, relationships, attitudes toward women, life goals. That sort of thing. An expanded *Our Bodies Ourselves*."

Jim laughed and crossed his legs. "Not too ambitious, are you?"

Alix relaxed. "It would be great, sort of like facilitated consciousness-raising groups for teenagers. The girls I see are so hungry for basic information."

"We can't do it."

"Why not?"

"Too much controversy. The funders wouldn't like it." He beamed at her. "I personally think it is a superb idea, but the timing is off. The political climate has changed." He put on a sorrowful face.

Alix nodded and arranged her own face to show sympathy with his sorrow, while rage radiated heat through her body. "I get these kids after they're pregnant, or raped, or so devoid of hope they're strung out. I want them before."

Jim stood. "I'm sorry, Alix. It is a good idea—but before it's time." He bent to take the folder with her materials in it, but she grabbed it first.

§　§　§

"Can you believe it?" Alix reached for her coffee, so angry the cup rattled in its saucer.

"So do it anyway." Emily swallowed her grapefruit juice. The four of them were having breakfast after working out at the Y. It had become an early Saturday morning routine to meet at the diner after their workouts. Of course, sometimes they skipped the workouts and just met at the diner.

"I can't simply 'do it anyway.'" This made Alix even angrier, so she decided to have butter on her toast. And jelly. Since the cancer, Emily sometimes made pronouncements with an edge that was unsaid, but not really unspoken, a silent, *What are you waiting for? Now or never. Stop whining and get on with it.*

"Just call the classes something else, like …" Emily paused as she added lox to her bagel. "Like The Art of Makeup."

"Or Skills Needed around the House," Gemma added.

"Or Be a Charming Woman." Vivian laughed.

Four weeks later, Alix held her first class. She called it Life Skills for Women and proceeded to do exactly what she wanted, just as Emily had suggested.

She started with six fifteen-year-old girls and they met in the basement of the center after school. Heating pipes crisscrossed the ceiling and loud hisses and knocks came from the boiler, but she'd made the group come and paint the walls bright colors, and Vivian got an old rug donated for the floor. She'd set up folding chairs and a table, and laid out a snack of cheese, crackers, cookies, and soda.

"My father caught me kissing my boyfriend." The girl who sat across from her had blond hair that fell in soft waves around her face. Pale soft curls against the black leather jacket, black jeans, black nail polish. "He said if I was going to be a slut, I shouldn't bother coming home."

"For kissing?" the girl next to her asked.

"My parents won't let me date at all," said another girl with a pierced nose. "I have to sneak out at night."

Alix sighed inwardly. In 1984 the concerns were not all that different from when she was in high school.

CHAPTER THIRTY-TWO

May 25,1984
Two months later

V ivian dumped the top drawer of her dresser onto her bed, searching for her sunglasses. It was 3:30 and now she was late. She had left work early to get a workout in before packing to go to Provincetown for Memorial Day weekend.

After Emily's first round of chemotherapy, she'd come to group and announced, "I have cancer, but I am not dying." She had sat in the rocker and pointed her finger as if they had been arguing with her. "I am beating this. I am going to see my kids grow up." She rocked forward, planted her feet on the ground, and sat up straight as if for emphasis. "And I want to be able to talk about the cancer. I will gladly accept any help you want to give. But I am not dying and I am not pretending I don't have cancer." She resumed rocking and then stopped again. "Don't reduce me to being ..." She hesitated and then found the words. "Don't go treating me like all I am is a woman with breast cancer."

"Oh, good," Vivian had said to her. "Because for a while there, I was afraid you were going to make us take up running for breast-cancer marathons."

Vivian peeked in on Katie, who at fourteen was not happy she had to stay with Sam and Alix's boys for the weekend. At least she had begun to pack. Vivian went back to searching for those damn glasses. They were taking Emily to Provincetown for her thirty-fourth birthday. This year they'd decided they had better start celebrating.

Vivian pulled out a tank top and shorts, then sweatpants and a sweatshirt. She threw in another sweater. In May on the ocean, the weather could do anything. She took back out the pair of shorts that were tight last summer. No need to depress herself. She found her baggy shorts and put those in.

She checked on Katie's progress again. "Why can't I come with you?" Katie had asked last night before dinner.

"You have your swim meet tomorrow. And Sam is going as your honorary dad."

"But what are you going to do?" Katie almost wailed.

Vivian stopped putting out plates on the table. Gathering Katie in her arms, she led her to the couch to cuddle.

"We're going to talk." She smoothed Katie's hair back from her forehead, realizing Katie must imagine all sorts of wonderful, exotic women activities that were a mystery to her. "Honey, really, mostly we just talk. Eat some food, drink some wine, and talk."

Vivian drove to pick up Emily first. She was waiting outside on the stairs with her suitcase. Vivian got out of the car to help her. "I'm fine," Emily called, and waved her away.

Vivian opened the trunk and watched Emily walk down the path.

Her hair hung in thin, limp strands. She hadn't lost all of it and was proud of that. Otherwise she looked unexpectedly strong and healthy.

"Oh, wait," she said when she handed Vivian her suitcase to put in the trunk. "I forgot my sweater." She hurried back into the house.

Vivian leaned against the car, feeling the warm metal

through her jeans. Before Emily had lost any hair, at the beginning of the chemotherapy, Vivian took her wig shopping at Filene's. The wigs hung on a wall or were displayed on the counter like hats. The exceptionally expensive human-hair wigs were inside the counter, behind glass like fine jewelry.

Emily and Vivian tried on short hair, curly hair, blond and red and jet-black, laughing at each other. Emily's hair was so thick and full and long, getting a wig over it was a project.

"Can I help you?" A saleswoman hovered.

"No." Vivian detested hovering, unwanted salespeople. "We're just experimenting."

"The wigs made from real hair look so much better," the saleswoman said, turning a key to slide the glass open on her side of the counter. She wore glasses perched on the end of her nose.

"We're just looking," Vivian said. "We'll let you know if we need anything."

"What do you need the wig for?" the woman asked, peering over her glasses.

Emily stopped laughing.

"We're just playing around," Vivian said. *None of your fucking business.*

"I have cancer and will lose my hair," Emily said.

"You know," said the saleswoman, not missing a beat, "you could cut your braid and have a wig made for when you need it. And no one could ever tell."

Emily turned and walked out without saying a word. Vivian ran after her.

"Blond and curly out of the 1930s or '40s," Emily said when Vivian had gotten her to sit for a snack and tea. "If I'm going to wear a wig, I want everyone to recognize it." She tore open the sugar packet with her teeth. "Do you know they're developing a procedure where a woman will go in for a mastectomy and they'll build her breast from her belly fat, so no one will know?"

She stirred her tea so vigorously, it slopped over the cup rim. "Who are we protecting from this information?" She blotted the spill with a napkin. "The cancer patient knows. The doctors know. The families know."

Oh, Em sweetie, Vivian had wanted to say. No one wants to have it thrown in their face that people get sick and die. Not young, beautiful people. Actually, we're not too happy about the old, wrinkled ones either. The only stage of life everyone wants to know about is between twenty and forty. Fifty, maybe, if you can look forty. Get sick, forget it. Out of the race, disqualified. Vivian wasn't sure where all this came from, but Gemma probably would give a speech about it soon.

Vivian's fingers drummed a rhythm on the car. Gemma kept researching study after study about the latest treatments and insisted on reporting them, as if she could suffocate the cancer under reams of information. Emily seemed to move faster and faster, as if believing that if she were a blur of constant motion, the cancer wouldn't be able to land on her again. Alix simply accepted. It was what it was. And Vivian saw Emily relax around her. Vivian knew she was happiest in denial. Cancer was a minor bump in the road, awful and scary, but something you recovered from. She refused to consider another outcome

She watched Emily walk back to the car with her sweater draped over her arm. Even Emily, with all her insistence on being visible, had her illusions. Her once glorious hair looked like shit, sort of like those men who grow three strands of hair very long on the side and comb it over their shiny heads. Vivian got in the car.

Provincetown, on the eastern tip of Cape Cod, was a magical place, part old fishing village, part artists' colony, part gay and lesbian Mecca. The ocean, the air, the sun were just what Emily needed.

They arrived as the sun lowered over the harbor, and they went to the Crown and Anchor to drink martinis on the porch and watch people promenade up and down Commercial Street.

"I finally reached Jerry," Vivian announced, stirring the olive-laden toothpick in her drink. She'd been holding this news the whole ride in the car. Over the past month, she'd called him a number of times, but she had kept getting his answering machine and didn't think she could just leave a message.

She looked up. The other women's expressions were carefully neutral but expectant. She laughed at them. "It was a bit anticlimactic. He did remember me, which was good. I had a moment of panic when I wondered if he would. He sounds great, we caught up. He worked for years in a relief agency in Africa, which explains not being able to find him for so long. Not married, no kids, teaching history now in middle school in San Francisco."

"So, don't leave us hanging." Gemma angled her chair to be able to put her feet up on the empty one across from her. "What happened when you told him about Katie?"

"I couldn't do it. I'm flying out this summer for the computer convention. I'll tell him then. Face to face will be easier.

"But too bad," she continued, "that I didn't find him earlier when Katie was still my golden girl. Did I tell you she called me a demanding bitch to her friend on the phone, just because I had asked her to clean up the kitchen?"

Emily scooped up a handful of peanuts. "I sometimes wish Jessica would call me names, just get angry and storm out. But she can't afford to do that. She worries that I might not be around forever."

Vivian ate an olive. "I hated my mother because she was vacant, had no substance. I tried to be a woman of substance for my daughter, and she calls me a demanding bitch."

"Did she clean up the kitchen?" Emily asked.

"Of course."

"Then you're doing fine."

Vivian didn't think she was doing so fine. Occasionally she and Katie could still dance around together in their PJs, but lately Katie had been telling her she danced funny, and the other day she had asked Vivian to change her outfit when they were going to the mall together.

Of course, Vivian had known the closeness of the early years would have to end, but she'd hoped they could stay the twosome team they'd always been. With her own mother, she was careful to call at least once a month, but they were awkward and short phone calls, reminding her of conversations in beginning Spanish.

Como esta?

Muy bien, et tu?

Bien gracias.

They established they both were fine and ran out of things to say. She dreaded the phone calls.

"Let's have another round," she said, waving her almost empty glass at the waiter. "Last week, I overheard Katie and her friends discussing their body flaws. Her friend Chris told her her ass was too big and now Katie worries that no boy will ever like her. So I sat her down and explained how luckily there are ass men and leg men and breast men. The women's magazines make you think there is only one type of woman that men like, but that wasn't true."

"You didn't!" Gemma looked appalled.

"We were not feminists all these years just so my daughter can obsess about her looks. I won't have it. I cancelled my subscriptions to *Glamour, Cosmo*, and *People*."

Alix laughed. She'd cut her hair and the curls sprang to life in the humid sea air. "So that's why you've been coming over checking out my magazines. And I thought you liked my company."

"God, you sound like me when I caught Matt with *Playboy* last year," Emily said. "Wasn't it you who told me not to be so rigid?"

"And then." Vivian leaned forward; this was worst part. "Katie goes and asks me last night how she can get boys to notice her. It can't be happening already. Does motherhood mean I have to live through this crap all over again?"

Gemma pointed to the street where men in drag handed out flyers to the evening shows. "We could learn a thing or two about not being so rigid about looks and gender stereotypes. As so many of those guys would agree."

"You're right." Vivian drained her drink and stood. "As I've been talking, I've been watching, and it's just driving me crazy that many of these guys look better turned out than I do."

She stepped down off the porch and approached a beautiful man in a blue sequined gown. "Excuse me." She smiled her most alluring smile. "I couldn't help but notice how gorgeous you look. Would you mind telling me where you got your wig and makeup done?"

The next morning, at the West End Salon, Stuart put Emily in a chair, covered her with a black apron, and walked around her, appraising her from all angles. He lifted her chin, tilted her head this way and that. He walked behind her and cupped his hands over her forehead. "You don't even need a wig," he pronounced. "You have gorgeous cheekbones. Your bone structure is like Audrey's." He looked over at them all, hovering like anxious grandmothers, and added, "Hepburn." As if he was interpreting for himself.

"Out." He waved his hand toward the door. "Go get coffee or something and come back in one hour." He turned his attention back to Emily. "We'll get rid of this sorry mess on your head and do your makeup and then you will see." He snipped at her long strands. "Of course, if you want to try a wig, we have some beauties. But you don't want anything that will overwhelm that face. Gary, come here." Stuart used his scissors to wave over a colleague. "You could die from this bone structure. No?" His hand lifted Emily's chin again. Vivian could see Emily suppressing a grin. "What do you think? Should we try her in that nice little red-headed number that Tommy brought in?"

Vivian watched Emily's face carefully as Stuart took the buzzer and shaved a swath of her head. She seemed to be doing okay. She herded Gemma and Alix out of the shop before Stuart yelled at them again.

An hour later Emily emerged into the bright sunlight with her red wig gently curling around her face and with a light touch of makeup. She whipped off her wig to reveal her bald head and ran her hand over it. "Stuart said I was so beautiful like this, that I didn't need it." She twirled the wig on her hand. "But I figured a bald mother might be tough on the kids at school events." She pulled the wig back on and straightened it in the reflection of a storefront window.

The rest of the day they lazily wandered in and out of shops, with Emily's new curls bouncing. The sun was warm, the gulls screeched, the air was salty and smelled of the sea. They weaved around families wheeling strollers and men with muscle shirts and tattoos holding hands. Women sat nuzzling each other on the park benches; artists sketched historic buildings; kids on skateboards claimed the street, forcing the cars to slow down. T-shirt shops, art galleries, taffy shops, fancy restaurants, and shops of sex toys that they'd never even imagined lined the streets. And in between the buildings, down alleyways, were glimpses of the harbor and the sparkling water.

They stopped at Bubala Restaurant where they could eat outside and people watch. Vivian had fallen in love with P-town.

That was what the locals called it. She loved the harbor, the sad sound of the lighthouse horn, the flamboyance, the tacky and artsy side by side, the freedom, and the seagulls calling.

She and Emily made a quick trip downstairs to the bathroom. "Do you like it?" Vivian asked, gesturing to the wig as they washed their hands. "You look so beautiful."

"Do you want to see it?" Emily asked. "My scar?"

Before Vivian could answer, she lifted her shirt. Where her breast used to be were angry red lines and puckered skin. Vivian grabbed Emily and hugged her, hiding her tears, smelling the urine and stale cigarettes as she stared at the graffiti on the tiles reporting that Chris loved Tom.

CHAPTER THIRTY-THREE

August 22 1984
Three months later

E mily walked home by way of Harvard Square, the evening
sun warm. A cap of her own dark, very short hair covered
her head and perfect strangers complimented her on the style.
In the front gardens of the clapboard houses, day lilies bloomed
in red, salmon, and the usual orange, while patches of purple,
white, and pink cosmos waved in the breeze. Bike riders wove
dangerously through the congestion of pedestrians, cars, and
taxis on Mass Ave. Near Church Street, she gave the coins in her
pocket to Mary, who worked the corner. Tonight group planned
to hear Gloria Steinem speak at the Brattle Theatre, but first they
were meeting to toast Geraldine Ferraro, the first woman vice-
presidential candidate, and she had left the shop early. Bernie
would close up.

For someone intent on retiring and traveling the world, he
hadn't changed his schedule much. Some days he took off with
his camera and didn't come in until noon. That was it.

"Stop bugging me," he'd say. "This is all the traveling I want
to do." And he'd wave his camera at her and stomp into the
darkroom.

Bernie had transferred the ownership of the camera shop to
her in June, insisting they do it immediately, so that he could
retire at any moment. Emily told him he'd probably outlive her,

but it seemed Bernie wanted to insure, in *that* unlikely event, that the shop would go to her kids.

"What will my kids do with a camera shop?"

"Sell it," he said. "It'll give them cash to start them on their way. And if you don't die, you'll have it."

Emily had wept when she asked Gemma to do the legal work. "How did I ever get so lucky?"

Gemma didn't think Emily was doing all that well in the luck department, but she agreed to draw up the papers.

In the weeks since Bernie turned over the shop to her, he'd started taking pictures again. He even taught an adult class in photography on Thursday nights. He seemed content to leave the bookkeeping, the ordering of inventory, and the general running of the shop to her. He did fuss about the hanging of the photos in the front room, so she left that to him. He actually smiled at customers now.

And last week, with Bernie's help, she sold her first book of photographs to a mainstream press. It was all old people, which was why Bernie loved it.

Past the Cambridge Common, Emily turned left and waved hello to a toddler pushing her own stroller. For the book, she'd photographed women stooped over and wrinkled; seventy-year-olds jogging around the Charles or out walking in pairs, dressed in sweat suits, arms swinging; grandparents playing with children; solitary men and women on buses. She really wanted to get old.

Reaching her house, she bounded up the front porch stairs and headed straight to the bathroom. She could hear the buzzing of an electric razor and assumed Matt was shaving. She knocked.

"Give me a few minutes." It was Jessica's voice.

She needed to get ready for the evening. She put the kettle on for tea. On the kitchen table Matt had propped a note between the salt and peppershakers: Out with Holly. Don't wait up.

She knocked on the bathroom door again.

"Cool your jets. I said I'd be out in a minute."

"It's Mom."

"Oh, sorry. I'll be done soon."

The kettle screeched. Emily poured the water to let the tea steep and then picked up Matt's note. Matt had fallen hard for Holly, but next month she was moving out of state with her family. The two of them moped, expressing the scope of the tragedy with every phone call. Emily couldn't be more pleased. She knew what happened when people got together too young.

She took her hot tea into the bedroom and tried to decide what to wear for an evening with Gloria Steinem. She didn't have time for a shower now. She would have to do what Vivian referred to as a whore's bath and sprinkle perfume in strategic places.

She sat at her dressing table, put on some blush, and picked out dangly earrings. She heard Jess moving between her bedroom and bathroom and called out for her to finish already. Emily put on lipstick, decided against the hanging earrings, and rummaged through her box, looking for the gold studs group had given her for her birthday. She heard Jess come into the room behind her and looked up. She gasped when she saw Jessica's bald head reflected in the mirror. It was like seeing her worst cancer-self return in some grotesque caricature on that twelve-year-old face.

"What have you done?" She spun around to face Jessica.

"Do you like it?" Jessica, all skinny arms and legs, stood there smiling tentatively.

"I couldn't look at her," Emily said as the four women settled in the restaurant booth. "All that glorious dark hair, gone." She sipped water. "Obviously, Jessica's going to be harder on me as a teenager than Matt ever was. I really hate Sinead O'Connor."

"Who?" Gemma asked, laughing as she passed out the menus.

"Some bald-headed singer from Ireland," Vivian said. "Don't laugh, teenage girls are no joke. I came home from work on Wednesday and there was Katie on the couch with a certain pimply boy." She shook her head. "Poor kid, she jumped so high. I must've really scared her. I sent Mr. Pimples packing and then sat down with Katie and said no boys over when I'm not home and I tried to tell her how important it was to look after herself. And she screams at me about how I don't trust her and how I don't let her breathe."

Vivian slid her pendant back and forth across the chain around her neck. "This from the girl I swore would not spend one moment questioning her worth or her mother's love. And she says I don't trust her? So I say, of course I trust her. She's got a great head on her shoulders, and I know she won't do anything foolish. I was just surprised."

"Did you give her condoms?" Alix asked.

"Are you nuts? She's fourteen years old."

"Age is not the point," Gemma said. "Information, is."

Vivian buckled her seat belt, removed her book from her bag, and stashed her carry-on under the seat in front of her, waiting for takeoff. First, she had to get through the two-day computer conference and then she'd meet Jerry.

"Scotch," she told the attendant.

Her fantasies about what would happen when she saw Jerry were out of control. She hadn't told anyone about them. She knew she was being ridiculous. Jerry had become her one true love and when she found him again, all would be well. Emily would stay healthy and Katie would be happy forever. She secretly cut out clippings of couples that found each other again after fifteen, twenty, thirty years, and lived in bliss from then on.

§   §   §

"So, Jerry. I have some news." Vivian stood in front of the hotel mirror practicing what to say. "You won't believe what I have to tell you." Discarded outfits covered the bed behind her. She finally decided on the old standby of t-shirt and jeans. "This might come as a shock." They were meeting at a coffee shop in Berkley. "Did you ever want to be a father?" Rejected openings crowded her head. "Do I have a surprise for you!" Damn. Vivian grabbed a linen jacket and headed out.

She recognized him immediately. He sat at a corner table reading the newspaper. He wore a plaid flannel shirt, jeans, and work boots. His ponytail and beard were gone, but his smile, when he saw her, was just the same.

He rose as she reached the table and bent forward as if to kiss her hello, but then pulled back and awkwardly held out his hand. She laughed, shook his hand and then kissed him on the cheek.

They sat in that shop for hours while Vivian asked him question after question about his travels and his work overseas and what brought him back to the States and how did he decide to teach history, keeping him talking and laughing, while another part of her mind searched for the way to tell him. "Why did you never marry?" she asked.

"I did." He stretched and put money on the table. "But it didn't last." He stood. "Let's go get dinner at this great Italian place I know. And then it will be my turn to ask the questions."

He ordered a bottle of wine and over the antipasto, she talked about moving east, told funny stories about her job, about women's group, about everything, except Katie.

He re-filled her glass. "So? Why now? After fifteen years?"

Vivian sipped her wine. Now or never. "You have a daughter."

Vivian watched as his face registered astonishment and quickly added, "Her name is Katie and she's fourteen."

He just stared at her, looking dumbfounded and then he threw his head back and laughed. "I did not see that coming. Holy shit. Really?"

She nodded.

"Wow." He laughed again. Vivian remembered how she had loved that laugh, all warm and clear, no rancor, just joy. He signaled the waiter. "I think this calls for another bottle. Okay?"

She nodded.

"And let's order our dinner and then you can tell me from the beginning. Everything."

She'd been so afraid he'd be angry, but he seemed grateful, if sad, as she ended her story with her search and finally finding him.

"I would have been a terrible father," he said. "I wasn't ready. I probably would've abandoned you and Katie, so trying to meet her now, I would be full of guilt and shame and she'd be angry at me." He sipped his after-dinner B&B and then laughed. "But this way you'll be the one she's pissed at and I'll get off scot free."

Vivian thought of her spirited daughter and said, "Don't count on that."

They spent the next day walking the streets and catching up. Vivian had brought him pictures of Katie through the years, and she told as many stories as she could. It was fun talking to someone as interested in Katie as she was.

"You didn't happen to go to Canada to evade the draft?" she asked as they sat outside late into the warm night, sipping brandy looking over the bay. She had to get this over with.

"Why?" He looked suspicious.

"Well …" She twirled the liquid in her glass and told the daddy-as-hero story.

He laughed. "Wow, you're really going to catch hell." He added in a serious, if tipsy tone, that he would not start out his relationship with Katie with a lie, but they'd figure out something. And he then reached for her hand.

He came to her hotel room the night before she returned to Boston and handed her a sealed envelope for Katie.

Vivian congratulated herself on not opening it and reading it on the flight home.

"No way," Gemma had said when she told the story at group. "You're lying."

"I swear on Katie's life."

Katie had come to her weeping after reading Jerry's letter and hugged her. "Thank you for finding him."

"Can I see the letter?" Vivian asked, hoping.

Katie shook her head.

But that night they cuddled on the couch together and Vivian told Katie stories of Jerry before she was born. She didn't tell the group that after Katie left for school the next morning, she shamelessly searched Katie's room, wanting to know what magic this man had wrought.

But Katie must have taken the letter with her.

Two months later, Vivian used her knife to slice open the bag and dumped the bulbs on the ground. She used the back of her arm to clear sweat and hair from her face. It was too damn hot for October.

Letters from Jerry to Katie arrived regularly since she'd gone out to California, and she assumed Katie was writing back, but she didn't say. He also wrote letters to her describing his years in Africa, his students in history classes. She wrote back telling more about Katie, about women's group, about Emily's cancer. Sometimes he asked difficult questions. Like in this last letter—

why had she cut him off without a word, why was she so hell-bent on doing life alone? She had started to respond, struggling to answer honestly, but it was all sounding lame. *I was young and I thought I could protect myself from being hurt. I believed needing someone was weak. I was afraid. I needed to know that I could take care of myself, by myself.* He was scheduled to come east for an extended visit over the holidays.

With her foot on the spade, she felt resistance as it passed through the thatched grass, and then it sank into the soft dirt. She angled the spade to hold back the dirt, dropped the bulb in, and patted the clump of dirt and grass back in place.

She was planting crocuses, snowdrops, jonquils, hyacinth, tulips, and daffodils in Emily's front yard. They would start blooming early next spring and continue through early June. By then it would be a riotous celebration of Emily being one-year cancer free.

So far she had planted one hundred bulbs. Only one hundred and fifty to go. Maybe it was excessive, but soon Alix and Gemma would be there to help. Vivian rested on her spade, and then started again.

Emily had taken her kids and Katie off for the day. They were bike riding to god-knew-where. Some path that led straight to Concord. They'd be gone for a long time, and after dropping off Katie and her bike, Vivian had sneaked back to do her planting.

Emily had become an exercise fanatic. That was one big change Vivian noticed from the cancer. Plus, she was spending as much time with her kids as they'd tolerate. And getting active in every goddamn cause. Last week she'd brought some weird energy-saving light bulbs to group. And of course, working feverishly on her photos, putting in endless hours in the darkroom. Vivian rested on her spade again. But she never talked about the cancer. Not since her chemo was finished. At least not to Vivian.

She sliced open another bag and out tumbled the little snowdrop bulbs. With the long spade, she lifted the grass near the southern corner of the house. Getting down on her knees, she dug shallow holes with her trowel, composing various versions of answers to Jerry's questions.

CHAPTER THIRTY-FOUR

October 27, 1984
One week later

"**S**it. The dishes will wait," Alix's mother said. "I want to talk to you."

Alix sat. She assumed this was bad news. Her mother had arrived unannounced from New York, right before dinner. "Why don't I get the boys to bed first?" Maybe by then Sam would be home from his meeting.

"No, the boys are fine watching TV." Her mother picked up her coffee cup. "But I'll take a refill."

Alix rose again to get the coffee pot, noting that her mother was as imperious as ever. Nothing to worry about, then. She looked healthy enough. She looked great, actually, with a new stylish haircut, her makeup tastefully done, well-fitting slacks, aquamarine sweater. Alix poured them both coffee and smiled. Maybe this was news of a different sort.

"I assume you're voting for Ferraro," Mimi said as Alix sat back down.

"You drove up from New York to talk about the election?" She couldn't resist teasing now that she imagined she knew the reason her mother had come. "Do you want a cookie?" She started to get up again.

"Sit still for a second, won't you." Mimi gave her look over the rim of her glasses, but said nothing more.

"So what's his name?" Alix asked. She'd help her mother along.

"Whose name?"

"The man you … I thought … Oh, never mind." Maybe she was wrong.

Mimi sipped her coffee. "I know I haven't always been the best mother. I have tried, though."

Shit. This was going to be bad news after all. Alix waited.

"I know I interfered too much, made you feel bad for going to work when the boys were babies. Told you I believed you had to sacrifice, that …"

"Mom, you—"

"But you showed me that a woman can be a phenomenal mother and have a life outside the house. And it's because of you that even I'm doing so well, that I got my license, am selling real estate, am having a life." She put her cup down and pointed at Alix. "Don't quit your job."

This was not what she'd expected. "I'll get us some cookies."

"I mean it. You love that job and you're good at it."

Alix put Oreos on a plate. "I've given it a lot of thought and I just can't keep up with it all. It's actually gotten more difficult as the boys get older, what with soccer, and homework, and drama club." She shrugged and sat down again. "Sam took that promotion because we needed the money, but his schedule is even more demanding. He and I are fighting constantly, the house is always a mess, and I miss at least half of the boys' games and school events."

"Stop letting Sam make you into a 1950s housewife." Her mother pointed again. "The boys are thriving and they have a mother who's engaged in the world. Don't worry about the goddamn house." She paused and added, "Or Sam."

Gemma ran the last block to their apartment and burst

through the door. "Willie," she yelled. "I'm not sterile." She found him in the alcove with his desk, surrounded by papers. She did a little dance.

"What?" He looked startled. "How? I mean…"

"I just got finished with the doctor."

"I didn't know you had an appointment. But of course that's wonderful. Great. Amazing. " And he got up and twirled her around.

"Do you really …." She interrupted herself and tilted her head to kiss him. "Do you really think it's wonderful?"

"Of course. Of course. Look how happy you are. We should celebrate. But first." He held her by the shoulders. "First, I'm going to tape this." He grabbed the floor lamp and talked into it like a microphone. "Leading Boston feminist lawyer is dancing now, in the privacy of her own apartment, at finding out she can, I repeat, folks, can follow a true woman's destiny and get pregnant."

He hammed it up, bending from side to side with the pretend microphone, and didn't see her stop smiling. "We are wondering, as we are sure all of you are, who will the lucky father be? Will she pick that striking black man she's been rumored to be cohabitating with, or will she return to the neighborhood and Vito?"

He finally realized he was the only one laughing. Took him long enough.

"Hey, babe. Do I offend?" He choked, trying to stop his laughter. "Sorry."

"You really are so dumb." She pushed him. He hated when she pushed him. She kept doing it. "How do you think I found out I'm not sterile? I'm pregnant."

He looked stunned. Then he smiled a big, goofy smile. He pulled her close and kissed her long and hard, his hands in her hair, on her back and then resting on her belly.

"We are going out to celebrate." He grabbed her coat and spun her around.

Over dinner they discussed baby names, moving to a larger apartment, who they should tell first, natural childbirth, until they were giddy with it all.

"We're having a baby," he announced to the waiter when he ordered dessert. "We need two crème brûlées for the momma and apple pie for me."

Dipping her fork into the pie, he said, "So, let's get married over winter break and then we can go honeymoon in the Caribbean."

Oh, no. Not this again. "Why don't we tell everyone we got married in city hall, just the two of us?" Gemma said. "We'll pretend to be married." She felt proud of this compromise. "And still go on a honeymoon?"

"You're crazy." He carefully scooped another bite of pie. "This kid has troubles. Big troubles and it's not even born."

"No one has to know. We'll keep it a secret. Just us. We'll know we didn't really get married."

"I'm sticking around like glue to flypaper. This kid will need a lot of help with such a crazy mama."

"I have boxes of baby clothes still in the basement. And the crib and high chair are there," Alix said the next night at group after they got past the screeches of oh-my-God and how wonderful, and the onslaught of questions about the due date and morning sickness.

"How's Willie doing with all this?" Vivian asked, her eyes teary with joy.

"He hasn't stopped grinning, and he arrived home last night with a life-sized stuffed lion."

"And you?" Emily asked. "How are you?"

Gemma laughed. "Are you kidding? How am I going to do this? This was not in the plan. Not in the plan at all." She stood. "I have to go to the bathroom. I guess that is one of the pleasures you ladies forgot to mention. Using the bathroom every five minutes."

FIVE YEARS LATER

CHAPTER THIRTY-FIVE

April 4 1989

"**H**ey babe, I'm leaving now." Willie put a steaming coffee mug on the bedside table. Pushing her hair off her face, he leaned onto the bed to give her a kiss. Travis bounded in right behind him, carrying a pile of books to be read with her morning coffee. This was their ritual before she took him to kindergarten, although today they were both playing hooky having been up so late unpacking moving boxes. Gemma stretched and sat up, already loving how the sun streamed in to this first floor apartment in Cambridgeport.

Willie picked up Travis for another hug good-bye and then tossed him, screeching and giggling, onto the bed. Gemma reached up and pulled Willie close for one more long kiss.

The apartment was full of boxes and furniture placed any which way. Willie tripped over a plastic front-loader on his way out. He swore under his breath and sent it rolling across the room.

After feeding Travis breakfast, Gemma drank her second cup of coffee as she watched him empty another carton of trucks and action figures. Emily was coming later to help unpack.

Gemma plucked a rose from the bouquet of flowers that Willie had somehow spirited in amidst all the chaos of moving day.

She hadn't realized, although she probably should have, what a wonderful caretaker Willie was. After Travis was first born, he'd bring her breakfast and read to her from the newspaper as she fed Travis. Then he'd carry the baby around all day long. She wasn't completely convinced that Travis had slept in his crib at all that first year. Willie just couldn't stop holding him.

When Gemma had gone into labor, she refused all drugs. She screamed. She hollered. She was not doing a nice Lamaze-style natural childbirth. She cursed at the nurses, at the doctors. She bared her teeth when they tried to shave her pubic hair. She threw her legs over the side of the bed and said she was leaving when they informed her they were giving her an enema.

"No visitors allowed in the labor rooms," the nurse told Willie when he arrived.

"I'm the father."

Willie stood guard. He did not threaten or create scenes. He just walked on through the swinging doors and down the hall, past the nurses' station, and found her. And he said the same thing to doctors, to orderlies, to nurses, to security. "I'm the father."

When Gemma told this story later to group, she said that if it weren't for Willie they would have restrained her and shot her full of so many drugs she would have been out for days. The hospital staff was so angry at her for not doing as she was told.

Another nurse came in. She was the sort of woman who flowed. Long hair, long legs, long arms, with a voice modulated to soothe.

She smiled. Gemma smiled.

She put a wet washcloth on Gemma's brow and gently washed her face. Gemma was grateful. And then another contraction started, and Gemma started with a low *oohh* that built and built until it was a wild bellow.

All the while the nurse told her to breathe. She breathed like

she wanted Gemma to breathe, little wisps of air pushed out—
puh puh puh. Going faster and faster as Gemma's voice echoed
and bounced off the white walls and sterilized equipment.

As the contraction subsided, she patted Gemma's hand and
smiled. "That was good, very good. For the next contraction, try
putting more into breathing and less into voice."

Gemma was loving her own voice. "Why?" she asked this
woman.

"If you breathe like I said, concentrating on the breath, you
won't yell."

That was all the conversation they had time for. Gemma felt
her belly tighten and started with her low *oooohhh.*

Another nurse came in and stood with Willie, watching as the
coaching nurse breathed and panted and Gemma shrieked and
howled through the contraction.

"Please," she said. "Try to breathe with me. You'll see it works
much better." She patted Gemma's face again with the washcloth.

Together they panted through the start of the next
contraction. Gemma concentrated on the woman's freckles and
puh puh puh—and then let her head drop back and her voice go.
It came from someplace deep. She had never sounded like this,
she had never made such a sound before. She knew it was power,
and she could feel it stretching her bones.

When the contraction ended, the woman was frowning. "You
must try harder. You must stop yelling."

"Fuck you."

"You're scaring the other patients and nurses on the floor."

"Fuck you." That was all she had time for. The next
contraction was coming, but this time instead of her low *oohh*,
she said, "Wil-lie. Get … her … the … fuck …out."

By the time she was ready to deliver, her doctor was there. He
was in his sixties, with white eyebrows so bushy they stood out
from his forehead at right angles. He seemed totally unfazed by

her noise. When she had first met him, he'd agreed to let her try natural childbirth. "Fine with me. I'll just be there to catch it." He did insist that she go to the hospital.

They shifted her to a gurney and started to wheel her out of the room. Willie grabbed her hand and held on.

"Sir, you can't come to the delivery room," a nurse said.

"I'm the father."

"Give him some scrubs and let him in," Dr. Haas said. "We don't have time to argue this."

"Gemma." The doctor looked at her and spoke sternly. "This next part is all up to you. Take that powerful voice and push and push hard when I tell you."

She could feel the contraction start, and Dr. Haas yelled, "Push." Willie grabbed one leg and a nurse grabbed another and she bore down with everything she had in one huge silent push. She could feel the muscles of her uterus contracting and the muscles of her abdomen pushing and then it was over. Her head flopped back.

"That was great. You are great," Dr. Haas said. "Get ready. Ready? Now push." And again she pushed until she felt her blood vessels would pop. "Yes, yes! Don't stop. Yes. There's the head!"

Nothing, no thing, nobody, no body had prepared her, had thought to warn her of the overwhelming attachment, the falling in love, the intensity of devotion to an infant.

It was terrifying. She could hardly breathe.

Because what was brutally, painfully clear the moment Travis was placed on her chest, was that her life as she had known it was over, forever done. She knew that her being, her self, her essence, would be forever entwined with this one. She would have to learn to walk in the world all over again.

She bought books. She needed voices, all sorts of voices to help her. Thank God for women's group during those first few months. She would have broken under the strain without them. She would have stuck her head in the oven like Sylvia Plath. She would have committed murder.

They came and fussed over her and Travis. Vivian brought her the best nightgown, with flaps that lowered to nurse, and Alix brought, well, everything. Emily took pictures—lots of pictures with Willie hamming it up in so many of them.

Then they'd kick Willie out for a few hours and curl up in Gemma's living room for group. Still, Gemma lived through Travis's first year in a miasma of worry, fear, anxiety, rage, and sleeplessness.

All that seemed so distant now. Gemma unpacked the dishes while Travis sat absorbed in his construction site on the floor. Gemma had finally left the DA's office and founded The Advocacy Center with a group of other women lawyers. They provided legal services to women in need, consulting services to police departments and justice departments. She worked reasonable hours, and Vivian's Katie had become Travis's favorite babysitter. The girl was a natural with kids, although now that she was a sophomore commuting to college, they didn't see as much of her. Luckily, Emily's Jess was happy to earn extra spending money and filled in. Alix's boys were Travis's heroes, teaching him how to kick a soccer ball and ride his two-wheeler. It was as close to a tribe as she could get.

"I'm here," Emily called as she walked in. Her dark hair was pinned up and covered with a red bandana. Her camera, as always, hung around her neck. She wore jeans and a T-shirt and looked ready for sweaty work. She waved an envelope. "Look what I found when I checked my mail." She put the letter down on the table and gave Travis a kiss on his head before hugging Gemma. "That gallery on Newbury Street is taking my hands series."

"Wonderful." Gemma laughed at how happy Emily was. "Let's get out of here and go for a walk, find a coffee shop and celebrate. Hey, Trav. Let's find a park, make some friends, and unpack all this later."

Emily coughed, a dry, raspy, awful sound. "Don't worry," she said when she could speak again. "I'm not contagious." She grabbed a glass out of a box and got some water. "I seem to have developed spring allergies."

With Travis running ahead, they walked up Pearl Street toward Mass Ave. A playground with swings, a sandbox, and some park benches was on the corner. Gemma listened as Emily described when the show would be and how the photos would be hung. Some teenage boys, who looked like they should be in school, were doing skateboarding tricks over on the basketball court.

Travis ran to the climbing structure where two little boys were swinging from a rope ladder. Nearby, toddlers played in the sandbox. Gemma figured that was a sign it wasn't full of broken glass. Two women, one in jeans and a T-shirt like Gemma and the other in a long skirt and sandals, sat on the edge of the sandbox.

"I'm going to take some quick pictures of the skateboarders," Emily said. "I'll meet you back here in a minute."

Travis and the two little boys slid down the slide, hopped off, and ran up to do it again. The three of them moving as a unit. Gemma joined the women by the sandbox, feeling bizarrely shy and awkward. She made herself smile. "Hi."

The two women smiled and nodded hello.

"How old?" Gemma indicated the children in the sandbox. She really couldn't tell if they were boys or girls. Both were dressed in T-shirts and denim overalls.

"Gabe is fourteen months and Chrissie is twelve months,"

said the woman in the skirt. "The other two"—she tilted her head to the running boys—"are four and almost five."

"Do you live near here?" Gemma asked, though she was distracted when she heard Emily cough from the basketball court.

"Over on Huron Ave."

"We just moved in yesterday."

"Hi," Emily said, out of breath when she came back and joined them.

"Travis is five," Gemma volunteered since they didn't ask.

"Oh." They both smiled and nodded. "He's a cutie," the woman in the skirt added, watching the boys careen from the platform and down the slide. "Where does he come from?"

Gemma's smile congealed. She turned as the boys ran to the swings. "There's this cutest little baby store on Mass Ave," she said with her back to the women. "And they sell the cutest black babies. Cheap too."

"Oh. I'm sorry. I didn't mean … I thought he was adopted from … Is he yours?"

Gemma was prepared to let her go on and on. But when she turned back, one of the babies was eating sand. "Is that your little one?" She pointed. "Probably don't want her doing that. Cats treat sand like kitty litter."

When the woman hurried to pick up her little girl, Emily pulled Gemma toward the slide.

"You can't do that, you know. You need these mommies."

Emily returned to the shop after a few hours of playing with Travis as Gemma unpacked boxes. She needed to make some prints and wanted Bernie to help her decide what would go into the gallery show. Bernie was with a customer and just nodded as she came in.

She flipped on the darkroom light. Clearly, motherhood

hadn't softened Gemma's edges one bit.

Sometime later, Bernie knocked on the darkroom door. "Alix is on the phone, she says it's urgent."

Emily clipped the last photo to dry, closed the darkroom door, and went into the office to pick up the phone. "What's up?"

"Katie came into the health center today." Alix sounded out of breath. "She told me she's pregnant. And she asked me not to tell her mother."

Emily sat down. "How can we not tell Viv?"

CHAPTER THIRTY-SIX

"**B**lue baller," a fifteen-year-old girl called out as the other girls collapsed in giggles. Alix smiled at the ten girls in the basement.

"Know your bodies," she instructed. "Know about birth control. Know it's okay to say yes, or no." She rose from the circle of chairs around her. "One sec, I just need to get some water." She had to get her mind off Vivian and Katie and focus on this class.

Her teen groups had become very popular. She held them four times a week, after school, in three different centers around the Boston area. Often, she was exhausted after these groups. They forced her to look at all her own beliefs, assumptions, and compromises. She had recruited other adult women to address the groups. Gemma came in every few months and taught protection against sexual assault and violence prevention. She raised funds so any teens that wanted to could take model-mugging classes. Emily taught photography. Vivian taught leadership, and Alix passed out condoms as the best protection against disease. Over the years she had trained colleagues and had been asked by a woman's organization in California to write a curriculum. She had great fun with these girls, but still it was discouraging, after so many apparent changes for women, how teenage girls kept having the same issues with self-worth, independence and sex.

How silly of her generation to expect that after being raised female, by mothers who were raised female in a culture that normalized the denigration of women, that these girls could then simply put that all away. As if the messages that girls were evil and bitchy and illogical were not deposited in their bones as they grew.

How naive they all were, not realizing they would have to break their own bones to ferret out those messages. Well, animals caught by trappers chewed their legs off to get free. What were a few bone breaks?

Over the years, Alix had decided to teach a little history about what she thought of as Sex Trap Number One. A long time ago, women were thought to be sexless. Just do your marital duties, mothers would tell daughters about to get married. Of course, even longer ago, women were supposed to be sex-crazed and the downfall of every righteous man starting with Adam, but she didn't get into all that. A nice woman wasn't supposed to like sex and would always say *no*, but the man would know that she really meant *yes* and so would force her, and lo and behold—she liked it. This was in a lot of movies before the 1960s. Then came birth control and the women's movement, and women could (even nice women) choose to have sex, could want sex, and could say yes. And then came the difficulty of saying no. Now if you said no, you were a tease.

The girls continued to call out the names they'd been called as Alix returned to the group circle. "Cock tease." "Frigid." "Ball buster."

She wanted to impart wisdom and share information, but she recognized her most important role in these groups was listening to the young women tell their stories. So she mostly let them talk about whatever they wanted—boys, sex, being attractive, boys, babies, birth control, drugs, boys.

"At least I've learned one thing," Alix told group. "If you can't do anything else for a human being, you can listen to their stories. People need their stories listened to. They need to be heard and to be believed."

Actually, she also finally understood the secret of being a good parent. All you had to do was listen. Not entertain, or impart wisdom, or be fantastically funny, or make fancy Halloween costumes. It was all in the listening.

Alix continued. "We started out adulthood believing we would live differently, do it better. Do you remember that? At what point do we recognize there are not that many different lives to live?"

Alix sat in a line of cars in front of the school, waiting in the twilight, in the cold wet drizzle, to pick up Dave from drama club and Mike from basketball practice, and acknowledged her marriage was over.

"I hate sex," she had told the group last week. "What's wrong with me? Here I am teaching all about sex to these young women and I can't stand to be touched."

"You don't hate sex," Vivian said. "You just don't like Sam."

"I love Sam," she insisted. "I've made my peace. We hardly fight anymore. It's really perfect."

"Yes, perfect. You don't ask for anything and he gives you nothing."

Alix watched through the blurry windshield as a few kids ambled out of the school, laughing and not hurried by the rain. This revelation about her marriage was an unexpected byproduct of teaching the teen groups. "Listen to your body, listen to your body," she told the girls over and over, and finally she had to pay attention to her own. Her body had rebelled

Sam said he loved her and he was a good father. He did good

work in the world. When Emily broke down on the road, Sam had gone at eleven at night without complaint and helped her. They had been together forever, and once—a long time ago—full of courage and idealism, they had set out to change the world.

But her body said, no more.

She banged her hand on the steering wheel. *Fuck.* And then she laughed. She wiped her tears. She had to get a grip before the boys saw her.

Could she simply decide at thirty-six, so sorry, wrong life?

Sam, she could say, you don't like me anymore.

Are you crazy? he would say. I love you.

Maybe, she could say back, but you're not happy with the way I dress, you don't like the way I keep house, you think I spend too much time at work, you criticize everything I do. You think my thinking is fuzzy.

But your thinking is fuzzy, he would say, looking confused.

You think I'm disorganized.

But you are disorganized.

You think I'm inconsistent with the kids.

But that is true, he would wail.

She knew how this conversation would go, because it had happened so many times before.

He would say, you have time to take care of everyone else except me.

She heard cars start their engines and more kids flowed out. She watched Dave and Mike walk toward the car. They were going to be tall like Sam and skinny like he used to be. She loved watching them when they didn't know it, getting a glimpse into their lives. They strolled in a clutch of boys, their walk a kind of slouch-slide as they pretended not to notice the group of girls who were practicing their hair tosses and lilting giggles. Alix smiled. Mike bent low to hear one of his friends who hadn't yet had his growth spurt and then straightened. His head fell back in a full-throated laugh, his braces twinkling even in the gloom.

They were on the edge here, just between boy and man. The man box was closing in on these boys. The women's movement hadn't been able to do much about it. The man box was strong—show no pain, shake it off, absolutely no crying allowed, not ever. The most athletic was still the most popular. Someday soon, she should start similar groups for boys.

Dave had had his first kiss; Mike had seen him and teased him mercilessly. It was someone from the drama club, which explained a lot. So just to get the pressure off Dave, she'd asked Mike, and you? Don't you have a crush on a girl too? And poor Mike turned red and stammered and grinned. Wow, pay dirt. Does she have a name? But he wouldn't give it up.

Mike and Dave broke from the pack when they spotted her Plymouth and raced to the car.

"Shotgun," Mike called, falling against the fender, beating his older brother.

"I called it first." Dave bounced Mike out of position.

"My turn." Mike pushed back.

They'd reverted to little boys so fast, her head ached from the whiplash.

Later that night, Sam was watching the eleven o'clock news when Alix returned home from a board meeting. The dishes from dinner were still in the sink, the dirty pans crusty on the stove.

She walked into the living room and sat across from him. He still had his beard, showing more and more gray.

"Sam, we need to talk."

She watched him frown, draw himself inward. This statement from her never boded well.

"Can I turn off the TV?" she asked.

"In a minute," he said without looking at her.

Alix got up and began doing the dishes, wondering how she would start this conversation.

He came into the kitchen after a few minutes. "What is it?"

"Things haven't been going so well with us."

He sighed. "Do we have to do this now?" He opened the refrigerator. "I told you I would do the dishes, you didn't need to do them."

"I'm not talking about the dishes." Alix dried her hands on the towel. "I'm talking about …."

"Why do you have to make a federal case out of everything?" He gulped from the orange juice carton.

"I think we need to talk about living separately." She just came out and said it.

"You can't be serious." He put down the juice carton.

She nodded, yes.

There was a long silence.

"But, you're my best friend," he finally said.

CHAPTER THIRTY-SEVEN

April 6, 1989
The next day

"These things happen," Vivian said to Katie, proud of her calm voice. She sipped her tea, trying to swallow her shock. Katie stood by the back door in the kitchen, looking ready to bolt into the rain at the first negative word. Vivian was careful. "I'm glad you told me. We can talk to Alix and figure out when to schedule the abortion." She got up to empty the dishwasher as she talked so she would appear more in control.

"I'm not having an abortion." Katie put her hand on the doorknob. "I'm keeping the baby." She looked defiant. As if having a child was a revolutionary act. As if she, her mother, should be proud. "Justin agrees with me."

Vivian dropped a plate; they both flinched. "But sweetie, you're so young, you haven't finished college. Justin is still in school." She bent and picked up the shards of ceramic. "You both have opportunities. Don't throw them away with this pregnancy."

"I'm the same age you were."

And look how well that turned out. But Vivian didn't say that. "Abortion wasn't legal back then." She threw the pieces of plate in the garbage.

"You would've had an abortion?"

"No. Of course, not." Vivian realized too late how that had sounded. "You have been the best, the very best, part of my life."

"Well, then shouldn't I give this baby"—Katie patted her belly—"the chance to be the very best part of my life?"

As soon as Katie left, Vivian called Alix, Emily, and Gemma. They rearranged their schedules, struggled through the rain, and arrived right after dinner. Alix brought wine, Emily brought ice cream, and Gemma brought a trashy mystery in case she couldn't sleep.

"Can you believe it?" Vivian said when they were all settled at the kitchen table. Katie had said she was going to the library, not that Vivian believed that for a minute. She figured Katie was out with that boy telling him how crazy her mother was, but she had chosen to let it go. They both needed breathing room.

She put down her wineglass and paced the length of the room. She stopped and glared at Alix. "And yes, I did talk to her about birth control." She resumed pacing, then whirled on them. "Can you believe she said that?"

Alix dished ice cream into bowls.

Vivian sat down and waved away the bowl of ice cream. "And then she throws back her shoulders and says: I will stay home with my child." Vivian stood again. "As if I were an evil monster. I thought I was giving such a good example of modern womanhood and she's throwing it my face." She gulped her wine. "And I wonder whose home she's planning to stay 'at home' in? Because, goddamn it, if I wanted more kids I would have had them myself."

"You're ranting," Emily said. "Take a deep breath."

Vivian sighed and sat down again. "I can't believe she did this to me."

Gemma licked her spoon. "She didn't do this to you."

"You know what I mean." Vivian picked up her ice cream.

"Listen to yourself," Gemma said. "She's pregnant and a wonderful young woman. She's not on drugs or a prostitute being raped by her pimp—"

"Your view of the world is fucking skewed," Vivian interrupted. "I wanted so much for her. I wanted her to go to college, to be a lawyer like you. Well, maybe not exactly. I wanted—"

"She can still do all that," Gemma said. "She's not going to be alone. She's got us. All of us."

Vivian turned to Alix. "Talk to her. She'll listen to you."

Two weeks later, Vivian unwrapped the package and began sticking plastic covers into electrical sockets. She was quite proud of how she had adjusted to Katie's pregnancy. Well, once she'd gotten over the initial shock, which luckily women's group had borne the brunt of. All their kids should praise the gods and goddesses for how often women's group saved them from the entirety of their mothers' craziness.

Last week, Alix had helped Katie find an obstetrician that she liked, and Vivian went with her to her first appointment. Katie called Jerry and told him that he was going to be a grandfather and afterwards, he called Vivian to congratulate her. He'd laughed and said, "Wow. The surprises just keep on coming. Luckily I'm coming out soon."

Jerry had begun spending summers in Boston as soon as he learned about Katie.

"I want to know my daughter," he'd said. "I can sublet my own apartment and not cramp your style, and then go back to California when the school year starts."

She loved the arrangement. The three of them spent a lot of time together going on outings, playing Scrabble, eating popcorn at the movies. And when Katie went off with her friends, she and Jerry got time to reconnect.

"So, what's up with you and Jerry?" Gemma had asked eventually, years ago, during the first summer he was there.

She had just smiled and shrugged.

"Not fair," Emily said. "We've listened to Jerry stories for almost fifteen years. Are you sleeping together or what?"

"Well, if you must know, yes. But I don't want to make more of it than it ever can be. I live in Boston and he lives in California. And Katie can't know anything about it. It would be awful to have her father come into her life, her mother and father get together, and then they break up all over again."

"Real positive thinking," Emily said.

"Unbelievable." Gemma shook her head. "What gives you the illusion that Katie doesn't know?"

Vivian inserted the last cover into a socket and went to get ready for group. She leaned close to her dresser mirror. At thirty-seven, the definition of her jawbone was starting to go. She tried not to care. What were her real concerns about aging? Jawbones were shallow. As a feminist she should know better than to get depressed. She knew she was still attractive. She just wanted her jawbone to stay.

She studied the wrinkles around her eyes, the puckering around her mouth and chin area. She felt her soft belly. On bad days she worried about offending people with how hideous she looked. On good days she felt glorious.

But aging meant giving up on limitless possibilities. Of course, the possibilities were never really limitless. That was an illusion the goddess gave you as a reward for surviving childhood. Because the minute you stepped on one road, the other roads grew dim. That was the depressing side of aging and that was why her bathroom was filled with moisturizers.

But she really didn't give a shit about her face. What she cared about were her identities, and grandmother wasn't one she wanted to choose just yet. She pushed away from the mirror. She might not want it, but it was happening anyway.

CHAPTER THIRTY-EIGHT

May 18,1989
One month later

As she reached the house, Emily paused to admire the profusion of daffodils and tulips in her small front yard. From now until early June, her yard bloomed with color. Vivian insisted she hadn't added any new bulbs, that they spread themselves, but each fall for the past five years, she'd seen evidence of new digging; and in the spring there were always surprises, like the dark purple tulips that opened yesterday.

Her cough had refused to go away. She had put off going to the doctor. Lots of people had lingering coughs. She dosed herself with cough drops and drank copious amounts of tea with honey, but at Alix's insistence, she'd finally called and made an appointment for the following week.

The news was not good. The cancer had spread to her lungs.

"I'm not telling the kids," Emily announced. She was curled up on Alix's couch. Vivian, Alix, and Gemma sat close around her. They nodded. They were all silent. What could they say? Outside it rained heavily. Through a break in the curtain, in the glow of the streetlight, Emily could see the wind whip the new leaves.

"Matt just finished his junior year. Jessica has her first

boyfriend and is almost in college herself. I'm not doing this to them."

"You have to tell them," Alix said. "Otherwise, they'll find out by accident and wonder about sudden stops in a conversation and will be filled with panic and distrust that you're holding back even more."

"What the fuck else could I be holding back?" Emily flopped onto the couch cushions. "This sucks." This was the one place she was completely herself. How did people live without such a place? She didn't have to be tough, or strong, or deny, or talk, or anything like that.

Vivian flopped next to her. "It really fucking sucks." She agreed so solemnly, Emily started laughing.

"What's the plan?" Gemma asked.

"Well, there's new treatment and different chemo, so at least I won't lose my hair again."

Emily told Matt and Jessica that the cancer had returned, but she made it sound like a minor development. She spent the next six weeks going to the treatments, working, and watching reruns on television. She had dealt with the divorce, with worries about money, and work, and the kids, and even not having a breast. But then, she had thought, she would get it all together and live on into old age, generous, a wise woman, open to what life had to offer. It turned out time was up. Are we wise women yet? No? Too bad, had your chance, say good-bye.

She sat on her couch, wrapped in a quilt, and stared at the street. She hated. She sat and hated. She burned with rage. It threatened to consume her, to turn her smoky inside so she became unclear about everything. She felt blind. It was so difficult to see with her eyes stinging, straining, through the hot, smoky haze.

But once started, a fire is hard to stop. Look what had

happened to Yellowstone. The fire had leaped from treetop to treetop and burned underground from root to root, erupting as trunks burst into flame.

The people in charge at Yellowstone let it go unchecked for a while because fires could be good. Lots of controversy exploded over that one. And yet, sure enough, the next spring pastel-green growth emerged among the huge blackened trunks. If she wasn't careful she'd be a blackened trunk—all burned up. No new growth.

"You're doing fine, Em," Alix had said the other day, squeezing her hand across the table at Brigham's. "You're functioning, taking care of the kids, working, and cleaning the bathroom. You haven't collapsed. Give yourself a break."

Alix's voice, soothing, insistent, went on and on as Emily sat in the restaurant, tears spilling over her cheeks, not bothering to wipe them away, not even crying, just tears spilling from her eyes.

So now she knew. Her cancer wasn't going to be the bump-in-the-road-whew- glad-that's-behind-me kind. She could no longer pretend she would live forever, just like everyone else did. Of course, everyone else was also in denial, but death was still an out-in-the-future kind of thing.

She was not surprised. Not anymore. She had no expectations that tragedy would pass her by. Life was tragic. Unplanned, terrible things happened. It was good to be careful, eat healthy, exercise, rest, quit smoking, not drive when drunk, and not walk in front of buses. That was a good way to live, but it was not a way to avoid tragedy. Not a good way to avoid death or loss or pain. It just made it easier to live if one was awake and breathing easily, and if her muscle tone was good.

"You and me have a lot in common now," Bernie said. "We both need to live as if there are a million tomorrows and as if tomorrow might be all there is." That's what Bernie said to her when she complained. "Listen, hon. Everyone lives between living and dying. Wasn't there some Dylan song, if you're not busy being born, you're busy dying? It's just that for some it's a wide expanse, and for others more of a narrow path. A thin line. You know, as you get older, you live with that all the time. It could be fifteen years, or ten or tomorrow, but it's finite."

She needed to discover Bernie's thin line.

In July, when Emily felt better, the group threw Katie an early baby shower and literally showered her with baby stuff, books, jewelry, and clothes for Katie for after the baby was born. Emily started taking weekly photos of the pregnancy.

Vivian wasn't sure what Katie planned, but there was no mention of marriage, and for that she thanked the goddess every time she remembered to. She liked Justin, although she never would admit it, but he was just a boy and cow-eyed in love with Katie. And Katie ran him ragged doing her bidding.

"Just listen," Alix counseled. "Let her tell you in her own time."

Vivian tried not to ask questions and just enjoy the long, cozy evenings with Katie, thinking of silly baby names while she cooked whatever Katie would eat. But she worried. She couldn't figure out how Katie would manage a baby, working, and college, even if she lived at home.

This month, Mandy, one of the women who worked under Vivian, had returned to work six weeks after her son was born. She looked peaked. Mandy never talked about her children during work. She was a firm believer in keeping boundaries. Especially around male coworkers.

Vivian respected that, but she worried about it also.

The men showed no similar constraints. They bitched about no sleep with infants and carsickness with toddlers, and she guessed when she wasn't around, they bitched about their cranky, overtired, sex-denying wives.

But Vivian, ever the realist, acknowledged the truth. When women talked maternal, their credibility went down; and when men talked maternal, their credibility went up. Mandy was just trying to hold onto her credibility.

In the ladies' room, though, Vivian could ask her how things were going. Was the baby sleeping through the night? Mandy might not want to acknowledge the strain, but Vivian was a firm believer in leakage. Let a little out, and the chances of the pressure building too high were lessened. It was her responsibility, after all, as Mandy's boss.

Vivian worried about Katie and tried to follow Alix's advice to just listen, to not ask, to cook healthy food and keep baby proofing the house.

Katie came into the kitchen as Vivian finished wrapping presents for Gemma's birthday celebration that night. "I spoke to the dean today. She thinks I should declare political science as my major if I want to go to law school."

Yay for the dean. But Vivian only said, "Mmm," and pretended to be concentrating hard on folding the wrapping paper just right.

"But I don't really know if I want to do that," Katie said, taking a jar of peanut butter out of the refrigerator. "All I really know is that I'm not ending up like you and Alix." She leaned back against the sink, scooping peanut butter out of the jar with her index finger.

"Alix? What's wrong with Alix?" Vivian handed Katie a spoon from the dish drainer and went back to wrapping Gemma's gifts.

"Nothing. I love Alix. I think she's wonderful and gentle. But she has spent her whole life in the service of others and maintaining those connections. And you?" Katie waved the spoon at her. "You've spent your life in determined disconnection. Except, of course, for me and women's group. I am not going to live like that." She licked the spoon clean and dipped it again. "I'm not running away from love."

Vivian bit her lower lip, trying just to listen. She tasted blood. She wrapped tissue paper around the bar of lavender-scented soap. On so many levels, she was angry. For one, she didn't like the idea that her life was over. The wonderful role model she was providing for her daughter, the model of independence and freedom, had just been dismissed as "disconnection." One of her most dynamic and fascinating friends had been dismissed as a doormat. Her nineteen-year-old pregnant daughter was—

"Mom. Don't stand there and bleed." Katie held out a tissue for her lip. "I think you're great. You raised me all by yourself and kept us together."

She felt Katie come close and dab at her lip.

"I know it wasn't easy, Mom, and I respect you for it. It's just that it cost too much. You're all alone. I don't want to end up all alone."

Vivian waved away the tissue. If she wanted to bleed, she would bleed. Did this girl-woman think she was making sense? She was pregnant, no money, no job, no plans—and she was making pronouncements about her mother's life?

"Mom. Do something. Breathe or yell or something. What's wrong?" Katie shook her shoulder.

"Stop shaking me. I'm fine." She walked to the sink and splashed water on her face. "So, what are your plans?" Fuck just listening. She was tired of being supportive and waiting until Katie was ready to think about things. "Tell me, what are your plans? Are you still going to school? What are you going to do for money?"

"I don't know. I don't need to know all the answers at once. I'm different from you." Katie pointed to the wall calendar that had every square filled for the month of July. She walked over and flipped to the next month; August was also filled. "I don't have to plan out every step. I'm open to what comes."

Vivian held onto the sink, the metal flashing digging into her palms. She needed desperately to talk to Alix. She turned her head to face Katie and spoke slowly and clearly. "You might not want to hear this, but listen and remember it for later." She took a deep breath. "You don't know shit."

She picked up the shopping bag of presents and headed out of the kitchen. "I need to get to group. Tell me if you're going out and tell me when you're coming home. While you live in this house, you at least need to make plans enough so I know whether or not to call the police when you don't show up."

"I'm moving out."

Of course. Why didn't she see this coming? That was what this whole conversation was about. Vivian couldn't move. She knew if she blinked, if she took one step, the world she had carefully made for the two of them would shatter. The oak furniture, the rose-colored rug, the photos, the books on the table, the cozy family of two, would disappear, revealing bare floors, a light bulb hanging from the ceiling by a wire, and cracked windows held together with masking tape.

She turned and looked at her beautiful Katie. "Do you know where?"

"Brighton. I can take the subway to school from there. We're going to share the apartment with Justin's brother and his girlfriend."

"When?"

"I'd thought I'd move a little at a time. I thought, maybe, I'd sleep there tonight."

"Phone?"

"Yes. Here, I'll write it down." She grabbed a pad. "Are you okay?"

Vivian nodded.

"I love you, Mom."

CHAPTER THIRTY-NINE

August 4 1989
One month later

E mily kept finding things to teach herself about how to be. Remember fear is the enemy. Remember to stay in the present. Remember how spring just came. Winter would hold on, fighting to stay, being all blustery and spitting ice. But spring just kept moving in, no big rush, melting a clump of snow here, swelling some buds there. Not being too pushy, simply sliding in where it could.

This was what cancer did for her, made her remember these things when the rage threatened to consume her, when Rick said some stupid, insensitive thing like, "Imagine what it will be like watching Jessica with her own kids someday." Why would he say that? All she could do was imagine.

Or when people said they couldn't live through what she'd been through. When she was feeling generous, she was sure they said that to pay tribute to courage and strength. She heard an element of disparagement too, though, as if they were saying, "If it were me, I would be too sensitive, too noble to keep going," as if it was better to fold under. Because really, either you lived through the events in your life—or you died. Living through was not an act of courage or will, it simply happened. You kept breathing, cooking, eating.

Matt was working long hours doing landscaping for his

summer job, and between that and his new girlfriend, Heather, wasn't home often. But when they all were together, sometimes she played a game as they sat at the kitchen table. She would watch Jessica blush as Matt teased her about being on the phone all the time and who was the boyfriend. Jessica tortured him back, telling him Heather had called but she was on the phone and wouldn't be off for a while. They fought over whose turn it was to do the dishes and who was supposed to have taken out the garbage. Emily stayed silent, watching, listening, as if she could glimpse into the future and pretend she was seeing them as they would be after she died.

Alix hurried down Brattle to Vivian's. She could see by the car in the driveway that Gemma was already there. When Vivian opened the door, Alix had to squeeze by the boxes and bags piled in the entryway.

"What is all this? You moving?"

Vivian led the way into the kitchen. "Katie and I picked out baby stuff and I got two of everything, cribs, car seats, and high chairs, so the baby can stay here as often as Katie and that boy need."

Gemma laughed as she placed mugs on the counter. "If you're not going to call him Justin, at least call him 'that man.' He's old enough to vote now."

Vivian made a face and thrust a plate of cut-up carrots, celery, and peppers at Gemma.

"Sorry I'm late." Emily had let herself in and leaned against the kitchen doorjamb, her sweater buttoned and her hands thrust in her pockets. It was eighty degrees, but Vivian had on the air conditioner and Emily was too thin and always cold these days. "I was out shopping with Jessica for dorm-room sheets and stuff." Emily crossed the kitchen and turned the burner on under the tea kettle. "When Matt left for college he had one duffle bag.

Jessica's going to need a truck."

They carried the food and tea into the living room and settled in. "I'll get some napkins," Alix said, and went back into the kitchen. When she returned, Vivian's eyes were wide with horror and she was pointing at Emily, saying, "You can't do that."

"What can't she do?" Alix asked, sitting close to Emily on the couch and taking her hand. She noticed that lately they all touched, patted, rubbed Emily whenever they could, as if they could hold onto her longer, or maybe transfer their health to her. Luckily, Emily didn't seem to mind.

"Emily bought tickets to Guatemala," Gemma explained in her dispassionate, just-giving-the-facts lawyer voice. "She leaves next week."

"Why?" Alix asked. She was not going to let herself get upset. She used to believe in the as-soon-as theory of life. As soon as Mikey was out of diapers, or Dave finished school, or they moved to a larger place. But aging cured a person of that. She now believed in the wave theory. Relax your body when the waves you didn't see coming tumble you, dive when you do see them, and swim like hell during the lulls in the breakers.

"Guatemala is having a civil war," Emily said. "The indigenous Mayans are being slaughtered. Violence is everywhere."

"Sounds to me like a perfect time to go," Gemma said.

Emily laughed. "People are needed to bear witness, to tell stories, to take pictures." She leaned forward. "Listen, I want to do this because I am going to die soon anyway. I have no reason to fear the danger. I want to do something big. Perhaps now I can."

"What if you get sicker down there?" Vivian asked. "Do you want to die alone?"

"What? You all were planning to die with me?"

"That was fucking obnoxious." Vivian looked at Emily's cup. "You want more tea?"

"I don't want to stay here being hovered over or wondering what every change in my body means. Or lie in bed, thinking, 'Oh, shit, what if there really is a heaven or a hell?'"

"Yeah." Vivian nodded. "That one worries me too, every once in a while."

"Last week, Jessica said she'd been thinking maybe she would postpone college for a year. So I asked what she wanted to do instead. She just shrugged and said we could hang out together.

"She's having a hard enough time leaving for college. She's going to feel guilty, half of her left here, thinking and worrying about me. This way she has to go off and start her life, because I'm in Guatemala."

"What are we going to do without you?" Vivian asked. Alix was grateful Vivian had said out loud what she was thinking. She squeezed Emily's hand.

"I don't want to resent your problems with living just because I am dying." Emily looked at Vivian. "We're at different moments in time now. You all still have to worry and make future plans. And not that I'm not interested, just that the future no longer applies." She smiled. "And don't worry, when I'm too sick to take any more pictures and am a burden on my Guatemalan hosts, I'll come home and be a burden to you all."

Gemma poured more tea. "So what can we do?"

"Water my plants," Emily said without hesitation, as if she had been rehearsing this. "Host Thanksgiving for Matt and Jessica, and write me letters."

"Are you scared, Em?" Alix asked.

"Sometimes. Mostly, I'm just pissed I don't get to see the end of the story. Meditating helps. You guys want to meditate with me?"

"Now?" Alix asked.

Gemma simply nodded. Gemma usually said yes when faced with a choice.

"I knew it." Vivian stood up. "I knew you could never take the hippie out of the girl. Eventually it all comes back. Today it's meditation. Tomorrow it's tofu and brown rice, then she'll ask us to sew our own clothes, weave our own cloth, dye our own thread, spin our own thread, and then raise our own sheep."

Emily directed the moving of furniture so they would all have room to sit comfortably on the floor.

"I don't sit comfortably on the floor anymore," Vivian said. "And every time we do something like this, I figure Gemma's going to make us learn karate or something."

"Now find a comfortable position," Emily instructed. "Close your eyes if you want. Take a deep breath."

"Unbelievable. I thought I gave all this up when I left Berkeley twenty years ago. I swore I would never do this again."

"Everyone close their eyes. Viv, shut your mouth."

Over the fall, they all received letters and brought them to group to read out loud.

I saw a volcano erupt as I flew into Guatemala City.

It's a contest who will survive longer, me or the rain forest. Depressing to think it may be me.

I found a love. He seems to adore one-breasted, short-haired dying women. Kinky enough for you?

CHAPTER FORTY

March 5, 1990
Seven months later

"You take the condom and roll it over the erect penis, leaving a little space at the tip."

Alix demonstrated by unrolling the condom onto a banana. The group of fifteen-year-old girls giggled, and Alix knew she definitely had their attention. She smiled.

"That isn't like any man thing I've ever seen," one of the girls shouted.

Alix frowned and studied the banana. "Yeah, I guess you're right. They're not usually such bright yellow."

More laughter and giggles, and Alix laughed along.

"Alix?" Maria stuck her head in the room. "Sorry to interrupt. There's a phone call for you from Guatemala. She says it's urgent."

Alix took the call in the director's office for privacy.

"Hi." Emily's voice sounded so clear, so close. "I'll be back in Boston tomorrow night. Group night, right? Let's be wild and hold it at Mass General."

Alix knew what this meant, but she kept her voice light. "I'll meet you at the airport. What time are you getting in?" She squeezed the banana and the skin split, oozing pulp. She put it down.

"No, all the arrangements are made." Now she heard the

strain in Emily's voice. "Meet me at the hospital. Bring me some warm, wonderful, cozy flannels. And Alix? I'm not telling the kids yet. I want group first."

It wasn't until late that night, after Alix had made dinner for the boys, cleared her schedule for the next evening, called Vivian and Gemma, and climbed into bed, that she remembered the banana-filled condom on the director's desk. She was going to hear about that.

The next afternoon Alix stood freezing outside the entrance to Mass General. She was not going in until Vivian and Gemma showed up. The sleet stung her face. March in Boston was brutal. The weather swung from winter to spring daily. People swerved around her, walking quickly to get out of the icy wet. She pulled up her coat collar, hunched her shoulders against the cold, and jammed her hands in her pockets. Inside the air was hot, sticky with sickness and people being tearful in the elevators. Out here they just rushed past, not caring that some lady was standing on the steps, freezing her ass off and getting soaked.

Vivian's green Honda sped into the drop-off section and stopped short. Vivian got out, wearing a bright orange slicker, both hands full of shopping bags. She closed the door with her hip.

"I don't think you can park here." Alix took one of the bags.

"Are you okay?" Vivian embraced her full around, and Alix felt sharp edges of packages bouncing against her back. "Listen, just hold these bags." Vivian did not wait for an answer. "I'll go park the car. And wait inside, for God's sake. You look like a drowned raccoon. I'll be back in a sec."

"Drowned rat."

"What?"

"The expression is: You look like a drowned rat."

"Fine, but you look like a drowned raccoon. Your mascara has run."

Vivian pulled away from the curb, sending a shower of water over a pedestrian's feet. She slowed down, lowered the passenger window. "I'm so sorry," she yelled to the retreating raincoat. She made sure never to let incidents like that pass. These small things added up.

She pulled into the dark tunnel leading to the parking garage and waited for the wooden arm to lift and let her through. She could not believe Alix was waiting outside, letting the weather flatten her curls and drip mascara off her chin. Probably making deals with God, Vivian figured. If I stand here and freeze, you'll make Emily okay.

It wasn't until the car behind her honked that she remembered she was supposed to push the button and grab the card that spat out. Her car lurched forward. Vivian found a space, took more packages from the trunk, and hurried outside toward the entrance of the hospital. She'd brought warm flannel PJs and a robe, flowers, pictures for the wall, even a quilt. She would rub oils into Emily's skin and massage her limbs to make her better.

Gemma got out of the cab and saw Vivian in a bright orange slicker hurrying from the parking garage. She waited for her to catch up. "Wow, in that slicker no one could possibly run you over." She stretched on her toes and kissed Vivian's cheek. "At least, not by accident."

Vivian stared. "You've been crying."

"No."

"Yes. Sunglasses in freezing rain are a dead giveaway."

"So?" Gemma pushed the sunglasses more firmly on the bridge of her nose. "Let's get inside."

Flinging words over her shoulder, Vivian walked ahead of

her up the steps. "Alix cries, pours buckets. That woman cannot control her tear ducts. I cry, too, although no one compares to Alix. Emily cries perfect little pearl drops and her nose never runs. You—" Vivian stopped and turned. "I've known you for almost twenty years and I can count on one hand the number of times I've seen you cry."

"Hmm." Gemma grabbed one of Vivian's packages.

"We shouldn't look upset." Vivian kept talking as she went through the door. "We should act like it's nothing serious. Anyway, it might not be serious. It could be a false alarm."

"Emily wouldn't come back from Guatemala for a false alarm." Gemma pointed to Alix waiting by the elevators, and she and Vivian hurried to join her.

Alix took Gemma's hand and held it.

As they waited, Gemma wondered if she could remember exactly when the group became central, their vehicle for making sense, their way of knowing what they felt and why. When the rest of their lives became stories they brought to group. When, at what moment, at what point, did they realize they could imagine living without family members, without other friends, work, even body parts, but not without group? In group they were all funnier, stronger, more real, smarter, prettier (or, as they said as they got older, "more attractive") and more successful than in any other place in their lives.

Lying in bed, surrounded by IV poles and bottles, Emily was connected to so many wires, she could barely move. She had been there less than twenty-four hours and already the room had that messy hospital look. She pulled on the sheet to straighten it. She was weak. The doctor promised she would feel better in a day; she had let herself get badly dehydrated.

She leaned over and pulled her hand mirror and makeup out of the little bedside drawer. She was down to one hundred and ten pounds. Her skin stretched over her face like cellophane; her eyes sank so deep in their sockets, eye shadow would be a waste. She dabbed on some foundation and rested.

She looked out the window at the steel sky, and before she knew it, even without closing her eyes, ten, fifteen minutes were gone. She tried mascara. She figured she couldn't be about to die any minute or she wouldn't care about the makeup. She didn't want to scare them too badly. And she wanted to wait until she saw them and saw how they reacted and had had the fluid for a day, before she summoned the kids. She'd made Rick promise not to tell them she was back. She had some vanity left. She figured that, too, meant time. When she was actually dying, really dying, like hours away, she wouldn't give a shit about anything. All desire would go. The desire to eat had gone already. The desire for cigarettes had come back.

The nurse came in. "Time for your blood pressure check."

"You do this every five minutes?"

"Oh, no. It was a while ago." She adjusted stuff behind Emily on the wall, and then lifted her arm and cuffed it.

"How do I look?"

"Beautiful. And as soon as we get more of that fluid in you, your face will fill out a bit." She put the stethoscope in her ears. "Special visitor coming?"

"My women's group."

"Oh?"

Emily studied the nurse. She probably wasn't much older than Jessica. Born too late for the era of women's groups. "Your mother may have had one."

"Oh, like a bridge club? My mother used to play bridge once a week with the women from church." She wrapped up the cuff, hung it on the wall, and took out her thermometer.

"Not exactly. We don't play games. We support each other."

"Oh, like AA?"

"Well, no." Emily opened her mouth for the thermometer. She was too tired to explain.

She heard their voices in the hall. They came in as the thermometer beeped and the nurse removed it.

Emily smiled and held out her arms. There had better not be tears. She was engulfed with hugs and then sank back onto her pillows. She scrutinized Alix. Nope, clear and dry eyed, although soaking wet.

"You have quite a weight loss secret going on here," Vivian said, waving her arm over her.

The nurse started to say something, but Alix grabbed the flowers. "Do you have a pitcher or something we could put these in?"

The nurse hesitated as if afraid to leave. "Sure," she finally said, and left the room.

"I've been gone for months," Emily said. "A more exciting time than you've ever had in your life, and all you can talk about is weight?"

"Look what we brought you." Vivian started opening up bags.

As Vivian oohed and ahhed over her own purchases, she started decorating the hospital room, laying out the quilt, which was really incredibly beautiful, and hanging up a photograph of Provincetown that Emily had taken. Alix sat on the bed, taking Emily's hand.

"Have you called the kids yet?"

Emily turned to the window. It was dark outside and the window reflected Gemma holding up the picture while Vivian hammered. It would make a nice photo. "Viv even remembered to bring a hammer. Isn't that something?"

"Time for your meds." The nurse came back with a vase and a paper cup with pills.

"What is this?" Emily asked.

"Something to help you sleep."

"I don't want it."

"It's written for you."

"I went through this with the doctor. He said I could wait and—"

"She doesn't want those now." Emily was startled by Gemma's voice.

"I'm just doing what's written in your chart."

"It can't wait?" Gemma asked.

"Later the pain might be too much. And the doctor has ordered them. I have a lot of other patients to attend to. It's written and that's all I know about it."

"Aren't those orders written 'as needed'?"

The nurse pivoted. "I need to check."

"Do that." Gemma returned to the task of hanging the picture.

Emily flopped back onto the pillow with relief. She didn't want to be drugged up. Maybe at some point, but not yet. "Alix, get my camera out. It's in the red bag. We're taking pictures."

"Now?" Vivian asked. "Like this?" She waved her hand at her clothes.

"Yes. Now get close together. Over by the door. Pull that curtain. Alix, push that thing that raises my bed. Good. Stop."

"Emily, this is too maudlin for words," Vivian said.

Emily grinned at Alix and Gemma as they all waited while Vivian took out her mirror and put on lipstick.

"Mom!" Jessica burst through the doorway. "Dad told me. You didn't call me. How could you not call me?" Jessica stopped and stared. "Oh, Mom."

Emily handed her camera to Alix and wrapped her daughter in her arms as Matt walked into the room.

"Get me out of here," Emily said a few days later.

Gemma made the arrangements for the hospital bed and other supplies. She arranged for hospice to come in once a week. Vivian brought flowers and good pillows and made sure there was tea and snacks to offer all the visitors. Alix was the gatekeeper, helping Emily say no if she needed to rest.

They were there round the clock, moving deftly aside into the shadows when other friends came, or when her kids were there, or when her Vermont family visited. And then they'd move back in again as people left. They provided the backdrop, the constant presence.

"I'm serious. You've got to promise." Emily grabbed Vivian's arm so hard, it hurt.

"Shit, Em, you are so strong. All that working out paid off. Half dead and you're still stronger than I am."

Emily laughed. "Sorry. I just wanted you to pay attention."

"I'm paying attention."

"Rick thinks the kids are all grown up now that they're both in college."

"So do they, by the way," Gemma said.

"But they're not. You all have to promise you will hound them. You will each call them once a week to check in. You will not wait for them to call you. You will call."

They all nodded. Vivian could tell that even Gemma was holding back tears. "And not just at the beginning either. You have to keep calling."

"So, what do you think?" Vivian asked. "When they're forty, forty-five, should we let up a little?"

Emily laughed again, but she shook her head. "I don't want you to ever let up. I want them to know that in this universe there are three women, who because they loved their mother, are caring for them as much as if she were around. Even if they think they are too old, or too together, or you all are too annoying."

Now Gemma was crying.

"I'm not asking for you to take them out to dinner or babysit their kids. Just check in. That's all."

By May, Emily no longer left her bed and was awake very little. Matt hardly stirred from her bedside. Vivian helped Jessica snip every daffodil and tulip in the front yard. They spread out a sheet and put the hundreds of blossoms on it, and then carried it to Emily's bed, so when she opened her eyes she would be surrounded by spring. They watched her sleep. Her breathing was rough.

Jessica leaned her head on Vivian's shoulder. "I'm not ready."

Vivian stroked her hair. "Oh, baby." And Jessica held on.

They had given each other more than they ever dreamed when they first started. Not least of all, one another's children. So Vivian held this girl, this part-of-Emily girl, and knew she would stay in Jessica's and Matt's lives forever. Such gifts. It was hard to know who was doing the giving.

They buried Emily's ashes in Vermont.

"I want them in chronological order." Bernie impatiently tapped his cane on the wooden floor of Emily's living room, making Vivian's head ache. "Why is the pile marked 1979 over here?"

"I don't know how Emily ever worked with you so long." She adjusted her granddaughter Emma on her hip and walked over to where Bernie pointed. Emma was just over four months and teething. She had Justin's dark hair, Katie's curls, and Vivian's attitude. "You are a grump."

Bernie was helping them put together a retrospective of Emily's work. Gemma was in one corner carefully making labels.

Alix sat cross-legged with Jessica and Matt, giggling over the commune pictures.

All around them were photos: the antiwar marches, the breast series, button lady, the protests at Seabrook, rocks in a stream bed, Provincetown, the garbage photos, the kids playing dress up.

Vivian picked up the picture of them when they first met in front of the Women's Center. She shifted Emma to her other side. So many ways to capture a life, a movement, a moment.

"Where should we put this one?"

ACKNOWLEGEMENTS

I can't be sure all creative works are collaborative efforts, but this novel certainly was. Of course, I am solely responsibly for the content and for any flaws; but without the help of many it would never have happened. I am indebted to all the friends, colleagues, and writers who offered their encouragement and wisdom during the writing of this novel.

I am forever indebted to my women's group, which has sustained and challenged me for over thirty years in all aspects of my life, including the writing of this novel. Thanks to Diane Butkus who never wavered in her enthusiastic endorsement of this project; to Randy Meyers who spent countless hours reading and critiquing the manuscript, generously sharing her brilliance and hard- earned knowledge of writing and publishing; to Susan Knight who took me seriously when I said I was writing, who listened often and with compassion to my struggles; but refused to let discouragement take over.

My sincerest thank you to Elizabeth Barrett, an inspirational teacher and exacting editor, who in her classes, fosters an atmosphere of acceptance and persistence which allows hesitant first drafts to eek their way to becoming completed manuscripts.

Special thanks to Joshua Kriegman, documentary film producer and brilliant story editor, who with a deft combination of praise and a "few tiny suggestions" kept me going through many, many rewrites.

Thank you to the many writers and teachers of Molasses Pond and my writing classes, especially Martha Barron Barrett, Elizabeth Barrett, Sue Wheeler, Margaret Sofio, Julie Horner, Sue Quinlan, Titia Bozua, and Emilie Spaulding, who patiently read and re-read and then read again the many drafts offering skillful critique and insight. And of course thanks to all who are part of our writing community, joining our 4:30pm Portsmouth weekly gatherings when possible, offering stories, laughter and commentary on the state of ...well, everything.

Thank you to all my family members who offered love, thoughtful feedback, and who cheered me on when I despaired, especially Orion Kriegman, Isaac Kriegman, Josh Kriegman, Cynthia Kriegman, Hannah Thomas and Kirsten DeLuca.

Thanks also to Nika Dixon who designed the cover that she somehow knew I had visioned.

I especially want to thank Tom Holbrook of Piscataqua Press and RiverRun Bookstore who made all this possible, who chose this manuscript as a winner in the Piscataqua Press fiction contest and then did such phenomenal work to create a published novel.

ABOUT THE AUTHOR

Virginia DeLuca has published short stories in *The Iowa Review* and *Currents Anthology*, and has won several prizes for fiction, including the Seacoast Writing Association and the 2011 Pirates Alley William Faulkner Wisdom Competition. She coauthored the nonfiction book, *Couples With Children*, and has contributed articles about parenting to various magazines.

Ms. DeLuca is currently the director of a violent-offender program in Maine. Throughout her career, she has worked primarily in violence prevention and intervention, assisting women of all ages as they struggle to change circumstanes in their lives. This work informs her novel.

She lives in Durham, New Hampshire

Made in the USA
San Bernardino, CA
15 June 2014